Praise for *The Great Pretenders*

"What a good book! Engagingly readable, full of Golden Age of Hollywood glitz—and a wonderful story of idealism, courage, and the price of love. Enjoyed every page!"

—Diana Gabaldon, #1 *New York Times*
bestselling author of *Outlander*

"In her riveting new novel, Laura Kalpakian has given us a heroine to cheer for in this juicy tale of Hollywood. Roxanne Granville's journey from diffident daughter of privilege to boundary-shattering career woman who takes on both the Hollywood blacklist and the racial prejudices of the early Civil Rights era is breathtaking and moving, even epic."

—Melanie Benjamin, *New York Times*
bestselling author of *The Girls in the Picture*

"Set against the glitter of Hollywood during the McCarthy era, one courageous woman, forced to start anew, reinvents herself as an agent and ends up selling blacklisted scripts. The screenwriters she represents are every bit as forbidden as the African American man she falls in love with. Kalpakian has written a timely story that deftly deals with racism and the fight for justice. *The Great Pretenders* is poignant, touching, and often filled with laugh-out-loud wit."

—Renée Rosen, author of *Park Avenue Summer*

"A fascinating journey into the intrigues and hypocrisies of 1950s Hollywood, coupled with an indomitable heroine who dares to shatter the rules. Exciting, fast-paced, and revelatory."

—C. W. Gortner, author of *The Romanov Empress*

"Both a wild romp through glittering 1950s Hollywood and a poignant journey of love and courage in the blacklist era of the silver screen. I was swept away by the passionate story and whip-smart writing. Laura Kalpakian's clever prose introduces us to a vibrant woman we can admire—a woman both brave and vulnerable. After one fearless choice, her life seems to career toward certain wreckage, yet Roxanne is there to show us that integrity and love are the conquering powers. Deeply moving, intelligent, and charming, this is a story to savor."

—Patti Callahan Henry, *New York Times*
bestselling author of *The Bookshop at Water's End*

THE GREAT PRETENDERS

LAURA KALPAKIAN

BERKLEY
New York

BERKLEY

An imprint of Penguin Random House LLC

1745 Broadway, New York, NY 10019

Library of Congress Cataloging-in-Publication Data

Names: Kalpakian, Laura, author.
Title: The great pretenders / Laura Kalpakian.
Description: First Edition. | New York : Berkley, 2019.
Identifiers: LCCN 2018037214| ISBN 9781101990186 (paperback) |
ISBN 9781101990193 (ebook)
Subjects: | BISAC: FICTION / Contemporary Women. | FICTION / Historical. |
FICTION / African American / Historical.
Classification: LCC PS3561.A4168 G74 2019 | DDC 813/.54—dc23
LC record available at https://lccn.loc.gov/2018037214

First Edition: April 2019

Printed in the United States of America
1 3 5 7 9 10 8 6 4 2

Cover art: car © Roger-Viollet /
The Image Works; Woman © AGIP / Bridgeman Images
Cover design by Vikki Chu
Book design by Elke Sigal

For Zai Pakradouhi McCreary
And for her great-grandmother,
Pakradouhi Kalpakian Johnson

Here's looking at you, kid.

—*CASABLANCA*, 1941

PART I

A DAUGHTER OF EMPIRE

1953

CHAPTER ONE

Will it rain? Though clouds glower overhead, I lift the black veil on my hat and put my sunglasses on so I don't have to meet anyone's gaze as we listen to the droning voice extolling Julia Greene's accomplishments as if she had just graduated rather than died. Errant, uninspired raindrops descend, enough that women pull their mink stoles closer, and many people look up, surprised. In this vast sea of celebrity—the stars who glitter in the cinematic heavens and the producers, directors, and studio heads who make their lives hell—no one believes there can be rain unless the director says, *Cue the thunder.* We, the family, are seated in front of the mahogany casket, which is bedecked with orchids. Beside me Leon is stoic, not an expression that reflects remorse. Does he regret breaking Julia's heart? Does he even care that she died alone in Paris? The thought makes me want to cry all over again, but hearing her voice in my head—*Never forget that you are Roxanne Granville, named for the romantic heroine of a great play*—I forbid myself the luxury of tears. I remind myself that she sent me to L'Oiseau d'Or, a Parisian finishing school for the contemptibly rich, where I learned one never admits there's anything one can't endure except for vulgarity. Like this vulgar send-off. Look at all this gaudy array of stupendously garish floral tributes. It's as though they were ordered by some freewheeling set designer operating without a budget.

Julia, with her standards, would have laughed at every ostentatious moment, but she would have understood that it could not be otherwise. This is Hollywood, after all.

She would not have been amused to see some of these faces, since Julia didn't share Leon's rabid anti-Red convictions. John Wayne, Ward Bond, Gary Cooper, Hedda Hopper, Cecil B. DeMille, Ginger Rogers, and all the rest of Leon's staunch allies from the Motion Picture Alliance for the Preservation of American Ideals, they're all here, looking stylishly somber. Every one of them is well aware that we are simultaneously the audience as well as the actors in this mourning drama. Even a funeral becomes a theatrical occasion.

Besides all the famous names, there are dignitaries from a dozen philanthropic arts boards that Julia generously funded. Their women look like moneyed bonbons. Our sweet neighbors, Fred Astaire and his wife, they're here, and dear Buster Keaton with his always-sad eyes. All of Empire Pictures is here, not just the production chiefs, the financial wizards, and Melvin Grant's whole law firm, but all of wardrobe, makeup, set design, down to the lowliest gaffers and carpenters. Empire people loved Julia; she always threw a massive Christmas party on the winter solstice and then insisted that the studio close down between Christmas and New Year's. Paid vacation for everyone! When she and I left California in '49, Leon ended that practice. Leon casts a long shadow over all these Empire people, hundreds of them. I have vowed to myself that before this terrible week is over, I will step out of his shadow. I hope I have the strength. Julia always told me: "The more strength you use, the more you will have." I'm counting on that to be true.

Leon takes my black-gloved hand and squeezes it as if I am three again, a child who needs to be reassured. My grandparents are the only real parents I ever knew. I call them Leon and Julia because that's what they called each other. Grandma and Grandpa are the sorts of names you might give to a tugboat. Leon and Julia are yachts, sophisticated, strong-willed, charming (manipulative, many would say), elegant, powerful personalities. The same cannot be said for the woman on my left, Florence, my mother, sitting beside her inebriate third husband, Walter. In the row behind us I cringe to hear my brother-in-law, Gordon, inadequately suppress a burp. He sits with my sister, Irene, and Jonathan. Jonathan and I have been friends since we were tots, brother and sister without shared parents.

I was basically orphaned and went to live with my grandparents when my father, Rowland Granville, returned to his native England and the West End stage, and my mother, Florence, decamped with a South African animal wrangler she met on a movie location. I was about three. Honestly, Florence was no loss to me. Then—and now—with a sidelong glance she can reduce me to self-hating pulp. That's why she's sitting to my left. On the right side of my face I have a birthmark, like rouge too eagerly applied from my temple to my cheekbone. It's easily subdued with makeup except when I am upset for any reason, and then it's an unfortunate barometer of my emotions. An imperfection I can never quite forget, certainly not in a city that worships physical beauty, and really, what other kind of beauty is there?

Standing together, at some distance from the rest of us, I notice many Negroes. I recognize a few cooks from the Empire commissary, and a few Empire janitors, and servants from Summit Drive, including Clarence, of course. Impossibly tall, thin, stoic, terse, his hair sprinkled with gray, Clarence runs my grandfather's house the way a conductor runs the Philharmonic. Perhaps the solid woman beside him is his wife. Only I didn't know Clarence had a wife. That strikes me as suddenly curious. I've known Clarence for twenty-two years, all my life, and I didn't even know he was married? The others, earnest-looking, middle-aged men decorously holding their hats, I don't recognize any of them. One older gent is in a wheelchair with a tall young man beside him who holds an umbrella over his head, as if protecting the older man is a solemn duty. He closes the umbrella as the rain ceases, but he does not lose his air of vigilance.

I shiver. Leon puts an arm around me and pulls me close to

him, and then I'm really afraid I will cry. I love him so much, but I still feel sharp little stabs of resentment. Was Leon with that slut Denise Dell when Jerrold Davies called him with the news of Julia's death? At least Denise and her pimp mother, Elsie, have the decency not to show their faces here today.

How could Leon have chosen Denise over Julia? For forty years, Julia was more than a wife; she was his partner in creating, maintaining, and advancing Empire Pictures. She read and evaluated scripts, helped to make casting choices, offered sotto voce comments on-set, and watched the endless boring dailies in our screening room while I slept in her lap. Who else but Julia Greene, with her enormous verve and charm, could have persuaded George Gershwin to write music for a frothy Max Leslie comedy in 1937? Sure, George agreed to write for Sam Goldwyn's *Follies*, but Empire is a much smaller outfit; Empire could never pay what Sam Goldwyn could pay—but George was happy to do it for Julia.

I close my eyes and think back to those childhood days and nights at Summit Drive when George and Ira Gershwin were among the not merely famous, but legendary guests, all of whom basked in the Greenes' hospitality. Actors, writers, directors, producers, composers, editors, cameramen, set decorators, and costumers, as well as the city's great philanthropists, they all came to croquet parties, tennis matches, late-night suppers on the candlelit terraces, musical evenings, movies in the screening room, lavish Easter egg hunts for the children, annual New Year's Eve galas, intimate dinners, leisurely lunches by the pool—oh, and the Christmases! Everything Julia did, she touched with glamour. If I think of that now, I will cry. I mustn't cry.

I glance sideways. Leon's profile is dignified, even regal, but I have come to see him not as a child regards a beloved grandparent, but as a grown woman judges a man who has disappointed her. My respect for Leon has ebbed, and like the beach at low tide, you see all sorts of trash and debris and garbage, mud you never knew existed while you floated on bright water.

Despite his dalliances, Leon and Julia stayed married. She always believed Empire Pictures was Leon's true mistress, but her stunning collection of jewelry testifies to his many infidelities—and his remorse. However, his affair with Denise Dell did not end like his other affairs. Denise absorbed his time and energy, and finally, his loyalty, and his love. As the affair went on—and on and on—Julia and Leon engaged in long bouts of screaming, oaths, and threats. Their anger then decayed into cold silence. Julia moved into her own suite at the opposite wing of the house. Leon was seldom home anyway. By my last year in high school the mansion on Summit Drive had fallen silent, a thirty-five-room cocoon of unhappiness from which no butterfly emerged. Julia cloaked her bitterness with the dismissive phrase "No fool like an old fool." But that old fool broke her heart. All she could salvage was her pride. She took that (and me) and moved to Paris in 1949. I could write a book about Paris, about the people I met at Julia's weekly soirees, Thursday evenings in our 8th arrondissement apartment near the Parc Monceau, about going to little smoky *boîtes* and hearing Sidney Bechet play, about L'Oiseau d'Or, for that matter. (I was the only student who rode a bicycle to the school—very much frowned upon by *les grandes dames*!) I would have stayed in Paris happily, but Julia insisted that an American girl needed an American education, so I went to Mills College in Northern California, where earlier this month Jerrold Davies made a transatlantic call to tell me that my grandmother had died of a heart attack.

But Jerrold is not here for the funeral. Jerrold can't even return to the US. He fled a subpoena from the House Un-American Activities Committee in 1950 and went to Paris, where his Best Picture Oscar for *The Ice Age* sits on the rickety shelf of a Left Bank apartment. He uses the Oscar as a hat rack. Simon Strassman fled to Mexico in '51. I think his passport was revoked. Nelson Hilyard is dead, a suicide. Of the old guard Empire writers who delighted my childhood, only Max Leslie is here, standing between his grieving wife, Marian, and his longtime secretary, Thelma Bigelow.

"Come on, Honeybee. Let's go home." Leon holds my hand, raises me to my feet. "We're done here."

He takes my arm, and as we start toward the cars, a swarm of uniformed drivers races up the hill, like infantrymen armed with open umbrellas to shield us from the light rain. Nothing can ward off the throngs of gawking fans, though police have cordons to keep them in place. Nothing can protect people like us from the press. Flashbulbs sparkle across our vision as Leon waves photographers away.

"Smile, Ginger!"

"Fred!"

"Over here, Miss Stanwyck!"

"Hey, Coop!"

We avert our eyes and hurry past. We know the press is merciless and always will be. The relationship between the press and the picture business is that of mutually voracious cannibals.

Our driver shepherds us to the Rolls, closes the door behind us, starts up, and drives off. We all fall back into the plush seats, sighing. Jonathan passes around his hip flask. Irene, in her cool, blonde, graceful way, takes a genteel swig from it. Gordon prefers to sip from a bottle of Pepto-Bismol. Leon declines the flask. I take a gulp. Walter finishes it off and hands it to Florence, who doesn't notice that it's empty. Everyone but me opens their sleek cigarette cases, gets out a smoke, and lights up.

Leon takes my hand in his. "I'm proud of you, Honeybee. You did fine. Julia would have been proud too. You are a credit to her, to me, to Empire Pictures."

Leon always talks like that, as though Empire Pictures is actually a living thing that can have credit bestowed upon it—or conversely, that can be diminished. He always reminds me I am a daughter of Empire, and while I recognize the benefits, I'm tired of the responsibility. I retrieve my hand from his, roll down the window, and breathe in. Deep.

CHAPTER TWO

The next day the family rode together in the Bentley to a lawyer's office in a shabby downtown district. Garbage blew along the gutters. Irene and Gordon both commented on the general decay, and Florence wondered aloud why Julia would have chosen this nobody lawyer.

"Mr. Wilkie," said Leon with a tight jaw.

"What's wrong with Melvin Grant?" asked Florence. "He's been your attorney for eons."

Leon did not reply. I too said nothing, though I knew very well why Julia chose someone else to represent her interests. Melvin Grant would protect Leon even if it meant protecting Denise Dell as well.

Our driver stopped in front of a dingy, four-story building. The street was packed with big cars illegally parked, and uniformed chauffeurs who stood by their vehicles, smoking. "We must be late," Gordon remarked. "It looks like everyone else is here."

"Well, they can't start without us, can they?" asked Leon.

We stepped out, evading winos who sidled up, panhandling, though they retreated when Leon exited the Bentley. Leon has always exuded authority with his erect, even regal carriage, broad brow, horn-rimmed glasses, his ring of wiry gray hair, and his elegant suits. We walked single file to the door, gingerly sidestepping wads of snot, old chewing gum, and cigarette butts. Florence and Irene pulled their fur coats close at the throat. I hate fur coats; I'm too young to be taxidermied. But like everyone else, I'm wearing unadorned black—black coat, black Dior suit, black gloves, black hat and handbag.

At the elevator an old Negro slid aside the metal grille. "Goin' to Mr. Wilkie's office, yes? All you fine folks goin' there today," he said as he punched the buttons with knobby, arthritic fingers. He stopped at the fourth floor and pointed to a door that read *Arthur Wilkie, Attorney at Law.*

Mr. Wilkie's secretary, a withered woman who introduced herself as Mrs. Wilkie, greeted us at the door and offered to take our coats, but we all declined. She asked if we wanted coffee or tea, and we declined. She led us down a dirty hall to a conference room where the ghosts of a hundred thousand cigarette butts lingered and dust motes caught the morning light. We were seated at a long table where places had been reserved for the six of us. I knew, or recognized, most of these over-upholstered ladies and gentlemen from Los Angeles arts foundations Julia had long supported. I certainly did not know the five well-dressed Negroes, though I had seen them at the funeral. They all sat together, their faces dark masks of discretion. Beside the old gent in the wheelchair was the man who had thought to bring the umbrella. He was not wearing sunglasses today. His face was so beautifully sculpted it ought to have been on a medallion. He and I were the youngest people here and our eyes met briefly before everyone turned their gaze to Mr. Wilkie, who began with conventional condolences.

Mr. Wilkie was small, disheveled, nervous, the carnation in his lapel the more pathetic for its being so wilted. Speaking in a high-pitched, hurried voice, not the sort to instill confidence, he rattled over as much background as was necessary for people to understand Mrs. Greene's estate. Before she left for Paris she had taken steps to untangle many of her own assets from those of her husband. "Her interest in Empire Pictures, the house at Summit Drive, and other properties held in common with Mr. Greene, the house at Tahoe, the Malibu—"

Leon coughed in a way that only Leon can.

Mr. Wilkie quickly wrapped up the list of those jointly held items, concluding, "Those properties are not under discussion. Today we are allocating Mrs. Greene's personal estate." According to the wishes expressed in her will, the first bequest was the furniture and antiques in the Parc Monceau apartment in Paris, and the Matisse on the wall there. Those she left to Jerrold Davies "to help finance his next picture," said Mr. Wilkie, reading from the document. He said he would contact Mr. Davies in Paris.

I stifled a smile. From the grave Julia was poking Leon in the eye again. However, Leon kept his gaze on a fly buzzing near the Venetian blinds. But when the next item was read—a big fat bequest to the NAACP—Leon and all the arts people drew a great, collectively horrified breath and stared at the Negroes. Leon coughed repeatedly, like he might choke. Gordon turned to him, murmuring something to the effect of *Did you know* . . . but Leon ignored him and turned to me, muttering the same question. No, I shook my head, and whispered, "Honest. I had no idea." And honest, I didn't. Julia did not share Leon's staunch anti-Communist ideals, but the NAACP? That was shocking!

The man in the wheelchair introduced himself as August Branch. He was bald with a round face and round body, and wore a bow tie. His voice had a Southern lilt as he thanked Mr. Wilkie and spoke at length of Julia's generosity over the years. If he noticed that Leon flinched, he gave no indication. "Mrs. Greene's long support for our Cause has been invaluable. On behalf of the NAACP and speaking as editor of the *Challenger*, I want to assure you that her generous contribution today will help racial equality prevail." The young man beside him leaned in and murmured in a low voice. Mr. Branch nodded. "Thank you, Terrence. Ladies and gentlemen, I am reminded that we have editorial deadlines to meet, and I'm afraid we must leave. The press waits for no man."

As he and his whole delegation rose and left, they each offered somber condolences to Leon. Leon nodded grimly. No one shook hands.

After they were gone a general murmur of indignation ensued, and there was a good deal of coughing and lighting of cigarettes as Mr. Wilkie went on detailing much smaller bequests of money to the various arts foundations Julia had favored and fostered. The rest of it came to me, some in a trust I could not access till I was thirty, some in a lump sum that took my breath away. Julia divided her jewelry collection between me and Irene, though I got the diamond ring, the diamond choker and bracelet, the ruby pendant and earrings, the long rope of perfectly matched pearls. My mother, Florence, got Julia's fur coats. An odd bequest, another poke in the eye, I assumed, for Florence's having always been so nasty about my birthmark, especially since Florence has lived in the Bahamas since 1946.

Late this afternoon Florence and Walter will catch a flight back to the Bahamas, and I won't have to see them again until I get married. Which I do not plan on doing. Maybe ever. When I told Julia I would never marry, she just laughed and said, "When you really do fall in love, Roxanne, I want to be there to see it. You will fall so hard, you'll make Cyrano and the original Roxanne look like cynics." Well, maybe, but honestly, why marry? Give me the lyrics of Ira Gershwin and the immortal lines from *Casablanca* any day. (I could recite the airport scene verbatim from the time I was twelve.) My parents, between them, have six marriages. Jonathan's parents have eight, that we know of. Julia and Leon's marriage endured, but it certainly wasn't a thing of beauty. Marriage has little to recommend it, that I can see, other than a mortgage and the missionary position.

The driver took us all back to Summit Drive. Irene and Gordon got in their teal blue Cadillac and drove home. Florence, leaning on Walter's arm, went up the broad staircase to their room.

Leon and I looked at each other, alone together for the first time since I had returned from Northern California.

"I have something to tell you," I said, taking a deep breath.

Behind his glasses, his eyes narrowed. "Not today, Roxanne. Whatever it is. Not today."

"Today."

His voice lowered to a growl. "It can wait."

"It's not about Denise Dell, if that's what you're afraid of."

"I am not afraid."

"Then hear me out. It's important."

"I'll join you in the library in twenty minutes." He turned and left.

I took off my hat and carried my gloves and walked among the drooping floral funereal tributes that had been moved from the cemetery to the Summit Drive foyer, a room with thirty-foot-high ceilings and marble floors, grand as any hotel foyer. Despite the vastness, there were so many flowers that the odor of their decay floated like miasma. The most gaudy of the displays had a card that said, *Vice President Richard M. Nixon and wife*. The rose-studded wreath was from my father, Sir Rowland Granville, London. After he left California, Rowland never forgot my birthday, and always sent me some extravagant gift at Christmas, but I didn't actually see him again till Julia and I stopped in London on our way to Paris. He was playing Malvolio in *Twelfth Night*, an absolutely astonishing actor, and a very charming man, kind, attentive, even courtly to both of us. I liked him, but I couldn't really bring myself to call him Daddy, and I couldn't abide his snotty third wife. Her name is on the card too. Lady La-Di-Dah Granville.

I started up the grand staircase lined with dark, ornately framed seventeenth-century paintings. All thirty-five rooms of Summit Drive are furnished with the detritus of ruined aristocrats, art and furniture that had been collected and shipped by Leon's agents in Europe before the War. As a child I thought nothing of this regal magnificence. Now, I find it stifling, as if the large, hoary hand of the skeletal past wants to throttle me. In Paris, the past and present are all mixed up, and I could live there happily in both. But Summit Drive is like a museum, like *Citizen Kane*'s Xanadu, though not quite that garish.

The library was my favorite room among all the thirty-five, filled with my most cherished childhood memories. Aside from the dark, heavy Flemish tapestries across one wall it was actually airy, comfortable, with roomy wing chairs, and bookshelves full of first editions. This is the room where my grandparents sat through many dolls' tea parties and never so much as blinked with restlessness. In this room Leon sat me on his lap and read to me: *Tom Sawyer*, *Treasure Island*, and *Alice in Wonderland*. He had such a rich, wonderful, rolling voice. This is the room where as a child I sat in on long story conferences with Leon, with Max Leslie, Simon Strassman, Nelson Hilyard, and Jerrold Davies. Half a dozen other writers came and went, but these were the core Empire writers, men who had brought the studio to its great heyday in the thirties and forties, who made millions laugh and cry with their words,

I remember those brilliant evenings as generalized sensations filtered through a fog of cigarette and cigar smoke, with the clink of ice in long-ago glasses, the splash of the soda siphon, the crack of pistachios, and the rumble of their deep, masculine laughter as yellow chalk dust floated down from the chalkboard where they kept their collective notes. Pads of yellow paper lay about, the pages ruffling, filled with words and doodles. They brought in an upright piano for Nelson Hilyard to pound out impromptu scores. Max and Simon would jump up from their chairs and enact scenes. Simon, in particular, despite his great weight, was a limber mimic and known to take the floor lamp in his arms as if it were a heroine, speaking words of passion to her while we laughed and laughed. I was enthralled there in the rowdy company of writers who would scribble, debate, cast, pour another drink, flip the pages on their pads, and start all over again. Their talk was salty, often raucous.

These men were free-wheeling storytellers, and funny as hell. Their fingers were stained blue with ink and brown with nicotine, but they proved to me, even then, and I was just a kid, that work and joy could be synonymous.

Jerrold Davies always had a director's eye for timing. Timing was everything to him. Simon Strassman was known for his big, bold dialogue, Westerns, pirate stories, tales of derring-do. Max Leslie wrote bright, witty comedies. Nelson Hilyard, probably the most brilliant of them all, was known for his deep, sensitive dialogue; if he were still alive, Nelson would be writing for actors like Monty Clift or Marlon Brando. The movies Leon and these men created kept audiences coming back year after year, earned a few Oscars, brought Empire renown and profits. While the rest of the world (I later learned) was suffering through the Depression, I was hoisted to the top of the library table at the age of nine or ten to do a tap dance as Nelson pounded out "My God How the Money Rolls In" on the upright and we all sang the ribald verses.

Now, the library was silent, no upright piano, the chalkboard long gone.

I cringed a little to remember that this was also the room where I waited with two cops who brought me and Jonathan home after I rolled the Packard down a ravine driving just a little bit drunk. Maybe more than a little bit—and we had open containers of beer. I was sixteen. When the cops shone their flashlights down the ravine and into the car, Jonathan and I were shaken, but unhurt. The Packard is a big, heavy car, and it too was unhurt, though the passenger side was badly scraped and scratched. Once the cops realized who we were, they put us in the squad car and brought us to Summit Drive. Leon and Julia came into the library wearing dressing gowns (they would never wear anything so banal as bathrobes) and glared at us while the cops related our sins. The cops took their payment and left. No unseemly charges were filed. Julia took Jonathan home to his father's house (also on Summit Drive) and I stayed in the library to face Leon's wrath. When he finished with me, I was filled with remorse, and was basically locked in a tower for the next six months.

Clarence knocked and entered, interrupting my thoughts. He carried a tray with sandwiches, a bottle of white wine, and a pot of tea, and set the tray on a table that had framed, signed photographs of Richard Nixon and J. Edgar Hoover, Leon's special friends and political allies. Leon especially admired Nixon, a fellow Californian, and the feeling was mutual. Leon and other Hollywood ultraconservatives, including Hedda Hopper and Gary Cooper, had been invited to the Republican convention in Chicago last summer, and Leon would have gone to the inauguration earlier this month if Julia had not so inconveniently died.

"Clarence, what happened to everyone who used to work here?" I asked. "Everyone is new. Except you."

"They have been replaced," Clarence said in his stentorian fashion. He had the gravity of a college president on graduation day.

"I know Denise and her mother moved in after we left for Paris," I declared dramatically. "Did Denise fire them because they were loyal to my grandmother?"

Clarence's sphinxlike expression did not alter, though he paused to consider his words. "New staff was preferred. However, Mr. Greene knows I am indispensable." He turned and left.

I eyed the sandwiches. I was actually starving, but you grow up in Hollywood, and you learn early on that you do not want to have stuff caught between your teeth when you're about to make a life-changing speech, a gesture so grand it must not be tarnished in any way, which is what I was about to do. Like Joan Fontaine in *Jane Eyre* telling Orson Welles, No! she won't live with him and be his mistress! Would Joan have eaten a crumpet before that speech? I sipped the wine and wondered briefly if everything important to me had to somehow first happen on film. The thought prickled, but I was spared any further discomforting introspection because Leon opened the door.

"What is it that can't wait, Roxanne?" He sat behind a desk that once belonged to a French abbé.

I placed the wineglass on the table. "I don't want to go back to Mills College."

Surprise briefly lit his face, but he was a master of concealment, and immediately he looked merely studious. "Julia would be so disappointed to hear you say that. She believed in higher education for women. She chose Mills herself."

"Julia's dead," I said, hoping to be cruel. "I don't want to go to Mills."

"All right, then. Something closer to home? UCLA? USC, perhaps?"

"I don't want to go to college."

"Something further away. NYU? Columbia?"

"You're not listening, Leon. I don't want to go to college."

"You have to be educated."

"To do what? Can you really see me conjugating French verbs for a room full of high school students?"

"There are many fields open to women nowadays."

"Name one."

Leon pondered this while he regarded me intently. He was unaccustomed to being challenged. Small wonder. For thirty-five years he had run Empire Pictures, and few had challenged him and fewer yet had bested him. "An education will broaden your horizons."

I thought that was a pretty weak comeback, but I didn't say so. I was on a mission here.

"You should return to college. That French finishing school was a waste of time and money in my opinion. What did they teach you of any use?"

"How to handle men. Every woman needs to know that."

He clearly meant to say something tart, but thought better of it. "If you don't want to go to college, what do you envision for your future?"

"Whatever I do, it will have to be here, in the picture industry. What else am I fit for? What else do I know? I can't be an actress." Reflexively I touched my right cheek.

"You are beautiful, Roxanne. Don't let anyone tell you any different."

I might have teared up. All my life Leon and Julia have told me I am beautiful. But I thought of Bette Davis and kept my resolve. "I'm not thinking of the future right now. I'm thinking of the present, and I'm only certain of one thing, and that's that I don't want to live here with you."

"Where do you want to live?" he asked, ignoring my pointed exclusion.

"Not here."

"This is your home, Roxanne."

I sat in one of the wing chairs in the best L'Oiseau d'Or posture I could muster. I was trembling with suppressed emotion, and blurted out, "Then why has Denise Dell been living here since Julia and I went to Paris?"

"I thought this wasn't going to be about Denise." He rose, came round the desk, and took a seat opposite me, so close he took my hand. "Roxanne, Honeybee, I'm sorry you feel this way. I don't think Julia would want you to leave Summit Drive."

"I will only stay here if Denise Dell leaves." There! Joan Fontaine could not have done better. This moment called for panache—the real thing, not just the cologne I was wearing.

Leon meditated on this. He withdrew his hand. He said at last, "I suppose you are old enough to make your own choices. I just hope they will be good choices and reflect well on me and on Empire Pictures."

"You are not the center of the universe. Neither is Empire."

"Well, Empire is the center of any universe that you belong to, Honeybee. This will be your home, forever, and if you change your mind, you can always come home—"

"Then why did you make her leave? You broke Julia's heart! You broke my heart. You broke her spirit!" I blubbered and choked.

"Julia left me, as you well know. You went with her."

"What else could she do? Stay here and watch you carry on with a girl forty years younger than you?"

"Julia had her own secret life. Her own betrayals."

"Julia was never unfaithful to you."

"Funding a Communist organization with my money? The NAACP! The NAACP is crawling with Red agitators stirring up the races. I'd call that an unforgivable betrayal of my every principle! Those Negroes this morning were laughing at me! All that money! And the Matisse to Jerrold Davies! Jerrold is a Red who fled to France rather than testify to a legitimate congressional committee. And Julia produced his *Les Comrades*. An outright Communist film!"

"Her name wasn't in the credits," I offered, though I certainly remembered how Julia had laughed to think that Leon would read of her contribution in *Variety* and go apoplectic—which he did. He actually made an international call to Paris just so he could rant at her! She listened, replying only with monosyllables while she filed her nails. I admired her coolness. "I don't blame her," I retorted. "She was angry when you fired Simon and Jerrold, and Nelson and the others."

"Julia knew very well I signed the Waldorf Agreement in forty-seven, along with the other studio heads. We vowed not to hire or to keep on any known Communist. The men I fired refused to cooperate when the Congress of the United States—the Congress!—asked them, under oath, about their affiliations."

"Why shouldn't they be able to believe what they want, even if it's Communism? I thought it was a free country!"

"It is a great country, and that's what we're preserving. The Communists want to destroy us, to undermine American values, and they mean to use the movie business to do it. Besides, Simon is a drunk and Nelson was a homo. If he killed himself, then that was why."

"He did kill himself, Leon! I was with Julia in Paris when Kathleen called and told us! It was awful! He shot himself in the head in his bedroom, Leon! His wife found him!"

Leon's features composed themselves. *Cue the thunder.* If I were a faltering director or an errant producer or a sloppy actor, I'd be afraid right now. "I have no wish to discuss the past with you, Roxanne. You want to leave home. Is that correct?"

"Yes." I reined in my tears.

"Are you prepared as well to part with the allowance I give you? Because if you leave home and don't go to college, that will certainly end. It is a generous allowance."

"You heard the lawyer. I have money from Julia."

"Fortunate for you, since without it, you would be hard-pressed to earn a living."

I did not reply, but certainly, I have no useful skills, and I have no talents. My L'Oiseau d'Or education had no employment value unless you count knowing how to slice off the neck of a champagne bottle with a knife like they do in the French Foreign Legion. I love to read, though I can't imagine myself writing, and my English major and a French minor at Mills? Don't make me laugh. Still, I managed to declare, "If I'm not living here and not taking your money, what do you care?"

He went to the desk, picked up the phone and dialed, and spoke for about twenty minutes with Melvin Grant. I stood up and walked to the window. I did not yet have the kind of mastery of my emotions that he did. That Julia did, for that matter. Maybe that only comes with time and age and practice.

He put the receiver down. "As you know, I own a lot of properties in LA. One of them is a bungalow, a cottage at Malibu. You can live there. You can go to Melvin Grant's office and pick up the key from the secretary, and sign the lease."

"Thanks," I said, my voice shaking. I started to leave, but he too rose, and took me in his arms, held me, pressed me to him as if he would never let me go. I held him too, breathed in his old remembered scent that spoke to me of being loved, cared for, a cherished child. I wanted to tell him how much I loved him, and how sad I was, and how I wanted everything to be different. But since it could never be the same, what was the use?

I broke from his embrace, picked up my hat, gloves, and purse, and went out to the garages, where I found my MG T among the dozen vehicles Leon kept there. The silver MG was a present for my twenty-first birthday, and though I loved it, it was fussy and unreliable. I had to coax the choke when it refused to start, and hope like hell I wouldn't have to go back inside the house after my grand exit. Finally the engine hummed to life, and I tore down the long drive, the long, winding hill, and out the gates, as I sped toward Melvin Grant's office on Wilshire.

"Miss Granville," said the receptionist at the law office. "I was told you'd come by and sign these papers and collect the key. Perhaps you'd like to pay the first year's rent now."

My eyes widened.

"That'll be a dollar." After I gave her a dollar, she handed me a receipt. "The rent for nineteen fifty-four will be due next year on January first." She put the key in my hand.

I drove down Sunset to Pacific Coast Highway. Though the Silver Bullet is a difficult English car, it has everything I love: speed, style, wire rims, a smooth purr to the engine, and grace on curves. On PCH I turned north toward Malibu, where I pulled off to the side of the road, and though it was January, I unsnapped the convertible top and pushed it back so I could really feel my freedom. Speeding up PCH, to my left the sea was a dolphin-gray, and blue-gray waves broke in a white, ruffled froth along the pale beaches. The wild wind seemed both soothing and invigorating as I snatched that stupid little hat off my head and flung it away. Then, one by one, I pulled off the black gloves, like a stripper. My short hair whipped around my face. Yes, I was bereft and saddened that Julia had died, bereft and saddened that I had lost my grand-father to that slut, Denise, but happy to be my own self, free of the antique past, ready for the future. No thought of what that future might be or mean, however, and at the moment, not caring either.

Two days later I returned to Summit Drive to get my things. I chose a time, mid-morning, when I knew Leon would be at Empire. I parked in the broad circular drive, opened the massive front door, and went in. I went up the staircase, and in the hall I was sur-prised to see Denise's mother, Elsie O'Dell, come out of a bedroom door. (Denise's real name was Dora O'Dell, a fact I knew because Julia used to make fun of it.) Elsie's overdone mouth opened in alarm to see me. Her hair was an impossible saffron color, and she looked like a Victorian sofa, all puffs and rolls and bulges on tiny little feet. I thought about making some snotty remark, but instead, I walked past her without a word. She didn't deserve to be spoken to.

In the spacious bedroom suite that had been mine for as long as I could remember, only the view—the tiered gardens, the swim-ming pool, the artificial lake—remained the same. The room was clean, but everything of mine was boxed up, labeled, and stacked; the drawers and closets were all empty, the canopy bed stripped and bare. Well, fine. I poked about in the boxes. The girl who had lived here seemed far distant to me.

Clarence knocked and entered. "Shall I instruct that all this be delivered to your new home?"

"All I want is my clothes, my books, my records, and the hi-fi. The rest of it can just go up in the attic."

"Very well, Miss Roxanne. Please give me your new address before you leave. By the way, this came for you yesterday." He handed me an envelope, nodded, and left.

The return address was Mr. Wilkie's law office, and inside there was a typewritten note with his signature saying that the enclosed was from Julia, but that this was a strictly private communication. He had been under instructions not to give it to me when the will was read, and many others were present. The letter inside was dated November of last year, two months before she died.

Roxanne, dearest,

If you are reading this, dear girl, then I am gone. Do not mourn. I have missed you every day since you left, but it is altogether right that you should have an American education, and find your own life in your own country, that you find work to give you satisfaction, and a man who will reward and return your love.

Though you suffered in our disintegrating marriage, Leon and I have always loved you. Even if for a while we did not love each other. Our love for you will never change. Life is short and love is long. Love is demanding and rewarding and aggravating, sometimes angering, but it is never finished or over, or done with, not even in death.

You and Leon are the dearest people in the world to me, and I do not want either of you to live with rancor in your hearts on my account. I am writing this so that you shall know, without any doubt, Roxanne, that I have forgiven Leon. You may wonder why I do not write to him. The wounds that Leon and I inflicted on each other are still too fresh, too raw for me to tell him. But you can tell him. And when you think the time is right, please do tell him I have forgiven him. You must also forgive him. Look after him, Roxanne.

I have and will always love you both. You must love each other now that I am gone. Do not cling to resentment on my behalf. Be good to him, and to your sweet and dearest self. You will be the shining star of any firmament you choose, dearest girl. You have been the joy of my life.

Love always,

Julia

If I had not seen Elsie O'Dell on the stairs, I would have gotten in the MG, right then. I would have driven straight to Empire Studios, gone right to Leon's office, and flung myself against his shoulder. We both would have wept and smiled to read the letter, wept and smiled for our love for each other and Julia. A heart-warming scene, something out of *It's a Wonderful Life*, or even a touching Max Leslie comedy. But, in fact, I had seen Elsie on the stairs. Everyone in this particular drama had made their choices. Maybe Julia had forgiven Leon for the pain and betrayal. I could not. I vowed not to return to Summit Drive, not even to speak to Leon as long as Denise lived here. I put the letter in my handbag and went downstairs.

Looking for Clarence, I passed through the breakfast room, and there sat Denise Dell, wearing a dressing gown, the pale half-moon of her right breast exposed and glowing. She was smoking and reading the trade papers. A bright shingle of brilliantly blonde hair fell forward, grazing her shoulder. She looked up at me, then she returned to *Variety*, as if I didn't deserve the slightest acknowledgment, not even the grin of the victor.

CHAPTER THREE

The cottage that was mine for a dollar a year was far north of the fashionable Malibu, the Colony. My place was a ramshackle affair that sat up high, with steps leading to a broad porch that gazed out to the beach and the sea—like being on a yacht without the seasickness. It and the few other cottages nearby backed up to Pacific Coast Highway and faced the ocean, separated from the beach by low, rolling dunes, half dirt, half sand, lit up by stubbly, colorful ice plants clinging as best they could, given the winds, the tides, the shifting sands. High winter tides had gnawed at the beach itself, and great bright coppery coils of kelp lay above the tide line and gray gulls circled overhead.

I had barely aired out the place when my neighbor, Mr. George Wilbur, came over with his wife, Mildred, in tow. I say "in tow" because she walked behind him, stood behind him, spoke when spoken to. She was better behaved than their dog, a big, friendly Irish setter who bounded up the porch, eager to make friends. The Wilburs were both of them pinch-lipped, middle-aged, and nosy. They insisted they'd only come by to be certain I wasn't a squatter. This place had been empty for months, they said, and before that a disreputable writer had lived here; they knew he was disreputable because various women were frequently overnight guests. Before that a disreputable musician had lived here. He too had various overnight guests. Once I convinced the Wilburs I was no squatter (did they want to see my lease?), they said they were happy to have me nearby. I personally wasn't so happy to have them nearby, though I liked their dog, Bruno.

My place was built a long time ago, judging from the narrow-slat wooden walls. The kitchen and living room had broad windows that opened onto the wide, high porch with a glorious view of the beach, the ocean, the horizon, and all the ongoing daily interplay of light among them. In the living room there was a battered upright piano, badly out of tune, and with keys that felt almost bloated with the salt air, but it still played. I wondered if it might actually be the piano that Nelson had played in the library all those years ago. In the grate of the big stone fireplace I found ash—the writer's drafts, no doubt. The writer left a bookshelf full of Dashiell Hammett, Raymond Chandler, and a lot of lesser authors, and assorted pencils. In the fridge there was a carton of milk, and a loaf of bread so thick with mold it looked like moss. A mouse-trap sat on the kitchen counter. I had my work cut out for me.

The smaller bedroom had a narrow metal-frame bed that looked to have come from an orphanage. The bigger bedroom was more cheerful, with a big south-facing window, a double bed, a dresser, and a couple of side tables, all in the rounded style of the twenties. The place had bamboo blinds and haphazard furniture. In the living room a desk fronted the windows, and a television with rabbit ears that could be made to work (sort of), sat across from a big, threadbare, comfy chintz-covered chair. All in all, more appealing to me than Summit Drive's antiques, reeking of the European past. Still, I know Julia would have been appalled that I was so ready to love this place. She was very much comme il faut, elegant, though not spontaneous. Me, I was ready to be spontaneous, bohemian, eclectic, my new favorite words.

The first thing I unpacked and put on the bedroom vanity was my half-empty bottle of Panache. The word itself was first used, ever, in *Cyrano de Bergerac*. When Empire made the talkie of the play in 1931, the year I was born, Leon commissioned a Beverly Hills *parfumier* to create this cologne, Panache, as a gift for Julia to celebrate. It's an intoxicating fragrance; the top notes are citrusy, the lower notes an earthy bergamot with a hint of vanilla. This cologne was Julia's signature; only she could wear it. On my fifteenth birthday, she gave me my own bottle, declaring that we both had panache. I felt very grown-up. That same day she drove me to the studio of Empire's makeup maestra, Violet Andreas. She sat me in the chair and told Violet I needed some lessons in what could be done with the artful application of makeup to conceal the blemish on my cheek, lessons I have used to my advantage every day ever since.

From Malibu I drove to the *parfumier* in Beverly Hills and collected his condolences when I ordered a new bottle of Panache. That same day I visited other boutiques where my name sufficed for credit. I ordered bedding, fine cotton sheets, dishes and silverware, and a set of cookware (though I'd never cooked for myself) to be delivered. My place was far from any restaurants, so on my way home I went to the small local market and stocked up on eggs (how hard could it be to scramble an egg?), TV dinners, fruit, potato chips, beer, champagne, and boxed donuts. The checker gave me my change and a sheet of something green.

"What's this?" I asked.

"Green Stamps," he said. "Everyone saves Green Stamps. You know," he went on patiently, "you get these stamps when you shop, and you paste them in the little books and then you take them to the Green Stamp store and buy stuff." He looked pleased.

I just laughed. "I'll never lick a bunch of stamps and paste them in a book! That's ridiculous. Here." I gave them to the woman in line behind me and left the place amused.

To cover the bare walls I called up the librarian at Empire's archives and asked for half a dozen movie posters, films from the old days. I specifically said nothing with Denise Dell in it. The librarian found for me the pièce de résistance, a gaudy poster from the 1931 *Cyrano de Bergerac* that I hung above the fireplace. As a child at Summit Drive, I would sometimes watch *Cyrano* in the screening room all by myself just to see my father. I was jealous on Rowland's behalf when José Ferrer won the Oscar for Best Actor in '51 for playing the title role. My father was far better.

The bad news of the Malibu place was that I had to park my sweet little British sports car behind the bungalow on Pacific Coast Highway, where the salt air would eat away at the paint and the leather seats and the polished wood dashboard. Without telling Leon or Melvin Grant, I paid an Empire carpenter to build a garage for the MG.

Wearing rubber gloves and scouring away, I finally vanquished the dirt and decay while loud music played on my hi-fi—Peggy Lee, Rosemary Clooney, Frank Sinatra, Perry Como. I hung the framed movie posters. On the living room desk overlooking the Pacific, I put two framed photographs—a studio photograph of Julia from the thirties, and a snapshot of the two of us in Paris. I particularly liked this picture, because you could see the family resemblance. We both have dark hair, wide-set, dark eyes, broad foreheads, and the same smile.

Only then, when I had imparted some order to the place, did I invite Irene, sans Gordon, and sans Gordon Junior, and sans her twins, who were even worse brats than Junior. She was in the early weeks of another pregnancy, and so she was pale and unwell. Naturally she pronounced the place absolutely dreadful. She and I split a bottle of champagne on the deck before going out to eat at the Farm Café, which she also pronounced dreadful. She's very refined, my Irene.

Five years apart in age, we are a study in contrasts. I was always painfully self-conscious about my birthmark, socially awkward, and slow to make friends. Irene was like Grace Kelly before there was a Grace Kelly: beautiful, blonde, bland, impervious to trouble of any sort. Irene's mother had run off with a stuntman, and her father, Walter, was one of those actors destined always to play roles where he smokes a pipe. When Florence married Walter in 1941 (her third husband, by the way), she insisted I leave my grandparents' house and come live with them and Irene in Brentwood. I refused to go, and threw tantrums; I was ten years old and Summit Drive was the only home I had ever known. Leon and Julia said absolutely no, they would not part with me, until Florence threatened legal action. That would have meant a scandal. Florence would have done it too. She had a long-smoldering resentment against Leon and Julia.

Florence's childhood had been blighted when her little brother, Aaron, died in a boating accident at the age of four. Leon and Julia were both shattered by the boy's death, emotionally catatonic for ten years, until I was born in 1931. Julia always said that just by being born, I had brought them back to life. They doted on me, indulged me, applauded all my little victories, and chastised my flaws, though they mostly overlooked my major faults, so much so that even though the stain on my cheek means I'll never be truly beautiful, I have a certain amount of confidence, even *esprit* that I probably haven't earned.

Quite apart from the fact that I usurped her parents' affection, Florence never reconciled herself to the birthmark on my cheek. She wept on the day I was born. On the Cyrano set, no less. Certain that my father was having an affair with an actress who played a nun, Florence had insisted on watching the filming even though she'd been having intermittent contractions. Cameras were rolling in that last poignant scene where Cyrano (my father) was about to expire in Roxanne's arms when Florence let out a terrible scream, and then several more in quick succession. They hauled in a divan, Florence lay down, and Rowland fainted when I was delivered by the studio nurse assisted by the wardrobe matron. Swaddled in Cyrano's velvet cape, they put me in my mother's arms. She kept brushing my right cheek with her hand, and crying. And how do I know this? She told me. More than once.

Florence never liked me, but *tant pis*. I hardly ever saw her after she went to South Africa. That is, until she married Walter, and (still throwing tantrums) I was forcibly removed from Summit Drive to live in stuffy Brentwood. I rebelled in every way I could think of. Irene did not rebel; she just waited it out with a serenity I came to admire, and then, to imitate. Irene refused to call Florence Mom, and I refused to call Walter Dad, so they just stayed Florence and Walter. Irene and I became true sisters, allies against The World of Florence and Walter. Julia and Leon came to love Irene like another granddaughter.

And then she married Gordon. She was not yet twenty. As soon as she moved out of the Brentwood house, Florence started eyeing my birthmark as though she—once again—wanted to "do something" about it. I'd already been subject to two of these painful, fruitless treatments. I telephoned Julia in tears, and she said, "Pack your things. You're coming home." Never were words sweeter to my ears.

When Florence found me throwing clothes in a suitcase, I (never averse to drama) declared, "I'm leaving, and you'll never be able to hurt me again!"

I was certainly wrong on that score, but it felt good to say it. On my St. Francis of Assisi days, I feel sorry for Florence. The rest of the time, I try not to think about her at all.

Like Irene, Jonathan too pronounced my Malibu place dreadful. He does not like the sand, or the ocean, for that matter. He's fastidious; so fastidious that he actually liked the military school his father sent him to. Military school, however, didn't make him a soldier, and as soon as he graduated he went to New York to study Method acting. When he came back to California a few years later he immediately moved out of his father's Summit Drive house and rented a big place in Laurel Canyon, quickly dubbed Casa Fiesta, where the parties give themselves. Everyone young comes to Casa

Fiesta to complain, to gloat, to boast, or carp, to preen, to get their egos stroked, to get laid, or to get drunk. The liquor bills alone probably eat up half of what Jonathan makes on any given picture, especially since his roles are still minor, and mostly in those dreadful sword-and-sandal pictures so popular nowadays.

"You should have come to last night's party," he said, brushing the sand from his cuffs and sitting down on one of the deck chairs after he'd dusted it off. "Perfect for you. Literary, even. Charles Bukowski came and recited his poetry while Bongo played, and a girl in a beret danced."

"A beret and what else?"

"Not much. I bagged her later that night." *Bagged* was Jonathan's personal expression for his trophy collection. I always said the phrase made him sound like some sort of grouse-hunting aristocrat, which he took as a compliment. "Monty Clift came," he went on, "and Natalie Wood was there, and that actor you dated a couple of weeks ago. What was his name?"

"I can't bear to remember. His breath would strip the *Queen Mary* of varnish. Anyway, I'm finished with actors altogether, except for Bill Holden or Burt Lancaster."

"They're too old for you!"

"Well, maybe. But I am getting bored with the usuals, the handsome, the uncomplicated, the good dancers, the good tennis players."

"And good in the sack," he finished up.

"Yes, fine. But I'm tired of actors. They are all egotistical, vain, and insincere."

"You describe me perfectly."

"You don't count. You are a Duckling and a Quacker."

Jonathan and I were once the Order of the Ugly Ducklings. The only two members. As a kid he was fat and had a stammer. Long gone is that stammering, insecure, pudgy youth. Jonathan Moore is tall, dark, and dreamy like Tyrone Power, classically handsome, with an arch, often cutting wit. However, I still have my Ugly Duckling birthmark. I handed him a beer, cracked open my own beer, and plopped down in the chair next to him.

"What do you do out here all day?" he asked.

"Read, walk, eat, drink, swim, play the piano. Watch television when the rabbit ears work."

"You'll get fat and stupid if you keep that up, Quacker."

Bruno, walking on the beach with the Wilburs, saw me, and dashed across the beach and up the stairs, slobbering great doggy kisses and immediately trying to befriend Jonathan too. Jonathan fought him off.

"Down, Bruno!" I pulled him away.

"God! Roxanne! How can you stand that dog!"

"I love you, don't I, Bruno?" I crooned, and petted the setter's happy head. I led him down the stairs, giving a halfhearted wave to the Wilburs as he ran toward them.

"Those are your only neighbors? Those two? They look like dried figs with feet."

I laughed. "They do, don't they?"

"How can you stand it out here with only those people and their big stupid dog?"

"I like it here."

"It's not Paris."

"True, but it's home."

We watched the waves in companionable silence, like two old people who have shared a lifetime together, which, I suppose, we have. Jonathan's mother had left when he was a toddler, and his much-married father, an imperious executive at MGM, was never interested in him. They too lived on Summit Drive, but Jonathan was much happier at my house, where Leon and Julia were fond of him. As kids, he and I had the run of Empire, the backlots, and any soundstage not in use; we played pirates on the studio's ships; we sailed our toy boats in the waist-deep water of the filming pool; we had gunfights and wrangled chickens on the Western sets, played cops and robbers on the New York street. We went anywhere we damn well pleased; the studio guards could reprimand us, but we were never punished, because Leon was always willing to forgive us our childish trespasses. We were golden, and ours was a childhood like no other. We took a vow at thirteen always to tell each other the truth, and never to kiss or be boyfriend and girlfriend. We did once kiss, but it was gross. Like kissing your brother.

"Speaking of Bill Holden . . ." He grinned conspiratorially. "You wanna hear a secret? My agent got me an audition for *The Bridges at Toko-Ri*! Bill Holden! Grace Kelly! Jonathan Moore!"

"You Quacker! Congratulations!"

"It's the great dramatic role I was born for; well, it's on the way to the great dramatic role I was born for—Hamlet. I'm every bit the actor that Monty is, that James Dean is, and all I get offered are sword-and-sandal crap."

"Not after *The Bridges at Toko-Ri*! The offers will come pouring in! Oh, I'm so jealous! You've found the thing you were born to do. You can say, 'I'm an actor!' Me? I'm fit for nothing."

"You're a girl. You just need to get married."

"Don't be stupid. I'm Roxanne Granville, named for the romantic heroine of a great play. My father has been knighted by the queen. Why would I want to change names?"

"All the girls want to be married."

"And live like Irene and Gordon in that big, sterile house crawling with servants, and a lot of brats underfoot? No thanks."

"It doesn't have to be like that."

"How would you know? Besides, can you think of a single man of our acquaintance who would make a good husband? Even one?"

Jonathan thought on this for a while. Then shook his head.

"Exactly."

"You could be one of those louche women who lie by the pool at the Beverly Hills Hotel and float on their money and their connections."

"Julia would be ashamed of me if I did."

"Well, what do you want, Quacker?"

"I want to be glamorous like Julia was. She always said glamour is nothing more than knowing how to talk fast, laugh fluidly, gesture economically, and leave behind a shimmering wake."

"What does that mean, exactly?"

"I'm not sure. But she could do it. She made it look easy."

"Maybe you'll grow into it, Quacker."

"Maybe, but what'll I do in the meantime? I need a job. Something."

"You could have any job you want at Empire, any job a woman can do. Editor, set decorator, costumes, makeup."

"You have to train for years for those! I'm too restless to be a student of anything. Besides, whatever I did at Empire, everyone would say, 'Oh, poor Roxanne, only her grandfather would give her a job.' And even if they didn't say it, they'd think it. I have to prove my own self worthy of . . ." I didn't know what. I swilled from the beer bottle in a manner that would have scandalized my grandmother.

"Well, why don't you try your hand at writing? You had to learn something from those old boys and their story conferences, Simon and Max and Nelson and Jerrold."

"'Story is all!'" I said, quoting Nelson. "'It doesn't mean your picture will be boffo at the box office, but without a good story, you might as well bend over and kiss your movie goodbye.'"

"All right. Get yourself a typewriter and have at it."

"I don't want to write. I don't have the discipline for it."

Jonathan sipped his beer thoughtfully, unusual for him. "Why not be an agent? Join one of those big agencies. Go out to lunch and let the waiters fawn over you and your handsome clients."

"I would never be your agent. I pity your agent."

"But you admit that I'm handsome."

"Sure, Quacker. Still, it's an idea. You don't hear of too many women agents."

"You don't hear of women directors either, but then there's Ida Lupino, and I know how much you admire her."

"I do admire her, but I don't have the . . ." Courage? Heart? Talent? Drive? I didn't know what I didn't have.

"Didn't you just tell me you are the famous Roxanne Granville, named for a heroine? Your father's a Sir. Why should you be afraid to be an agent?"

"I'm not afraid. I'm . . ." Not sure what I was.

"Everyone knows the studio system is crumbling. Believe me, I'm an actor. Actors, producers, directors, writers, we're not all living in our little slave cabins around the big house like we used to. We're more independent, but we need savvy intermediaries. Now more than ever. You could do that. Didn't L'Oiseau d'Or teach you how to be charming?"

"The word is *charmant*! Agents aren't *charmant*. They are mercenaries."

"Mercenaries in a good cause. Pity the poor, struggling actor or writer, Roxanne." He folded his hands in prayer and looked out to the horizon. "They have talent, ambition, high hopes"—he smashed out his cigarette and added—"but they need someone to look after them, to make sure they're always working. You're Roxanne Granville who knows all the right people! You should become an agent and help these poor, lost souls."

"I told you, no more actors."

"Okay, writers! You like to read. You actually like writers, and you did learn from the best of them."

"That's true."

"They're clever. You're clever."

"That's true too," I said, pleased.

"There's your answer, Quacker."

Two days later the prestigious Rakoff/Holtz Agency hired me without a blink, though I had no experience, no references, couldn't type, and hadn't graduated from college. Perhaps they were impressed that I could speak French and Italian fluently, that

I had once mastered Debussy on the piano, that I had gone to L'Oiseau d'Or finishing school, that I wore couture clothing (Dior and Balenciaga). Perhaps they were impressed that in modeling myself on the late Julia Greene, one of the city's most renowned philanthropists, I had the aristocratic confidence to wear a diamond ring in daytime. Or perhaps because my grandfather is the legendary Leon Greene of Empire Pictures. Or maybe because my father is Sir Rowland Granville, recently knighted by the new queen and currently wowing West End audiences in *Macbeth*. Let me put it this way: I didn't have to drop any name but my own. And I sure as hell didn't start in the mail room.

CHAPTER FOUR

Rakoff/Holtz had a high-rent address on Sunset, four floors over-looking the boulevard, and twenty years' worth of cinematic history to its credit, with a dazzling roster of actors, directors, and writers. The offices were traditional as a pair of spats. Irv's partner Sidney Holtz had died the year before, and an enormous oil portrait of him hung in the reception room. Bad art and bad taste, if you ask me, though, of course, no one did. When I have my own agency, I intend to have splashy modern art on the walls.

Far from where any Rakoff/Holtz clients might see us, we five trainees shared an undifferentiated, nearly windowless room that we called The Farm. We were the Farmhands. Each gray metal desk had a hulking typewriter, a telephone, and an address book that popped happily open when you put the arrow on a certain letter. A bulletin board across one wall listed our assignments color-coded to our names. As the only girl, the guys teased me about how badly I typed. To their gibes I would reply: *Does Swifty Lazar do his own typing? No. When I have my own agency, I won't have to type.* However, I kept an empty desk drawer so the trash can would not visibly fill up with my mistakes.

Three fans hummed on low, but we were sweltering on this August morning. The guys took off their jackets the minute they arrived, loosened their ties, and rolled up their sleeves. Joe Roberts even had his shoes off and his feet up on the desk as he read the *Hollywood Reporter.* No such mercy for me: stockings, heels, slim skirt, and a crepe de chine blouse. Tom Willis's desk was empty, and we all wondered if he was too hungover to come to work. He drinks more than all of us put together.

"Hey, Roxanne," Joe called out. "It says here that over fifteen million Americans now have television sets, and by nineteen fifty-five there'll be another fifteen million. What does Leon Greene think of that? I bet he's trembling in his boots, isn't he?"

"Probably crying in his beer," offered Dave.

"Leon Greene is not trembling in his boots, nor crying in his beer," I retorted, though in truth, since I moved to Malibu, I had seen Leon only on three public occasions honoring Julia's gifts to the arts, galas where Denise was emphatically not present. My grandfather and I were not on the best of terms, but I wasn't going to let these two think they could belittle him. "Leon has had thirty-five years in the film business, and that's like a hundred and thirty-five anywhere else. He survived the talkies. He survived the formation of the unions and the strikes that followed. He survived the costs of Technicolor. He survived the War. And when the courts made the big studios divest themselves of the theaters they owned, he survived that."

Joe made a snorting noise. "Oh, he prospered from that, Roxanne. The smaller studios like Empire and Paragon, they never owned theaters. That leveled the playing field for them. What I want to know is, will he survive television and the Red Menace?"

My phone rang before I could reply.

"Come up to Mr. Rakoff's office at ten forty-five," said Bonnie, Mr. Rakoff's secretary. "And it's too hot for coffee. He wants champagne this morning. Three glasses."

Today was the first time Mr. Rakoff had asked for champagne, and I wondered if there was a special occasion, or just the heat. In the kitchenette I put the bottle in its crystal ice bucket and the flutes on the tray, and started up the stairs. L'Oiseau d'Or taught me how to master the stairs in high heels, though, admittedly, as a student there I did not carry a tray. The other Farmhands actually envy me this part of my job. The guys are almost never face-to-face with Irving Rakoff himself (to say nothing of the firm's most illustrious clients). But after working here for six months, I know exactly what will happen. While I pour coffee, Mr. Rakoff will say something like, *Of course you remember Roxanne Granville* . . . And I exchange pleasantries with whoever it is, usually someone I remember a lot younger with less paunch and more hair.

Despite her cheery name, the secretary, Bonnie, looked more like a mother superior. She never wore anything but navy blue or black. "He's expecting you."

"Who's the client?" I asked.

"Richard Neville."

Richard Neville was an aging actor best known for swashbuckling other men's wives. "And the third glass?"

"Who knows, maybe for you, Roxanne." She rose, opened the door to Irv's office, and closed it behind me.

Irv Rakoff didn't get to be a legend in this business because of his looks. Middle-aged, with a graying crew cut and pasty skin, he had heavy, dark jowls that spread across the collar of his shirt and drooped over his tie. Coatless in this heat, he sat at his desk. "Good morning, Roxanne. Why don't you open that now and pour some for yourself?"

I turned to the table and popped the cork expertly while inwardly crowing, *Promotion, promotion! I've worked here six months and I'm getting a promotion!* But as I poured the third glass, I felt Mr. Rakoff behind me, pressing, pushing himself into my behind, in fact. Unmistakably he had an erection. His arms encircled my waist, his hands stroked my hips and moved up to fondle my breasts. He breathed heavily. His lips, at the back of my neck, nuzzling, damp. Accelerating revulsion and disgust ripped across my brain like a car chase in a silent movie. I could feel my birthmark flood with color, but I just stood still, frozen, uncertain, bottle in

hand, thinking: *If I turn around, he'll kiss me. If I stand here, he'll . . .*
So I turned around and poured champagne all over his boxer
shorts. He wasn't wearing any pants.

"Sonofabitch!" he cried, jumping backward. "Goddammit,
Roxanne!"

"Oh, Mr. Rakoff! I'm sorry. Did I just—"

"Goddammit!" He fluttered his boxer shorts over his erection.
"You're not so very special, Roxanne."

"Maybe not," I retorted with more bravado than I felt, "but
I'm not just off the bus from Arkansas either. Imagine if I told my
grandfather about this."

"You won't."

He was absolutely right. I would not tell Leon. Suddenly the
humiliation of the situation crashed upon me. I dropped the bottle
onto the carpet, moved to the door, and flung it open.

There was Bonnie at her desk, and sitting in a chair across from
her was Richard Neville, all bronzy-tan and shock of cinnamon-
colored dyed hair, with his mouth dropped open to have a view of
me with champagne all over my skirt, Rakoff standing there in his
underwear, and the bottle lolling on the floor.

Bonnie leapt from her desk, pulled me roughly into her office,
closed the door with a thud, and told Neville without so much as a
blink, "Mr. Rakoff will be just a moment. Roxanne, I have a
bunch of scripts that need delivering."

Richard Neville started to laugh, a deep, throaty, theatrical
laugh, and Bonnie gave a smirk. They were not laughing at Irv
Rakoff in his underwear. They were laughing at me, knowing exactly what happened in there. A comic scene. Just another Hollywood day. I wanted to protest, to yell or cry out, but, as if I was
suddenly struck dumb, no sound came from my lips.

Suddenly Tom Willis popped into the room. Grinning, handsome in a crisp new wide-lapel suit, he offered Richard Neville a
hearty, masculine handshake while ladling fulsome praise all over
his latest unremarkable picture. Bonnie rose and opened Irv's door.

He was back behind his desk (and I assume he had his pants on). He called out in a jovial fashion, totally in control of himself and the situation, "Richard, come and meet Tom Willis. He'll be your new liaison while we work on this deal. He'll see to it you're very well treated. He's a Dartmouth man."

The mirth died from Neville's lips, and color drained from his face. He knew this meant Irv Rakoff, the name partner, would no longer personally represent him; he was passé, maybe even finished, handed off to . . . "What did you say your name was?"

"Tom! Tom Willis, your new agent."

"Plenty of time to get acquainted," Irv said. "Come into my office."

Bonnie closed the door after them. She took from her desk a stack of scripts and placed them unceremoniously in my arms. "Deliver these, then come back to the office and take up the rest of your duties."

"You think letting Mr. Rakoff feel me up is part of my duty?" I rasped. I know my mouth was gaping, but I couldn't help it. "You think I'm supposed to—"

"If you know what's good for you, you'll shut up right now." As if on cue, her phone rang, and she picked it up. "Mr. Rakoff's office."

I went downstairs feeling rickety, uneven, tottering in my heels, knowing I had to go back to the Farm to get my purse and keys before I could leave. I went first to the women's bathroom and washed my hands and saw Julia's diamond ring flash in the harsh light. I started to cry, bringing my wet hands to my face until I all but heard her voice. *Not here. Not now. Never forget you are named for the romantic heroine of a great play . . .*

After I collected myself (which took some doing), I strolled into the Farm, where the guys were all underemployed—reading the newspaper, chatting on the phone, doing a crossword—but when they looked up and saw me, their collective expression was sympathetic. Did they know? Did they guess? "I spilled champagne on my skirt," I stammered.

Dave handed me the newspaper. "I know Max Leslie is a friend of yours," he said.

My heart sank as my eyes devoured Hedda Hopper's shrill column excoriating Max as another Red serving the ambitions of the Soviet Union, another cowardly Red who had taken the Fifth before the House Committee and refused to name his Communist comrades.

"His ass was cooked when his name showed up in the pages of *Red Channels.* Anyone, everyone whose name is there, well . . ." Joe sliced across his throat.

"He'll probably have to leave the country like so many others," said Dave.

"Or shoot himself like Nelson Hilyard," said Joe.

"Hilyard was a homo," Dave clarified. "At least Max Leslie isn't an actor, or a director. They're really screwed. A writer can always find someone to front for him—put a new name on the script and who knows the difference? Sometimes the studios themselves slip a different name on the credits, and keep their own men working."

"Leon Greene would never do that," said Joe. "Is it true that he makes everyone at Empire recite the Pledge of Allegiance every morning, Roxanne?"

I collapsed at my desk.

"To name names, or not to name names! That is the question!" cried Dave, shattering the dour mood by leaping to his feet and striking a Shakespearean pose. "A story in three classical acts: First, you abase yourself before the Committee, then you swear it was a rotten mistake in your rotten youth, which you deeply, truly, tremendously regret—pause here for sackcloth and ashes." He crossed himself and looked skyward. "Then you blather the name of every face you can remember, and some you can't. The more names, the better. The more they love you. Mea culpa, the gang's all here! Or there. Or about to get subpoenaed. The Committee then thanks you for your courageous and forthright testimony, and you thank them for the opportunity to serve your country and for their fine work serving our country, and everyone is just so delighted to serve their country that 'Stars and Stripes Forever' blares over the loudspeakers." Dave hummed a few bars and saluted. "Be a friendly witness, and you go on working. Do it not, and your life is over!"

Joe picked up a pencil, brought it down on the desk like a gavel, and barked at me, "Are you now or have you ever been a member of the Communist Party? Speak up! Don't think you can claim the First Amendment! Men have gone to prison for that!"

Tom Willis ambled into the Farm, beaming, happy to inform them all of his promotion in glowing terms. "Lunch and drinks are on me, boys! Success will make me invincible!"

I collected my purse and keys, thinking, *How goddamned stupid can you be, Tom?* But maybe they don't teach you at Dartmouth that Hollywood is like a huge hothouse, steamy and enclosed. Everyone's lives and loves, their fortunes, their so-called sacred honor, their sins, their failings, their bad judgments, their bad breath, their bad debts are like the steam that rises on the hothouse walls, dripping with what everyone—actors, writers, agents, producers, directors, the press, the critics, the musicians and the carpenter, the sound man—knows. In Hollywood fame, money, reputation, friendship, even love and marriage are conditional, flimsy, and often for effect. *No one is invincible, Tom. The film business is like the house of straw where everything can be blown away with one foul gust. Just ask Max Leslie.* Which is what I intended to do.

CHAPTER FIVE

By the time I arrived at Max and Marian's, the hot August air had dried the champagne from my skirt, leaving the barest outline of a stain. As I pulled into the driveway of their big two-story faux Tudor house on Carolwood Drive, my own ordeal paled in comparison to the scene before me. Someone had splashed buckets of red paint across the front porch, the door, the lower windows. It looked to have dried, but I certainly wasn't going to step on the porch. I went round to the back, through a rustic gate and arbor draped with red climbing roses. "Max," I called out. "Marian? It's me, Roxanne!"

Max, sitting on the edge of the pool, his pants soaked to the knee, looked up. His bare feet were in the water, which was an odd color; a sickly mauve ribbon rose up from the deep end and floated like a banner toward the shallow end, where he sat. He had a glass on one side, a bottle on the other. He smiled, though his eyes were deep-ringed with misery behind his glasses, his gray hair hung lank across his brow.

"Max, what's happened? Who did this to your house? Who could have done this?"

He rose unsteadily and dripped over to me, took me in a great, warm hug redolent of Scotch and sweat. "Roxanne, dear little Roxanne."

"Max, have you called the police?"

"The police won't lift a hand. I'm an avowed Communist, remember? A marked man."

I glanced over at the pool and saw underwater in the deep end the patio furniture, table, a few chairs, and great sodden cushions that had sunk to the bottom. And a couple of gallon cans of red paint.

"Those zany Marx brothers came by," he said. "But instead of Groucho, Harpo, and Chico, it was Karl Marx and his brothers, Nikita and Stalinski. They just went wild," he added with a small, scruffy smile, though the joke fell flat. "It's good of you to come, Roxanne, but you shouldn't have. I'm assuming Leon doesn't know you're here."

"Leon doesn't get to tell me what to do. I have my own place now at Malibu. I won't go to Summit Drive as long as Denise and Elsie live there. So I don't care what Leon thinks."

"Then you're the only person in Hollywood immune to what Leon Greene thinks."

"Where is Marian?" I asked, now seriously worried.

"Visiting Norman." Max wobbled back to the shallow end, sat on the steps, his feet in the water.

I had never met their son. Only heard about him. I kicked off my high heels and put my feet in too, stockings and all. "How is Norman?"

"Norman's the same as he ever was, or ever will be," he said with a shrug. "Marian always wanted to keep him living with us, no matter what. She thought that she could love him into being like other kids. But once he got to be sixteen, well, we had to put him in a home. That's what they call it, and it is a home, I suppose. Beautiful, serene, secure. Expensive." He sipped from his glass. "Marian and I just about broke up over Norman. More than once," he added. "Now Norman is well cared for, and Marian goes to see him five days a week. She feeds him. Like a baby."

"That is a sad story, especially for a comedy writer."

"The screenwriter's Buster Keaton."

"Max, what happened yesterday with the Committee?"

"I got my dick put in the wringer—begging your pardon, dear girl." He sipped more Scotch and looked at the nearly empty glass as though it might be about to speak. "I should never have let Melvin Grant handle my case. I wanted one of those left-wing lawyers like Wilkie, but Melvin Grant insisted he should represent me, swore he could make it all right. He set it all up. An executive meeting of the Committee convened just for me in a discreet hotel room, no press. He said it was all just a formality anyway, and if the Committee asked me to name names, I wouldn't be telling them anything new. They already knew who these people were. They just needed to hear it from me. Marian wanted me to do it. So I could go on working. She begged me. Even though I would have had to give up her name, she insisted. So I told Grant I'd co-operate."

"Why didn't you? I mean, if they already had the names . . ."

"That's what they told Vic Hale, I'm sure."

"They didn't know about you till Vic gave them your name?" Vic Hale had come to Empire in the years I'd been gone. I didn't even know him, but I despised him now, and I always would.

"Vic Hale named names because his agent told him it would be a good idea. His agent and his attorney, Melvin Grant. How could he resist the two of them?"

"I know why Melvin Grant would think that—he works for Leon—but why would the agent care?"

"Because if Vic isn't making money, the agent isn't making money either. That simple."

Had Irv Rakoff stooped to telling his clients they should name names if the Committee asked? Did all agents? The thought made me sort of sick.

"It's like the La Brea Tar Pits," Max went on, "a great pool of sludge that sucks people into it, and when they climb out, no matter what they did or said, they're covered in sludge, and they leave tracks wherever they go. That's what's happened to me. To Vic. To any of us." A dry, hot breeze swept over us, ruffling the weirdly colored waters. "You want a drink, Roxanne? I should have asked."

"No. No, I'm fine." I patted his shoulder.

"Melvin Grant and I got to the hotel room, one of those big downtown hotels, so old even the walls have nicotine stains, and the elevators creak, and the radiators leak rusty water, room number—whatever it was—and the Committee men, they're already there. It's set up like it's all supposed to be dignified. We engage in a lot of greasy formality before I swear on the Bible, and we finally get to it. Am I now or have I ever been a Communist, and I say, yes, sir—I really did call that little rodent "sir"—I was once a Communist, but I left the Party in thirty-nine when Stalin made his pact with Hitler, and I never went back. I am a dedicated American. So far so good. We exchange a few lines about how great our country is. All the time I'm sitting there, the cigarette smoke is getting thicker by the minute, and I'm thinking, what the hell right do they have to ask me any of this? Then they wanted names, and I realized that Melvin had sugarcoated the turd. If I named names, lots of my friends and comrades would also get their tits and dicks put through the wringer. I've been writing dialogue my whole adult life and I just couldn't seem to make the lines they wanted come out of my mouth. I'm sitting there, wondering what I should do. I can't invoke the First Amendment, free speech. I know that for damn sure. Look what happened to Dalton Trumbo, Adrian Scott, Ring Lardner, and the rest of the Hollywood Ten. They insisted the First Amendment protected them. That defense and the appeals went through the courts for a couple of years, and when the Supreme Court declined to hear their case, well, guess what? They all went to federal prison. So if the First Amendment is no good, what's left but the Fifth? I kept looking around that hotel room, the rusty radiator underneath the window, the pigeons crowded on the sill. The mirror had a little crack in it. And then I looked at the bed, and I knew that no one but prostitutes had ever made love in that bed, no one but whores had ever made love in this room. So I took the Fifth."

I listened to the pool water slurp along the sides for a few minutes. "What will you do now?"

He sipped in silence. "Well now I'll lose my job with Empire, and no one else will ever hire me. They're the only studio I've ever worked for."

"But you have a contract with Empire! You've been there . . . longer than I've been alive."

"The studios have dumped better writers than me, and all those writers had contracts too. The studio heads are a law unto themselves. When Leon Greene wants you gone, you're gone."

"It's tragic."

"It's actually comic. There was never any serious Red threat in the movies, no matter what Ayn Rand and the rest of them think, and the party never advocated overthrowing the government. The only people who made those kinds of outlandish statements at meetings were FBI spies, stooges who would show up to foment insurrection and collect names. That's the comic part."

"But it's tragic what's happened to you and Simon and Jerrold and Nelson."

Max draped his arm over my shoulders. "How can I explain it to you, what it was like twenty years ago in the thirties? Oh, sure, there was a lot of ideological struggling, Trotsky versus Stalin, all that sort of thing, but really, here in Hollywood, the Communist Party was a big social network. That's where I met Marian. She was a script reader and I was a writer, and we were all very serious, hardworking people who believed we had the right to unionize. Simon and Nelson were always more committed to the party and its principles than I was—Simon was actively raising money for the Abraham Lincoln Brigade fighting in the Spanish Civil War. People forget now that in the thirties, the Communists were the only ones standing up to the fascists in Europe. Here in Hollywood, the Communist Party gatherings were where you went if you had a social conscience, if you wanted to act on behalf of the poor, the disenfranchised, the despairing, if you wanted to fight racism and fascism." He gave a rueful, halfhearted chuckle. "It's also where you went if you wanted to get laid. People who went to Communist Party meetings believed that all of us, writers, actors, the men who moved the sets, that we should speak with one voice through a union. I'm not ashamed of that." He drank the last of his Scotch. "Now all that youthful fervor for social injustice, on behalf of labor's right to organize, including the right to strike if need be—oh yeah, there were heads and hearts broken over that twenty years ago too—that has condemned me. Condemned us."

"You still have your self-respect," I offered, uncertain what else there was to say.

"I don't regret the choice I made to take the Fifth. But it's only been one day. I might change my mind."

"Is there some way I can help?"

"No. Thanks. You always were just the sweetest kid, but I don't want you involved in this. You're too young yet to have a past you'll have to pay for, Roxanne, a past you'll regret."

"Well, I'll get older, won't I?" The water lisped at the edges of the pool, sibilant, like baby talk. "Oh, Max, when I read Hedda's column today and all those terrible things she said about you—"

"Forget it. Tomorrow that paper will be on the bottom of the birdcage. But I'm still under subpoena. If I don't leave the country soon, they may take my passport. It's happened to others."

"Jerrold told us his passport was revoked after he got to France."

Max nodded sadly. "Simon and Leah have to stay in Mexico for the same reason. Well, Simon does, and Leah will never leave him." In the distance a siren sounded. "The FBI are around here for sure. You better go, Roxanne, now before someone sees that smart little car of yours in the driveway and takes down the license plate. You still drive that sweet little MG T?"

"I do."

"You were a pretty reckless driver, as I recall. Didn't you roll the Packard down a ravine one night?"

"I'm much more responsible now. That was a long time ago."

"Yes." He smiled. "A long time ago. We had some good times then, didn't we? You know, you remind me so much of Julia. You have her mannerisms. You're wearing her cologne."

"Panache."

"Ah, yes."

"You'll give Marian my love, won't you?"

"Sure." He waved the bottle of Scotch at me. "Go on now, Roxanne. Thanks for coming."

I picked up my shoes, though I didn't put them on. I said goodbye and left him there, and when I got to the gate, I heard a splash, and I turned to see that Max had waded into the pool, fully clothed, and was standing there in the shallow end making patterns in the water with his hands.

CHAPTER SIX

I drove away from Carolwood and up the narrow leafy roads toward the canyons. Between the anguish of seeing Max Leslie and the memory of Irv Rakoff pressed up against my butt, I hated the thought of delivering scripts. I went instead to Irene's ultramodern glass-and-steel house in Benedict Canyon, where I didn't even have to knock, I could just walk in and say, "I'm here!"

She was pleased to see me. She's always pleased to see me. Though she was many months pregnant, wearing a housecoat, and barefoot, with her hair in shiny metal curlers all over her head, Irene looked younger than her twenty-eight years. We chatted inconsequentially as I followed her through the cool, high-ceilinged rooms, the billiard room, the sunroom, and out to the circular flagstone patio, covered with a thick, thorny bougainvillea arbor. Off in the distance beyond the tennis court some men were using bulldozers and pickaxes and tearing up the lawn.

"Did you have a water main break or something?"

"No. Gordon's afraid the Soviets will set off the bomb, so he's having them dig a bomb shelter. I told him it'll have to have enough room for Josefina too." She nodded toward the pool, where the nanny played with the children. "Gordon says we gave the Soviets far too much when they were our allies, and in Korea—"

"Even the word *Korea* makes my head hurt." I felt cross and unsettled. The heat bore down, even through the bougainvillea arbor. "I voted for Stevenson."

"Don't tell Gordon that." She lit up, took a deep drag.

"When do I ever talk to Gordon? To him I'm just your immature kid sister."

"I have informed him you're not immature, you're a romantic with an overactive imagination, and you'll grow out of it when you get married and make someone a fine wife just like me."

I've no idea how she met Gordon. Polo grounds, maybe? At the country club tennis tournament? Someone's yacht? He was from Chicago, candidly ambitious, handsome in a freckled, red-headed way, good on the tennis court, and an avid sailor. He was still wearing his naval officer's uniform at their wedding in 1945. After the War, Gordon didn't merely go to work for Leon—within a year he became the de facto operating chief of Empire Pictures. He also became the son Leon lost, precious and beloved. Gordon can do no wrong in Leon's eyes. Gordon's children can do no wrong in Leon's eyes. I think Leon must be going blind.

"What are you doing out and about?" Irene lowered her pregnant self on the chaise. I plopped down beside her. "Isn't it a workday?"

"I'm supposed to be delivering scripts," I said sourly. I couldn't bring myself to tell her about Irv. "But I'm playing hooky."

"I've never understood what would possess you to want to be an agent, but it doesn't matter." She waved a graceful hand, as though dusting cobwebs. "Your career days are coming to a close. It's time you got married, and I'm looking for your husband. You're twenty-two, you know. If you don't marry soon, you'll fade like a dress left too long on a shop-window mannequin."

"Is that why you married Gordon? Because you thought you were fading? You are beautiful, Irene! You've always been beautiful."

"Doesn't matter. A woman has to choose. It's the one important life choice we get to make, so it had better be good. Gordon was the best-looking and the most persuasive man I'd ever met. We wanted the same things. I knew I could count on him to fulfill for me what I couldn't do for myself. Look around you, Roxanne. This is all Gordon's success, and I get to bask in it." She gazed out over the vast, shady garden, the pale-blossomed crepe myrtle trees lining the paths, the palms, the pool where the screaming three-year-old twins twisted in Josefina's arms, struggling, flailing with pudgy little fists.

"How can you let the twins do that," I asked, "and not tell them to stop?"

"I don't want to undermine Josefina's authority."

"Well, I pity Josefina when your next one is born."

"Oh, save your pity. We're hiring her sister to come when the new baby is born. They're happy to have the work. I can't deal with the kids."

"I been through your closet, Miz Conrad," said Eudonna the housekeeper when she brought us two lemonades. "What'll I do with all the red dresses? Some of them are mighty nice. I don't think the people who come to the Salvation Army will be wearing Chanel."

"Keep them, or give them away, I don't care. Just get them out of the house." After Eudonna left us, Irene lowered her voice. "Gordon said I had to throw out all my red clothes. You walk into a party in a red dress, and it makes you look un-American. People whisper about you."

I glanced at the table beside the chaise, where Ayn Rand's *The Fountainhead* lay, its spine cracked open. "You're not reading that, are you?"

"I told Gordon, 'Isn't it enough that I sat through the movie?' But he says no."

"All the characters are insufferable. You wouldn't want to ride an elevator with them." I leaned to the side and stuck my finger down my throat.

"Thank god Ayn's gone back to New York now, but she still

lingers here like the smell of an intellectual fart. After you left for Paris, Leon used to host dinner parties for the Motion Picture Alliance people, and Ayn Rand and Hedda Hopper were constantly competing for the most dramatic woman in the room. Exhausting, even just to watch them."

"Hedda Hopper, America's basset hound," I grumbled. "Did you read her long screed about Max in the paper this morning?"

"Someone should have told Max an actor is supposed to deviate from the script, not a writer."

"You're not usually that unkind, Irene." Prickly with heat, I stood, reached up under my skirt, and, never-minding the bomb shelter diggers and the team of Japanese gardeners snipping, clipping, and mowing nearby, I rolled my stockings down my legs, unhooked my garter belt, and let it drop on the ground. I shimmied out of my sticky, silky half slip and sank back into the chaise. "I went to see Max this morning. Someone has smeared the whole front of their house with red paint and poured the rest of the cans in the pool."

Irene lit up a cigarette and took a satisfying drag. "I'm sorry to hear that. Really, I am, and I know you loved those old writers, and they loved you, but they did it to themselves. They act like martyrs, but they're not. Melvin Grant set everything up for Max, just like he did for Vic Hale. Executive session in a hotel room, discreet, no reporters, no crowds, just a nice friendly conversation. It was all going to be easy, and then Max took the Fifth. Melvin won't even defend anyone who takes the Fifth, so you can imagine how that made him look. Whatever you do, don't mention Max to Leon, and, for god's sake, don't tell him you went there. He's in a rage over the whole thing."

"How would I tell Leon?"

"He's coming by to pick me up. We're going out to lunch."

"Oh god . . ." I moaned. I could feel my birthmark flushing.

"What is it?"

"The last time I saw him we were the guests of honor at a Philharmonic luncheon where they unveiled the plaque to Julia."

"And? Please tell me you didn't make some awful comment about Denise."

"I didn't call her a whore, if that's what you mean. I just said she wasn't a great actress."

"Oh, Roxanne, you know Leon thinks she's Jean Arthur, Rosalind Russell, Bette Davis, and Vivien Leigh all put together. Well, maybe not Bette Davis. But if you make this into a contest . . . well, Denise has already won, don't you see? She's not so bad, really."

"It hurts me to hear you say that."

"You are a reckless romantic. I am a married pragmatist." She blew out a fresh plume of smoke and put her hand over her belly, where the baby kicked. "I'll be so happy to have my body back once I get through this awful childbirth. Why can't it be like the scene in *Stagecoach*?"

"You mean, why isn't real life like the Hays Code? No swearing, no white slavery, no miscegenation, no venereal disease."

She laughed. "No nakedness, not even in silhouette, and if two people are on the bed, they each have to keep one foot on the floor, and absolutely no one can get knocked up and have a baby. So in *Stagecoach*, the married lady's face contorts, and they cart her off camera."

"And the next thing you know, without so much as a maternal peep, there's a clean, sleeping little cherub in her arms."

"Trust me, the real thing is goddamn messy, bloody, and painful. And the kid they hand you when it's over? It hardly looks human, much less worth all that work and pain. It's all gross and disgusting, and then once they're born, kids are nothing but trouble."

Eudonna led Leon to the patio to join us, and his face lit up to see me. He held out his arms, and he held me close till I squirmed out of his embrace. "So good to see you girls together, Snow White and . . . her sister," he said. I assumed he couldn't bring himself to say the words *Rose Red*. Too close to Communism. Irene rose, kissed his cheek, and excused herself to get ready. I stayed put. The Japanese gardeners had finished, the children were gone from the pool, the men digging the bomb shelter had taken a break and left the yard.

"Are you coming to lunch with us, Roxanne? Denise will be so happy."

He must be getting senile, I thought. "No, I just stopped by. I have scripts to deliver to Rakoff/Holtz clients. I have to go."

"Really?" Leon's broad brow furrowed.

"Yes. I'm working now, remember? I have been for six months."

"I meant you shouldn't be delivering scripts. That's the errand boy's job. You should be assisting one of the firm's partners, getting to know the business."

"Oh, I'm getting to know the business." I thought of this morning's sickening incident. If Leon knew, he would shred Irv Rakoff into a hundred pieces. Or would he? I glanced sidelong at him while he sipped the lemonade Eudonna brought him. Had Leon ever done such a repulsive thing? I knew he'd had affairs, lots of them, but I could not imagine Leon Greene pressing himself up against some unwilling girl as a condition of the job. His essential dignity, his pride alone would have kept him from any such gruesome display of power.

"Why do you look so grim?" he asked.

"I'm tired of serving coffee," I said, which was certainly true.

"You are serving coffee? Like Clarence? That's degrading."

If you knew the half of it, Leon . . . I felt woozy. "Oh, it's not so bad. It's like a play. I mean like George Bernard Shaw without the wit. We all have our lines."

"What kind of lines?"

"Well, Irv says: 'I'm sure you remember Roxanne Granville,' and whoever it is says, 'Yes, of course,' and I say, 'Yes, of course, I remember you from—'"

"What? They're parading you around like a monkey on a

string!" He stood and started pacing, always a bad sign. "Don't you see? How that reflects on you! On us! It's such an insult! Serving coffee like a maid! Do any of the others serve coffee?"

"No. But they're all guys." I was not at all immune to what Leon Greene thought of me. My birthmark suffused with color, and shame overwhelmed me.

"I ought to call Irv Rakoff and give him a piece of my mind. That would get some results!"

"Don't. Don't interfere. It's my job."

"How could you let them treat you like that and not protest? I didn't bring you up to accept insults. It's as much an insult to me and Empire."

The enormity of the affront, the ongoing, *daily* affront, racketed through my whole body. The mortifying spectacle! I thought about how many times I'd bent low to lay a tray on the table while Irv and his cohorts looked down my blouse or ogled my backside. No wonder none of the guys got asked to deliver coffee. *Oh yes, and I am Roxanne Granville, named for . . .* Shame and anger and the desire to deflect humiliation away from myself made me snap at him. "What do you intend to do about Max? Are you going to fire him?"

"I already have," he replied without a single qualm. "We have to protect our priceless heritage, our American ideals. Max did it to himself. We can't have Communists, radicals, and crackpots—"

"Leon! I'm talking about Max! He's not a crackpot. He's your friend!"

"I have to think of my country. There is a higher loyalty than personal relationships. We must stop the people who want to overthrow the United States government, maybe not by outright revolution, but by something more insidious. A Communist college professor corrupts his students. A Communist author like Howard Fast corrupts his readers. And movies, well, movies are the most powerful medium in the history of mankind. If movies are tainted with Communist messages or propaganda, then America itself is tainted. Moreover, I gave my word. We all did when we signed the Waldorf Agreement. We said we would never hire or keep on the payroll a known Communist." Behind his glasses his gaze was utterly without regret.

"Julia would spin in her grave if she heard you," I retorted, picking up my shoes and my clothes.

"And what would she do if she knew you were carrying coffee like a maid? I wonder if she'd think that fine French finishing school was worth it."

Trembling with rage and shame, for myself, for Max, for Julia and Leon and Empire Pictures—oh yes, I was a daughter of Empire, like it or not—I said goodbye and went into the house. I passed Irene, who was dressed, her hair in a smooth, perfect pageboy.

She took one look at my face. "You did it again, didn't you?"

"Enjoy lunch with that slut Denise."

I went into the bathroom to wait till I could hear them leave. In the mirror I stared at the birthmark that had made my mother hate me. Once when Jonathan and I were kids, we were underfoot on the Western town set. We just joined the extras in front of the sheriff's office when they called "Action." But suddenly, some underling, a guy, called out, "Cut!" and strode on-set, took my arm, and yanked me away, saying I couldn't be there, not with a face like that. Everyone—cameramen, script girls, gaffers, the director—held their breath. Clearly, he didn't know who I was. Simon Strassman got out of his chair, dismissed that guy, put his arm around me, and told me to go back and play the scene, that I would be fine. Simon told the cameraman to reshoot and the director did not dare object. The director knew who I was. But I could not move, and I could not hide my tears. I could not hide my tears now either. Alone in the bathroom, I started to blubber and cry. Irv Rakoff also knew who I was, and he had not one qualm about pushing himself up against me and putting his lips at my neck and his hands all over my boobs. I splashed water all over my face and came up dripping to look in the mirror and stare at Roxanne Granville, the stupidest girl on the planet.

In the kitchen Eudonna was chopping onions and listening to a Negro preacher railing on the radio. I asked her to turn it down as I picked up the phone and dialed Rakoff/Holtz. I shivered on one of the hottest days of the year, crying because Eudonna's damned onions were stinging my eyes.

"Put me through to Irv," I said to the agency operator.

"Mr. Rakoff's office," said Bonnie, all crisp business. "Who may I say is calling?"

"Leon Greene's office," I replied. "Mr. Greene wishes to speak with him."

"May I know what this is in regard to?"

"You may not."

"Leon!" said Irv when he came on the line at last. "What's this about?"

But I heard it. That little quaver of fear in his voice. *He thinks I might have told Leon.* Oh yes, cue the thunder. He was afraid of Leon. So that's what this was all about: power. Who had power, and who didn't. At this moment I did—fleetingly, yes, I wasn't so stupid as to think I could maintain it—but I let the silence linger for a moment to let him break a sweat. "I quit, Irv. You'll never humiliate me again. I know that you hired me so that you could tell your clients you had Roxanne Granville fetching and carrying for you, bowing and scraping, 'Of course, sir. Sugar? Cream?' And you must have thought that little escapade this morning would shame me so much that I'd be in your power—well, you can go to hell, and the next girl you press your dick against, I hope she turns around and knees you in the balls." I hung up and looked over at Eudonna, who was shaking her head and chopping her onions. I turned up the volume on her radio, and left.

I got in the MG and drove straight to the LA River, possibly the ugliest spot in all of Los Angeles, possibly the ugliest spot in the whole world, and parked near a stunted palm. I picked up the scripts from the passenger seat and, holding them in my arms, I made my way to the chain-link fence separating the city from the gray moonscape that lay before me. The LA River is not a river at all; it's nothing more than a gray-brown rivulet trickling between gray concrete banks. The sky overhead was a blue-bronze bowl, and the parched earth beneath my feet cracked, so dry no dust raised up. A razor-sharp wind cut through my short hair and along my stained cheek. I pulled the scripts from their envelopes and, one by one, I grabbed handfuls of pages, ripped them from their little pronged paper holders, lifted them high, and flung them over the chain-link fence, snagging my wrist now and then, the sharp points tearing at my flesh, my skin bleeding. The pages blew and danced in the wind, falling down the concrete slopes to the bottom of the channel, where they rolled beside the brown seam of dirty water. I felt a fresh crack of energy with each handful I tossed aloft, delighting in the destruction as the wind snatched them. Hundreds of them blew along the concrete alley, where they twitched and desiccated. I felt a small thrill of vindication or vengeance, or some emotion I did not quite recognize, to think of all these words that no one would ever read. All these lines no one would ever speak. All these scenes that would never see film. All that gone with the wind. As they say.

CHAPTER SEVEN

I drove home, took off the champagne-stained skirt, threw it in the trash, got in the shower, and washed off the rage and shame from the morning. Afternoon sun still burned across the beach as I stood on the high porch overlooking what I'd come to think of as my own domain, drying my hair with a towel. Bruno, the Wilburs' dog, jumped over the enclosure where they kept him and bounded up the steps. "What do you think, boy?" I asked, kneeling down and rubbing his ears. "What's next for me?"

Bruno only barked in reply, and the two of us took a long run up the beach, splashing in the surf. I had quit my job. Okay. Now what? The thought of trying other agencies made me wary. I'd never before experienced the sort of thing that happened this morning, even though I had lived in the heart of the Hollywood maelstrom all my life. As Julia and Leon's granddaughter I was protected as a child, a young girl. But now I had stepped into the adult world, the working world, and not even Leon could protect me there. If I got hired at another agency, wouldn't there always be some man, some boss who would assume I'd be willing prey? (Is there such a thing as willing prey?) What if I went independent? Could I beat Irv and men like him at their own game? In the six months I'd worked at Rakoff/Holtz, I certainly hadn't seen anyone do astrophysics or brain surgery. Agents brought together people with complementary needs, like Julia used to do in her salons in Paris. How hard could it be? As the surf washed over my ankles and Bruno barked happily beside me, I thought wistfully back to those Thursday evenings at the Parc Monceau apartment, smiled to think of the films and books and musical collaborations all given their first embryonic momentum there. Julia went out of her way to cultivate artistic people, not just Americans like Jerrold, but anyone who might mutually benefit one another. And they did. If the name Roxanne Granville had such panache, why shouldn't I use it myself?

And hadn't I learned from those story conferences in the library? Max, Simon, Nelson, Jerrold, taught me, early on, that the dramatic core of any film is characters who are being tested. Whether high drama or slapstick, *High Noon* or *Duck Soup*, the characters don't have to be saints, they just have to be interesting, have interesting motives, and respond to unlooked-for challenges. I knew a hundred hungry writers who could write stuff like that, writers who camped out at the lunch counter of Schwab's Pharmacy and were party regulars at Casa Fiesta.

I went to Casa Fiesta that night, where, as usual, there was a fluid cast of people who all resembled one another—young, eager, restless, ambitious, beautiful, looped on drinks or drugs, oversexed, or some combination of all of that. Ice jingled in glasses, and neat little marijuana joints passed from hand to hand. Casa Fiesta is the only place, other than Central Avenue, where you'll see race-mixing: Negro musicians and flamenco guitarists, artists and actors and writers, dancers and hangers-on. A bespectacled bongo player named, in fact, Bongo, seemed to live at Casa Fiesta. By day there was always some leftover guest lounging on the back patio or someone sleeping (or screwing) on the couch. I'm not sure Jonathan ever noticed.

Tonight, though, something special was afoot. Every actor Jonathan knew who had ever wielded a spear in a sword-and-sandal picture was there, all of them wearing robes or togas, costumes from these roles. In the back patio they had stoked a bon-fire in the firepit, and by the time I arrived, the flames were snapping high and the smoke was rising above the eucalyptus trees.

Someone put a drink in my hand and introduced me to a handsome Negro actor named Clayton Strong and his girlfriend, Rita, a PE teacher at Jefferson High. She wore a tattered bedsheet to suggest a Nubian slave, and he wore the costume of a Nubian king. Clayton towered over everyone here; he had played football for the UCLA Bruins, and even played pro football for a while.

"But I quit football. It's easier to be an actor and deal with bigots instead of dealing with bigots and getting the shit kicked out of me," he said.

"Yes," said Rita, bristling, "but it's a damned shame you can't be anything but a slave or a savage king. As an actor you have no . . . no . . ."

"No scope," he filled in for her. "It's true. I'm too old to be a shoeshine boy and too young to be someone's pappy."

"I can't imagine you as either one," I said.

Girls moved through the crowd, handing out finger cymbals and gongs to everyone. They turned out all the lights so our faces and bodies were lit only by the flames, and suddenly there burst among us Jonathan in a loincloth, shirtless, and barefoot, doing a wild dance. Amid the din and clang of instruments, the cheers and shouts, he finally snapped the loincloth off and fed it to the flames. Applause roared up with smoke. The sword-and-sandal actors each brought something symbolic to feed to the flames while they recited lines that had everyone clutching their guts with laughter. Clayton Strong shouted, "No more slaves!" and flung in some feathers. Some of the women who had appeared as snake-dancers or slave girls stripped down to their underwear. Diana Jordan, who had played a Roman prostitute who converted to Christianity, tore off her toga—and everything else. That was when we heard the sirens.

I got out of Casa Fiesta without being noticed because I didn't have to put my clothes back on. But my hair smelled of smoke all night long, and I had a hangover.

The next morning, hair washed, hangover defeated, I got on PCH about eleven. I had the top down and the ocean waves breaking on the beach to my right, dry-stubbled hills rising up on my left. I turned up Sunset, drove to the Garden of Allah, parked the MG there (with such a smart car, no one would ever know it didn't belong there), pushed the seats forward to protect the leather from the heat, and walked to Schwab's. I was a woman on a mission.

Just in front of Schwab's, Al Gilbert, who covered scurrilous stuff for a rag called *Secrets of the Stars*, was walking out. He was a big, wheezy man; I always thought of Al as sweat-stained even if you couldn't see the sweat stains. He held the door for me like he was Charles Laughton playing Captain Bligh. "Hey, Roxanne, care to comment on last night's orgy?"

"It was a church social and we all had strawberry ice cream."

"Come on. It was a race-mixing debauch where people were naked."

"I have a real story for you, Al. I heard it from a friend of mine."

His bloodshot eyes actually brightened, and he reached in his coat pocket and took out a pencil and scrap of paper. "Speak."

"A certain powerful man—"

"Who? I need names, Roxanne."

"I'm not saying. I heard it from a friend. He called her into his office and when she got there, he wasn't wearing any pants, and he comes up to her, and—"

Al gave a great guffaw. "That's not a real story! That happens all the time!"

"Well, if you published her story, maybe it wouldn't happen all the time."

"Who would believe her? Boo hoo, little me and the big, bad producer." He started to put his pencil away, then stopped. "I hear

Leon Greene fired Max Leslie within twenty-four hours of his taking the Fifth. Care to comment?"

"Would you like to quote me, Al?"

"Sure!"

"Then take this down. You and your kind are the enemas of the picture business."

"And we always get our shit."

I brushed past him and into Schwab's. The place was smoke-laden as usual, never mind the overhead fans. When I'd first started at Rakoff/Holtz last winter, I used to come to Schwab's for lunch just to hang out among the young writers. I always had a Coke and a ham sandwich and nursed the fantasy that someone would recognize me as a person with exquisite taste and terrific commercial instincts (knowing full well that those two things could cancel each other out). I daydreamed that a brilliant but unsung writer would come up to me and press into my hands a script that would turn out to be the next *Casablanca*. I liked to imagine that the story of how the script had come to me would itself become legend. Kind of like Swifty Lazar getting his name from Humphrey Bogart for having made him three deals in one day. That didn't happen, of course, at least not yet. Anyway, now I was an independent, and the daydream shone all the brighter.

As I went up to the counter, people were popping in and out of the phone booths, jumping up, jostling one another, eager, noisy. Schwab's, though an actual pharmacy and a soda fountain, is a de facto club, a regular rendezvous, a fish tank of sorts for enterprising, unemployed writers. There's camaraderie here, but there's competition too. You can all but taste it. Writers of all stripes and varieties are always on the lookout for someone to read their stuff, but mostly they come here to exchange gossip and ideas, to sniff out opportunities. The place percolates with ambition and energy. The mood at Schwab's is always upbeat. If you're down in the dumps, go someplace else and drink in the dark.

I ordered a Coke from the girl behind the counter, a beautiful girl with curled, cascading light brown hair, a red, voluptuous mouth, perfect teeth, and expectant blue eyes. Everywhere you look you see these perfect specimens of femininity, oozing Ava Gardner smolder or percolating Debbie Reynolds wholesomeness. It can be damned discouraging, having a face irredeemably marred in the world's capital of beautiful women.

I took my Coke and wandered over to a booth where many writers had parked themselves. I had a nodding acquaintance with most of these guys—and they were all guys. "There's a new agency in town," I announced. An expectant hush fell over the crowd; if I am not mistaken, the very fans overhead stopped in their revolutions. "Yes, boys, I have hung out my shingle. The Granville Agency is new and independent, and I'm taking on writers."

"On your back?" asked Art Luke with a moody laugh. Art doesn't usually make jokes. He was older than the rest; he had grown up in a Mormon enclave in Mexico and fought in the Pacific. He wrote hard-boiled films: lots of jaded detectives and gorgeous dames.

"Granville's Folly," scoffed Maurice Allen, an acerbic, displaced New Yorker who hated Southern California. "You'll never make it work."

"Don't be so sure. I know everyone in this town."

"A girl agent?" scoffed Jimmy Ashford, a pale young man who came from a family of walnut growers in the Valley and feared having to go back. "That'll be the day."

"A woman. My name is Roxanne Granville, and I have more panache in my little finger than you have sperm count in your left testicle." I waited for the laughter to die down. "I'm open for business. I'll be back here tomorrow at noon and every day this week just to collect your scripts. I'll read them all."

Charlie Frye wandered in, tanned, blond, a little disheveled as usual, handsome in his surfer way. I had met him at the lunch counter my first week with Rakoff/Holtz. He was writing dialogue on a napkin.

"Roxanne's just telling us she's opening her own agency," said Jimmy.

"I quit Rakoff/Holtz."

"You sure they didn't fire you?"

"Here's what happened." I lowered my voice in the manner taught by L'Oiseau d'Or, so that my words seemed musky and important even before I spoke them. "I went to a fortune teller the other night. She looked like Ava Gardner's going to look in thirty years. She held her hands over a crystal ball." I formed a tent with my fingers and closed my eyes. "'*Ma chère,*' she said, 'you are not meant to labor in the service of others. You are a true original. You are an independent. You are destined to represent the writer of the next *Casablanca*, and to do that you must be free.' Honest, guys, that's what she said, in French. I offer you my rough translation."

"I got a script right here in my front pocket, Roxanne," said Jimmy.

"Keep it there, along with your hands and your dick," said Charlie. "Roxanne, read my *Coast of Fortune*. It's the best!"

"I'll read it all," I said. "If it's any good, I'll represent you. I'll find you work. I can't promise Paramount or MGM, or even Empire or Paragon, but I can promise I will work for you, and I'll take ten percent of everything you make from here to eternity." Everyone guffawed at that. "We're all in the same boat, aren't we? All starting out. We need each other. Bring me your tired, your poor, your huddled masses of words. Tell your friends," I added, glancing around Schwab's. "I'm open for business."

My announcement had its intended effect. Pleased, I walked out of Schwab's, turned down Sunset, and went to church.

That is, I went to the first movie theater I came to. *From Here to Eternity* was playing, and the girl in the ticket booth (another simmering beauty) said it had already started. I didn't care. I had already seen it. Besides, I don't go to the movies for the film. I go for the religious experience. The Church of Rick and Ilsa, as Julia used to call it.

I bought some popcorn, stepped into the dark, and took an aisle seat, delighted that I hadn't missed the rolling-on-the-beach scene where for a few brief, ecstatic seconds Burt Lancaster and Deborah Kerr clasp each other in the surf. Oh, I long to meet the man who could do that for a woman! I sighed, nibbled the popcorn, and sank happily into the film.

For Leon, watching movies was work. Every night after dinner he went to the screening room at Summit Drive. Julia also sat through all those daily sessions, but pictures were never simply her profession; they were her passion. She shared that passion with me. A darkened theater was our favorite place on earth. She used to take me to matinees when I didn't weigh enough to hold down the seat. Sometimes we'd go to the glamorous palaces like Grauman's Chinese, but often we'd take in a double feature at a little music box of a theater in Westwood. We believed that theaters were a place of worship where magic washed over us, a world heightened, made brilliant with music, with action and romance, where all the sounds are crisp, and all the words are meaningful, and all the endings are happy or poignant, and you walk out bathed in emotions you didn't have to suffer for, or struggle for, or take any risks to feel so wonderfully enhanced. A gift. The false opulence, plush carpets, stale air, and palliative darkness combine to create a sacred space. A place of solace, hushed and holy. I recognized this same consecrated ambience the first time I walked into Notre-Dame in Paris, except that Notre-Dame did not have stale air, and the stories glowing in the stained glass windows were not nearly as exciting as the coming attractions in a darkened theater.

PART II

THE CHALLENGER

1955

CHAPTER EIGHT

'm sitting on an orange couch in Larry Sanford's office on Poverty Row, those little low-rent studios hunkered near Gower that make B Westerns, gangster flicks, monster movies, and Saturday-morning serials. Larry's office, like all the rest of them, is smelly, smoke-filled, with filthy windows; the Venetian blinds are missing slats, and lurid posters dot the walls (men looking resolute, women wailing in terror, slimy creatures). Larry and I are chatting away about Charlie Frye's *Return of the Cat People* and a couple of second-rate Westerns that Jimmy Ashford wrote. Larry isn't exactly committing to them, but he's enthusiastic about both my clients, and last year he bought one of Jimmy's Westerns, and a gangster script by Art Luke. The pay was mere *merde*, but he actually produced them. Now he's talking about Charlie's *Return of the Cat People* like it is *Citizen Kane*.

Larry stands up from behind his desk and moves to the couch where I'm sitting. The arms on this orange couch and the cheap coffee table in front of it have scorch marks where people have left their cigarettes to burn. Larry takes the cigar from his mouth and smiles, sits down and flings his arm across the back of the couch and toys with my hair. He puts his cigar in a nearby ashtray, and his hairy hand on my knee.

I am no longer the girl I was two years ago, speechless as Irv

Rakoff pressed up against my butt, but right now, I can't help but think of Diana Jordan. At a Casa Fiesta party, Diana told everyone that her recent elevation from sword-and-sandal to an earthy Bad Girl role in a new MGM noir picture happened because Mr. Moore (yes, Jonathan's awful father) got her on his couch, and, as she said, "All I had to do was moan." Then, to demonstrate, she leaned back and moaned. Very convincing. Should I lean back and moan in exchange for this opportunity? (I can all but hear Charlie: *Do it, Roxanne, it's great for me. If you care for me, Roxanne—and I know you do—lie down with Larry Sanford.*) In the world I live in, sex is a kind of currency. I very definitely remove Larry's hand from my knee. But if I am honest with myself, I wonder if I'm acting on principle or because Larry Sanford is small potatoes, and his orange couch is really appalling. If it were Jack Warner . . . ? "Sorry, Larry. No go. I can take this script somewhere else." But he pushes me back on the couch, rummages all over my blouse, yanking off the buttons while his cigar-breath covers my face, my mouth, until I can turn my head away. Larry grunts, one hand goes up under my skirt. I'm pinned there beneath him. I struggle to free my right arm. I smack his head, his ear, and then again, hard enough to make him cry out in pain. I slither out from underneath him and kick the coffee table over. Ashtray and cigar go flying.

Larry gives a rough laugh and sits up. "Well, it was worth a try. No hard feelings."

"Sure, Larry," I say casually, though I am trembling, sweating. I'd never let this bastard guess how much he has rattled me.

"Rethink my offer, Roxanne." Larry ambles back to his desk while he plays with his pants.

I put Charlie's script in my briefcase and snap it shut. I see one of the buttons from my blouse on the floor, but will not deign to bend over and pick it up.

"Your agency is barely getting by. Who else but me is going to buy your rotten little scripts?"

"Television, Larry," I say with a lot more bravado than I feel.

"Why should anyone pay to go to a Saturday matinee serial when they can stay home and watch the same thing for free on television?"

"Get out."

Blouse buttoned the best I could manage, dark glasses on, and without another word, I walk out to the parking lot. I silently pray the MG will start without fuss, and it does. I put on my hat, stick the gear in reverse, and back the hell out of there, speeding toward Sunset, darting in and out of traffic, hoping there are no cops nearby.

Finally, on PCH, just the sight of the ocean calmed me, and I felt like I could slow down. Up ahead on the side of the road I saw a pickup truck; the hood was up and steam was pouring out of the engine. A small, forlorn woman with short-cropped gray hair stood in front of it. The least I could do was give her a lift to a gas station so that some creep didn't come by and pick her up and try to jump her. I pulled over.

She ran up to the MG exclaiming her thanks. Then she said, "Roxanne?"

I took off my dark glasses. "Thelma?"

"My god, Roxanne, what's happened to you? You look awful, and your blouse is all undone."

"Oh, *merde*! I'm all right. Shaken. That's all." I gathered my blouse together.

"Who did this to you?"

"No one. Really. A total nobody. A total nobody with a gruesome orange couch. Get in. What on earth are you doing out here with this truck?"

"I work for my brother now. He owns a farm out in the Valley. I deliver produce. Or at least when the truck doesn't overheat, I do."

"I had no idea you'd quit Empire."

"Oh, I didn't quit. They fired me the same day they fired Max two years ago. Escorted me off the lot without my address book."

"That's so unfair! You didn't do anything."

"I was Max's secretary for fifteen years. That was enough."

"I've heard Max and Marian are in Mexico City with Simon and Leah." I pulled back onto PCH and drove as Thelma told me the long, sad story of four people I had loved, how they and a whole crowd of blacklisted writers and directors who had fled to Mexico were drinking too much, running out of money, quarreling among themselves about the finer points of Communist doctrine, and nursing old grievances—in short, leading the bickering, unproductive lives of café expatriates.

"It's really just a gawd-awful way to live." Thelma added, "No one but Simon even speaks Spanish. Max and Marian are miserable."

"What happened to their son, Norman?"

"They moved Norman from an LA institution to one in Riverside County so Marian's sister could visit him." Thelma was a tiny woman, with spindly arms and bags under her big gray eyes. "But the sister died last year so no one goes to see him now. Marian is a mess, worrying about Norman, and Max is a wreck worrying about her."

"Heartbreaking."

"Yes. I drove out there once to see Norman, on their behalf, but he didn't know me at all and, well, let's just say I never went back. Anyway, I've got all I can do to haul produce six days a week for my brother."

"Look, Thelma, quit that job and come work for me. I have my own agency now." I took a business card from the glove box and handed it to her.

"There's no address on it."

"That's because I have to work out of my home. I live in Malibu, up that way." I pointed north. "I'm doing all right—well, truthfully, not great. I waste a lot of time trying to be organized. I'm not any good at keeping books, and I can't type except with two fingers, and my calendar is a mess. I can't pay you anywhere near what you earned at Empire, and I know I can't pay you what you're worth, but I can probably do better than your brother."

"Whatever you're paying, I'm in. I'm too old for hauling potatoes. Besides, I love bringing order to chaos. I had a lot of practice,
working for Max."

"That's great! When can you start?"

"Tomorrow, at eight, and I'll make the coffee!"

Is this the way fate works, then? Larry Sanford tries to jump
my bones, I flee, and fate hands me Thelma Bigelow, secretary
extraordinaire. I didn't immediately tell her the bitter truth of my
little agency. Larry was right. Though I worked hard, and my
name was enough to get me invited to galas, to premieres, parties
where I met important people, in nearly two years of being independent, my dream of discovering the writer of the next *Casablanca*
seemed like a fatuous illusion. I would have welcomed a little nepotism. I couldn't help but wonder if I was on some sort of weird
blacklist, that maybe the other studios thought if Empire wouldn't
buy from the Granville Agency, why should anyone else? My writers relied on Poverty Row and television. Sad to say, the closest the
Granville Agency came to a big studio contract was last year. A
wonderful script of Maurice Allen's generated extravagant enthu-
siasm from Paramount, lots of meetings, talks. Maurice did the
changes they asked for. I had the pen inked up to sign, but the
producers just sort of vanished, along with their promises. From
that crushing disappointment, I learned what every agent and
every writer knows: Nothing is real till money changes hands.
Without Julia's inheritance, I'd be broke.

The following Friday at our weekly lunch at the Ambassador, I told
Irene about finding Thelma on PCH and hiring her on the spot.
She looked pensive. "I wonder if it's wise for you to hire Max
Leslie's secretary. She might be a Communist too. You never
know."

"She's not a Communist."

"You don't know that for sure."

"Well, maybe I don't. Who cares? She's incredibly organized and efficient, and I'm in awe of her talents."

"Leon won't like it."

"How would he find out? I have hardly spoken to Leon in a year."

"That's your own pigheaded fault. You're the one who made this a contest with Denise, and you've lost. Just admit it. Make up with Leon. He's an old man. He's besotted with her. He's never been happier. He told me that."

"Forty years of marriage to Julia, and he's never been happier?" I gulped down the lump in my throat with a swill of Campari. The bitterness was bracing.

"Denise isn't so bad."

"I would have thought you'd be more loyal to Julia."

"Julia's gone, little sister. She has been gone for two years, and if you don't want to lose Leon forever, I suggest you rethink your opposition to Denise. Leon misses you. He loves you. He was heartbroken you didn't come to Thanksgiving. You didn't come to Christmas. You didn't come to his birthday celebration in February."

"I told him I'd never return to that house as long as Denise was in it." The dramatic declaration that had once felt so Vivien Leigh grand now struck me as overblown.

"Do you think you are a Daphne du Maurier character, Roxanne? In case you hadn't noticed, you live in the real world." Irene ordered us each another cocktail and lit up a cigarette as only Bette Davis and Irene Conrad could. She gave me a long, hard stare. "Leon and Denise got married last week up at his place in Tahoe. They'll announce it publicly in a few days. He asked me to tell you. He didn't want you to read it in the papers."

I felt my innards turn to chalk. "How could someone as smart, as powerful, as Leon Greene be felled by such a little gnat?"

"She's not a gnat. We underestimated her. So did Julia, for that matter. It was never enough for Denise just to be a rich man's mistress. Denise and Elsie both have clawing ambition. They see a shelf full of Oscars in their future, and so does Leon. He truly believes she's a gifted actress who just hasn't yet found the right film. Don't roll your eyes at me, Roxanne. She's not that bad, and you know it."

" 'Mediocre' is hardly a bouquet of praise."

"Look, I don't want to argue with you about Denise's gifts. Let's talk about you and Leon, about our family. You need to come down off your high horse. He misses you. He really does. He loves you. He wants us all to be a family again. He sent me with a peace offering." She reached in her handbag and drew out a long, flat velvet box, the sort that would hold a diamond bracelet.

"I already have a diamond bracelet in my safe-deposit box. One of his many remorseful gifts to Julia."

"Just open it."

It was a key, two keys actually, to the front door and the back door of a modest house on Clara Bow Drive in Culver City. "But I don't want to leave Malibu. I love it there."

"It's not for you to live in, silly. I told Leon you can't go on running your business out of that ramshackle place in Malibu. Use the house for an office! Clara Bow Drive is perfect for the Granville Agency. I checked out a couple of Leon's real estate holdings before I found it. Two bedrooms, big living room. Nice big oleander hedge to shield you from the street. Rent is a dollar a year, which I already paid when I signed the lease, so now you really owe me."

I fondled the keys. Smiling. I couldn't help it. A secretary. An office. I was established.

"For Leon it really was a gift, but I'm insisting on a condition. I want you to make up with him. Think about it, Roxanne, Leon is not going to live forever, and—"

"Is he sick?" I asked, alarmed.

"He's not sick. He's old. Make up with him, Roxanne. Don't lose your grandfather because you're so pigheaded and stubborn. Be reasonable. All families are complicated. Be nice to Denise. You can do this. Otherwise Julia wasted all that money on that fine French finishing school, didn't she?"

"I suppose if my father can play Lear, I can be civil to Denise Dell."

"Better than civil. Nice."

"Nice."

"Good. Next weekend there's an exclusive party at Summit Drive to celebrate Denise's new picture, *Banner Headline*. Be there, and be nice to Denise. I mean it." She kicked me gently under the table. "I have my own reasons for wanting you to come to the party. I want you to meet one of Gordon's friends. Elliott Dunne."

"Oh, Irene, you know I can't abide any of those crew-cut types that Gordon hires. They're all so . . . so starchy."

"Elliott Dunne is single, smart, and ambitious, and I want you to marry him and live in a lovely ranch house with a pool in Encino."

"And serve hubby his mashed potatoes wearing a little apron over my Dior dress and high heels? Dream on."

"Well, I'm tired of seeing you out and about with Charlie Frye these past few months."

She and Gordon had met Charlie and me at the Cocoanut Grove a few times. Irene found him boring, but he was fine for me, good-looking, and a good dancer. He's a good writer too, though not so wildly ambitious that he loves to work. We started dating after he invited me to a surfing competition (where he came in fifth). At first I thought Charlie was attracted to me on behalf of his scripts, and that might have had something to do with it, but now I sometimes wonder if it's because he can leave his surfboard at my house when he goes home to his nasty Hollywood walk-up.

"Do you want to hear something funny about Charlie?" I whispered.

"Always."

I lowered my voice and told her how making love with Charlie was like an athletic event, like he expected to feel a ribbon break across his chest as he crossed the finish line, especially since he in-sisted on having John Philip Sousa marches on the hi-fi. I hummed a few bars of "The Stars and Stripes Forever," and Irene and I laughed so hard we started crying, and the waiter came over and asked if we needed assistance.

"No, no." I waved him away. "We're fine."

Irene wiped her eyes and caught her breath. "Well, whatever you do, don't bring Charlie Frye to the party."

"Don't worry. I never take writers to anything important. They drink too much. I'll come with Jonathan. He's always pre-sentable."

"He's certainly collecting an unpresentable reputation. He might work more if there were fewer orgies at Casa Fiesta."

"Oh, don't believe what you read in the gossip columns. Anyway, actors need a whiff of scandal just to keep the publicity machine oiled so people don't forget them."

"Actors need to be up and in the makeup chair at five a.m. Without a hangover. If Jonathan wants serious roles, he should be a serious actor. I must run, I can't be late for my meeting with the principal at Junior's school." She gathered up her purse and gloves. "Leon wants you to call him and thank him personally for the keys to the new office."

"I can do that."

"Now." She reached into her handbag and gave me a dime and a piece of paper with the Tahoe number on it. She nodded toward the row of pay phones in the lobby. "Tell him you're happy about his wedding. Can you do that?"

"Yes."

"Promise."

"Yes."

"Good. Call collect."

CHAPTER NINE

In Hollywood, the term "exclusive party" means you invite everyone you owe money to, and everyone to whom you owe favors, as well as everyone you might want to ask for money or a favor in the future. Knowing this, Jonathan and I sat in the back seat of the limo, wordlessly passing his hip flask back and forth, nursing our anxieties. My anxieties were personal. I'd promised to accept Denise as Leon's wife, to be nice to a woman I detested. Jonathan's anxieties were professional. Jonathan intended to use this party to kiss whoever's ring, or tush, needed kissing to get a good role. He hadn't got the role in *The Bridges at Toko-Ri* or any other decent picture, and he was madly jealous of friends like Rock Hudson whose careers were on the ascendant while Jonathan's talents were still confined to clunkers like *The Silver Chalice*.

At Summit Drive we stepped out of the car into a herd of photographers snapping pictures as we entered the high, marbled foyer. Tall, austere Clarence, looking more like a senator than a butler, gave a slight smile and nodded to me. The place looked exactly the same as when I left it two years ago as we passed into the long salon at the back where French doors gave onto vast, tiered gardens. In the high upstairs gallery ringing the salon, an orchestra played movie themes from recent pictures. The people who made those pictures collected below—there was more star power here than you can see at the Griffith Observatory. Leon's close allies in the Motion Picture Alliance for the Preservation of American Ideals gathered in their own galaxy. When the orchestra took up the theme from *The High and the Mighty*, on cue, John Wayne turned from his conversation with Gary Cooper and Hedda Hopper and waved to everyone present. Standing there between those twin pillars of American masculinity, Hedda, who usually bristles with righteous indignation, looked like a delighted damsel.

Jonathan bent his head to mine and murmured, "You are the only woman here in red."

"Mais oui." I had chosen this red dress particularly for tonight, just for a bit of *tant pis* to Leon and all the rabid Red-baiters I knew would be here. A strapless bodice, full at the hips, with two layers of shimmery, brilliant red-patterned voile over silk, it rustled softly when I walked, and it screamed Dior. I carried a small, chic Dior handbag and accessorized with elbow-length red gloves and Julia's diamond choker, diamond bracelet, and ruby earrings, retrieved from the safe-deposit box. I didn't wear them with Julia's grace or glamour. How could I? How could anyone? My hair, longer now, was swept up into a fashionable French twist, except for one long lock that fell down the right side of my face, à la Veronica Lake, obscuring the birthmark.

Waiters hoisting trays sailed through the salon, and the effervescence in crystal glasses caught the light cast by sparkling Venetian chandeliers. Women's high heels clicked percussively on the black-and-white marble floors. Tall French doors led out to the portico that opened to a view of the terraced gardens and the artificial lake with its leaping Versailles fountain. Strings of colorful Chinese lanterns illuminated the April twilight in the reflecting pools.

Natalie Wood walked up to us, glowing. "Come with me, Jonathan, I want you to meet my director."

"Nicholas Ray?" Jonathan and I exchanged a quick, intense glance. *Rebel Without a Cause*, not even yet released, was already rumored to be an Oscar contender. I quickly crossed my fingers for him as she led him away.

To my surprise, Hedda Hopper, the queen of gossip glory, came up to me. "Isn't it wonderful," she gushed, "Leon and Denise just eloping like a couple of youngsters."

"It's wonderful—so romantic."

"How is the Granville Agency doing, Roxanne?"

"Beautifully. Just fine."

"Any great deals to report?"

"I'm not at liberty to say right now." I have discovered this is a wonderfully evasive phrase suggesting, teasing, titillating that great things hover in the offing, awaiting only some small formality to emerge. "But when I am, you'll be the first to know."

Hedda blew a smoke ring, making me think she'd seen right through the ruse. "It can't be easy being an independent woman agent."

"It's not easy being an independent woman, Miss Hopper. As I'm sure you know."

"No one knows that better than I. Men are always trying to shut me up."

A snappy retort trembled at the edge of my lips, but I said nothing of the sort. Hedda Hopper can and has made reputations, and just as swiftly rendered them into ash.

"You must have learned a lot from Irv Rakoff when you worked for him."

"I learned nothing at all from him, thank you." Unless it was how to pour cold champagne over a man's dick, and how to sniff condescension at a hundred yards. I smiled at her.

"It's hard in this business for a woman to deal effectively with men, and to remain a lady."

"Remaining a lady is not a priority for me."

"Really?" Hedda's bright little eyes lit, and I could all but hear her cranial wheels turn.

"To be a lady is to confine oneself to a certain set of expectations that belong to others. At the L'Oiseau d'Or in Paris, they taught us it's more important to set one's own expectations—in short, to be clever."

"Clever girls often overreach themselves," she said with an implied *tsk-tsk*.

"But clever women do not. It's a matter of knowing what tools to use for each purpose. You wouldn't use an oyster knife to stir your tea, would you?"

I took some small malicious pride to see confusion momentarily cross her face. Perhaps that's what Julia meant about glamour: Talk fast, laugh fluidly, gesture economically, and leave behind a shimmering wake. Wake or not, I freed myself from that asp in a hat and wandered the stellar gathering, champagne glass in hand. I exchanged false effusions of noisy affection and false promises to have lunch soon with all sorts of people, and when they waxed on about how wonderful *Banner Headline* was, I agreed without ever observing that the story was a pale imitation—actually a shameless derivative—of the Cary Grant/Rosalind Russell classic, *His Girl Friday*.

Denise had made three pictures a year for Empire since 1948, and many of them had done well. Particularly in the bright comedic roles, even I had to admit, she had flair. But was she the equal of Rosalind Russell or Carole Lombard? No. *Banner Headline* (written by Vic Hale, and directed by Phil Tobin) was, in my opinion, only workmanlike, though Leon had filmed it in Technicolor so luscious every frame brought to mind ripe fruit. And of course he had spared no expense on publicity. Witness this party.

I saw Irene sitting on one of the Louis XVI divans in her white gown with emeralds to complement it, her smooth blonde hair in a perfect pageboy. She had collected an admiring coterie, but when she saw me, she rose and excused herself. Arms linked, we floated through the throng, Empire's daughters, envied and admired. A colored waiter paused in front of us with an assortment of canapés, dollops of pâté, and pale pink prawns. I passed on the canapés, but took a third glass of champagne. Irene beamed to see a slick, hand-some blue-eyed man approaching us.

"Elliott Dunne, do you know my sister, Roxanne Granville? Elliott came to Empire when you were away in Paris, Roxanne. Elliott's just had a promotion, haven't you?"

"Vice president for production." He grinned.

"I might as well tell you both," Irene confided, "I am making it my mission to see that you two have an affair. I've decided, so don't quarrel with me."

"No quarrel here," said Elliott, smiling.

Unlike most of Gordon's cadre of imports, Elliott was not crew-cut; he had a luxurious mop of sandy hair and an ingratiating smile. Irene's idea of a *petite affaire* was suddenly appealing. At least I'd be spared "The Stars and Stripes Forever."

"You're the agent, aren't you?"

"Yes," I said, pleased. "What is Empire looking for these days?"

"Well, another big hit to follow up on *Banner Headline*," Elliott replied loyally, going on to glorify the film as though it had the critical clout of *East of Eden*, the poignancy of *Marty*, the five-million-dollar box office of *Magnificent Obsession*.

"And you think Vic Hale can give it to you?" I asked with dramatic disbelief.

Elliott evaded this topic while his eyes cast over me, frankly admiring. I'm sure Irene was delighted to note that the conversation meandered pleasantly down flirtatious paths. Across the room I saw Leon and waved. A momentary look of pain crossed Leon's face, which I have to assume was occasioned by the red dress, but he moved through the throng to join us. He kissed my cheek, and Irene's.

"You girls look like fire and ice," he said, beaming.

Elliott respectfully excused himself. Gordon beckoned to Irene, and she left us.

Leon and I moved out of the main currents to a place near the French doors, and never mind the red dress, his voice filled with its old warmth. I told him how much it meant to me to have a real office.

"Yes." He smiled. "I thought that house might suit you, though you know it's not zoned for business. It's a residential block, so you have to be discreet."

"The Granville Agency doesn't exactly have limos full of movie stars pulling up in front of the house, so I think we're safe."

His eyes lit with tender affection. "I can't tell you how happy I am to see you, Roxanne."

"I've missed you, Leon." I hugged him, and I knew Irene was right: I didn't want to lose Leon. Of course I could accept Denise. I didn't have to like her or respect her, just accept her.

My resolve was immediately tested when Denise joined us, taking Leon's arm possessively, dwarfed by his height and intellect. Enormous blue eyes set in her perfectly oval face; fresh, full ruby lips; blonde hair waved up high; spit curls the size of quarters stuck to the sides of her face. By any standard, Denise was a ravishing beauty, broad shouldered, with enormous breasts. I liked to think in ten years, say, around 1965, she'll look like Ma Kettle, but in the meantime she radiated fleshy vitality in a Technicolor-yellow gown set off by a necklace of yellow diamonds and a yellow diamond bracelet gleaming on one of her long white gloves. She gazed up adoringly at Leon, and he beamed at her like Joseph Cotton seeing Dolores Costello again in *The Magnificent Ambersons*. "My beautiful wife." Leon savored that last word as if it were a piece of toffee.

As the daughter of Sir Rowland Granville, I said, "Congratulations on *Banner Headline*. It's a great picture."

"You've seen it, then?" asked Leon, clearly pleased.

"Yes, Jonathan and I went together. We both loved it."

"I've heard so much about you and Jonathan," Denise said in her low, trilling voice, "running wild all over the studio when you were kids."

"It was our playground."

"They were sweet kids," said Leon.

Her mother, Elsie, clad in a gown of an unbecoming salmon color, joined us and offered me a gloved hand as Leon introduced us. *"Enchanté,"* I said.

A photographer approached and asked Denise and Leon to pose with Phil Tobin, the director of *Banner Headline*. Elsie followed them.

"That's a very daring dress," said a voice behind me. I turned around to see a short man with thinning hair and sharp features. "Red is a dangerous color these days."

"It's a dress, not a metaphor."

"Are you a Communist?"

"Are you the FBI?"

He laughed, a genuine, self-deprecating laugh. "FBI men are rumpled and sweaty, and they wear glasses and hats ten years out of date. They're generally unshaven and chain smoke. I assure you, I'm not FBI, Miss Granville."

"You know who I am?"

He chuckled. "That's why I thought the red dress was especially provocative—daring, given your grandfather's patriotic zeal."

"Have we met, Mr. . . ."

"Carleton Grimes."

I could not place him. He had hooded blue eyes, a thin, elegant moustache, and receding ginger-colored hair, and he carried himself with a kind of low-key sophistication.

"Everyone in Hollywood knows Roxanne Granville. Or knows of her. You're an independent agent, aren't you? Who do you represent? Anyone here?" He gestured around the gilded gathering.

"I don't do actors." Unfortunate phrasing. "I don't like them very much as a tribe, I mean. My clients are writers."

"Yes, actors have no substance if they're not reflected in someone else's adoring eyes."

"You must be a writer."

"No, I work at Paragon. Noah Glassman was my father's college friend at NYU." He paused when I frowned. "Noah's the president of Paragon Pictures."

"Oh yes, I remember now."

"I came out here from New York to make plays into films. I wasn't fast enough with *The Country Girl*. But I did manage to meet Grace Kelly, and we got to be friends, so that was some consolation." He nodded in the distance to where the statuesque Miss Kelly stood like a pale flame collecting admiring moths. He took another glass of champagne from a white-gloved waiter. "This must be quite a good moment to be an independent agent. Films need stories. Stories need writers, and all the old guard, the really reliable talent, they've been swept out by the Red-hunting broom. We should have lunch sometime, Miss Granville. I'm always looking for interesting properties."

"I'd like that, Mr. Grimes. I happen to have interesting properties," I said as Gordon joined us.

"Look at all the television people," Gordon muttered angrily. "I can't stand them. Irene insists everything has to come to a stop once a week to watch *I Love Lucy*. I keep telling her, it's crap! Lucille Ball was a failed chorus girl! What makes her so funny? They're taking bread out of our mouths."

Carleton and Gordon immediately dove into a rant on behalf of butts-in-the-movie-theater instead of butts-on-the-couch.

"My perspective is a little different," I offered. They both looked surprised. Men are always surprised when women differ with them. "I quite love television. Sure, the pay is poor, the prestige is nil, and the hours are brutal, but on behalf of my young, ambitious writers, I am grateful to television. Television, gentlemen, is the great, roaring beast in the basement of the entertainment industry. You just keep throwing chunks of meat at it, and it roars the louder, and wants more."

"A rather odd way to describe your writers' work. Meat?" Carleton observed.

"Television doesn't need deathless dialogue. Just lines to fill up the box."

Carleton laughed. "You know that the dialogue on *Dragnet* is so wooden because they're too cheap to pay for rehearsals and they read it off of the prompter as they're filming."

" 'Just the facts, ma'am,' " I said, imitating deadpan Jack Webb.

"But just look at what Disney's done with Davy Crockett, and all those little buckaroos," said Gordon, a despairing note in his voice. "Three million annually!"

"Pity the fucking raccoons," said Carleton.

"I hate it when my kids go around singing *Davy Crockett: King of the Wild Frontier*," Gordon grumbled. "Who would have ever dreamed some old frontier tale would make that much money?"

The gods of irony intervened as the orchestra on the gallery broke into a rousing version of the *Davy Crockett* theme song. Throughout the huge crowd, uncomfortable laughter rippled, and then everyone went back to pretending that they hadn't noticed that every one of them—from the oldest to the youngest, from the studio mogul to the Negro waiter—could probably sing every verse.

"We're negotiating now with that man." Gordon pointed to a slick, handsome man with gleaming hair and a five o'clock shadow. "Ernest Todd from CBS. He came out here from New York last year. CBS is interested in showing some of our old films late on Saturday nights." Gordon nabbed a shrimp off a passing tray. "Todd bought Max Leslie's old house on Carolwood Drive."

Ernest Todd ambled over to us. Gordon introduced us and again told the story of how Irene insisted life come to a halt so everyone could watch *I Love Lucy*. Only this time he left out the bread-from-our-mouths bit and told it in a bright-eyed, cheerful way intended to elicit the goodwill of this New York guy who had bought Max Leslie's house.

I excused myself and went to the French doors, searching for Jonathan. I saw him down there on the second terrace surrounded by a bevy of the young, beautiful, and ambitious, some of whom frequented Casa Fiesta, though they were certainly better behaved here, and better dressed as well. I meandered down to them, and came in the midst of Diana Jordan raging against her agent, Irv Rakoff. Diana had a raw energy about her, a sort of sexual swagger few women would dare to parade; not perhaps what Julia would have recognized as panache, but unmistakably brassy charisma. Given this venue, she was more restrained than usual. "As soon as I can get rid of Irv, I'm coming to you, Roxanne. I want a woman agent."

"I only handle writers. Writers are easier than actors, not as needy. More grateful," I said as all these actors laughed out loud.

"A woman agent?" chuckled Rock Hudson, still glowing from his starring role in *Magnificent Obsession* (which, for all its magnificent profits, was a corny, one-hanky weeper). "What'll they think of next? Women directors?"

"And why not?" I retorted.

"Men don't want women ordering them around."

"Well, I have two words for you, Rock," I said. "Ida Lupino. She is a genius. She directed *The Hitch-Hiker* a year or so ago. Didn't any of you see it? That's no teatime drama. She directed that picture with such a sure hand, it gave me nightmares for weeks—oh, and it was an all-male cast too, in case you missed it."

"Women lack authority," Rock insisted.

"Don't get Roxanne started," Jonathan warned.

"Where is it written in stone that just because we have ovaries, we have no balls?" That got a laugh, and I might have gone on being outrageous (and, of course, amusing) but Clarence interrupted us with a white-gloved tap to my shoulder.

"Miss Roxanne, Mr. Greene would like you to join the family on the gallery for the toast."

I excused myself, and returning to the salon, I could hear the musicians hurrying through "Three Coins in a Fountain" so fast it sounded like a polka. I lifted my luscious red skirt and went royally up the stairs to where the family had gathered, along with Vic Hale, *Banner Headline*'s writer; Phil Tobin, the director; and the leading man, a harmless hunk.

I joined the luminaries in the gallery. To my right I saw Irene gazing with the calm of a blonde Buddha, and beside her, Gordon with his worried-cobra look. To my left I saw Elsie exuding the smug exultation of a woman who has succeeded beyond her wildest dreams. Beside her stood Denise, proud as a gilded figurehead on a full-sail clipper ship, oozing confidence as Leon addressed the gathering below, extolling the picture and all the many people he wanted to thank for its glorious success, beginning with his lovely wife. *Applause. Applause.* Denise blew kisses. Perhaps she was rehearsing for her Oscar moment.

And yet, as I stood there, looking across this constellation, I knew that for all their cool sophistication, their jewels, their gorgeous good looks, each man and each woman here knew that beauty wasn't enough to crown you with success. In the fight for screen credits and star billing, for sex and swimming pools, for love and glory, as they say in *Casablanca*, you couldn't be stupid and survive. You couldn't be scandalous, or at least you couldn't be caught. You couldn't cling to the past, not even to past greatness. The present shone. This season's box office. This season's awards. And the future? I wondered if Davy Crockett and the blurry gray light flickering across American living rooms would make coonskin caps of us all.

CHAPTER TEN

Music blared out of the hi-fi: sounding brass, piping fifes, crashing cymbals, the roll of drums, peaking, ebbing, peaking, ebbing, then blasting gloriously forth . . . bright bells . . . no, wait. That was the phone. Great tubas resounding across vistas of marching . . . the phone.

"Charlie, that was the phone."

"Wait, Roxanne, no, just wait, please . . ."

"I have to get the phone. In my business the missed call is the lost deal."

"Just wait," he panted, working hard. "Just wait, please . . . please . . . Ah! Ah! Ah!"

I scrambled out from underneath Charlie, raced out to the desk in the living room, and picked up the phone, surprised to hear Thelma's voice on a Sunday morning.

"Is that 'Stars and Stripes Forever' I hear in the background?"

I hotfooted it over to the hi-fi and turned it off in the middle of the march, then ran into the bedroom and grabbed a T-shirt. I couldn't imagine talking to Thelma naked.

"Is Charlie there?" she said when I returned to the phone.

"Well, yes. It's Saturday night. I mean, Sunday morning."

"I have an important message for you. I'm coming over tonight to talk to you about something important, and you need to be alone. Do I make myself clear?"

"Are you a Soviet spy?"

"Roxanne, please go find your underpants and your brains, and put them both on." And with that, she hung up.

Brewing coffee in the kitchen, I could see George and Mildred Wilbur out walking on the beach with their dog. They waved at me in their sickly, middle-aged fashion. Bruno, the huge, stupid, loving, gorgeous Irish setter, barked at me to come out and play. George called him back and told him to heel. Bruno, eager to please, did so.

I opened some windows to let the stale air out, and when the coffee was done, I started to take a cup out to the porch before I remembered I was only wearing a T-shirt. The Wilburs wouldn't much like that.

I went into the bathroom and took a shower, where I made a lot of noise—flushing the toilet, slamming the towel cabinet door. Nonetheless Charlie only just rolled over on his back when I came back into the bedroom. I raised the shade, and sunlight fell across the bed, glowing on his long, tanned legs. Grinning, he pointed to his upthrust dick, the ornament of the brilliant white patch between his tanned hips and his muscled thighs.

"No. It's nearly noon. I'm throwing you out of the house. I have work to do."

He sat up, drew me toward him, and held me, murmuring against my throat, "I like you better when you're all woman and not part agent."

"But if I were all woman, you wouldn't eat."

"I barely eat now." He released me. "I should be earning fifteen hundred a week, not a measly two fifty a pop for an episode of *Dragnet*. Why did Larry Sanford turn down *Return of the Cat People*? It was perfect for them."

"Larry missed his chance," I replied, never having told Charlie the truth.

"Why can't you get me something that's not television and not

Poverty Row? What about my *Coast of Heaven*? You've read it. You know it's as good as *On the Waterfront* or *Rear Window*."

"I'm going to trust your own good sense that you know that isn't so."

"But it is!"

"It needs polish. I keep telling you, it needs polish."

"You know I'm the best of your writers. I'm certainly the best of your lovers."

"Time to go," I said, freeing myself. I reached in the drawer for my lacy, satin lingerie and then pulled on a pair of pedal pushers and an oversized USC T-shirt.

Charlie got up, put on his swimming trunks, and took his surfboard out for a quick dip, returning an hour later, salt-splashed and glowing. He left his surfboard leaning against the porch rail, collected his clothes, got in his beat-up '48 Dodge, and drove back to his Hollywood hovel on Sycamore Street. I never stayed at his place, not after I saw the Murphy bed and the cockroach.

Like the rest of America on a Sunday night, I had *Walt Disney's Disneyland* on the television when I heard footsteps coming upstairs to the high porch. A knock sounded at the door, and I opened it to find Thelma, and with her, to my utter surprise, was Max Leslie. He was grizzled, paunchy, and pale. His hair was too long, and his shoes were scuffed, and he was stooped in a way I did not remember. Behind his glasses his hazel eyes were ringed with dark circles, and his manner was subdued. I hardly recognized this man who had once filled Leon's library with words, laughter, and cigar smoke, with antics and ideas. He apologized for coming, and I protested, "No, I'm so happy to see you!"

Max gave a slight laugh. "I doubt that's so."

"No, it's true! I just can't believe it's you!!" I felt like a child, lying shrilly to avoid getting in trouble. I showed them both to the small sofa and sat across from them in the overstuffed chair. "Everyone thinks you're in Mexico. How long have you been back?"

"Better you don't know." He had a long, appreciative look around the walls, taking in the framed movie posters, two of them films he wrote. "You're looking swell, Roxanne. Marian sends her love."

"Oh, give her mine too!" I got a bottle of Scotch and three small glasses and poured us each a splash. I noticed the briefcase at his feet. "How was Mexico?" I asked, instantly wishing I had not.

"A hellhole. By the time Marian and I got down there, all our friends who had been there a couple of years were drinking too much, sleeping with one another's wives, rehashing tactics, the Fifth versus the First. Stalin versus Trotsky. The meaning of the Nazi-Soviet pact. Was Albert Maltz's nineteen forty-seven recant a real recant? Simon is killing himself with drink and party politics, he . . ." Max seemed about to say more, then didn't. He bolted the Scotch.

"Where are you living? Maybe I shouldn't ask."

Max and Thelma exchanged glances. "Marian and I have a little rented clapboard house in an old neighborhood in Riverside, sixty miles east of here," said Max. "Out back we have a view of the alley and the neighbor's trash cans. Marian has a vegetable garden, and she fusses over whitefly and leaf rot."

"And Norman?" I asked, half-afraid to hear the answer. "How is he?"

"How is he ever?" Max sighed as though pulling some sorrow up from his solar plexus. "Mexico was hell. Marian went half-mad with missing Norman. Especially after her sister died and there was no one to go visit him. Now that we're back here, we go to see him four, five times a week. He's in a nice place in Riverside, but it costs a lot to keep him there."

"I'm so sorry, Max."

"You had nothing to do with any of this."

"But Leon did."

"Then let him apologize," Thelma snapped.

Max's whole body seemed to sag, and his gaze rested on the old upright piano, but I felt he was looking into some long-distant past I could not share.

"That piano looks like the one Nelson used to play."

"That's what I thought too."

"You still play?"

"Now and then. I don't want to forget everything I once knew." The silence between us prickled with the unsaid. "It's dreadfully out of tune."

He placed a hand over the briefcase. "I have an enormous favor to ask of you, Roxanne. As an agent. As a friend. I guess you know what it is."

"Max, if I can help you in any way, I will."

"Listen carefully, Roxanne," said Thelma.

"If you're found out, you'll come under the scrutiny of the Red hunters, the Un-American bloodhounds, the FBI. So I do not ask this lightly. Whatever you decide is fine with me. Really."

"Why don't we turn on a record?" suggested Thelma, getting up and bringing down the bamboo shades.

I went to the hi-fi and lifted off the album of John Philip Sousa marches. (I sure as hell didn't want to have to explain that!) Frank Sinatra's *Songs for Young Lovers* was nearby—not exactly suitable, but so what? I returned to sit across from them.

"Everyone knows the rumors," said Max. "Writers get black-listed and the studio revenues go down, and sometimes even the studios collude to put another name on scripts so that writers can go on working. That'll never happen at Empire, and Empire is the only studio I ever worked for. Only studio Nelson or Simon ever worked for. I've heard that Empire sold off the old Western lot last year."

"Empire isn't making Westerns anymore."

"They're building tract houses where the Western lot used to be," said Thelma. "They're building tract houses everywhere. Some-one offered my brother five hundred thousand dollars for his farm."

Max poured himself another Scotch. "I told Thelma I didn't

want to come to you, but you're the only one I can turn to, Roxanne."

"And I told Max you make your own decisions," said Thelma.

"Roxanne, if I don't write, something inside me dies. I learned that much in Mexico. I've got two brand-new scripts here. I think they're good. I'm hoping that you'll read them and think they're good, and maybe give my work to one of your young clients. A decent writer. He puts his name on it. He takes the credit. We all split the money. I'm sorry to ask at all, but I'm desperate to make some money. All our savings are gone. If I could do anything else but write, I would, but I can't."

"Maybe you could go to England. I've heard lots of blacklisted writers are doing well there," I said. "Maybe not well. But they're working. Or Jerrold in Paris! He would love to see you, I'm sure of it."

"I can't go to England. I can't go anywhere. I can't leave Marian, and she can't leave our son. If I don't get some money, Norman will have to move to a public insane asylum. That would kill my wife."

Sinatra crooned, filling up the silence. "They Can't Take That Away From Me" seemed all the more poignant. Finally I said, "It's so unfair, Max. You're the screenwriter always known for sparkling wit and the funny lines and madcap stories."

Max shrugged as though dusting defeat from his shoulders.

"If you decide to do this, Roxanne," said Thelma, "and I do mean if—really, if you don't want to, we all understand the risks—but if you do, then we need to find a writer we can trust."

"There is no one we can trust," said Max, "present company excepted. We have to take a chance." He ran his hands over his face. "I'm still under subpoena, and if the FBI finds out I'm not in Mexico, I could easily be indicted for contempt of Congress. They can revoke my passport. If it weren't so tragic, it would be comic. It would be a comic movie full of misunderstood intents."

"A movie like you would write." I rose, took the needle off the record, and turned off the hi-fi. "Leave the scripts with me. I'll read them. Still, I mean, the kind of witty comedies that you wrote, who's doing those now? No one. Everyone's flinging themselves into musicals or biblical epics, extravaganzas they can splash across the screen in Cinerama or VistaVision and Todd-AO, 3-D, or any of the other cinematic marvels the studios are flogging."

"Movies people can't watch at home on that little grainy-gray box," said Thelma.

"Exactly. These big glamorous pictures, well, look at last year's *The Egyptian* or *The Sign of the Pagan*, they're terrible, but they're making money, and that's the only standard. Sadly."

"I saw *Banner Headline*," said Max, shaking his head. "Vic Hale and Phil Tobin might be all-American, but they're sure turning out limp-dick pictures. These, at least"—he nodded toward the briefcase—"these are charmers, like the old Cary Grant comedies. But I don't expect miracles, Roxanne." Max got slowly to his feet. "I'm grateful for whatever you can do. Truly grateful. And if you decide it's too risky for you, I still thank you."

I promised to read them and get back to him. I walked them outside, said good night, and watched them go down the steps. I stood there for a while longer, watching the waves roll in and fling themselves on the moonlit beach like true believers fling themselves into causes lost before the tide changed, ebbed, and went elsewhere.

CHAPTER ELEVEN

D espite its sexy name, Clara Bow Drive was an uninspired residential street of houses that all looked alike. The sole grace was a line of still-spindly jacaranda trees lining the parkway between street and sidewalk. Between the sidewalk and the two-bedroom stucco house we rented there was a thick line of six-foot oleander bushes that shielded us from view. Once you walked inside, the eye went directly to the modern art I had all over the walls. Big, clean bands of color, work by artists I'd met at Casa Fiesta who lent me paintings that would otherwise be stacked in their studios. The rented furniture too was clean and modern. On a more utilitarian note, the house had a washer in the back porch and a clothesline in the backyard. Thelma and I both did our laundry at work.

Thelma's office was the front room, and she looked up from her typewriter when I walked in late Monday morning. "Well?"

"I loved them both." Max's scripts were witty Empire comedies in the best tradition. *Fly Me to the Moon* was about a highly intelligent young woman lab assistant, Maisie, who falls in love with her boss, the brilliant scientist Dr. Bleeker, who is so completely wrapped up in his work, he has no thought or care for anything or anyone else. Clever Maisie invents a series of electronic signals so that Dr. Bleeker thinks he's getting messages from the moon, and Maisie helps him "translate" them. Love and hilarity ensue. *You Make Me Feel So Young* was *Miracle on 34th Street* without Santa. "They're both fine, frothy pictures. Amazing that Max can write something so sparkling under the circumstances."

"Oh, Roxanne, this will make Max and Marian so happy!"

"Did the songs come first, or the stories?"

"Max said he had notes for these stories for a long time. But when he heard that song, 'Fly Me to the Moon,' the whole thing came together in his head, and he wrote it in a couple of days. He wrote them all longhand, like he always does, and I typed them for him. I knew we could trust you."

"Of course I can be trusted. Max and Marian have been dear friends since I was just a kid."

"Who will you offer them to?"

"Empire. We'll offer them to Empire!"

Thelma's face fell. "Are you feeling all right, Roxanne? Got a fever? Food poisoning? PMS? Empire is not what Max had in mind."

"Think of it as a coup for irony! Max is a writer. He would appreciate the irony. A bright comic film like this is the perfect follow-up to *Banner Headline*—which, by the way, is not making anywhere near the box office Leon hoped for, given all the money he threw at it. Vic Hale can't write decent comedy. Max Leslie is a genius. Besides, I have a new contact at Empire, Elliott Dunne."

"Aren't you listening to me? Leon would recognize this instantly as Max's work. Leon would . . ." She floundered, seeking some adequate description. "Gordon and Leon will read these and know they belong to Max. No, you should take them somewhere else." When I failed to reply, she pleaded, "You're not serious, are you?"

"Oh, but I am. I read these last night, and I kept thinking of everyone Leon cast off, cast out without a shred of loyalty. Not just Max! I kept remembering when Kathleen Hilyard called us in Paris, and Julia trying to calm her, and when she finally understood that Kathleen was telling her that Nelson had killed himself, shot himself in their bedroom, then Julia started shrieking. I remembered the letter Julia got from Simon and Leah that they were in Mexico, and how Simon made a big joke of it, the señoritas and muchachos and how there were so many Reds in Mexico City they had their own Rojo Fiestas. I remembered Jerrold, laughing, and telling a French director how it took him a year to learn to toss his hat on his Oscar in that crummy Left Bank apartment. They all made light of what they went through, because they are big-hearted, but we, Julia and I, we knew the truth of it. I thought on all that, Thelma, and I just got angry all over again. I couldn't sleep. I mean, for twenty years these writers made Leon rich, they made Empire great, and he had his lawyers terminate their contracts in twenty-four hours?"

Thelma was thoughtful. "You might be too hard on Leon. He wasn't alone in what he did."

"You, of all people, can say that? He fired you for nothing more than being Max's secretary."

"You don't know what it was like. You weren't even here. You were in Paris. You can't imagine what it was like for the rest of us in fifty, fifty-one, fifty-two. Before that, everyone thought, oh, the First Amendment! We'll stake our very lives on the First Amendment, and in nineteen forty-seven all those big-time actors—Bogart, Bacall, Paul Henreid, and the rest of them—they all flew to Washington to show moral solidarity for the Hollywood Ten. They were there, in the audience for the hearings. Great theater! The Hollywood Ten were so witty, so many clever retorts to the Committee's questions. And then, you know what? That slimy Parnell Thomas, the chairman, indicted them for contempt of Congress. They appealed through the courts, still believing in the First Amendment. But the courts supported the Committee, and by nineteen fifty the Hollywood Ten were in federal prisons. So when the Committee hearings started up again, here in LA, everyone was too afraid to do anything at all. People would cross the street to avoid being seen talking to anyone who had even a blush of Red. It could be your brother, your best friend, your ex-wife, and you'd still cross the street. It was like living in a pressure cooker. If you didn't want your career shredded, your life ruined, if you didn't want to see your work, your reputation smeared, to see your livelihood disintegrate in front of your eyes, then when the Committee called, you stepped right up and vowed your allegiance to the Motion Picture Alliance for American Ideals. You kissed the flag and pressed it to your bosom. And if the Committee asked if you were once a Communist, you said yes, and if they asked who else was a Communist, you coughed up names like the goddamned phone book. And if you didn't, then you could flush your life, your work, your reputation right down the cosmic toilet. I'll say it again. Leon Greene was not alone in what he did, and Jerrold and Simon and Nelson knew it. Max too."

"I can't believe you're defending him!"

"All the studios fired anyone who didn't cooperate with the Committee." Thelma took out a match and lit her cigarette. "Take these comedies to Paragon. They're a smaller studio, like Empire. They're perfect. You said you met Carleton Grimes the other night, their new managing director."

"If Empire turns me down, I will take them to Paragon."

"Look how good Leon has been to you, Roxanne," she implored, gesturing around the living room of the tract house. "How supportive. You'd still be stacking up file cabinets in your back bedroom if you didn't have this office."

"Don't confuse the issue. I made a bargain that I would accept Denise, be nice to her. I was nice to her, and I will be nice to her, but . . ."

"But what? Out with it."

"I will never think of her as Mrs. Leon Greene."

"So, you're still smarting on behalf of Julia."

"I suppose I am," I said, remembering seeing Denise Dell in the Summit Drive breakfast room just days after we had buried Julia Greene. "Julia shouldn't have died all alone in a foreign country while Denise lived in her house and slept with her husband. I can't forgive him for that," I said, even though I knew Julia *had* forgiven him—a fact I had never parted with, not even to Irene or Jonathan. I kept Julia's letter in a desk drawer.

"Forgiveness works both ways. What if Leon reads these scripts and guesses what you're up to, and he never forgives you?"

I thought about how Leon had declared Julia's gift to the NAACP a betrayal, every bit as bad as adultery. An unforgivable betrayal. I said with false insouciance, "It'll be a test for him, won't it? If he truly hates anything with the tiniest Communist tinge, he'll turn them down no matter what, even if they are perfect for Denise. When I was reading them last night, I could see her in these roles. She's no Bette Davis. Bette Davis can do anything, but Denise can deliver a comic line."

"Love or patriotism. You'd make Leon choose. His wife or his principles."

I shrugged. "Life is full of choices."

"You are tempting fate."

"My middle name."

"It's too much to risk. What about Max?"

"What about him? He's still in Mexico as far as anyone knows."

She stubbed her cigarette out with more energy than the act required. "I want to go on record that in my opinion this is a reckless act."

"Not my first."

"And, no doubt, not your last." She went back to typing so I knew she was sulking. I sorted through the mail till she finally spoke again. "Who will you ask to front for Max?"

"Charlie. He'd be grateful. He can be trusted."

"He can be trusted because you're sleeping with him?"

"That has nothing to do with it. No one else will know."

"What about your pal Jonathan Moore? You and he are thick as thieves. He's a bad influence. All those wild parties where people drink too much and dance around bonfires and take off their clothes. Everyone in this town knows about Casa Fiesta. The FBI could hang out there and—"

"The FBI at Casa Fiesta?" I laughed. "Those grim middle-aged men in their sweaty suits driving gray sedans? Not likely they could infiltrate Casa Fiesta. Besides, I won't tell Jonathan, or anyone else. This stays strictly within these walls."

When, later that afternoon, I offered Charlie the prospect of fronting for two comedies by Max Leslie, his clean-shaven jaw dropped. "I know Max Leslie's work! I've always wanted to be that witty, that smart." He jumped out of the chair and started pacing around my office. "Wow, I get to take the credit for a Max Leslie comedy?"

"There's a lot of risk. If anyone finds out, we'd be branded as Communist sympathizers."

"Yes, and you'd end up working at Pink's Hot Dogs." He grinned. "I'd move to Australia to surf."

"Not funny."

"Hell, Roxanne! Of course I'll do it! I'm a true-blue American! Everyone knows that. I played football at Huntington Beach High. You can tell Mr. Leslie I'm honored. I hope one day I can meet him and shake his hand."

"That won't happen. He's in Mexico." Charlie didn't need to know the particulars of Max and Marian's situation, much less that they were living sixty miles from LA. "This has to stay an absolute secret, you understand. You know what's at stake."

"You'd have to be living in a North Dakota root cellar not to know what's at stake."

When I was in high school I was so well known at Empire Studios I could drive the family Packard around the lineup at the gates with just a wave at the guard. Now I waited in line watching the heat needle of the MG rise. The huge Babylonian gates were two pillars in the shape of elephants, connected across the top with a frieze of fanciful palms. Leon inherited the gates when he bought out Babylon Pictures back in 1918 and turned it into Empire. I finally pulled up to the booth, but neither my car, nor my name, nor, for that matter, my distinctive face, were known to the uniformed guard. Not till I said I had an appointment with Elliott Dunne did he allow me to pass.

Once you drove past the fanciful Babylonian gates, Empire Pictures was as utilitarian as an army base. Sunlight bore down on the stark walls of soundstages and glimmered up off ribbons of asphalt. Men pushed trolleys laden with costumes of all sorts, and sets and trucks idled in doorways where costumed extras stood outside smoking. (Only the brass and the big stars got to ignore the No Smoking signs posted everywhere inside.) Small trucks and vans, some stacked with scenery and lighting, plied the lanes between buildings and soundstages. Beyond the soundstages were the various offices, the Writers' Building, Wardrobe, and Editing, and they too looked like an army base: two-story barracks with metal stairs. I drove past the commissary, where the patio was bedecked with tables sheltered by red-and-white umbrellas and tall palms that cast little shade. Beyond this was the Executive Mansion (yes, that's what they really called it), three stories of cream-colored splendor, a stupendous contrast to the rest of the place, and a colossal waste of real estate. A path lined with palms and lacy jacarandas led to the broad steps, and a pale marble fountain burbled out front. A sharp-faced gorgon sitting at a desk by the door demanded to know my business.

"I'm here to see Elliott Dunne," I said. "I'm Roxanne Granville."

"Second floor on the right. I'll let them know," she said, pressing on a button.

As a kid I had bounded up the tiled staircase, taking them two by two, to go up to Leon's office, where he welcomed me anytime, opening his arms and calling me Honeybee. Now I walked slowly and soberly, woozy with anxiety over what I was about to do. I paused, my hand on the mahogany rail. I might have turned around and left, but I looked up. All the framed posters lining the staircase were films starring Denise Dell.

"Roxanne!" Elliott himself came out to greet me and usher me into his carpeted office. "I'm so glad to see you so soon after the party."

We rattled along with the usual exchanges prefacing these encounters. At L'Oiseau d'Or they taught us a useful feminine art, a mannerism said to have been perfected by Josephine and practiced on Napoleon. A woman, especially when speaking to a man, would drop her voice, gently, not quite to a whisper. The art lay in the nuance. Her listener would have to bend closer to hear, evoking both a sense of intimacy and an air of importance to whatever was being said. The woman was thus made to seem both alluring and imperative in the same moment. I used it with Elliott. "I have here a couple of scripts by one of my writers, Charlie Frye, one of my finest writers, and I just think they're perfect for Empire."

"Tell me about them." He leaned in closer. We sat on a couch of Italian leather.

I offered up the stories in an appealing way, and he listened, clearly charmed, but finally, he stopped, shook his head. "Sorry, but Empire is looking for something bigger."

"Like *The Robe*? It cost four million dollars to put all those Roman centurions in their cute armor up on the screen in CinemaScope. Empire is too small to do something on that scale. These are cheap. Easy to film. Easy to market. We've always been known for the clever comedies, the—"

"We?"

I flushed. "Force of habit. I grew up on this lot. Empire was my playground."

"Yes, I've heard the stories. You and Jonathan Moore."

"Kid stuff. We were terrors."

"Not childhood sweethearts?"

"Oh, no."

Elliott seemed pleased. He took the two scripts from me and leafed through them. "I'll read them and get back to you. Actually, we have an unexpected hiatus in production right now, and something like this might suit us."

No doubt the less-than-stellar box office of *Banner Headline* had Empire executives scurrying around like lemmings, but I said nothing of the sort.

"What else has Charles Frye done?"

"Well, his *Return of the Cat People* just sold," I lied. I skipped the *Dragnet* episode altogether. "This sort of comedy is Charlie's great forte, you know, the kind of film where you get misty at the end and walk out of the theater thinking that the world's a better place. One of these could be the next *Sabrina*. Four-million-dollar box office." I went on at length, lauding Charlie's many gifts as a comedic writer, astonished at the ease with which these lies tripped off my tongue. Had I made a sentimental mistake with Charlie? Maybe I should have asked Maurice Allen to front for these comedies. Maurice, while a little astringent, was a more sophisticated writer, a more sophisticated person. I felt a stab of remorse, and a flutter of anxiety jelling into fear, but the scripts were literally in Elliott's hands, and it was too late to turn back.

CHAPTER TWELVE

I drove to Summit Drive on a sunny Saturday afternoon wearing a broad-brimmed sun hat and a pale yellow sundress that complemented my tan. The family was celebrating Gordon Junior's ninth birthday at Leon's house with a party by the pool. By the time I arrived, Gordon Junior had already gotten his big present, a miniature car that he was barreling around the pool area and over the grass, honking the horn, scaring the hell out of his younger siblings, crowing with delight, and alarming the servants who were bringing drinks and food. All Irene's children are brats, even the two-year-old, Cindy. I put my present on the table, and set myself the task of being genial while I braced myself for the possibility that my grandfather would guess I was representing the work of a man he thought to be a traitor to America. In the two weeks since I'd sent the scripts to Elliott, I'd had more than one attack of sender's remorse, made worse because I could share my anxiety with no one, not even Thelma. After all, she was on record as disapproving.

There was an empty chaise beside Irene, who looked as though she had been carved in white marble. She wore a sort of beach peignoir, since she burned easily, and smoke lazed up from her cigarette. "Where's Jonathan?" she asked.

"Probably nursing a hangover." I thanked Clarence as he

handed me a Campari and soda. "I went to a party at Casa Fiesta last night where everyone but me was beautiful and drunk."

"You are beautiful."

"Oh, come on. I might be smart. I might have a French education and a father knighted by the queen, I might own a diamond ring, a diamond choker, ruby earrings, and a rope of perfect pearls, but you know as well as I, I will never be beautiful."

"Then why weren't you drunk?"

"Al Gilbert was camped outside in his car taking names, and it just struck me as tawdry. I think I might have outgrown Casa Fiesta."

"About time. Jonathan should be outgrowing it too."

"Oh, I doubt that will happen." I didn't say more. Didn't want to be disloyal and admit that Jonathan's need for an ever-shifting entourage of affection sauced with competition was just short of insatiable.

Denise floated over to us. She wore a turquoise beach cover-up cinched at the waist that emphasized her long, shapely legs. She adjusted a table umbrella to shade her fair skin. We chatted, cotton candy talk, sweet but insubstantial, as she settled into a chair by my side. Then she said, "Elliott Dunne gave me two scripts by your writer, Roxanne. Tell me about this Charles Frye. Why haven't I ever heard of him?"

"He's young, like me. Like you." I was glad we were all wearing sunglasses.

"Does Charlie write comedy?" asked Irene, coming suddenly to life. "The last time I talked to him, he was touting his *Coast of Heaven* like it was *On the Waterfront*."

I gave a blithe chuckle and burbled on about how he could do drama, but he loved comedy, pretending he had gone through twenty drafts to achieve the frothy perfection of *You Make Me Feel So Young* and *Fly Me to the Moon*.

Leon and Elsie joined us. Elsie was pale and puffy and clad in a flowered tent. Leon looked as if he had stepped off the Riviera, dressed in shorts and a sailor's jaunty, striped shirt, with a yachts-man's cap atop his wiry gray hair. He placed a hand on Denise's shoulder, which she reached up and stroked as he sat down beside her. He too wore sunglasses, so I could not read his expression, but I could feel sweat pop on my brow that had nothing to do with heat.

"We're talking about Charles Frye, Pooks," Denise said, using their pet name that always made my skin crawl. Imagine calling a man like Leon Greene a name you might give to a Pekingese lap-dog. "Elliott sent them on to me. I think they'd be great for me."

"He sent them to me too. I'm not convinced," said Leon in his executive voice, which I took as a bad sign. "I'm surprised you'd bring them to Empire, Roxanne. You don't want to look like you're relying on nepotism, do you?"

"Oh, nepotism." Irene brushed that away. "There's nothing wrong with nepotism. Hollywood is one big happy family. Well, maybe not happy."

Elsie offered, "I think both these scripts are perfect for Denise. They highlight her best gifts."

"They're old-fashioned," said Leon. "*You Make Me Feel So Young* is like *Miracle on 34th Street* without Santa."

Since this was exactly my own estimation, I quickly put my drink to my lips and hid behind the glass.

"All those wise-cracking dames from the thirties, they're passé now," he added.

"Yes," said Irene, sighing, "now women are content with dia-logue so dry it might as well have come from Egyptian tombs. 'O mighty Pharaoh, my lord, I beseech thee . . . ' Why can't the girls have any spirit?"

"Maisie in *Fly Me to the Moon* has spirit," I said. "A character like Maisie, a lowly lab assistant, falls in love, but she has to do something smart, something unconventional to get her man."

"She lies to him," said Leon. "She deliberately misleads him, creating messages from the moon. I don't think we should make pictures that celebrate subterfuge. It's un-American. It sends an un-American message from the screen." His brow creased in a frown.

"No one wants characters who are saints," I said. "Look at *Casablanca*. Everyone in that movie is morally compromised."

"That was wartime," said Leon. "This isn't."

I could feel the birthmark flush.

"But she does it for love, Pooks," said Denise, placing her hand on his knee. "She lies because she loves him. And if you think about it"—Denise paused for effect, thinking about it—"she's actually lying when she lets Professor Bleeker think she's just really dim. Really, she's very smart."

"These comedies," Leon scoffed, "they're throwbacks. I mean, we used to do them in the old days, crank them out, five or six a year. I want something more elegant for you, angel, more modern, something sleek. You'd be wasted as the frumpy Maisie, wouldn't you agree, Roxanne?"

Panache will sometimes suffice when real courage fails. "It's true Maisie doesn't start out in an evening gown, but—"

"Nor does she end up in one," Leon reminded us.

Sunlight blinking up off the pool played across my field of vision, and I wished like hell I'd listened to Thelma, but I went on, "*Fly Me to the Moon* has a lively woman at the center, not some tough private eye, not some oil-chested Pharaoh, but a woman who grows more beautiful because she has brains. I think that's a picture women will want to see."

"That's exactly what I thought," said Denise. "They're wonderful scripts, charming, and funny and endearing. They suit my talents. You do know how great I'd be, don't you, honey?"

"Of course." Leon took off his sunglasses and beamed at her.

"Well, Pooks, you're the boss, you decide, but I think I would shine."

And with that Denise stood, dropped the cover-up, and poised herself for a moment, her voluptuous glory molded in an aquamarine swimsuit, before she walked to the diving board, treating it like a model's runway. She executed a dive as perfectly as Esther Williams might have done. We all watched, spellbound.

"I want the best for her," said Leon, speaking directly to me.

Denise burst to the surface, shining. The bright blonde mane of her hair cast back and the sheer energy she radiated sparkled all over her, sunlight reflecting rainbows on every drop of water that beaded on her skin. Her glory reflected in Leon's eyes, in his face, in his smile.

"I want your next picture to be the one people are still talking about in ten years," Leon said as she gracefully hoisted herself from the water. "I want you to shine."

"That's exactly what I want, Pooks."

"I want an all-American comedy for you."

"Oh, Charlie Frye is all-American," said Irene with a trilling laugh. "He likes John Philip Sousa. You know . . ." And she started humming "The Stars and Stripes Forever" as she marched off like a drum majorette rounding up her brood, because Clarence was wheeling out the birthday cake.

Perhaps ten days later I put the phone down and staggered up from my chair and into the front office, where Thelma sat typing away. She looked up at me, her face lit with alarm. "Who died?"

"That was Elliott Dunne on the phone. They're buying both of them! *Fly Me to the Moon* and *You Make Me Feel So Young*! And," I crowed, "they're paying five thousand each!"

"Five. Thousand. Each!" Thelma stood up, hooting, and we linked arms and did a little victory dance we'd devised whenever we got a sale, even for *Dragnet*, until Thelma stopped dancing, and frowned. "Five grand is nothing compared to what Max used to get."

"But it's more than Charlie ever dreamed of!" I insisted. "And they want to give Charlie a studio contract, a three-year contract! To come work at the studio! Oh, Thelma! We've never had a writer get a three-year contract! I'm going to call Max right now!"

"No. Don't call from this phone," Thelma cautioned.

"Right. Okay. I'll call Charlie and tell him the good news. You cancel everything for the rest of the day. We're locking up and driving out to Riverside with some French champagne!"

I returned to my office to get my keys, when the phone rang. "Granville Agency," I said jauntily.

"You have done quite the coup, little sister," said Irene, her voice tense, her words terse. "Gordon's just told me they bought your two pictures, the so-called Charlie Frye comedies."

"What do you mean?"

"I read them last night, Roxanne. I've met Charlie Frye, re-member? So I know for a fact that Charlie wouldn't know wit like that if it tickled him in the testicles."

I laughed out loud. "Oh, Irene, how can you talk about testi-cles? Of course Charlie—"

"These were written by Max Leslie, a Communist, and it's no good pretending they aren't."

"Max isn't a Communist. He quit the party in thirty-nine when—"

"Spare me the history lesson! How can you be so reckless? Why are you doing this?"

"Well," I offered with a bit of sass, "I thought I'd just see which of Leon's two passions would win out. If he loves John Wayne and Richard Nixon more than he loves Denise Dell."

"And now you have your answer. So what? What in the hell have you proved? Who have you hurt? What have you done, Roxanne?"

Silence lingered between us. I was stunned at her anger. Irene always kept her calm.

"If anyone ever finds out—oh, and they will, somehow—can you even imagine what will happen to Leon? The American Legion will attack him like he was Iwo Jima."

"The scripts are perfect for Denise," I said in my own meager defense.

"One day you will get caught out in one of these foolish gestures, and the world will deal with you unkindly, and you will have only yourself to blame." She hung up.

"Who was that?" Thelma called out from the front room.

"No one," I replied.

Word of the Granville Agency's success rippled everywhere. I sold three more scripts from different writers that same week (albeit all to television). Telegrams fluttered in, delivered sometimes three or four at a time, congratulating us. Our phone rang off the hook. People offered praise, some of it laced with snide asides: Charlie Frye? The guy who wrote *Return of the Cat People* now had a dual-picture deal with Empire and an actual three-year paying contract as well? Amid this flurry of praise when I came into work mid-morning about ten days later, I was surprised when Thelma looked up from her typewriter with a peculiar expression on her face.

"You have a visitor." She nodded toward a woman sitting on our couch, her shoulders hunched.

Kathleen Hilyard, once a glamorous, high-kicking, long-legged dancer, sat before me. I scarcely recognized this wisp of a woman. Her hair was clipped close to her head, her face lined. She wore a nun-gray dress with long sleeves, little white gloves, and sturdy shoes. "Forgive me for just showing up, Roxanne."

"Mrs. Hilyard—Kathleen—there's nothing to forgive."

"Bachman. I'm Kathleen Bachman now. My maiden name. I took the girls back to Phoenix and we had to change our name. Nelson . . . his . . . well, the disgrace, you know? The Oscar Nelson won for *The Ice Age*, I have to keep it hidden in a drawer. We can't even speak of him to anyone. It's very hard on the girls." She knotted a handkerchief in her gloved fingers.

"It was tragic, Kathleen."

"I'm a manager in hosiery now," she said with some dignity. She put her hand on an elaborate hatbox that had *Goldwater's* in fancy lettering on it. "Ironic, isn't it? I left Phoenix in nineteen thirty-six to come to Hollywood and be a dancer like Ruby Keeler, and I went back fifteen years later the wife of a suicide. However, I'm not here to dwell on the past. I'm thinking of the future." She picked up the hatbox and put it in my hands. "Marian called me with the great news. Yes, I know they're in Riverside. I've known for a while. You made them so happy, Roxanne, and I thought, I mean, Marian too, she thought, we both thought—" Kathleen cleared her throat. "Nelson was such a fine writer."

I walked over and placed the hatbox on Thelma's desk. "Kathleen, the kinds of dramas Nelson wrote, no one's doing those now. There's no *The Best Years of Our Lives*, or *How Green Was My Valley*. His great, Oscar-winning film, *The Ice Age*, would never get made now. Everyone wants epics or musicals so bright they hurt your eyes."

"*On the Waterfront* did a clean sweep at the Oscars this year. Look, please, please, Roxanne, just read these. My girls are teens now—they're hoping to go to college. They ought to have something from their father's estate, something from his long career." She gulped with emotion.

"Nelson's name can never go on anything ever again," I said, regretting the cruel finality of it, but what other choice was there?

"I don't expect his name to be on it. Someone else's name. A front. Like you did for Max. No one else would know."

"Then what can your daughters be proud of if they can't say it's their father's work?"

"They would know. We would know. There's six scripts there. *The Devil and the Deep Blue Sea* is the best thing he ever wrote. It will kill you, it's so . . ." Kathleen bit her lip, collected herself, and placed one gloved hand primly over the other. "Two of these scripts aren't even finished. Nelson was in such despair for a long time. Especially after the Committee came after Simon and he had to leave the country. Nelson and Simon were true comrades. Nelson was dedicated to social justice. He was a good man, and a good father, no matter what else he was." She rose, walked to the desk, opened the box, and lifted the scripts out of rustling tissue paper, as though they were newborn babes. "It's wonderful work. He really was so very talented, you know. I'll accept whatever you say, Roxanne. I just ask that you read them. Please."

"You came all the way from Phoenix to bring me these?"

"I should have called ahead. I'm sorry. I thought if I saw you . . ."

"Can we get you something, Kathleen? A cup of tea, maybe? Coffee?"

"A drink?" said Thelma.

"No. Thank you. I have to get back home. I have to catch the afternoon train."

"You want a ride to Union Station?"

"I came here in a cab. I can take a cab back. Could you call me one, Thelma?"

Thelma reached into the drawer and took out her purse. "I'll drive you."

I said goodbye to Kathleen, then took the box, the scripts, the tissue paper into my office and started to read. I could hear Nelson's voice on every page, could all but hear his hands fluttering over the keys of the upright piano. I knew the very sort of music he would have played. *The Devil and the Deep Blue Sea* was an especially moving story, a drama that might suit Maurice Allen's talents. That is, if he chose to do it.

I walked to the window and opened the curtains to the spring twilight. If I could go back to my child-self, how could I possibly tell that little girl, *One day these men who seem to you like big friendly giants, who seem so brilliant, who create so many stories from their own great imaginations, one day they will need you, Roxanne. One day there will be no one to protect them, to advocate for them, except you.* How could I possibly have foreseen that those men who basked in the protection of the great studios—studios that had laid garlands at their feet, given them grand homes and gleaming swimming pools, glamorous cars, powerful friends—that all that would have dis-solved? How could they—how could I—ever have guessed that their gifts would be devalued and their names tarnished, that of those glory days and gala nights, nothing would remain? HUAC had swooped down on Hollywood like the flying monkeys in *The Wizard of Oz*. Those like Vic Hale who atoned by abasing them-selves went on working and became virulent in their own defense. Those who didn't suffered, sinking into obscurity or fleeing like refugees. Whatever choices they'd made, they were all diminished now, and they would never be golden again.

When I was looking for a lawyer for the Granville Agency, I wanted someone independent, someone to read contracts and keep secrets. Not someone old like Melvin Grant who had ushered his clients into Congressional hearings and on to disaster. Not some-one too cozy with the studios. Not someone whose standing in a big corporate firm might be instantly improved if he were to let some bit of information drop to another colleague. I knew that Julia had trusted Mr. Wilkie, but my needs were not her needs. Jonathan recommended his attorney, Adam Ornstein. Adam had the gravity of a rabbi. He had two doors to his office, like a psycho-analyst: one you went in, and one you went out. This was a man who understood secrets.

I spent the morning going over several of my writers' contracts with Adam, then returned to Clara Bow Drive in time for my one o'clock appointment. Thelma and I made sure that no one else but she and I would be in the office. Maurice Allen was early, and the ashtray in front of him was full of butts when I walked in.

We went into my office, closed the door, and after the obliga-tory prelims—how wonderful our lives were going, the usual art-ful pretense—I had only come to the word *discretion* when Maurice raised a hand.

"I think I know what you're going to ask me, Roxanne. Who is it?"

"What makes you think . . . ?"

"Because you wanted to see me in person and in private. Because fronting for blacklisted writers is the new Hollywood vice—not as pervasive as adultery or drugs, but just as wicked, and even more risky." He blew a smoke ring.

"Nelson Hilyard."

"Hilyard was a homo, wasn't he? Not a Red."

"He was a Red too," I said.

"Great." Maurice stubbed out his cigarette. "I'm in. I need the money. I don't have any politics other than that."

"Don't you want to read them first?"

Maurice shrugged. "Give them to me, I'll read them, but I can tell you right now, I'm happy to pick up the pen that once wrote *The Ice Age*, even if he was a Commie and a homo. I need the credit, Roxanne, I need the money. I need to get the hell out of Poverty Row and television. I don't want to go back to New York as a failure."

"Remember—you tell no one."

Maurice rose and picked up the envelopes that held Nelson's scripts. "I hear Charlie's moved out of that Hollywood dump, and he's renting a place right on the beach in Venice, and he has a new car. I suppose all his success is something on the same order."

"Something like that."

"Well, silence is my middle name," said Maurice on his way out the door.

It was true that before the ink on his Empire contracts had even touched the page, in a burst of elation, Charlie had moved to a beachside apartment in Venice, bought a new custom surfboard, and put a down payment on a 1950 Buick Roadmaster station wagon to carry it in. But privately, success had had a strange, unlooked-for effect on Charlie Frye. His supreme surfer confidence withered, and his inner anxieties suddenly surfaced. I was the only one he could turn to, and though I saw less of him now (I'm pretty certain he was out impressing other women), turn to me he did. He would call me, sometimes late at night, sometimes in the middle of the workday, demanding that I drop everything and attend to him, assure him, prop up his ego, assuage his fears.

Charlie's needs reached a new, exasperating peak the day before we were to have a celebratory lunch with Elliott Dunne. I held the phone to my ear and played with a pencil while he nattered on for twenty minutes, anxious and needy. I broke the tip of the pencil. "Listen, Charlie. Tomorrow Elliott Dunne is going to give you the key to the Writers' Building at Empire Pictures. This is your great chance to be the screenwriter you always wanted to be. Don't screw it up. We bought you that nice new suit and tie. Tailor-made, remember? The same tailor Leon goes to."

"Yes."

"Then you just wear that, look handsome, and let your wit and good humor shine through."

"What if I can't?"

"I'll see you at Pierino's at one o'clock." I hung up, irritated. More than that: angry, really. If I'd loved Charlie I would have been more supportive. But I didn't love him, and I never would. Constantly stroking his ego made me too tired to stroke other things. I couldn't go on waving pom-poms and bouncing away to John Philip Sousa.

CHAPTER THIRTEEN

~~~~~

Fate had something else in store the next morning. I went out to the Silver Bullet, and it only barely coughed to life. I knew (bitter experience) better than to turn it off until I got to Reg's Auto Repair in the Valley. Wishing I'd been brought up to pray, I urged the MG along the back roads.

Reg is a displaced Brit with smoke-stained fingers, bad teeth, a thin nose, and bright blue eyes. He only works on foreign cars, specialty cars, and fussy and unreliable sports cars. Like mine. His place, a big dusty lot overhung by eucalyptus trees and aged sycamores, takes up an acre in what was once a chicken ranch. I had the MG's top up so I wouldn't get blown to bits, but when I stepped out of the car, dust, no doubt left over from the chickens, swirled up and coated my white shoes. In the small office an open window let in a dry breeze, ruffling the receipts and invoices, and girlie calendars that were pinned to the wall. A colored man reading a newspaper leaned back in the desk chair, his feet up on the desk, resting atop the phone book. He bent the page and looked over it.

"Where's Reg?" I asked.

He waved in the general direction of the garage outside and returned to his newspaper.

Why didn't he get up and go find Reg for me? He didn't even look up again. Cursing him under my breath, I stomped through the dusty yard as my shoes turned a dingy brown. In the big garage where the mechanics were all bent over the engines of sports cars, I stepped into a grease puddle. "Reg! Reg!" I called again over the clang of tools and an unseen radio playing Hank Williams. "Reg! I need your help!"

Reg emerged from under the hood—the "bonnet," he would have said—of a Triumph. He wore oil-stained overalls and wiped his hands on an oil-stained rag. He plucked a cigarette out of his mouth and grinned at me. "Miss Granville. Oh no, more trouble with the Silver Bullet?"

"I'm in a hurry, Reg. Really. You have to look at it right now. I have a lunch date at Pierino's and I have to be there. I can't be late."

"Let's have a look at her." Cars were always female to Reg. He walked out with me, opened the MG's hood, and poked about, muttering to himself. He tried to start it, to no avail. "Sorry, Miss Granville, it's the electrical system. It'll take me a couple of days. Parts, you know. Hard to come by." The colored man strolled out of the office, and Reg turned to him. "Your Porsche is ready, Mr. Dexter. I've just asked Bob to take it round the block once, just to be sure all's well while I do your paperwork."

"Thanks, Reg," said Mr. Dexter without a glance at me.

Blood pounded into my face from embarrassment, lighting up my birthmark. Everything I'd assumed was wrong. The Negro man did not work here. He was a customer. He carried a sport coat over his shoulder; he was well dressed, certainly not in greasy overalls, but I had not seen that behind the newspaper. Moreover, something about him was oddly—not familiar, exactly, but, well, something . . . I said again to Reg that I had to have the car, and I had to have it fast. "I have a very important lunch appointment. I need to be there."

"Sorry, miss. You know what these electrical systems are like." He began explaining how English cars used two six-volt batteries and American cars used one twelve-volt and . . .

I just wanted the damn thing to run, to be reliable. Too much to ask of a British car. I regretted not driving a Cadillac like everyone else. A cab into the city would cost me a fortune, more cash than I had with me.

Reg went into the office, and Mr. Dexter came up to me. He was tall, broad-shouldered, solid, his hair cut short and close to his head, his skin a deep mahogany. His large dark eyes were expressive and flickered with mirth. Then he was instantly serious. "Where is your appointment?"

"Pierino's on La Cienega."

"I know where Pierino's is. My Porsche is done. I'll drop you off there if you want."

I flushed even more deeply. "Thank you."

"Of course, the Porsche is a sports car, no back seat." He frowned, as though puzzled. "You'll have to sit beside me. You can't pretend I'm your chauffeur."

"That really won't be necessary," I replied with what I hoped was dignity.

Mr. Dexter went into the office with Reg, and one of the mechanics drove into the wide yard in a cream-colored Porsche convertible spewing dust all around, coating my navy blue suit and my white gloves.

Reg and Mr. Dexter came outside, and Reg held the Porsche door open for me as I lowered myself into the leather seat. I wanted to ask the driver to please put the top up, but something about him did not invite the asking of further favors, and besides, I was still smarting from my awful gaffe.

Reg chuckled, reached round to his back pocket, and handed me a coarse blue foursquare kerchief. "It's clean, Miss Granville. Ironed, even. The wife just gave it to me this morning, and I swear, I haven't used it yet."

I tied Reg's kerchief under my chin. The car hummed to life, and we pulled out of there in yet another cloud of dust.

"I really do appreciate the ride. I'm Roxanne Granville, by the way."

"I know who you are. Leon Greene's granddaughter."

"Don't believe everything you read in the society pages," I said, assuming he had seen photos of me at the Cocoanut Grove or some such place.

"If it's in the newspaper, it ought to be true. Isn't that the standard for journalism?" he asked as though I had some sort of answer. I didn't. He continued, "I'm Terrence Dexter. I'm a columnist and reporter for the *Challenger*. Your grandmother was a big supporter of our paper and the NAACP."

Oh god, now I remembered his face! "You were at my grandmother's funeral. You brought the umbrella."

"I did." He looked over at me, rather surprised, and I wondered how I could ever have forgotten his face. He smiled, and I noticed he had a gold canine tooth.

"You came to the lawyer's office with the man in the wheelchair."

"Mr. Branch. He's editor in chief of the *Challenger* and a leader of the NAACP."

"I had no idea that Julia supported those causes."

"Judging from the looks on the white folks' faces there, no one else did either. Your granddaddy surely didn't." He barely suppressed a chuckle.

He wrapped his long fingers around the steering wheel and drove with an easy certainty, double-clutching when necessary. The Porsche didn't ride like the MG; it seemed to sit lower to the road, and the engine had a deeper tone. The leather seats had their own peculiar odor. Terrence Dexter was a fearless driver, downright scary. I held tight to the door handle. He was speeding and taking curves faster than he should. Certainly faster than I would have taken them, and I consider myself an experienced driver.

"You have to master a Porsche or it will master you," he said laconically.

"Well, my MG has mastered me. Sometimes I swear it stays more at Reg's than it does with me."

"An MG is like a little-bitty firefly that has some magic. But a Porsche isn't like that. A Porsche is like an eagle. No magic, but it has strength."

"That's an odd, imaginative way to talk about a car."

He shrugged, and gave me a look that made me vaguely uncomfortable. When I see this sort of look on people's faces, I always assume they're looking at the stain on my cheek and thinking, *Oh, that poor girl with her ugly cheek.* But he couldn't see the birthmark on the right side of my face, and his assessment was of an oddly different nature.

"My brother, Booker, and I used to do valet parking for parties at your granddaddy's when we were in high school. Summit Drive is where I acquired my taste for fast cars and pretty women. We drove some fine sets of wheels till Clarence caught us driving the cars without white gloves, and, well, there was hell to pay. Said we had to promise we'd wear the gloves, all valets gotta wear gloves. So we quit. Just walked off laughing while he . . . well, he was plenty steamed."

"Why would he insist on gloves?"

"So our black hands wouldn't be touching the white folks' steering wheels."

This had never occurred to me. Of course servants wore gloves. I might have said something, but Terrence Dexter passed a lumbering Buick on a curve, downshifting for a burst of speed, rousing a blast of the Buick's horn. I clung to the door.

"Clarence is the squarest of the squares. Everything gotta be just so. He's my uncle, married to my Aunt Ruby."

Clarence had nephews? I knew nothing of his life. "Does anyone else in your family work at Summit Drive?" I asked for want of anything else to say other than *Please slow down.*

"Well, over the years some of my cousins have been waiters at the big parties. And they wore white gloves, you can bet on that. Aunt Mavis used to be a cook there."

"I remember Mavis," I said, a little embarrassed I had no

recollection of her last name. "She was always nice to me, had warm tapioca pudding for me when the chauffeur brought me home from school."

"Yes. Aunt Mavis used to say how sweet you were, but spoiled rotten, and your grandparents let you run wild. She felt sorry for you that you didn't have your own mama and daddy."

"I didn't feel sorry for me," I replied with a touch of hauteur. I could feel my birthmark flooding with color. "My mother . . ." How to say *My mother can't stand the sight of me*? I let that thought pass. "My father went back to England. My father is Sir Rowland Granville, the famous British actor."

"My father is James Dexter, the famous American auto mechanic," Terrence replied.

"Then why do you take your car to Reg's?"

"He's dead. Both my parents are dead."

"I'm sorry to hear that."

"Thanks, but you don't have to be. I don't need your sorry."

He was awfully testy for what was after all a mere conventional expression. "I don't remember when Mavis left Summit Drive."

"When Mr. Greene put a loyalty oath in front of everyone in nineteen forty-seven. They all had to sign it, swear by Almighty God that they had no intention of overthrowing the government. If you didn't sign it, you got fired, and probably your name turned over to the FBI." He glanced over at me. "Why do you look surprised? Your granddaddy is great friends with J. Edgar Hoover."

"I'm . . . I mean, I know the studio requires everyone to sign a loyalty oath. I just didn't think Leon would ask it of people who worked in his home."

"Clarence was happy to sign it, yes sir, and happy to have the job there for twenty-five years, and looking forward to the next twenty-five, thank you. Everyone signed except Mavis. Mavis said, 'I'm a freeborn American, and ain't no one gonna make me sign an oath.' Easier for her than for some. She's a great cook. She cooks for Lana Turner now." He drove for a few minutes in silence, then added thoughtfully, "The loyalty oath impinges on the First Amendment, and it'll go through the courts, and be defeated, but that'll take forever. Seems like everything takes forever."

He talked some more about the courts—appeals courts and the Supreme Court, subjects in which I had no interest whatever, as we started up the Sepulveda Pass, a two-lane highway bordered on either side by woods. He took another curve at alarming speed. The glove box popped open and a book fell out. *The Negro Motorist Green Book.*

"What's this?" I asked, leafing through it, state by state.

"When was the last time you peed in a field, Miss Granville?"

"I have never peed in a field, thank you."

"If I gotta travel, drive someplace far from where and what I know, I need this book to tell me where can I stay. I gotta know where I can eat. Where can I get gas? Lots of Shell gas stations won't even sell gas to us. Others, if they sell gas to Negroes, they won't let us use the toilet. You look surprised," he said again.

"I would never have thought of that."

"Well, you wouldn't, would you? A girl like you, you go some-where and the guy pumping gas, he's white, the waiter, the butcher, the baker, the candlestick maker. Everyone except the shoeshine boy and the janitor or the maid. But me, I have to be careful. Even here in LA, we all do. I'm not talking Alabama, I'm talking Glendale. Right up the road. That's what's known as a sundown town. Your black ass better be out of there by sundown. My brother once played a gig in a club up there, and he had a hell of a time getting home at three in the morning, couldn't get a cab to save his soul. Had to spend the night under a bus bench."

"In Glendale? What— Oh god!" I screamed as a huge deer leapt out of the woods, antlers and all, right overhead, its hooves flying, its eyes rolling crazily as Terrence swore, leaned on the horn. I ducked and clutched at his arm and he downshifted, swerved, sped up. The deer landed in the opposite lane, and that driver nearly hit it. Both cars fishtailed, squealed, and burned rub-ber before Terrence righted the Porsche, and shook off my hand.

"Oh! Sorry!" I cried.

"No! No! I had to steer and shift at the same time!"

That brief moment of physical contact crackled between us like experiencing an electrical shock. The deer. The danger. I was trembling. I could not catch my breath. His hands coiled around the wheel, and he kept shaking his head and cursing the deer.

"I didn't mean to grab on to you," I said. "I shouldn't have. I have never been so close to dying. Your driving saved our lives. Thank you."

"At least you had your gloves on."

"If you mean because you are colored—" My voice quavered.

"Please, Miss Granville. I am not colored. Look at me," he insisted. "No, really, look!" I turned and met his eyes, which were dark and fierce. He was about my age, and he bristled with an intensity I had seldom experienced in anyone. "I'm not blue or pink or green. I'm black. I'd rather be a black bastard than a colored boy."

"I only meant . . ." But then I wasn't sure what I meant, and I was still in shock. After a short silence, I said, "I hope I haven't kept you from anything important."

He did not reply, but reached in his suit pocket and put on his sunglasses.

I opened my purse and put on my dark glasses. It wasn't my job to entertain him. And then I thought, *Well, Roxanne, it's not his job to entertain you either.* In a silence that felt ominous we crested a hill, and the city fanned out before us. He gave the car one last burst of speed before we came down into the broad city streets, where he slowed, mindful of the speed limits and traffic lights, and, I feel pretty certain, keeping an eye out for cop cars.

As he pulled the Porsche in front of Pierino's flagstone circular driveway, he remarked, "I hope you don't expect me to get out and open the door for you."

I had no opportunity for a retort, because just then I saw none other than Gordon Conrad standing under the awning by the valet's podium, handing off the keys to his Cadillac. Gordon gave me a weird look just as the valet opened the door to the Porsche. I got out, and the Porsche roared away before I had the chance to thank Terrence Dexter.

Gordon asked with no other greeting, "Who is the jungle bunny? Your new chauffeur? And what's that on your head? You look like a farm girl just back from a hoedown."

I snatched the kerchief from my head. "Really, Gordon, do you have to be vulgar?"

"No, but I like to. What are you doing here?"

"I'm meeting Elliott and Charlie at one."

"You're early."

"I had car trouble, and he—that man—gave me a ride in from Reg's."

"I always told you to drive a Cadillac. Well, you might as well have a drink with us till Elliott gets here."

"Who is us?"

"Leon, Denise, Elsie, and me."

This prospect shook me up even more than driving with a speed demon and having a deer leap right over my head. My throat tightened, but I stuffed Reg's silly kerchief into my purse along with my sunglasses and followed him in.

They were naturally sitting at the best table in Pierino's, Denise looking like a camellia in a bouffant skirt that brushed the floor, Elsie like a great flowered pillowcase. Leon rose and embraced me, and, though no one but me would have guessed, his hug was perfunctory.

"Roxanne just got out of a fancy car driven by a boogie," said Gordon after the waiter brought the drinks.

"Don't call him that. He was very kind. I had trouble with the MG, and I had to leave it at Reg's. He was picking up his car and offered to bring me into town. He's a reporter. He writes for a paper called the *Challenger*." I decided not to mention his connection to Clarence, or that he had been at Julia's funeral and the reading of her will.

"The *Challenger* is the voice of the NAACP," said Leon. "The NAACP pretends to serve colored people, but they're a Communist front, roiling up race relations."

"Now, now, Pooks," said Denise, tapping his arm. "Let's talk about my new picture, *Fly Me to the Moon*."

Leon glanced over at me briefly, uncomfortably, then looked away.

"Who will play Professor Bleeker?" asked Elsie. "Gary Cooper?"

"He's too old," Gordon protested, though with a quick look to Leon, he corrected himself. "I mean, why should we pay for the star power of an established actor when there are so many young actors who are cheaper? Rock Hudson. We're thinking of Rock."

"Dreamy," said Elsie. "Positively dreamy."

"He's too tall for me," said Denise with a small pout. "Every time I stand beside Rock, I'd look like a Munchkin. I'd look . . ." she sought the word.

"Diminished," I offered without an ounce of irony.

"What about Alan Ladd, honey?" Denise tucked her hand through Leon's arm. "He's not very tall."

"What about Jonathan Moore?" I volunteered.

"He has no comedy credits," said Gordon. "Just a lot of sword-and-sandal crap."

"Hardly comedic," said Elsie. "I'm for Alan Ladd."

"If Jonathan wants to audition, that's fine with me," said Leon. "Just because he's never been in a comedy doesn't mean he couldn't do it."

Talk turned to the cameras rolling in August and for the production schedule to be fast-tracked so *Fly Me to the Moon* could be released at the end of the year. "To qualify for the Oscars," said Denise with a delighted smile.

I was relieved when Elliott and Charlie entered Pierino's together, Charlie looking especially handsome, like a surfer Bill Holden in his new suit, his blond hair neatly brushed back and gleaming with Brylcreem. He was the perfect young writer, deferential, respectful, calling the men *sir* and the women *ma'am*, and telling Denise how much he had loved her in *Banner Headline*.

"You know the script needs rewrites, don't you, Charlie?" asked Leon in a prosecutorial voice. "A few more contemporary touches."

"Rewrites, sure," said Charlie, his teeth flashing white in his tanned face. "I'd do anything to make you and Miss Dell happy."

Denise rewarded him with one of those smiles movie stars master, the goddess from on high toying with mere mortals. Elliott escorted Charlie and me to our table and ordered a bottle of champagne to celebrate the giving of the keys to the Empire Writers' Building to Charles David Frye.

That lunch was the apex of my career to date. Charlie's too. After lunch Charlie drove me home, both of us bathed in the glow of cocktails and great expectations. He was so happy when we got to my house, he came in, loosened his tie, and took me in his arms. He didn't even put on John Philip Sousa.

CHAPTER FOURTEEN

Jonathan dismissed my idea that he audition for the role of Professor Bleeker in *Fly Me to the Moon*. He insisted he was a dramatic actor and would not discuss it further. But I'm not so easily dissuaded. I went to Casa Fiesta the following Saturday night, thinking I might have better success there, that others would chime in and tell him how foolish and stubborn he was being.

I parked my car on the street and wandered in; someone put a drink in my hand, and I drifted over to where Jonathan and Diana Jordan were arguing. Diana was fueled with alcohol and fury. She had just axed her bastard-louse agent, Irv Rakoff. In addition to heaping verbal *merde* on Irv (which, admittedly, I enjoyed), she and Jonathan and Bongo were arguing about the best jazz club in LA. Bongo was all for the Dunbar Hotel.

"Wrong! It's the Comet Club," Diana insisted, flinging her glass into the fireplace. "The Comet Club has the best jazz in this town, in this whole state!"

Jonathan put his glass down and said, "Prove it!"

And that's how I somehow ended up with him, Bongo, and two handsome actors, Dwight and Dennis, or Don and David, or whoever they were who had played high school students in *Blackboard Jungle*. With Diana at the wheel we were on our way to Central Avenue. In the front seat Diana raged on, swearing at Irv, every name in her vast arsenal of insult. Occasionally she'd shout into the back seat to me, "No offense, Roxanne. I know you're an agent too."

"None taken!" I hollered back. With Jonathan pinned (so to speak) to the back seat, I worked on him all over again about the audition.

"You know I don't do comedy!" Jonathan shouted at me over Diana's harangue.

"You've never tried."

"I don't *want* to do comedy. I'm a serious actor."

"Oh, come on, how serious was that last role? Wasn't your name something like Gluteus Maximus? Would you rather go on saying lines like 'My little dove of Canaan'?" I was pleased that he visibly squirmed. "You need to audition for Professor Bleeker."

"What a disgusting name."

"What if I told you his name was Hamlet Bleeker? Auditions are Friday morning. Do it! Working is always better than not working."

"Isn't Leon afraid that Denise will fall in love with me? I am so much better looking."

"But you're not richer and more powerful, and you never will be. Audition."

Diana drove through the Central Avenue district, known for its raffish cafés and jazzy clubs, its after-hours cabarets and jam sessions. I'd been lots of times with groups of friends to the Dunbar Hotel, or the Club Alabam, places where the music was cool and the reputation was hot. I'd never heard of the Comet Club, which is where we stopped. She handed the guy five dollars to park her car, saying it shouldn't be too far away. She'd need it again soon. She also threw money at the big guy manning the door and collecting for the cover charge, and the six of us sashayed into a dark club full of roiling jazz, where the musicians played their instruments the way a moth plays with a flame, daring it to kill him.

"See what I mean about cool, daddy-o?" said Diana, giving us all a knowing grin as we followed her to the bar.

Galaxies of planets and orbs were painted across the ceiling in dull gold and amber and a dirty white. The chandelier twirled slowly, rotating shards of starlight over all, and splashed along the walls were comets with fierce, beautiful tails. All this was dimmed by thick clouds of cigarette smoke and the scent of reefer. We crowded at the bar and ordered drinks while money and liquor and music flowed all around us. The crowd was perhaps two-thirds Negro and one-third white. Many tables had black and white people together, something you never publicly see except on Central Avenue. Though there was a dance floor, no one was dancing except for one lone woman, who nodded and rocked, eyes closed, hips swaying. Everyone else, unless they were talking or flirting, succumbed to the rhythms, enchanted. The jazz was nothing I recognized, nothing I could groove to, and it was so loud that everything had to happen by way of expressions or gestures like a silent film.

The Negroes were indeed cool cats, wearing formfitting jackets, their slim legs in tight pants, their women in luxurious clothes that clung to their bodies, their hair sleek and shining, even in the smoky ambience. Most of the white men wore tuxes, their women in evening gowns and long white gloves; expensive furs lolled over the backs of chairs like animals at rest. The six of us were more casually dressed—Bongo in nonstop black and a beret, Jonathan in a shirt open at the collar. The two actors wore sport coats. Diana's silk trousers swayed when she walked, and I wore the proverbial little black dress with a gold belt.

Diana turned to us and shouted, "You see that man on trumpet? That, my friends, is the sexiest man who ever drew breath. Don't you doubt it. I've never had it so good as I have with him." She nodded toward the bandstand as she rolled and thrust her hips.

The band took a break, and the trumpet player ambled over to us, and right there in front of God and everyone, he took Diana in his arms and kissed her on the lips for a very long time, as much an act of ownership as passion. She laced her arms around his neck and went nearly limp in his arms. Admitting publicly to an affair with a Negro? That was over the top. Even for Diana Jordan. Bongo and the two actors put down their drinks and left without another word.

"You lily-livered stupidshits!" Diana called out, laughing at their retreating backs. Then she introduced Jonathan and me to Booker Dexter.

Except for the name, I wouldn't have known him immediately as Terrence Dexter's brother. He was not as tall, nor as handsome, as Terrence, who at that very minute I saw across the room, deep in conversation with none other than Clayton Strong and his girl-friend, Rita. Something Clayton said made Terrence throw his head back and laugh out loud, very unlike the man who had given me a ride in his Porsche. He turned and saw me, and as his eyes met mine surprise lit his features. An unlooked-for frisson of delight rushed through me as he crossed the smoky room with a smile on his face.

"Miss Granville."

"Mr. Dexter. I'm so sorry I didn't thank you for the ride the other day. It was unforgivable."

"No, really, I'm sorry I drove off in a huff. That deer had me really rattled."

"I've never been so scared."

"I lost my cool. I apologize."

"You know this chick?" asked Booker.

"We've met." He gave me an intimate smile.

"Crazy, man! My uncle working for your grandfather," said Booker after all the intros, connections, and exclamations were exchanged. "Terrence tell you all we used to park cars at your grand-daddy's? 'Yessir, lemme park that Jag for you, sir!' Terrence, he once drove a Jag halfway to Santa Barbara and still had it back when the party ended."

"Don't ever let Clarence know," said Terrence seriously.

"You dig the music?" Booker asked Jonathan and me. "West Coast Cool."

"Sure," said Jonathan. "Can't dance to it, though."

"Don't have to. It gets you here"—his hand splayed over his heart—"and here"—down to his guts—"and here." He grabbed his groin and laughed, then threw an arm over Diana's shoulders, and they meandered away, probably out to her car.

Jonathan and I followed Terrence to a table, where we crowded in with Clayton Strong, Rita, and two others, friends from UCLA. For the friends' benefit, Clayton and Jonathan recounted the loincloth-burning party at Casa Fiesta, and commiserated over toga roles. Clayton recited the stale paeans reserved for Negro actors, nearly all of which began with "Master," and Jonathan offered up some of the god-awful lines he and Paul Newman and Jack Palance had recited in *The Silver Chalice*. Jonathan had everyone laughing till it hurt, then he bought another round of drinks and invited all of them to Casa Fiesta next weekend.

"Laurel Canyon?" said Terrence. "We better not show up there unless we're parking cars."

"No," I said, "everyone comes to Casa Fiesta."

"That's true," said Clayton. "I thought Rita and I were goners the night of the toga-burning party when the police and fire department showed up. We could have been busted, and it would have gone hard for us, but"—he nodded to Jonathan—"he sent us upstairs to wait till the coast was clear."

"We put the bedroom to good use," said Rita.

Musicians gathered again on the stage and tuned up. Booker was the last to appear, while Diana came to our table, where she all but oozed sexual surfeit. We could smell it on her.

"What do you think of the music?" Terrence asked me once they started in on a new set.

"When I think of jazz, I think of Louis Armstrong, Ella Fitzgerald. I saw Sidney Bechet play in Paris a few times."

"That old-timey stuff? That's New Orleans crap. Sidney Bechet is old enough to be my granddaddy. Nobody but squares digs that anymore! Everyone who's cool digs bebop, hard bop, progressive jazz. West Coast Cool, that's what we call this." He nodded toward the bandstand, where, even if the musicians were cool, sweat gleamed on all their faces. "The greats all got their starts here on Central Avenue, grew up around here. Buddy Collette, Art Pepper, Chico Hamilton, Charles Mingus, Dexter Gordon."

The names meant nothing to me, but I nodded as though they did.

"When I was a kid, you'd ride up and down the streets delivering the evening paper, and you'd hear all these kids practicing, and playing in church. That's where they learned their licks, most of them, playing hymns in church."

"A hymn in church seems a long way from what they're playing here."

"No, see, Roxanne, you gotta know your hymns before you can bust them up into something else. A hymn is comforting because every chord has its expectable chord right behind it, every note has its expectable note right in front of it. Jazz takes all that, shatters it. Jazz don't comfort. Jazz wakes you up, because you never know what's coming next."

"Did your brother play hymns in church?"

"Oh, believe it! Booker and me both. We had rented instruments and Mama said to pay our part for them, we had to play in church every Sunday. People would come to that church just to hear Booker Dexter play! I tell you, the old ladies wept in the aisles."

"And the young ladies too, no doubt."

"No, the young ladies got damp and frisky." He grinned. "My brother and I, we were every Sunday in those pews, no matter what we'd been doing on Saturday night."

"I won't even try and imagine what that was."

He laughed. "Music kept us out of real trouble. We played in church and at school. At Jefferson High there was Dr. Browne. Man, he turned out more jazz musicians than any school ever has in the history of the whole world! I play a little piano, a little sax, but my brother has God-given genius. Oh, children! When Booker puts that trumpet to his lips, he leaves you slain! Well, you can hear him! He could bring down the walls of Jericho. He's a progressive jazz man."

"It certainly sounds progressive."

"Dig it!" Terrence nodded in time to the beat. "They are cookin' tonight!"

Later, the band took another break, and Booker and Diana again disappeared. A different drummer and piano man came out and seated themselves at their instruments. A vocalist shimmered out from behind flimsy curtains and took the mic. She wore a white strapless evening gown and long white gloves that contrasted vividly with her dark skin. She had orchids pinned in her hair, which was upswept with lots of escaping curly tendrils. The piano man introduced her as Miss Jaylene Henderson. As soon as she opened her mouth and the first notes of "The Man I Love" poured out, the Comet Club came to a standstill, and even the musicians lapsed into something of torpor. She lit into "How High the Moon," and everyone in the room seemed to rise on the tide of her voice. Throughout her set, she alternated sad with soaring till I felt like my emotions had been through the wringer. She could do anything with that voice, silky one moment, rasping the next. She sang "Smoke Gets in Your Eyes" in a voice like molten honey. Terrence asked if I wanted to dance.

He held me in a practiced embrace, and he danced well, though not like anything I'd been taught at L'Oiseau d'Or, and certainly not like free-form bop to Bill Haley and the Comets at Casa Fiesta. His arms wrapped round me like you would feel a silk scarf around you. His physical warmth penetrated my skin, down to my very bones. He responded to the music, and I responded to him. He had, I noticed, perfect, small ears.

She finished "Smoke," nodded to her musicians, and her voice, like a ribbon of lyrics, rolled out, " 'You must remember this . . . ' "

" 'As Time Goes By' is my favorite song," I said, "from my favorite movie, *Casablanca*."

"Never heard of it."

"You never heard of *Casablanca*! Why, that's like . . ." But I could think of no equivalent.

"Well, I heard of it, but I've never seen it."

"You don't know what you've missed."

In reply, he gave a light laugh and pulled me closer. "Maybe you'll have to show me what I've missed."

"Maybe I will."

"What's that cologne you're wearing. It's . . ."

"Panache, and you have to have panache to wear it."

He gave a slight laugh, and a twirl, and when the vocalist lingered over the last few lyrics, he laid me back in his arms, and I let myself trust him.

Jaylene bowed her head and accepted her applause with the same aplomb that Cleopatra might have shown to a throng of unworthy Romans.

We returned to our table, and Jaylene descended on us in a cloud of Arpège. She lifted one of Terrence's cigarettes and lit up. She blew the smoke in my direction, giving me a long, hard assessment.

"Jaylene Henderson," said Terrence, "this is Roxanne Granville and Jonathan Moore. Jaylene and I went to Jefferson High School together."

I nodded. I couldn't imagine this woman as a high school girl.

"And the church choir," she added, giving Jonathan a flicker of interest, which he reciprocated. "I was a soloist."

"I was never that good," Terrence admitted.

"He was good at other things." She exhaled knowingly, then added, "He was in the top five in typing class. Fast, but not accurate." An admiring white man came up and asked if he could buy her a drink, and she drifted away on his arm.

We stayed so late that Clayton and his friends had all left, and other musicians were coming in and setting up for an after-hours jam session. Booker played his last set and joined our table. Jonathan swooped up the last tab and paid it with a fat tip. We five exited the club, Booker and Diana in the lead, his arm over her shoulders. We had no sooner stepped out on the street than we were swarmed by photographers, shouting and blinding us with flashbulbs.

"There she is! Get her! Get her, boys! Get 'em together! That's right! Hey, Diana! Kiss him, Diana! Let's see you—"

"Bastards!" yelled Diana, freeing herself from Booker and using her full girth to ram into one of the photographers. He stumbled back, and fell. Booker used his trumpet case to smack another in the guts. Curses rained down. A photographer blinded me with his flashbulb right in front of my eyes, and I swung my handbag at him, knocking the camera out of his hands onto the sidewalk, where it landed with a gratifying crack. I felt a smack across my face, a blow that made my ears ring, and I reeled and fell with a thud to the pavement. With one hand Terrence pushed the guy away and with the other he pulled me to my feet, wrapped his arms around me, holding me close. Though mayhem raged around us, we seemed briefly isolated as I looked up into his eyes, and suddenly remembered the deer jumping over us, and our frantic physical clutching at each other, but just then police sirens blared and cop cars descended. Uniformed men with nightsticks poured out of the vehicles and swept through the crowd, some invading the Comet Club, crying out, *Raid! Raid!* Terrence and I were yanked apart, and he was marched toward the wall while I was thrust roughly in the other direction, stumbling when my high heel broke off. I could see Diana, bent forward, a cop twisting her arm behind her back as he marched her to the car and thrust her into the back seat. I was prodded with a nightstick into that same car. While Diana spewed invective, I watched as Jonathan was dragged along the sidewalk by the back of his coat and flung into the car beside me. His beautiful face was a mass of blood. My face was smeared with blood too. The door slammed shut.

From behind the grille we watched as white and black people were marched out of the Comet Club, pushed, punched by armed cops, everyone screaming and swearing over the sirens. The white people were thrust toward the curb, the Negroes, the men flung up against the wall, the women treated a little less brutally. From around the corner I saw another cop leading Booker in handcuffs. The cop held his trumpet case and now and then hit him with it, once in the head, once in the stomach, once in the groin. Booker crumpled. The last I saw of Terrence, before the car we were in sped away from the scene, he was lined up with other Negroes, men and women, facing the wall, feet spread, hands behind his head.

Jonathan, Diana, and I were dumped at the police station. We were told to sit in a line of benches that felt like pews in the Church of Stink and Wallow. All around us were moans, men peeing themselves and women so spent with tears they were hiccupping. I ached everywhere, my eye throbbed, blood had dried on my dress, my face hurt, and I hoped my nose wasn't broken. Diana was a nonstop fountain of curses. Jonathan kept hollering through his bloodied lips, *Do you know who I am! Do you know who my father is?* until some cop came along and told both of them to shut the hell up.

"You can't tell me to shut up. You can't hold us," cried Jonathan. "We haven't done anything wrong."

"Resisting arrest."

"We weren't resisting arrest. We got in a fight with photographers."

"It was a drug raid. They had drugs."

"That's not true."

"That's what they told me."

"We are important people. You will regret this."

"Not as much as you will. Look at that lip! Now shut up or it will get a lot worse."

We could see that was true. White people swept up in the raid streamed into the station, some the worse for wear, but few were badly bloodied. The Negroes shambled in, pushed with nightsticks, their clothes stained with blood, their heads too. Many limped or leaned on one another. Men and women who just hours before had seemed so graceful, so joyous, so in command of the Comet Club and their music, shuffled in, abject. They were told to sit separate from the white people across an irregular aisle. Jaylene Henderson was not among them. Terrence was one of the last. His right eye was swollen shut and bloody, and his shirtfront was red. The cop nudged him with the nightstick to the small of his back. He moved forward, but without haste. He glanced at me, and looked away.

From down the hall a voice bellowed out, "My horn! My horn, gimme back my horn, goddammit!"

Two cops thrust Booker in front of them. He was badly beaten. Terrence jumped to his feet and started toward his brother till a cop blocked his path. Diana leapt up and cried, "Motherfuckers! Dirty bastards! Sonsofbitches!" She kept swearing and shouting till they led Booker away, down a long hall.

Terrence sat down, bent over, his head in his hands. I rose and started to hobble toward him till a cop roughly took my arm, marched me back to Jonathan and Diana, and told me to stay put and shut up. Jonathan put his hand over mine.

"This is Irv Rakoff's doing," Diana said, her voice thick with rage and pain. "This is his revenge. I should never have . . ."

"Fired him?" I asked. "Of course you should have fired him! Look what he was doing to you every time you wanted a new role!"

"I should never have let him know about Booker. That's what I meant. I was drunk and angry when I called Irv. I wanted him to know what a piss-poor lay he was, and so I, well, I let him have it, right where I knew it would hurt the most."

"You told him about Booker?" asked Jonathan, incredulous. "And the Comet Club?"

"When they print those photographs," I said, "they're going to slay you."

"I slipped up," she admitted. She gulped, her shoulders shook, and she collapsed into an emotional heap. Brassy, brave, charismatic Diana Jordan, weeping, blubbering? Not a sight I ever thought I would see. She wiped her nose with her hand. "Irv must have called every slimy rag in town and told them to show up at the Comet Club at closing time if they wanted to catch me with Booker."

"Who called the cops?" I asked.

"Who knows?"

We watched, horrified really, as the Negroes were processed, one by one at the high desk in front of us. Most of them—patrons, musicians, even the waiters and bartenders—were arrested and booked. They would stay overnight in the slammer. Terrence rose wearily when his turn came. As they led him away, his gaze rested briefly on me, but I could not read the expression on his face, which was battered and bloody, his eye swollen, but the set of his jaw suggested a cold, abiding anger.

Except for Jonathan, Diana, and me, the white people arrested at the Comet Club all got processed, made their calls, and left. When at last the three of us were the only people left from the raid, still in handcuffs, our bruises puffing, our clothes torn, five photographers came in, including dear old sweat-stained Al Gilbert, and snapped what felt like a hundred pictures while we cursed them and their misbegotten mothers.

After the photographers were done, the cops took our handcuffs off. They let us go to the bathroom. A uniformed cop stood there at the open door of the women's room while Diana and I each did our business in stalls with no doors. Then they herded us back into the waiting room, where we huddled together, beat-up, stinking, filthy, caked in dried blood, silent and spent. Only then did they tell us we could each make one phone call.

Diana called someone from MGM. On behalf of Jonathan and myself, I called Irene. Who else was there? Thelma didn't have the money to pay off the cops, and that's what needed to happen. I grew up here. I know how this works.

Gordon showed up near dawn. Diana asked for Gordon's help, and he said nothing doing. She was MGM and not his problem. He called us all goddamned morons then he marched up to the desk sergeant. I'm sure he was armed with many envelopes of cash, suitably spread around among the undeserving. He spent a long time talking, though I couldn't hear what was said. They released Jonathan and me to Gordon. He even got my handbag back. Diana was left alone. I felt sorry for her. I hoped MGM would come to her rescue.

Gordon had a lot more to say to us in the car, heaping abuse on our stupidity and saying how the newspapers and gossip rags were going to love this. It was full morning by now, and the bright light hurt my eyes. Hell, my whole face hurt. My whole body. Our defense about being ambushed by photographers? He didn't want to hear it, even though he knew—everyone in our business knows—that the cops and the press were dirty-hand-in-dirty-glove, always had been, always would be. He left Jonathan off in front of Casa Fiesta in Laurel Canyon with a few choice remarks about auditioning for *Fly Me to the Moon* with a great big fat split lip. I started to get out too, to go to my car, but Gordon stopped me.

"Irene says you're not driving home. She told me to bring you home with me. Oh, and by the way, Leon is furious with you."

"He knows?"

"Of course! You think I'd let him read shit like this in the papers? I called him. He said he bailed you out when you rolled the Packard, but you're not sixteen anymore, and if you're going to go on making reckless choices and stupid decisions, then you should take the consequences."

"So who paid off the cops?"

"I did. You and Jonathan can pay me back. Five hundred. Each."

"Really? That much?"

"No, but you can just pay up and shut up. Both of you."

"Gee, thanks, Gordon. You paid it yourself. I'm kind of sur-prised."

"Irene made me do it," he said as we pulled up the long drive to his Benedict Canyon house, where the lights were all on, and Irene opened the door and took me in her arms.

CHAPTER FIFTEEN

ossip about the Comet Club raid and the arrests ran through the streets of Hollywood like the bulls of Pamplona. By the time the afternoon papers came out, barbs, gibes, and photographs peppered the pages, including pictures of the three of us looking like sodden criminals. *"Merde!"* I cried, reading the afternoon newspapers in Irene's kitchen while swilling orange juice, wearing one of her peignoirs, and holding an ice pack over my left eye. Our names and ages and occupations were printed, and I was explicitly referred to as Leon Greene's granddaughter.

"Why did you go in the first place?" Irene rebuked me for the hundredth time. "A Central Avenue jazz club with Diana and her Negro boyfriend?"

"I keep telling you! We didn't know she had a Negro boyfriend."

"Well, now the whole world knows it. She's finished! Professional suicide. She'll be a waitress in El Monte this time next year!"

"You wouldn't believe how the police treated the Negroes, Irene. Much worse than they treated any of us. I was stunned. They—"

"Oh, please, Roxanne. I don't want to hear it. Will you please just show some sense next time? Better yet, no more next times! Understood?"

"Yes," I replied, chastened.

I borrowed a dress of Irene's (mine was ruined), and she drove me over to Jonathan's to pick up my car so I could drive home, where I went straight to bed.

At Clara Bow Drive on Monday, Thelma had the newspapers spread out on her desk. She regarded me with an appraising look. "Back in the old strike days, a shiner like that was called the Red Badge of Courage. All the Reds had them."

"Yes, my makeup took me an hour this morning. I felt like Picasso—one color for one side of my face, another color for the bruises."

She handed me a stack of phone messages from Terrence Dexter. "He keeps calling. Who is he?"

"He was arrested at the Comet Club with me."

"With you and Jonathan and Diana Jordan and her Negro boyfriend. How could you have been so stupid, Roxanne? That whole Casa Fiesta crowd is bad for you."

"I keep telling everyone! We didn't know she had a Negro boyfriend! We were ambushed by photographers! We went for the music."

"And stayed for the raid."

I went into my office, closed the door, and dialed the number; it belonged to the *Challenger*. I asked for Terrence Dexter, only to be told he wasn't there. I called three or four times and always got the same answer. Then I said, "Listen, this is Julia Greene's granddaughter, and I want to talk to Terrence Dexter."

The next voice that came on belonged to none other than August Branch. "Miss Granville," he said in his softly Southern-inflected voice, "I hope you weren't too badly hurt in that fracas at the Comet Club."

"I've felt better. I'm concerned about Terrence. How is he?"

"A few stitches over his eye. Booker got the worst of it. They're recovering at their sister's place. I'll have Terrence call you."

"Can't you just give me his number?"

"'Fraid not. We don't give out numbers here. But I'm sure he'll call."

I thanked him, hung up. Twenty minutes later, the phone rang. But when I picked up, it wasn't Terrence, but Mr. Branch again, who said that Terrence couldn't talk right now, but he wanted to know if I would like to come to the *Challenger* tomorrow around noon, and he would take me out to lunch.

By day Central Avenue looked entirely different—no neon, no jostling crowds. More just an ordinary street, only everyone was colored. I left the Silver Bullet in a parking lot between a dry cleaner and the offices of the *Challenger*, a two-story brick building. Emblazoned across the windows and the door were two stylized figures, one large and overbearing with a club, one small but strong, arm upraised, rock in hand. Inside I saw orderly rows of desks, but very little else orderly: stacks of paper, books falling over, files lying atop cabinets, an arsenal of phone books, and an array of lamps. I didn't see Terrence anywhere.

"If you'll just have a seat," said the receptionist, a matronly woman who didn't seem to pay my shiner the least mind, "he'll be back soon."

The *Challenger* itself was spread out on the coffee table in front of an aged leather couch. Leafing through a few issues, I got the impression that, like a small-town chronicle, it covered local high school heroics of both sporting and musical varieties, the meetings of social and service and church clubs, the awards collected by church choirs, the travels of pastors, the closing of a pawnshop, and the arrest of three inept men who tried to rob a shoe store. However, the *Challenger* also lived up to its name. Its pages described questionable police activities, including bribery, extortion,

and cruelty. Its editorials called for the immediate universal imple-
mentation of last year's Supreme Court decision, Brown *v.* Board
of Education (which I had never heard of). Terrence Dexter's column talked about the integration of the black musicians' union
#767 with the whites' #47 two years before, not just the advan-
tages, but the clubhouse camaraderie that black musicians forfeited
with the merger.

Terrence came in the front door and said my name. He had
stitches over his eye that looked raw and painful. He wore a jaunty
fedora, and he bristled with energy or indignation, I couldn't tell
which, but not that cold anger I had sensed at the police station. He
commented ironically on my shiner.

"All the girls are wearing them this spring." I pointed to the
newspaper and asked why there was no mention of the Comet
Club raid in the *Challenger.*

"Next issue. We only come out three times a week. Used to be
six days a week before the War. Ben Tupper's writing the article.
I'm writing the column. I have more leeway with the column.
Come with me; I know Mr. Branch would like to meet you."

I followed Terrence through the low gate and toward the back,
where August Branch had a glassed-in office with a door wide
enough to accommodate his wheelchair. Like the rest of the
Challenger, his office was a melee of stacked papers, folders, over-
flowing inboxes, two telephones, a typewriter, an array of fountain
pens. On the wall were photographs of serious-looking Negroes
shaking hands in front of NAACP banners, framed plaques honoring the *Challenger,* and August Branch personally. Mr. Branch
righted the carnation in his lapel as Terrence introduced me. He
spoke in a formal fashion, his accent left over, he said, from his
childhood and youth in Alabama. He went on at length and with
respect about Julia Greene, her courage, and her commitment to
racial equality. I replied with vagaries. Certainly I did not say that
in all the years I had lived with her, I knew nothing of this commitment.

Then he turned to Terrence. "Did Booker get his horn back?"

"Well, yeah, sort of. After you called the station I went back there, and they said there'd been a mistake and they had mislabeled his horn, and that's why they couldn't find it. But when they gave it to me, there was a mop handle shoved up the bell. Bastards charged me for the mop."

"No!" I cried. "That's terrible. That's absolutely awful!"

"No shit. The only thing more important to my brother than his horn is his dick." Terrence coughed and excused himself to Mr. Branch and to me. "I paid it. But I'm not giving the horn back to Booker till it's fixed. He won't be playing it for a few days anyway. I dropped it off at Corelli's to have it fixed."

"A wise choice. Now take Miss Granville to lunch at Ruby's, and be back in time for the editorial meeting." To me he said, "Ruby's is Central Avenue's best-kept secret."

As Terrence and I passed the dry cleaner, a small brown woman stuck her head out the door and said, "Terrence, your shirts're all clean and pressed, lotta starch, just how you like 'em. Your suit's ready too. Oh! Look at your face, Terrence! Those bastards! They didn't even find no drugs, did they?"

"Hard to say, Sally, if they found them or brought them to the party."

"It was our fault," I said as he and I walked on. "Diana fired her agent, and he knew about Diana and your brother. He wanted to bring her down, but just look at the terrible things that happened to everyone else."

"Including you," he reminded me with a nod to my shiner. He grinned so broadly his gold tooth gleamed. "Don't worry. It'll go away and you'll be pretty again."

On the other side of my face I could feel the birthmark flush, pleased that he had called me pretty.

As we walked down Central Avenue, many people greeted him, some calling him Terrence, some calling him Mr. Dexter, some merely tipping their hats. They all looked rather askance at me. These were well-dressed people, the women wearing hats, the men in suits. At the same time, many of the businesses we passed were shuttered, and in those doorways drunks sprawled, or men squatted, their faces to the sun, their eyes closed, their shoes broken, their pants stained with urine.

As we passed one of these derelicts, Terrence said, "When I was a kid, this was a great place to grow up. My brother and sisters and I, we had a fine childhood here, my mother's family all around, Bowers and Goodalls, and Prestons. In these neighborhoods, doctors and lawyers lived next door to plumbers and carpenters. Kids went to the same churches, the same schools. We all took piano lessons or sang in the church choir. We all went to Jefferson High. Everyone looked out for everyone else. But since the War, everything's changed. Now . . ." He stopped to light a cigarette. "Now heroin's moved in. And with the old covenants breaking down, lots of people are moving out. It's all different."

"Covenants?"

"Don't you remember Hattie McDaniel fighting those covenants on West Adams? Took her years in court, but she won, and now there's no more covenants saying where Negroes can live or rent. I mean, now they're illegal, but we're still fighting for fair housing."

"Hattie McDaniel. You mean Mammy from *Gone with the Wind*?"

He gave me a look I can only describe as pained, more pained than the fresh stitches over his eye, as he pushed open the door of a large café.

Ruby's had a long counter and a lot of booths (everything upholstered in maroon) lining the walls with tables in the middle. The air was full of cigarette smoke and scents I couldn't immediately identify—frying, I expect. A big colorful jukebox blared out music I had never heard, a raucous voice I can only describe as Not Perry Como. It was like a foreign country. I was relieved, though I'm not sure why, to see a mixed group, two whites and two Negroes, come in and take a table in the center.

A colored woman, full-bodied and broad-shouldered, strode out from the kitchen at the back. She wore a neat uniform in black and white trimmed with red. Terrence introduced her as his Aunt Ruby, Clarence's wife. "Oh! Look at you!" she cried. "Look at you both! Miss Granville! I heard you was caught up in that nasty business the other night. How is Booker, Terrence?"

Terrence shrugged. "He'll live."

"And the horn?" she asked urgently. "You get the horn back?"

"I did, but don't mention it to him yet. I gotta have it fixed first."

"What was Booker thinking! Carrying on in the open with that . . ." Ruby slowed and turned to me. "You remember your grandmother bringing you in here when you was just a kid?"

"I'm sorry, I don't."

"Well, she did. Yes, she'd come in here now and then after she'd had a meeting with Mr. Branch, and sometimes she brung you. You was just a tot. You had a root beer float. Sit right here"— she gestured to a booth—"and I'll be right back with some corn fritters and a root beer float." She gave me a warm, welcoming smile.

"Your aunt seems so unlike Clarence," I said when she had left us. "I mean, she's so warm and friendly. The staff at Summit Drive lives in fear of him."

"Clarence knows how to make people tremble, all right. He made me and Booker tremble when we were kids. He stepped in to help raise us after our daddy died, and it wasn't easy. The girls were mostly grown up, but me and Booker, we were a handful, high spirited and full of ourselves. Clarence is stiff and stubborn, and things have to be just so."

"Like the white gloves."

"Oh yes, the white gloves. We tried his patience something awful. He was always saying he was giving up on us, but he never did." He handed me a menu that was sticky with use. A thickset woman, her hair pulled into a tight, shining bun, appeared at our table with a pad in one hand, coffeepot in the other. "This is my sister, Coralee Winters."

She looked to be a good deal older than Terrence, forty at least, and she licked her pencil with the gravity of a judge writing a verdict rather than a waitress taking an order. She nodded toward my shiner. "Cops do that to you? What's the world coming to?"

"Not the cops. I got in a fight with a photographer."

"She got him good," said Terrence, easing back with a lazy grin. "Knocked him down, busted his camera."

"Hmm," said Coralee. "They teach street fighting in Paris, Miss Granville?"

"Please. Call me Roxanne. You knew I lived in Paris?"

"Clarence keeps us up on the Greenes," said Terrence, and though Coralee's expression remained unchanged, her balance shifted slightly, and I could swear she kicked Terrence under the table. I flinched to think of the tales Clarence might have carried out of Summit Drive in those years that Julia and Leon were screaming at each other. I let Terrence order for us, and she wrote it down and left.

"You'll like the food here," he said. "The women in my family pride themselves on their cooking."

Cooking is not something I can talk about, or care about, really. I don't even much care what I eat (as long as it isn't liver or cauliflower or Brussels sprouts). But the food that day was a revelation. We had corn fritters still sizzling from the pan and with a spicy sauce of some kind of tomato and horseradish. A big messy sandwich full of pork cooked so soft it was almost buttery and a tangy sauce and crunchy greens and little crispy potatoes.

While we ate, all sorts of people came up to our table, all of them indignantly commenting on the black eyes and the Comet Club raid. I didn't catch all the names when Terrence introduced me. Some were his cousins, or second cousins, his friends from

Jefferson High School, his colleagues at the *Challenger*, or just people he knew. He had an easy, noisy camaraderie with each of them, and a capacious memory for the details of their lives.

"Do you know why my grandmother was so supportive of the NAACP?" I asked, after he had introduced me with a note of pride as Julia Greene's granddaughter. "Or how she connected with them?"

"How would I know?"

"I just wondered. The day her will was read in the lawyer's office, I just assumed she had supported the NAACP to offend Leon to his conservative core. But now, here with you, and what Mr. Branch said, and Ruby saying Julia used to bring me here when I was a kid, I think she must have truly believed in what she was doing. I wish I could ask her."

"You still miss her?"

"I do. She and Leon were really my parents, and I was heartbroken when they split up."

"Even if you got to go to Paris?"

"Even if. Paris was wonderful, though, and I'd love to go back, but now I have a job."

"Yeah, what exactly does an agent do? I didn't quite hear you at the Comet Club, the music was too loud."

So I told him how the Granville Agency was an intermediary. "I'm like the feeder in the zoo," I said, "the guy who walks around with the bucket full of meat and throws it at the lions, and the bucket of bananas for the monkeys, and the bucket full of palm fronds for the giraffes. Occasionally I wear a pith helmet. It's a jungle out there." I told him the story of how I went independent, dumping Rakoff/Holtz's scripts in the LA River. I had long since shaped the story into something amusing, leaving out the part where Irv pressed his dick up against me.

Terrence too had a lot of humorous anecdotes about growing up around here with lots of aunts, uncles, cousins, grandparents, everyone nearby. Except for his father, who had come from Alabama after serving on the Western Front in World War I, his family had been in California for generations. He told a story about an ancestor, sly, smart Nana Bowers, brought here as the slave of Mormon pioneers in the eighteen fifties, outwitting her owner in court, getting her freedom because California didn't recognize slavery. The story was meant to elicit smiles, but *slavery* was a word I'd never heard except as part of a dry, academic past. I couldn't imagine that word being part of your family's story.

"Terrence and Booker was spoiled rotten, both of them," Coralee said when she brought dessert, apple pie with ice cream. "Only two boys in a family of girls? And the youngest at that! These two boys, they couldn't do no wrong in that house. All their lives they had women looking after them, me and my sister, Bonita, my mama, my grandma, the aunts, the great-aunts. My mama like to die of the happiness the day Terrence graduated from UCLA. She always knew Terrence gonna do something really fine one day. He was always a reader, a thinker, good with words. Mama was so sure he's gonna be a writer, she made him take typing in high school. Shorthand too." Someone called to Coralee and she left us.

Terrence chuckled. "I fought Mama something fierce on the typing and shorthand, but then, well, I go to school, and just lookie here! I was one of three boys in a typing class full of girls! Sixty-five words a minute," he added. "And shorthand, well, I use shorthand every day on the job. My mother knew me better than I knew myself."

"My mother doesn't even like to look at me," I said, surprised at my own candor. I brought my hand up to my right cheek. "From the time I was born she hated the sight of me."

"Then you know what it is to be judged for your skin, don't you?"

"I never thought of it like that."

"Think of it," he said. He smiled at me in a way that made me feel we were intimate allies. "You like the pie?"

"It's wonderful. I've never tasted anything quite like it." I sipped the last of the root beer float. "Did you always want to be a writer?"

"I'm not a writer, not like James Baldwin or Richard Wright. I'm just a reporter. International correspondent, that's what I wanted to be, to see my byline in the *New York Times*. I was so certain that's what I'd be, I got a passport the day after I turned eighteen. Then, well, time goes by, and hell-bent as I am on being an international correspondent, I begin to understand that the only way the *New York Times* gonna hire someone like me is to be pushing a broom, daddy-o." He shrugged. "Anyway, I been working for the *Challenger* since I was eight, delivering papers on my bike, running stats for the sportswriters when I was in high school, writing obits, and filling in weekends when I was at UCLA, so taking a job there was just like stepping into a shoe already comfortable. It's a great paper, and August Branch is a great man. He insists that your copy's on time, that it's the truth, and that you haven't violated the code of ethics or the English language. He's very particular about the code of ethics and the English language. Other than that, what I write, well, that's up to me. The column is my own."

"Are you the colored Hedda Hopper?" I asked, thinking myself witty.

"I'm not the colored anything, Roxanne, and I'm sure as hell not a Red-baiting gossipmonger." He swooped up the check. "I need to get back to the office."

We left, and walked back to the *Challenger*'s office in silence, the moment of alliance shattered with my stupid comment. Here was the most interesting man I had met since Jerrold Davies, who didn't count since Jerrold was old enough to be my father. If I didn't speak up, apologize . . . A premonition of regret wavered before me, almost visibly. At the parking lot Terrence said a crisp goodbye. I put my hand on his sleeve. "Terrence, I'm sorry for what I said about the colored Hedda Hopper, I wasn't thinking."

He actually looked suddenly tired; his shoulders sagged. "People like me get tired of hearing 'sorry' from people like you."

"Well, next time I'll think."

"Next time?"

"Look," I said cheerfully, "it's Tuesday. Why don't you come out to my place on Saturday? I live in Malibu," adding awkwardly, "at the beach."

"Can I bring my wife and kids?" he asked, suddenly solemn.

Keeping my face frozen to conceal my shock, I said, "Sure. How many?"

"Three."

"Well, sure, bring them all. I'll make lunch."

"What's your address?" He took out a pen and opened his palm, and wrote down the address. "See you Saturday around one."

I drove back to Clara Bow Drive wishing I hadn't made the invitation, though I told myself: *Just as well he's married, Roxanne.* After watching the chaos sown by adultery in my own family, I stay away from married men. No chance now I'd have an affair with Terrence Dexter, who could prove very dangerous. Not only was he married, he was a Negro. Just look at what happened to Diana Jordan, with her beautiful, battered face spread all over the papers and her promising career in tatters. Even apart from his being black, I don't like complicated men, and clearly, Terrence Dexter was too complicated, too smart, too deep, and too intense by half. So why did I find him so compelling, and why did the very sight of him raise my heart, my spirits?

Irene was already sipping a cocktail when I arrived at the Ambassador that Friday for our standing lunch date. "Tsk-tsk, Roxanne, if the shiner weren't enough to make you conspicuous, you're wearing trousers too? No hat. No gloves?"

"A black eye is its own fashion accessory this spring." I sat down and signaled the waiter for a Campari. "Besides, Betty Bacall wears trousers. Kate Hepburn wears them."

"I don't think you're quite Kate's equal yet, are you?"

"Who is?" We ordered, and then I noticed a new sapphire solitaire ring on her finger. An enormous sapphire solitaire.

"From Gordon," she said, nodding toward Julia's sparkling diamond gleaming on my hand. "A present, and for exactly the same reason. I found out because Gordon isn't as smart as he thinks he is, and he slipped up."

"Oh, Irene, this makes me so mad. Who was it?"

"Some twit with a twat. Gordon is a powerful man, and there are ten thousand girls who don't care if he's married."

"He ought to care that he's married," I said, thinking of the married Terrence Dexter, of the way he had danced with me, the way he had held me in the middle of the mayhem.

"Actually, he does. Gordon's been contrite, really sorry. He promises it'll never happen again. It will, of course. This ring is a sort of business proposition, even if Gordon doesn't yet know it. I have to get smarter as I get older. I'm almost thirty. I have to think of him less as a husband and more as a business partner, and the business is Us. That's what Julia and Leon had for years. Of course, she detested Leon's little peccadilloes, but together they were their own corporation, and that corporation was worth preserving."

"Until she walked away from it, from him, from everything, and started all over again in Paris."

"At least she had you."

"And I had her. To Julia," I said, lifting my glass to Irene's, though I did not add that I now knew my grandmother had helped out the NAACP for years, or that I had met August Branch, the man who had accepted Julia's bequest.

Suddenly Jonathan Moore burst into the restaurant, halted briefly by the maître d', who was unaccustomed to men with big fat bruised lips bounding in. We waved, and the waiter let him pass. He was flushed with excitement, calling out in his imperious way, "Waiter! Bring us a bottle of champagne!" He gave us each a hurried kiss on the cheek, plopped himself down in a chair, and beamed. "I got called back for the Dr. Bleeker role!"

"So you took my advice and auditioned for *Fly Me to the Moon*," I said, feeling smug. "I'm waiting for your abject gratitude."

He laughed. "I've never done comedy, but I thought, well, what the hell? I wore a rumpled coat and a pair of thick horn-rimmed glasses and greased my hair up and let it hang in my eyes. I slouched and muttered and looked generally brilliant and unworldly. And even with my busted lip, I think they were really impressed."

"Did they say anything about the Comet Club?" I asked.

"I made some lighthearted reference to the raid and the cops, but Phil Tobin, the director, didn't think it was funny. And Leon definitely didn't think it was funny."

"It's not funny," said Irene, blowing out a plume of smoke. "Getting beat up and arrested in a Negro jazz club is never funny."

"We weren't arrested, Irene," I insisted. "We got beat up by the photographers who were there to snag Diana."

"Let that be a lesson to you. Don't befriend women who are sleeping with Negroes."

"Oh, I don't want to talk about lessons or Negroes!" cried Jonathan as the waiter brought the champagne. "I want to talk about how I'm going to get the part! I couldn't believe it when I read *Fly Me to the Moon*. It's a damned fine script, crisp and witty. I never thought Charlie Frye was that smart, Roxanne. You must have been sending him to one of those Learn to Write in Your Spare Time courses you see advertised on the backs of matchbooks."

"Ah, Charlie Frye!" sighed Irene with a snide, sidelong glance to me. "Tanned and handsome, and now an irresistible success! A three-year contract at Empire! Everything a young writer could ever want. What a great client! What a great lover! I wonder what dazzling script he'll turn out next."

I kept my gaze on the bubbles rising in the champagne glass. I could admit to no one, not even Thelma, my fears about Charlie, my mistake in choosing him to front for Max.

"Am I missing something?" Jonathan asked in the long, awkward silence.

Irene and I assured him he was not and returned the conversation to reflect on him while we women dutifully basked in his masculine glory. We clinked our glasses, toasted him, and then toasted ourselves together and individually. We had each in our own way emerged unscathed from what could have been, would have been, ruinous for anyone less fortunate, which, I reflected, was probably most of the world.

CHAPTER SIXTEEN

Why would a man with a wife and three kids drive a Porsche? Maybe the wife drove a station wagon. Why hadn't he shown me pictures of his kids? Even Gordon carries pictures of his kids in his wallet. Though these and other questions nagged at me, for Saturday I bought some beach balls and a kite to amuse the kids, and a big basket of strawberries from the Farmer's Market, and potato salad and chocolate cake too. Saturday morning I made ham sandwiches, about a hundred of them. Or at least that's what it felt like. What do I know of kids other than Irene's? And they don't count.

I was reading a script on the high front porch when Terrence Dexter came up the stairs. I peered down the steps behind him. "Where are Mrs. Dexter and the three kids?"

He burst out laughing. "Oh, Roxanne, I was funning with you! I'm not married! I am so not-married I live in a rented room on Naomi Avenue with a hot plate and a garage. I live there so I can drive the Porsche."

"A worthy set of values," I said, happily relieved.

"Brought you a present." He handed me a record album—Buddy Collette. "Buddy's a Central Avenue man. Put him on the hi-fi. See if you like him."

"Thanks, I'll do that," I said, feeling pretty certain I'd like

Buddy Collette better than John Philip Sousa. Buddy and his mellow quartet filled the little cottage with music that seemed to spark intimacy. Or maybe that was my own mood and Buddy just helped it along.

"Nice place. Sure different than Summit Drive, with all those antiques."

"I was tired of all that heavy hand of the past. I want to be chic, modern." I had a serious look around. "Or, if I can't be chic and modern, then bohemian-eclectic."

"Are the movies in these posters by your writers?"

"No, these are Empire films from a long time ago. The men who wrote these movies are long gone."

He stood in front of each one studiously while I nattered on, anecdotes about the making of this one or that, saying nothing of who had died or fled the country or been shamed or professionally maimed, or any of that. I didn't want to tarnish the afternoon with any sad stories.

"I don't know shit about movies. I hardly ever go. Not even as a kid. My sisters sometimes took us to the Saturday-morning serials, but my mother, the women of my family in general, always say, 'You need drama, children? Well look no further than the Baptist church. King Kong got nothing on the Baptist God. In the Baptist church, you get your religion in Technicolor.'"

"Well, I got my religion in the Church of Rick and Ilsa," I said before I remembered he had never seen my favorite film. "They're the main characters in *Casablanca*, and the lines they speak amount to Holy Writ."

"Well, Roxanne, if you had grown up with Addie Dexter, you would know your Holy Writ and your hymns, or you wouldn't eat."

"And if you had grown up in the Church of Rick and Ilsa, you'd know that the true Ten Commandments have to do with happy endings and snappy dialogue. You'd be able to recite the whole airport scene, along with big chunks of *Citizen Kane*, my little Rosebud."

At the fireplace he examined the huge, framed, florid poster of the 1931 talkie *Cyrano de Bergerac* where my father played the title role. I told him about being born on the set and named for the heroine.

"If your father is Sir Rowland Granville, what does that make you?"

"Lady Chopped Liver." I laughed and took a deep bow. "Truth is, I throw my father's name around when I want to impress people. He's certainly good for that, but I hardly know him." I detected in Terrence's eyes a flash of condolence, or something very like it. I hastened to add, "I was lucky not to grow up with my parents— with my mother, anyway. If I had, I'd spend my whole life maundering to a shrink. My mother has a long-standing grudge against me. I thwarted her destiny and ruined her career. She always said if she hadn't been pregnant with me, she would have played the beautiful Roxanne in nineteen thirty-one, and she would have been so absolutely stupendous she would have won an Oscar and landed the role of Scarlett O'Hara that went to that trollop Vivien Leigh a few years later. Oh, and then, there was this . . ." I brought my hand up to my stained cheek. "She hated the imperfection."

He reached over and touched my face. "You ever think that this just means yours is a face no one will ever forget?"

"I have never thought that. It's been the bane of my life."

"Yours is a face I will never forget."

His touch was so tender, I wanted to reach up, to hold his hand there forever, but instead I said, "You better come in the kitchen with me and get started."

"On what?"

"You have to eat your weight in ham sandwiches."

We ate lunch out on the high porch. I was surprised at how mercurial Terrence was: cool and laconic when he drove me from Reg's, warm and romantic in the Comet Club, seething with emotion in the police station, charming to the old ladies at Ruby's. The man sitting beside me was relaxed, warm, expansive in the sunshine.

"I love the ocean," he said. "I love to look at it, I love to hear it, but when I was a kid, we hardly ever went."

"Why?"

"Well, Roxanne, I'm already tanned. Those few times Mama took us to the beach, we'd get weird looks. Made us all real uncomfortable. My mama, my sisters, they were not women who looked for trouble. They always told me and Booker, even if you stand still, trouble will come to you." He shook his head. "But I have to say, that raid the other night, overnight in jail, that was a first for me, though I don't suppose it'll be the last."

"Why do you say that?"

"Because it's just a fact of black lives like mine. Mama was right. Even if we stand still, trouble will find us."

"Well, I hope I never have to see another jail. And those rotten photographers taking pictures that made us look like criminals."

"Yeah, you looked pretty damn pathetic in the papers."

"Did your brother get his horn back?"

"He did. Corelli fixed it fine, but Booker knows something happened to it. A musician feels his instrument's pain like he'd feel his lover's pain. I mean, if he had a lover."

"Diana Jordan?"

"Oh, that's over. You better believe that's over."

I went in and got us each a slice of chocolate cake, and when I brought it out I said, "I thoroughly intended to take credit for this cake and the potato salad, but I bought them at the Farmer's Market."

He nodded. "Yes, it's better to start out with the truth."

"Is that what we're doing? Starting out?"

"Well, we do have matching shiners. For starters, I mean."

We took off our shoes and brought the kite down to the beach, where we had some luck getting it aloft and no luck keeping it aloft. The Wilburs' dog, Bruno, leapt over his small enclosure and bounded over, joyously greeting me. He was mad with doggy delight to meet Terrence, who responded to him right away. Bruno ran in and out of the surf, barking, chasing driftwood sticks that Terrence threw to him.

"You know," he said, "I've never walked on a beach barefoot before."

"There's an art to it, you know." I minced along under an imaginary parasol so that even Bruno quit racing and regarded me with some wonder. "Dig your feet in and the sand crabs will nibble on your toes."

"Not sure I want crabs nibbling my toes."

"I'll show you how." I dug my feet into the soft, wet sand, and so did Terrence. His eyes lit with mirth. "But they'll only nibble a little. Then you have to find new ones. See?"

"And there's an endless supply?"

"Endless."

As we meandered past great beds of bronzy kelp that had washed up on the beach, I said, "I always think there must be whole tribes of mermaids somewhere, and these are their braids. When they cut their hair, their braids are carried away by the currents."

He stopped and regarded me quizzically. "You are the living end, girl! Who would ever think of that?" Bruno brought the stick back and laid it proudly at his feet. "Good boy, Bruno!" Terrence flung it again, and the dog dashed off.

On this sunny May afternoon, those few people who saw us or passed us, white people, of course, all of them, gave us odd, disparaging looks as we ran barefoot on the shoreline and played with the dog. We wandered perhaps a mile up the beach before turning back and ambled south, a sense of connection between us as vivid as if that deer still somehow leapt, poised overhead. Our conversation roamed aimlessly over our respective pasts. He told three different stories as to how he'd come by the gold tooth, each one more outlandish than the last. Then he just laughed and said the truth was so dull, it wasn't worth telling, like using your grocery list for the page one headline. As we walked back we marveled that Julia's death had brought us obliquely together two years ago, and that Clarence, who had so loomed over my young life, had been a rock of Terrence's childhood.

"When he'd get angry with me and Booker, Clarence would say, 'You two are nothing but a handful of gimme and a mouthful of much-obliged, just like your daddy.' "

"He didn't like your father?"

"Nobody liked my father. Not even my mother."

"Did you like him?"

"I don't hardly remember him. I was just little, six or so, when he died. Clarence did his best with me and Booker, but he had these standards that made us crazy. Still, he kept us in line for the most part. We had a couple of scrapes, of course—nothing too serious. Kid stuff. Then."

This seemed an odd addition. "And since?"

"Booker's in serious trouble." He picked up a stick and tossed it for the dog. "Remember when I told you that heroin moved into Central Avenue and things were never the same? I know whereof I speak. Nothing we can do; no one in the family can stop Booker. He's not as bad off as Bird, Charlie Parker, who just died a few months ago, but one day he will be. No one can reach him, no one can protect him." Bruno brought back the stick and danced around us till Terrence took it from his doggy jaws and flung it down the beach again. "It's terrible, watching someone you love be in such pain, and being powerless to help them, powerless to stop them."

The sun had lowered in the sky and spilled a sheet of gold across the water by the time we returned to my place, and Bruno dashed up the steps ahead of us. We closed the door behind us. I leaned against it. Outside, Bruno yapped. Terrence took me in his arms and pressed me against the door, and we kissed for a long time, a long, slow, luxurious kiss, until the phone on the desk rang and rang. Finally I picked up.

Charlie Frye, full of anxiety, nagging me to offer his *Coast of Heaven*, now, while Empire loved him. I responded with random *uh-huh*s. Terrence went outside and sat with Bruno, staring out to sea, his dark profile highlighted in the unleavened sunshine. I told myself: *Roxanne, this is your chance to be free of "The Stars and Stripes Forever" forever.*

"Listen, Charlie, the *Coast of Heaven* is brilliant, and I won't rest until it's sold for ten grand," I said, stunning him into momentary silence. "I'll always represent your work, and be your friend, but the affair is over. No, I haven't heard about you and Margie Becker, and really, I don't care. No. I haven't heard about Shirley or Enid either, and I don't want an explanation." I took the phone in one hand and, extending the long cord, stood in the open doorway with it. "I'll still be your agent, of course. Of course I believe in *Coast of Heaven*, and I believe in your career, but the affair is over." Terrence turned, and his eyes met mine. While Charlie nattered, I smiled and walked back inside. "Yes, yes, Charlie. No, the affair is finished."

Terrence shooed Bruno down the stairs, came inside, and closed the door. He brought his lips to my neck and moved down my throat. The warmth of his hands penetrated my back, my shoulders, just as they had in the Comet Club. I caressed his close-cropped hair, his small, perfect ears. His bruised cheek against my stained one, he started to move as though he heard music, as though we were dancing, and then, in a manner of speaking, we were dancing, and I somehow said goodbye to Charlie as he blathered into oblivion, and I would have put the phone back on the desk, but it dropped from my hand as I wrapped both my arms around Terrence, who murmured against my ear something about being sure. *Yes. Yes. Yes*, I said as my personal tectonic plates shook, and the silverware rattled in the drawers as the walls waved and rippled.

He stayed till Monday morning. We ate all the ham sandwiches.

. . .

From that very beginning, our love affair was like a high tide sweeping everything in its lunar path. We fell in love the way that winter waves crash on the beach, a great whoosh of joy and discovery and emotion as our lives and bodies melded that summer. My better judgment constantly nagged at me, *You saw what happened to Diana Jordan; this is madness.* But it was a complicated madness, a rich, rewarding, and brilliant madness. Terrence Dexter endowed me with happiness such as I have never known. Loving him was like wine, a deep, complex melding of scents and flavors, swirled. We learned from and of each other, and in spite of—perhaps because of—all the vast differences in our lives and backgrounds, we each brought something fresh and resonant to the relationship. He loved my stories of the library conferences with the old writers, of Empire studio itself as my personal playground, of Julia and the Parc Monceau Thursday evenings, of L'Oiseau d'Or and the exiled, eccentric aristocrats who taught there. For all the fine private schools I'd attended, I'd never had a teacher like Dr. Browne of Jefferson High, who so shaped his students' lives and values. I loved the stories of Terrence's lively extended family, and the many times he and Booker did their best to outwit Clarence's rules.

At night I would lay spooned beside him, listen to the sound of his shallow breathing, somehow in the same tempo as the waves outside, and wonder if all lovers knew this happiness. Surely we alone experienced this. With Terrence I let my emotions loose in making love, all sorts of emotions, the fine and socially acceptable ones and the ones I never guessed at, emotions that brought me to the edge of everything I had ever known or hoped to know. Our lovemaking could be tender love or rushed love, rough love, sweet love, rollicking, frolicking love; every time we made love, we deepened the bond between us. I taught him French, words, phrases best murmured in darkness, or by candlelight, and under the covers. He taught me things I never guessed at.

That little Malibu cottage itself seemed to throb with the happiness we created. Buddy Collette's version of "Over the Rainbow" became my new favorite song. Terrence pounded out infectious high-spirited tunes or old hymns on the upright piano, improvising, especially lively variations on "Little Liza Jane," for which he and I both made up verses, and soon Liza Jane came to be his sweet name for me, radiating so much warmth and easy affection that I glowed just to hear him say it. His tunes wove in and out of our daily lives, like "Wade in the Water" when we'd take naked midnight swims. In the mornings we would shower together, wash each other down and leave each other breathless. Then, my hair still wet, I stood behind him, my arms around his chest while he shaved; I laced his back with kisses while he smiled into the mirror. When he left in the morning, I stood on the porch wearing a robe, my hands wrapped round a coffee cup, and Terrence gave me a final swift pat on the ass and a kiss on the cheek and popped down the stairs singing, " 'O little Liza, little Liza Jane!' " By the time our respective shiners had healed, we had declared our love for each other, and I had given Terrence a key to the Malibu cottage. Home.

I liked the sound of it. *Home.* I enjoyed a little frisson of happiness every time one of us said the word *we.* In our working lives we each kept odd, nonstandard hours, and I would find myself looking at my watch when I had meetings or events that went late into the evening, finally begging off, popping into the MG, and racing up PCH, delighted to see the Porsche parked there behind my house and knowing that Terrence was home. If I came home and he wasn't yet there, I waited to hear the rumble of the Porsche behind the building, when I would run down the stairs and he would catch me in his arms, and we would go inside, closing the door on the rest of the world.

Some nights he returned to the hot plate and garage on Naomi Avenue to be close to the *Challenger,* but he kept his starched shirts in my closet and his shaving gear in my bathroom, and, perhaps most intimately, he brought his portable Royal typewriter and set it up on the desk in the living room beside the two framed pictures of Julia and me. I liked to think she was smiling at him, and I knew she would be pleased to know we had found each other, loved each other. I read his columns at home and subscribed to the *Challenger* at the office. I smiled to hear him working in the evenings, the mad tap of the keys a kind of percussion against the jazz on the hi-fi, where I grew acquainted with Chico Hamilton and Art Pepper and Terrence learned to love Peggy Lee, though Sidney Bechet was still too old-fashioned for his taste, and he didn't like Bill Haley and the Comets at all. The Sousa marches, needless to say, went in the trash.

We shared a sense of being somehow destined, fated for each other. We met at the right time. The longest and stormiest of Terrence's affairs, the on-again, off-again liaison with Jaylene Henderson, had ended in January with a dramatic incident of infidelity on her part. As for me, the affairs of the heart I had known, they were like soda water, men who might have briefly sparkled but then went flat, dull, brackish as the local tap water. Charlie Frye was history. He only called occasionally when his confidence needed boosting. Professionally I obliged, usually while Terrence listened, grinning.

But I was grateful for the surfboard Charlie left on the porch. Terrence put it to good use all that summer, teaching himself to surf. He would lie on it and paddle out beyond the swells and sit there for a long time, his back to me, looking at the horizon. I lay on an old towel on the beach reading scripts, and one afternoon I looked up to see that Terrence had drifted far to the north. I ran down the beach and waded into the surf. "Terrence! There's a riptide! Be careful! Terrence!" I cried, not even certain that my voice would carry that far. When at last he looked back and saw how far the current had taken him, he turned the board around and paddled hard toward shore, fighting the current. I ran up the beach, paralleling his progress shoreward. I plunged into the waist-deep waves to meet him as he jumped off the board and took me in his arms, and we made our way, waves washing over us, exhausted, to the beach, where we fell to our knees in the foam, wrapped our arms around each other, kissed and rolled on our backs, and caught our breath. I laughed out loud.

"What's so funny?" He jumped up and ran after the surfboard before the sea reclaimed it, returning to me shaken and out of breath. "What is so damn funny?"

"The rolling-on-the-beach scene in *From Here to Eternity*! I always hoped I'd find a man who made me feel like that, and look, I have!"

"What are you talking about, girl! I could have died out there! And look at you! Flopped here like a piece of seaweed."

"Yes! Don't you see? That's why it's perfect!"

Terrence didn't. The humor lost some of its luster when I had to explain the scene and the movie, and finally I just gave up. Terrence's life, clearly, wasn't reflected in film. Mine was.

We took long, almost-daily sunset walks on the beach, ignoring the stares of people—white people, who naturally were the only sorts of people there. Terrence made me think: *Why is that only natural? Why does a Negro on the beach at Malibu so defy expectations?* But mostly I was too happy to give a damn what anyone thought. And though I had not forgotten what Diana Jordan's transgressions had cost her, I banished such thoughts and reveled in the summer days and summer nights.

On our sunset walks, Bruno always jumped the low fence and tore down the beach to be with us. Terrence knelt and rubbed his ears. "Hey, boy. Good dog. Good dog, Bruno."

"He likes us better than he likes the Wilburs," I said. "They're small-minded and mean-spirited and Bruno knows it."

"We're young and beautiful, and in a hurry," Terrence said, giving me a slight nudge with his hip.

"We are! And we're going to do great things!" I cartwheeled

twice down the beach, then returned to him, breathless and happy. "I'm going to find the next *Casablanca*, and you're going to win the Pulitzer Prize."

"Oh yeah," he said, laughing and tucking my arm in his, "a black reporter winning the Pulitzer will be for his coverage of hell freezing over."

The sun sank at the horizon, leaving a gleaming path across the sea, and I went into the kitchen to make us something to eat that wouldn't tax my limited repertoire. I had pretty much mastered scrambled eggs, and I knew not to burn the bacon. From the living room I heard Terrence give a loud groan. I went out to see him sitting in the big chintz chair, the script of *Fly Me to the Moon* in his hand.

"What is it? What's wrong?"

"Not another goddamn shoeshine boy and his jive dance!" He pointed to a scene in the script. "Clayton Strong is right, Cecil B. DeMille needs a couple of Nubian kings, and a lot of slaves to build the goddamned pyramids, but otherwise?" He pointed to the page. "Where are we? Chopping cotton and singing 'My Old Kentucky Home.' We're prim Aunt Jemimas or cuddly Uncle Toms, or kids doing tap dances for an extra nickel from 'de good ole white gentleman.'"

I glanced at the scene on the page, seeing it suddenly with new eyes. No wonder Terrence's life wasn't reflected in film.

"Your Church of Rick and Ilsa, it's the Beverly Hills Country Club. Whites Only."

"One day movies won't be like that." I didn't know what else to say.

"Really? You think one day you'll find a screenwriter who'll tell a story like *Up from Slavery*? Like James Baldwin's *Notes of a Native Son*?"

These were books I'd only just read this summer—writers, honestly, I had only heard of since I'd met Terrence, never mind the private schools and Mills College. "Why don't you write something that powerful? That true. No, really. You write it, Terrence. I'll sell it."

He scoffed. "You really think your granddaddy would buy a script by a black man? That any of your people—I mean it, Liza—from those Poverty Row cats, to the head of Paramount—would any of them produce a script by a man who looked like me?"

"We could say someone else wrote it, put another name on it. No one would have to know. Happens all the time." I looked at him expectantly.

His expression suddenly changed, and his eyes narrowed. "Do you have some secret, Liza Jane—I mean other than the secret we're keeping right here, right now? The two of us."

I went back to the kitchen, turned off the stove, poured us both a stiff drink, and sat on the couch, my feet in his lap, while I told him the whole story, not just about Max and Thelma and Kathleen Hilyard coming to me, but the whole long story about the men whose names were on the movie posters in this living room. I told him who had died or fled the country or been shamed or professionally maimed, everything I had not told him that first day. Full dark had fallen by the time I finished.

Terrence stood and paced. He was a restless sort of man. "I gotta ask, why did you do it, Roxanne? I don't mean finding fronts for your old friends, I dig it, you got gumption, girl. No, I mean, why take Max's work to Leon?"

"I was still angry about Denise breaking up his marriage to Julia—well, I'm still angry about that—and I thought . . . well, I had all sorts of reasons, and they all made sense at the time."

"And now?"

My shoulders sank, and for the first time I uttered the words, "I'm wondering if maybe it was a foolhardy gesture."

"Why did Leon buy them? The man who makes everyone in a ten-mile radius sign a loyalty oath? Leon should have taken you to the woodshed and given you a good whupping, but no, he offers your writer two pictures and a three-year contract? Crazy."

"Thelma thinks it's so they can keep Charlie close by. Keep an eye on him."

"Everything you've said about Leon Greene, one thing we know for sure, he ain't stupid. He knew, didn't he? He guessed Max wrote these. Why would he buy these scripts?"

"For Denise. Denise wanted them. I have to admit, they are great roles for her."

"Does Denise know Max wrote them?"

"Hell no."

"Leon might have told her."

"He's too proud to admit to a weakness. Any weakness. And he would see it as weakness that he chose to please his young wife, and never mind his sworn allegiance to the Motion Picture Alliance for the Preservation of American Ideals."

"Does anyone else know?"

"Maybe Gordon guessed. But he'd never part with any secret that could hurt Leon."

"Anyone else?"

"Well, you and me and Thelma. And Max and Marian, and Charlie, and Maurice, and Kathleen Hilyard." I did not include Irene, who had guessed.

"And Jonathan?"

"No. I'd never tell Jonathan. He's too free and easy, and he has too many parties."

"But did he guess? Jonathan got the role of Professor Bleeker. He knows Max Leslie's work, doesn't he?"

"He does, but Jonathan . . ." How to say this without looking disloyal to my oldest friend, and the only friend who knew about Terrence and me. "There's lots he doesn't notice. He's not exactly astute about anything outside of himself."

"They call that being egotistical."

"I'm used to it. It's just who he is. No one's going to change him. He's like my brother. You can't change your brother."

"Don't I know it." He rose, came to me, and took me in his

arms, held me close, his cheek against my hair. "I hope you know what you're doing, Liza Jane. It all sounds pretty rickety to me. I hope it doesn't crash around your ears."

There in his arms, though the beat of his heart comforted me, I thought just the same about the famous house of straw and how little it would take to blow it apart. I had more to lose now.

CHAPTER SEVENTEEN

Though the filming was taking place in exotic locations far distant from Hollywood, that summer everyone was abuzz with talk of the massive costs of Cecil B. DeMille's *The Ten Commandments*. Terrence and I, however, asked each other more plaintively, where is it in the Ten Commandments that we should not be allowed to fall in love? How had we so completely transgressed? We were forbidden to each other, not like adulterers skulking behind their spouses' backs, but by pressures, dogmas, assumptions, openly hostile undercurrents we could not fight. On our own beach (for that's how we thought of it, our very own beach, our own waves, our own horizon where the sun went down every night for our own pleasure and delight), the sight of the two of us together made other people walking the beach stare as though we were freaks or look away as though we were lepers. The pinch-lipped, fig-faced Wilburs never failed to bristle with spite, and they never once spoke to Terrence. When he and I were together publicly, we somehow roused deep, endemic anger in our fellow mortals who clearly felt they could revile us with impunity. Sometimes they would look at us as if they would just as soon throw us both to the ground and kick us as give us the time of day. Sometimes they muttered ugly things. And sometimes outright aggression popped out of people's pores like sweat. This was entirely new and scary to me, but

Terrence, I quickly saw, had navigated it all his life. I had new understanding of the necessity for *The Negro Motorist Green Book* for travelers, but there was no guide for lovers of different races to tell them where are the safe places, where might they be allowed just to love each other as ordinary people and not black and white.

One evening he picked me up at work, and we went to a dim little bar off Venice Boulevard for a drink before he had to return to the *Challenger*. We'd no sooner walked through the door than the bartender called Terrence a vicious name, and me a worse one. Terrence jumped, as though he'd been goosed, and marched me out of there so fast my head started to spin.

"Are you going to take that?" I demanded as he opened the door of the Porsche, shoved me in, and slammed the door. "Are you going to let that bastard talk to us like that? Who does he think he is?"

Terrence got in the Porsche and sped away. He did not answer me till I again demanded why he hadn't stood up to that bastard.

"Did you see his hands?"

"His hands? No. What's that got to do with it? He—"

"His hands were under the bar. Ten to one he had a gun under the counter. And he would have used it and been proud of himself."

"No. That's not possible."

He glanced over at me with a look of near desperation. "This isn't a goddamn movie, Roxanne, where you walk down the street at high noon, and make fine gestures, and in The End the good guys win while a bunch of trumpets play in the background. Shit like that will get you killed. It will sure as hell get me killed."

There was nothing I could say to that. I did not recognize the danger that Terrence instantly sensed because I had no frame of reference at all. After all, in the movies I had never seen a white woman and a black man out together, arm in arm. Of course I hadn't. There never was such a scene. There might not ever be such a scene. The Hays Code did not allow miscegenation on the screen. *Miscegenation.* Is that what we were doing? What an ugly word. So ugly that even the scandal rags that had excoriated Diana Jordan hadn't used it, preferring to highlight a blonde actress and her black lover. *Miscegenation.* As he drove me back to Clara Bow Drive, I tried but could not think of a single movie or play or novel where a white woman and a black man defied custom, expectations, and fell in love. None except *Othello*—a tragedy.

If we wanted to go to a movie, Terrence and I had to buy separate tickets, apart from each other, enter separately after the lights had gone down, sit together, and leave separately before the lights came up. And at that, especially in a crowded theater, we attracted unwanted attention just sitting side by side. We couldn't eat a meal at the Farm Café, or anywhere near Clara Bow Drive, without nasty looks seasoning every bite. We found a couple of restaurants in Chinatown, dark, quiet, painted in red and black and gold, with little glass wind chimes that tinkled with the breeze of every passing waiter. No one in Chinatown cared who we were, since we weren't Chinese. Neither of us had ever eaten Chinese food, and we both liked it, and we learned to use chopsticks. We drove to Baja for a couple of weekends, and there we could go wherever we wanted, dance to our hearts' content, and not attract any special notice (except for nasty looks from the border guards). Jonathan insisted everything would be fine at Casa Fiesta, reminding us that Clayton Strong and his girlfriend sometimes showed up at the parties. But Clayton's girlfriend wasn't white, and I reminded Jonathan that when Bongo and those two actors saw Diana and Booker together at the Comet Club, what did they do? They bolted, afraid to be anywhere near a white woman who loved a black man. By the end of the summer, Terrence and I agreed it was easier to stay home, to keep to ourselves.

We made an exception when the Comet Club reopened months

after the raid, an important night on Central Avenue. The club was packed and pulsating with excitement that night, full of white and black patrons, and the band was in fine form. Terrence and I got a few odd looks when we came in together, though we were not the only interracial couple, and that eased my mind a bit.

We joined a big group crowded round a single table. Clayton and Rita, Ben Tupper from the *Challenger* and his wife, Terrence's sister Coralee and her husband. Coralee was cool to me, not at all chatty and friendly, as she had been before Terrence and I were a couple. Her husband was a small, lithe man who did not talk, just quietly grooved to the music. We all applauded wildly when Booker soloed. Everyone commented how the Comet Club was the same old place, as though the raid had never happened. But for me, things were decidedly different.

Jaylene stepped out and, with a nod to her musicians, performed George Gershwin's "A Woman Is a Sometime Thing." She made the song—sung by a man in *Porgy and Bess*—the saddest any woman could imagine, as though it were a dirge for her and a warning for me. As Terrence and I danced, my head against his shoulder, I glanced over at Jaylene, and though her concentration on her song never wavered, I saw a light flash in her eyes and a quick, grim curl to her lips.

After her set I excused myself to go to the women's bathroom, where an older woman—a total stranger—snapped at me, calling me an ofay bitch, and others, also strangers, applying lipstick in the mirror, shot me looks meant to slay. Maybe they were friends or admirers of Jaylene. Maybe it was because I was clearly Terrence's date. Maybe it was because I was the only white woman in the bathroom. I certainly didn't let on that I was shaken, but I was, and I guess I knew now what it was like to be judged solely for the color of your skin.

I returned to the table and felt suddenly self-conscious about the music itself. West Coast Cool, progressive jazz, would never speak to my deepest instincts. Of the music that Terrence loved, I preferred the hymns and the old songs he played on Nelson's upright. I could not truthfully groove to what the Comet Club adored.

The band took its break. Booker Dexter strolled over, drink in hand. Coralee jumped up and hugged him. He pulled up a chair, wedging himself between me and Terrence, and sat down. I could feel him looming over me in a way that had nothing to do with his height. He accepted everyone's enthusiastic praise in a surly way. I saw Terrence and Coralee exchange a look of unease. "What do you see in her, Terrence?" asked Booker.

"Stay cool, daddy-o," said Terrence.

Booker grabbed my jaw, turning my head sharply. He ran his hand roughly over my stained cheek. "Always wanted to do that. Feel it." He picked up his drink, his cigarettes, and left us.

Terrence rose, kicked his chair back, and followed. I sat there stunned. Everyone was stunned. A great silence descended on all of us in the midst of the crowd and the smoke and the noise.

"Booker's unpredictable," said Coralee, putting her hand over mine in a way unexpectedly tender.

"He's a drug addict," said her husband. "It's true, Cora, and you know it."

At the bar, Booker and Terrence spoke angrily, their voices rising and then falling into a growl. When he returned to the table, Terrence took my arm and steered me from the smoky murk of the club into the warm summer night, where panhandlers beseeched us for money.

"It was nothing, Terrence," I said as I stumbled behind him.

"It wasn't nothing to me!"

"It's all right."

"It's not all right!" We got into the Porsche. The engine roared and the dash lights played over his somber face as he gunned the motor and pulled out. "Booker didn't used to be like that."

"Then maybe he didn't mean it."

"Of course he meant it! And I just had to stand there and watch him. I hate standing by! I stood by while Daddy took after my mother, slapping her around when she got too uppity. Mama would say, 'Oh, he doesn't mean it.' But he did! He meant it! I was just a boy, and wanted to jump him and fight him, but my sisters held me back, said there was nothing I could do, so I just witnessed, and I been witnessing ever since. Even for the *Challenger*, I'm nothing but a goddamned witness, just there to watch and report and never act. I hate being powerless, a powerless witness to what heroin has done to my brother, and now, here, I'm powerless when I see what he did to you."

"He didn't do anything to me," I insisted. "My mother was forever taking my face in her hand and asking what is this, and how does it feel, and can we get rid of it. It's happened before. It'll happen again."

"Not with my brother, it won't. We're not going back there."

"I don't want to cut you off from your family."

He gave a deep, throaty, scoffing laugh. "You think the whole tribe of them haven't chewed my ear? You think they haven't been telling me from day one that I gotta give you up for my own good? They're like the Hallelujah Fucking Chorus, girl! Wailing warning and hymns of doom. My aunts, my sisters! And Clarence! Oh you should hear Clarence Goodall on the subject of Miss Roxanne Granville." In the light from the dashboard I saw his jaw tighten. "Last time I saw him, Clarence handed me a pair of white gloves and told me to wear them when my black hands touch your skin."

I was appalled to hear this. I could so picture Clarence's cold correctness. "You never said that they knew about us."

"Oh, they know! My family, my friends, they don't need no *Secrets of the Stars* to be up on all the gossip. In my family, everyone's doings get poured out with your morning cup of coffee. I been taking shit about you all summer long."

"Why didn't you tell me?"

"Why should I? Just to make you unhappy? Your people sure as hell don't know about me, do they? And you don't need a diploma to guess what they would do, what they would say. What would they say, Roxanne?" he demanded, glancing over at me. "Really. I'm asking. What would they say?"

"Their wrath would be . . ." When I thought of Leon's response, the image that leapt to mind was Godzilla destroying Tokyo.

He turned his gaze back to the road. "Well, I'm not giving you up, no matter if Ruby and Clarence, Coralee and all the rest of them think that the butler's nephew shouldn't be sleeping with the little princess of Summit Drive."

"Please don't call me the little princess. It makes me feel stupid, and I'm not."

"You're not stupid," he said, taking a deep breath, "you are beautiful and brave, and I've never met anyone like you."

"Do you love me?"

"You know I do."

"And I love you. Isn't that all that matters?"

"No, and you are crazy to think so."

"I'm only crazy for you, Terrence."

"Well, sign us both up for the loony bin, Liza Jane."

"As long as we have a room together," I added, hoping to elicit a smile from him, but silence crackled between us. Anger bristled off of Terrence like static on a radio. After a while I said, "The world is never going to be kind to us, honey. I guess we need to accept that, and live around it."

"Can't ever live around it, Liza. It's there, like a great big pothole in the road of life." He put his hand over mine. "Loving someone, it's like you dance along this fine, smooth, paved road, and then, oh shit, you stumble, you fall into a pothole, and the person you love helps you out, and you're both the stronger for it. And if you're not stronger for it—the both of you—then you might as well pull up your pants and go home."

PART III

THE RED AND THE BLACK

1955

CHAPTER EIGHTEEN

They say that all the world loves a lover, so perhaps that's why that summer of 1955 everything I touched seemed to glow. No longer Granville's Folly, my little agency enjoyed a spate of good news, sale after sale for my clients who were moving out from Poverty Row productions. (Poverty Row itself was rapidly withering, thanks to television.) Television was still my writers' bread and butter, but I snagged a fine coup with Maurice Allen's—that is, Nelson Hilyard's—*The Devil and the Deep Blue Sea.* I sent it to MGM, to Jonathan's odious father, Mr. Moore. (I still think of him as Mr. Moore, though I've known him all my life.) When he called to say he wanted to meet to discuss the script, I insisted on meeting him at a restaurant—and not one that was part of a hotel. (From the actresses he'd invited to his hotel suites, to the script girls he'd accosted in on-set trailers, his reputation was whispered among women all over Hollywood.) We met at Ciro's, and I must say, he treated me with nothing worse than dripping condescension. However, he was brimming with excitement for *The Devil and the Deep Blue Sea.* He had a director in mind! Ambitious casting in mind! He wanted to meet the writer, Maurice Allen.

When we all three had lunch, Maurice conducted himself like one cool cat, which is to say, the jaded New Yorker he truly is. After that, of course, it was all hurry up and wait, but the contract with MGM did wonders for Maurice's generally caustic personality. He rented a house in the Hollywood Hills with a pool and a view. His mother left New York and moved in with him. Kathleen Hilyard (whom I called from a phone booth) was so delighted she wept with joy.

One night in late July, the Saturday before they would commence filming *Fly Me to the Moon*, Leon threw a soiree under the stars at Summit Drive. I attended with Jonathan, and we were stuck for what felt like hours talking to Mr. Moore who (surprise, surprise) actually had kind words to say about Jonathan's upcoming starring role. Jonathan's father could do to him what my mother did to me, and it wasn't pretty. Denise Dell came to our rescue, taking Jonathan's arm and saying she wanted to dance with her leading man.

I took the opportunity to escape Mr. Moore, though I shortly found myself marooned instead with Elsie O'Dell, who mentioned sotto voce that today was Denise's birthday. She was thirty. Elsie must have been pretty soused to part with that fact. No actress will ever willingly acknowledge a birthday. Look at Mary Pickford. She stayed in ringlets, hair bows, and flounces till she was old enough to be someone's granny, and then she simply vanished and became part of Hollywood's collective unconscious. Denise waved to her mother from the garden tier above us. Elsie rose to join them. "Are you coming, Roxanne?"

"No, I don't think so. Thanks anyway." I meandered alone among the guests, most of whom I knew, stopping to chat with those I liked best, like Buster Keaton and Fred Astaire.

For the first time in my life, I watched the waiters at a party. I wondered if they too were relatives of the Dexters and Prescotts, the Goodalls, the Bowers. Where was it written, on what tablets of social stone, that the help should all be black, and the party guests all white? The orchestra, however, was mixed, and the leader was black, and they all seemed to be enjoying themselves, and that cheered me. I knew from Terrence's columns that the only reason they could play together in public (integrated after-hours jam sessions were an open secret) was that the two musicians' unions had combined into one. I noticed Clarence standing at the French doors, overseeing his particular empire. I would have waved, but he averted his gaze immediately. *Well, tant pis,* I thought, still angry at the idea of those white gloves he'd handed Terrence with instructions about touching my white skin.

Irene interrupted my thoughts, taking my arm in a no-nonsense fashion. "You've been positively beaming all summer long, every time I see you, and it's getting tedious. You're sleeping with someone new and fascinating, aren't you? Tell me."

"We'll always have Paris."

"Don't deflect. You turned Elliott Dunne down when he asked you for a date. Twice. You know I had my heart set on a big white wedding, little Cindy as a flower girl, and the twins as ring bearers." She toyed with her amethyst pendant; she was wearing a pale mauve strapless gown. "So who is it? You might as well tell me. I'll figure it out. Someone"—she frowned—"someone's husband?"

I waved to Carleton Grimes, who had looked over from across the fountain. He nodded to me. He was with a bejeweled woman I assumed to be his wife. I laughed. "I'm having an affair with Carleton Grimes from Paragon Pictures." That ought to shut her up.

"Isn't he a little old for you? He looks forty, at least, and he's not that good-looking, even with the Errol Flynn moustache."

"He's sophisticated. And, well, honestly, Ava Gardner and Frank Sinatra have nothing on me and Carleton. A forbidden love affair. But oh, Irene, he . . ." I might have gone on at sexy length about my newly unleashed libido, but Carleton and his wife ambled over to us. He introduced his wife, and we all had the expected Hollywood exchange. I was beginning to understand Julia's dictum on glamour—talk fast, laugh fluidly, gesture economically, and leave behind a shimmering wake. The "talk fast," that was easy, but I certainly hadn't mastered "laugh fluidly" or "gesture economically," and only when I watched Carleton and his wife walk away from us did I realize that he had done exactly that. He was more accomplished than I gave him credit for.

"He's not your usual pretty choice for a man," said Irene critically. "Are you growing up at last?"

"Yes. I like them deep and dark and difficult these days. And that's the truth."

"Well, I'm going to tell anyone who will listen to me that you are having an affair with Carleton Grimes, and hope it will get back to his wife. That'll put an end to it, and you'll go out with Elliott Dunne."

"Speaking of straying husbands, how is Gordon these days?"

"Like an angel."

"I can't quite picture that."

"All right then, like a thoughtful husband."

"Can't picture that either."

Irene's cool laughter echoed with her shaking the ice cubes in her glass. "Wait till you get married, little sister. Love, honor, and obey. Well, maybe not for you; not obey anyway. You always make the rest of us look like we settled for the trolley car while you go off on a rocket."

"Fly me to the moon," I said with a laugh as the orchestra lit into the song the film was named for.

From where we stood I looked up to see Denise and Jonathan dancing, her bright blonde clarity beautifully highlighting his slick dark hair and fine features. She might be older than Jonathan, but they would look gorgeous together on film. On the strength of the champagne and the warm summer night, everyone here with a stake in *Fly Me to the Moon* was full of high hopes and high spirits. As was a certain writer in Riverside, no doubt. I pictured Max sitting on the back porch, smiling, watching his wife's tomato plants gleam in the moonlight.

But when actual filming started, in truth, an unhappy miasma surrounded *Fly Me to the Moon*. And it did not dissipate. The thirty-six-day shoot (requiring no locations, and thus, no vagaries of weather or transport to contend with) ought to have popped right along, but the production was plagued. Stalled with unending technical problems, gaffes in scheduling and budgeting, an electrical failure, a collapsed set with an injury to one of the carpenters, and a couple of days when Jonathan was late (and hungover). Each, all of these instances drove up costs and shortened tempers. Often in the evenings Jonathan came out to Malibu to rail and moan, a font of irate gossip. He told us the filming was like the fighting at Guadalcanal, and when Terrence asked how he had any idea what Guadalcanal was like, Jonathan said he'd seen the movie.

For all the accidents and incidents, the root of the picture's troubles lay with Leon. For over thirty years Leon had led Empire Pictures like a general, giving orders from behind a desk. But for this film he was leading the troops on the ground. He was on-set daily, and he did not bother finessing his decisions to smooth feelings or soothe egos. No one dared argue with him as he insisted on the best of everything for Denise, the perfect lighting, the luminous close-ups, the good lines. Every night Leon would look at what had been shot during the day; if he didn't like it (and invariably he did not) it would have to be re-shot. Moreover, much of it had to be rewritten, driving Charlie Frye to desperation.

Charlie called me nearly every day, sometimes twice a day, at work, at home. I was the only person to whom he could confide, since I alone knew his secret. Leon had totally shattered his confidence, pointing to a scene, describing the changes he wanted, and demanding rewrites, some to be done overnight, some in a matter of hours. I'd seen Max Leslie do rewrites on-set while everyone else was taking a smoke break, but Charlie froze up.

"I can't do it, Roxanne! It's like trying to take a shit in front of him!"

"Where are you now?" I took the phone to my office window and stood there watching laundry flap on the line.

"In the Writers' Building." Charlie's voice was wheezy with

anxiety. "He sent me back here to work and I can't. He's like Captain Queeg, Roxanne. I need help."

"How can I help? I'm not a writer."

"You got me into this."

"You wanted in, Charlie!"

"Well, now I want out."

"You don't mean that."

Silence crackled between us. "You're right. I don't mean that. I want the screen credit. I want the money, even if I have to split it with Max Leslie."

"Don't say that name."

"Vic Hale isn't here."

"Don't say it at all. Just go back to work."

"How can I? Leon humiliates me on-set. He actually asked me today if I needed help to pick up my pen or my prick."

I knew that Leon could be ruthless, but such crass cruelty I had never seen. Small comfort to Charlie. I hung up and wandered out to the office, where Thelma was typing away. "It's getting desperate at Empire. We may need to bring Max in for rewrites."

"Are you crazy? That is foolhardy. No. Too dangerous."

"We have to save the picture."

"You mean save Charlie."

"No, well, yes. Save Charlie and save us. If this is a disaster, all of my clients will suffer. My reputation will never be the same."

As the days wore on, the woes afflicting *Fly Me to the Moon* escalated, and repeated crises on-set undermined everyone working on the picture. Jonathan often came out to Malibu to let off steam. I was his oldest and most trusted friend, and he knew he could rant with impunity, but Terrence was less patient than I. Terrence would go on writing, pounding at the Royal while Jonathan flopped in the chintz chair and told his tales of woe.

"Two weeks into the shoot, and I want to kill myself," he said.

"Don't exaggerate." I brought out three beers from the kitchen.

"I hate comedy. I always have. I told you I'm a serious dramatic actor."

"You're working, aren't you? You're not wearing a toga."

"No one takes me seriously."

"I don't think that's true."

"It is! Look at Rock Hudson."

"You're twice as good-looking and three times as talented."

"Yes, but he's the studio's creation. The studio sent him to the star-farm, acting lessons, dancing lessons, fencing lessons for grace, horseback riding so he can play George Armstrong Custer!"

"Really? They're making a—"

"No, Roxanne, don't be stupid. What I mean is he goes up on the screen trailing all this glamour that's been created for him! It isn't real! But everyone believes in it, everyone takes him seriously. Directors, producers, they look at me, and they think, Hell, we don't have to take Jonathan seriously. Someone will always give poor Jonathan a job. After all, his father's an MGM executive. How could he possibly be any good?"

"But you are good! This picture could make you!"

"Maybe, but it's killing me in the meantime. It's killing everyone except Denise. I've never seen Leon so angry as he was today except the night you rolled the Packard down the ravine and the cops brought us both to Summit Drive along with the open cans of beer."

"I was sixteen and there was no arrest and no record," I explained to Terrence, "and Leon made a big fat donation to the Policemen's Ball."

"Policemen don't have balls," said Terrence, returning to his typing.

"Leon was angry that night," said Jonathan, "but he wasn't outright cruel and nasty like he is now. Watching him day after day now, I wonder if he's going senile."

"He's only"—I did the math—"sixty-five or so."

"He's not the man I remember." Jonathan lit a cigarette, and took a long, thoughtful drag. "Why don't you ever go to Summit Drive anymore, Quacker? You wouldn't have to bring Terrence, though that would wake them all up, wouldn't it? Ha! Just think about old Clarence! Your dear old uncle, Terrence. Imagine that!"

"Clarence knows about us," said Terrence without looking up from the Royal. "All my family knows, and they ain't happy."

I wandered over to him, put my hand on his shoulder. "I'm happy." Terrence absently patted my hand and returned to his typing.

"Well, whatever's driving Leon, he's making sure *Fly Me to the Moon* belongs to Denise. She's not such a bad kid, you know. Denise."

"You aren't telling me you like her, are you?"

"Sure, I like her."

I studied his face. "You're not going to fall for her, are you, Quacker? She will chew you up and spit you out!"

"Don't be ridiculous. Besides, I'm bagging Barbara Marsh regularly."

"Who is she again?"

"She plays the girl behind the perfume counter when Maisie goes shopping, trying to make herself more attractive for Professor Bleeker. It's Barbara's first role since she left the Pasadena Playhouse. She's delighted that Al Gilbert had a mention in his column last week about our little romance." He grinned like the Cheshire cat. "We were both late to the set the next day, and you should have heard old Phil Tobin. I thought he was going to sprout hemorrhoids he was so mad."

"I'll tell you what gives me hemorrhoids," said Terrence, turning from the Royal and taking off his glasses. "That fucking shoeshine boy who does his little dance there for Professor Bleeker and gets a dime for his trouble. That boy, just a-grinning and a-hoping for a handout from the nice white gentleman, that's shit. That kid is standing in for the whole Negro race."

Jonathan looked perplexed. "That scene isn't making a race statement, it's just to show that Bleeker has a kind heart."

Terrence gazed upward. " 'Why, thankee, massa, thankee.' "

"Don't look at me. I didn't write it."

"But you didn't notice it either," said Terrence. "Before I met Roxanne, I never used to go to the movies much, but the more I see, the more I think Leon Greene is absolutely right. Movies are powerful. They don't just reflect, they shape. Leon wants movies to save America from the Reds. I want movies to save America from ourselves." He turned back as though he were about to type again, but changed his mind. "I'm telling you, every Negro who coughs up the price of admission for *Singin' in the Rain*, for *Magnificent Obsession*, that person is crying out"—Terrence looked to heaven— " 'Erase me, O Lord, from America itself! Make me even more invisible, Lord! I been erased from history, and now, I beg you, erase me from the myth as well!' "

"What about *Carmen Jones*?" asked Jonathan. "That picture had a lot of colored people."

Terrence looked suddenly tired. "That picture was just as segregated as any other, and offered itself like a vacation destination with voodoo. That's not what I'm talking about. Movies ought to help America grow up. That's going to be my column this week."

"Please don't say Leon, or this movie in particular, honey," I said. "If they think you've read *Fly Me to the Moon*, people will wonder how you saw the script."

"Don't worry, Liza Jane. Here's what I'm going to write: Why doesn't someone make a movie of *Up from Slavery*? You remember that scene, Liza, where Booker T.'s mother somehow finds a chicken, cooks it, and wakes her children in the middle of the night so they can eat it on the spot? That's pretty goddamn dramatic."

"What's *Up from Slavery*?" asked Jonathan.

"Just what it sounds like," I said before Terrence could say something sharp. "Booker T. Washington was born a slave and went on to do great things."

"Oh," Jonathan said, waving his cigarette in the air, "a movie like that wouldn't make any money."

"Maybe what needs to change," I said, "is the audience, what people are willing to pay to see."

"Themselves!" cried Terrence. "Don't you understand? Except as sexpots or servants, we don't exist. What do you think that does to little black children? Maybe they're out there singing 'Davy Crockett' now, but in ten years they're going to grow up, and they're going to say, to ask, 'Why don't I see anyone who looks like me anywhere on that television? Why don't I see anyone who looks like me being something other than a slave or shuffling yassir-man?' There's going to be some hell to pay. One day."

"It's a question of changing what people expect, breaking hab-its, breaking customs," I said. "If people expect only white people to be on the screen, then when there are black people, it's like they don't belong. If a female Robin Hood swooped in, people would be dumbfounded. But Maid Marian is fine being bartered about."

"Isn't that what women have always been?" asked Jonathan, laughing lightly. "Bartered, baffled, and dim but kissable?"

"Maisie isn't dim," I insisted. "That's why the picture has such charm. It upsets people's expectations. Women are either passive pawns or they're scared of everything." I brought my hands to my face in mock horror. "Outrageous things happen to women all the time, and no one seems to care."

Terrence shot me an odd look, but the conversation went on, and not until Jonathan had left did he ask me what I meant. "Did someone do something outrageous to you, Liza Jane? Something you haven't told me?"

"No, I just meant . . ." And then I thought, why shouldn't I tell him? Why should I keep this all bottled up for two years, a nasty secret? "It was before I met you."

"Somebody hurt you?"

This was the first time I'd told the Irv Rakoff story to anyone except Thelma. I told him about hairy-handed Larry Sanford too, and all the rest of them, their easy assumptions that women, any woman, could be had because men had the power, and we knew it. I started to cry, and stopped myself, but Terrence kept his arms around me, held me, and told me to go ahead, cry, get it out. And when I was done, he said, "You gotta promise me, Liza Jane, if shit like that happens again, ever, you gotta tell me. I'll never let anyone hurt you again."

CHAPTER NINETEEN

The next day, I'd no sooner walked into my office when the phone rang. "Just one minute, sir," said Thelma. She came to my office door and mouthed, "Leon."

He got right to the point. "Charlie Frye doesn't always show up when he's wanted on-set, and when we have to send someone after him, they find him in his office, sharpening pencils and throwing darts. If he is there at all. He doesn't make the changes when they're wanted, which, as you know, is instantly. He's costing us time."

"But he does make them."

"He's costing us time," Leon repeated, "and time is crucial. He wrote a brilliant comedic script. Why can't he make some brilliant comedic changes? He's your writer, isn't he?"

The question hung there between us. "Sure, Leon. I'll talk to him."

"He's already been talked to, Roxanne. You set this in motion. You need to see he acts responsibly. This would never have been tolerated in the old days."

A chill pierced my very bones. "I will take care of this," I promised, not knowing if I could deliver. Or if Charlie could deliver. Max, of course, could deliver, but he was in Riverside, sixty miles away. I hung up and said to Thelma, "There's no choice. We need to have Max do the rewrites, and somehow we'll have to get them to Charlie."

"That means Charlie will know that Max is in Riverside."

"He'll only know for sure Max isn't in Mexico. We couldn't do it at all if Max was in Mexico. You see what's at stake, don't you?"

"I do," Thelma conceded, "but I feel like we're turning on the fan and waiting for the shit to hit it."

We set up a relay system that stayed in place for the rest of the filming. Charlie telephoned me with the changes Leon wanted, right down to the page numbers. I went to a pay phone, armed with about ten thousand dimes, and telephoned Max, who did the writing. When he was done, Marian phoned the office from a pay phone, asking for a different name every time. Thelma said, "Wrong number." Marian drove from Riverside. Thelma or I drove from LA. We met halfway and passed the envelope in that cosmopolitan hub, Covina. We met at a different gas station each time. I checked out the *Negro Motorist Green Book* and refused to meet at any gas station not listed there. Marian thought I was nuts, but since I'd first seen that book the day I met Terrence, I never pass a Shell station without thinking about squatting in a field to pee.

These treks to Covina left me parched and cross; they ate up chunks of my time, and often Marian was late. I sat in the sweltering heat reading scripts, wondering if fate was punishing me for my arrogance in offering to Empire. Or perhaps I was being punished for my stupidity in asking Charlie Frye to front for a comic genius writer like Max Leslie. Charlie, for his part, guessed that Max was living in Southern California (how else could we have the pages so swiftly?), and he once asked me where, to which I replied in French, "None of your damn business." The grueling handoff/edit/return went on for weeks, especially since the film did not wrap in the allotted thirty-six days, but went on so much longer that it could not be released at the end of 1955. Jonathan told me that when Denise heard this news on-set—in short, no hope of the

Oscars for 1955—she went into a full-throttle rage, throwing things and cursing everyone, including Leon himself. She wrecked the set, and they had to rebuild it before they could shoot again. That took time, and tempers frayed all the more.

One night Marian was very late, and I didn't leave Covina till ten. I called Charlie from a pay phone there. I told him I'd bring the rewrites to the studio the next morning, that he should leave my name with the guard at the gate. I could hear John Philip Sousa playing in the background.

I drove through the Empire gates early, but Charlie wasn't in the Writers' Building. Vic Hale told me he was on-set, Stage 17, adding for my benefit, "Charlie's not much of a writer."

"He's better than you on his worst day, you scum-sucking toady," I retorted.

Approaching the cavernous Stage 17, I entered quietly through a small door, and I stayed at the back in the darkness gazing at the well-lit set, Professor Bleeker's futuristic lab. They were filming the scene where Professor Bleeker first notices what he believes to be messages from outer space. Jonathan's comedic timing was perfect. He delivered his lines with airy efficiency as he swathed the emotional ignorance of Professor Bleeker in intellectual innocence. Unfortunately, Leon hated the scene, and he made his views known to the director, Phil Tobin, who instantly called, "Cut!"

Charlie, clutching his clipboard to his chest like a small surfboard in a big storm, joined me in the shadows so I could surreptitiously hand him the revised pages. He walked away without even reading them, and handed them to Leon. Leon told Charlie to wait in the tone of voice you'd use for a cur you ordered to sit. Leon read the revisions, and grunted, nothing more, before he called for a typist. He wanted ten copies made. He wanted to shoot the scene right after lunch. She hustled out at a run. Leon dismissed Charlie, who melted into the shadows.

I stayed in the back where I could watch without being seen. Between takes the set teemed with activity. Jonathan and Barbara

Marsh got their makeup refreshed by underlings while Denise was attended by the maestra, Violet Andreas. Violet held her makeup palette as if she were Monet in front of a haystack while Elsie hovered nearby checking each swipe of the brush. Violet was not accustomed to being instructed by novices, and had Elsie been anyone but Denise's mother, she would have been swatted like a fly. Phil Tobin, a big, balding man with the wide, still-nimble gait of a former athlete, barked and snapped at everyone, but there was no question as to who was the true director of this picture—in fact, who was the director of any universe in which this picture might be made. Leon strode around the set like the lion tamer at the circus, cracking the whip while various minions froze or scurried. His acerbic perfectionism was painful to behold. And as he quarreled with the set decorator, a young man who affected an ascot and sported a pencil-thin moustache, all I could think of was *cue the thunder.*

"What did you say your name was again?"

The set decorator replied so low I couldn't hear his response.

"Oh, good," Leon said, "because I was afraid that you thought your name was Cedric Gibbons, you know, the really brilliant set decorator, because if you are not Cedric Fucking Gibbons, then you'll do exactly as I say, or you won't be here tomorrow."

Cameras rolled again, and I watched take after failed take as Leon intervened to comfort Denise or to chastise whoever was impeding her abilities. At last it was time for lunch. With some relief, I stepped outside and blinked in the sunshine.

Charlie bolted out right behind me. "I hate you. You and your grandfather, and Max Leslie too."

"Shut up."

"I wish I'd never agreed to this." Charlie stalked off.

"What's wrong with Charlie, Quacker?" asked Jonathan, who had meandered outside, still wearing his Professor Bleeker costume and makeup. "Every day he's more like Boris Karloff in *Bride of Frankenstein.*" He closed his eyes, cinched his lips, and stuck his arms out, marching. I had to laugh in spite of myself, but, eager to avoid talking about Charlie (and terrified Jonathan might have heard Max's name), I immediately complimented him on his performance.

"I must hear more of this. Let me buy you lunch."

My entrance at the studio commissary ought to have felt like a homecoming, considering the number of years I ate there almost every day during summer vacations, but a lot of time had passed since then. I knew or recognized few people except for Violet Andreas and Frances Hargrove, the costume designer. Nostalgia might have overwhelmed me if I hadn't seen Vic Hale come in. He sat by himself. Ate by himself. No one would go near him. So perhaps he had saved his job, but he had lost his soul. I felt badly that I'd been so nasty to him. There is more than one kind of career death.

rotic became my new favorite word, supplanting *panache*. That little house at Malibu couldn't contain all the erotic happiness Terrence and I filled it with, the music and laughter, playing with Bruno on the beach, long walks, long talks, even the arguments, high-spirited back-and-forths, card games, and after the shoot for *Fly Me to the Moon* ended—and Jonathan ceased coming over to complain—we were alone again, and content.

But I did invite Thelma in for dinner one September evening. She had guessed about Terrence as soon as we subscribed to the *Challenger*, and I did not deny it; in fact, I felt wonderfully liberated to be able to say, yes, I'm in love with Terrence Dexter. He seldom came to Clara Bow Drive, but when Thelma drove me home that day (the MG was at Reg's), I insisted that she stay for dinner. Thelma's second husband was a jazz aficionado, so she knew of Buddy Collette, Chico Hamilton, and Dexter Gordon, and had heard them play in Central Avenue bars years before. Terrence adored her, and the feeling was mutual. The evening was a total success, except for my cooking, or rather, my learning to cook. Trial and error, to put it kindly. Tonight's error included the baked potatoes exploding all over the oven, causing smoke to come wafting out. I was humiliated.

"Don't take it so hard." Terrence nudged me after we had opened all the windows and fanned the smoke away.

"You need to use a fork and poke holes in potatoes before you put them in the oven," said Thelma. "You'll get the hang of it, don't worry."

"Come on, Liza," he chided me, "smile." He glanced over at the desk, where he'd set the camera he sometimes took on assignment with him, and handed it to Thelma. "Here, take a couple of pictures of us, will you?" He came back and stood beside me while the shutter snapped several times, and the flash went off. I could not have guessed how precious those snapshots would one day become.

The next day at work, Thelma handed me a parcel in a plain brown wrapper.

"What is this? A sex manual?"

"My mother's nineteen twenty-three Fannie Farmer cookbook. A gift. My mother was a great cook, and she swore by Fannie Farmer." Thelma lit her first cigarette of the day and wound clean paper into the typewriter. "Terrence is a good man, Roxanne, a fine man, brains, looks. Someone taught him manners, all right. He seems like a man of real integrity too. You just don't find men like that nowadays. Especially not in our business. They're more like Jonathan and Charlie, all riddled with ego and ambition and insecurity, men who drain the life out of their women, and then they move on to a new woman. I admire Terrence, and if he were white, I'd tell you to marry him."

"Marry him! I can't even go to the movies with him."

"Yes, and that's why I think you should end this affair. You two are playing with fire."

"We're not playing. We're in love."

"There's more at stake here than you getting your heart broken, dear."

"I suppose you're going to remind me about Diana Jordan and how her career is finished. Do you think that doesn't cross my mind every day? I think about—"

"Did I say anything about career? No. You've proved that you're willing to take risks with your career. I'm not even talking about you. He is in grave danger. Terrence." She pointed to the front page of the *Challenger*, another headline about the grisly death of fourteen-year-old Emmett Till in Mississippi that summer. At his funeral in Chicago, the boy's mother had insisted on an open coffin. The whole world sickened to see what they had done to her son.

"Terrence wants to go to Mississippi to cover the trial, but Mr. Branch won't let him, says the trial is a travesty. And it's too dangerous."

"And he's right. Those white men they arrested, they'll get off. You watch. No one will pay for this boy's death. You be careful, Roxanne, you and Terrence both. If that can happen to a boy"— Thelma again pointed to the page—"imagine what can happen to a grown man."

"We live in California, not Mississippi."

"Yes, and just why are you keeping your relationship a secret from everyone?"

To that question, rhetorical or not, I had no reply.

That night I woke to see Terrence sitting on the edge of the bed, his head in his hands. I glanced at the clock: two thirty.

"Terrence, what is it? What's wrong?"

"I'm sorry, Roxanne, but I can't stay here. It's not personal, but I have to go back to Naomi Avenue."

"Now? It's the middle of the night."

"Now."

"What's wrong, honey? What's happened?"

"They keep asking me at the office why I don't answer the phone. It looks like I don't care, like I can't be bothered when they need me."

"You could give them my number. It's fine with me." I stroked his back.

"It's not fine with me. I can't be driving down from Malibu while we're covering the Emmett Till case. It's not right. They need me at the paper." He stood, reached for his pants, and slid them on. "I'm going back to Naomi for a while. It's not personal, baby, but it's not right either. I need to be where I'm needed. You understand, don't you?"

I wanted to protest, to fling myself across the door and beg him to stay, but I watched him go and I did not resist. At least I'd learned that much, hadn't I? Max and Simon and Nelson and Jerrold had all learned the hard way that the unstable alliance of passion and principle, of responsibility and integrity, would inevitably exact costs. Someone like Terrence Dexter, well, he had known that for generations. Someone like me? My lessons lay ahead.

Ten days passed (and I was counting). I didn't see Terrence, but we talked on the phone often. The crisis created by the death of Emmett Till in faraway Mississippi kept him working nonstop at the paper and with the NAACP.

On the eleventh day Irene breezed into Clara Bow Drive, nodded to Thelma, and called out that I must cancel all my appointments this afternoon and go with her to UCLA Medical Center.

I panicked. "Is Leon sick?"

"It's Clarence. Yesterday they found him writhing in pain on the floor, and they took him to the hospital. No one even knew he was sick again."

"Again?"

"He was off work for about three months a few years ago. You must have been in Paris. A bad scare, cancer, but he's fine now. Well, not fine right now. Obviously. He had some sort of obstruction of the bowel and they operated yesterday."

"And is he all right?"

"He's recovering. Leon insists we both go see him on behalf of the family."

"Leon wants me to go too?" I asked, heartened at the request.

"Well, you're family, aren't you?"

"Leon hasn't exactly embraced me of late."

"And whose fault is that?" she snapped.

I got up and closed the door to my office. I had never told Thelma that Irene had guessed about Max. "Why can't Leon go?"

"Because he's Leon Greene! He can't leave the studio to go sit at the bedside of some old family retainer."

"That's a terrible thing to say."

"What?" Irene looked genuinely puzzled.

"To speak of Clarence like he's a pet or something. Summit Drive would fall apart without him. What does it matter if he's black or white?"

"I didn't say it mattered. What's got into you?"

"You would have never called him an 'old family retainer' if he were white."

"Oh, Roxanne! Did you put pepper in your Wheaties? What do you care? Just come with me. Let's get this over with and go out and have a drink. I could use a drink. We'll get some flowers in Westwood. They don't have anything decent in Culver City."

I asked Thelma to cancel my afternoon appointments, but I had an awful premonition that this was a very bad idea. My anxiety was confirmed when we walked into his hospital room and saw Ruby sitting on one side of his bed, Coralee on the other side, and Clarence, shorn of command, wearing a hospital gown. They all three glared at me.

"How nice to see you again," I said awkwardly, absorbing their ill will. I turned to Irene. "This is Clarence's wife, Ruby, and his niece, Coralee. They came to Julia's funeral." Coralee hadn't been there, but Irene didn't notice, and she nodded to each politely and asked how Clarence was feeling.

A little girl, Serena, with a book and a teddy bear, sat in a chair at the foot of the bed. She was Ruby and Clarence's granddaughter. She asked to see my diamond ring. "You engaged?" she asked.

"No, it belonged to my grandmother." I took our enormous bouquet of scentless hothouse roses and put them on the windowsill beside an immense floral arrangement of overpowering white lilies; the card read, *Get well soon, Leon and Denise Greene.* Also on the sill was a peanut butter jar with a few scraggly mums and asters from someone's garden. I was struck with the vivid contrast: the expensive gesture versus the felt tribute.

It seemed indecent to me to be talking about Clarence's bowels. I would have rather talked about the mop handle stuck up Booker's horn. Clarence himself sat stoic in the bed, grim, while Ruby and Coralee rattled on about his internal viscera. Irene listened, her face a perfect mask of concern.

Suddenly Terrence burst in. "I came as soon as I heard! Oh, Liza Jane!" he cried with undisguised happiness before he saw Irene.

I could feel a deep flush, not just over the birthmark, but over my whole body from the sudden pounding of my heart, and a gushing sensation between my legs that made my eyes widen in surprise. "This is my sister. Irene, Terrence, Mr. Dexter. This is . . ." *The man I love? A sonnet? Erotic poetry? Something in French?* I stood there speechless.

"Terrence is my nephew," said Clarence in a cold, corrective tone.

Irene looked from me to Terrence and back again and I could tell from the expressions fluttering across her face that she had assessed everything instantly. Her outrage and anger electrified the room. In her cool blonde-Buddha way she gave Terrence's hand a wan shake. She was wearing gloves.

Coralee saw the implicit derision in the gesture. "Terrence is the star reporter for the *Challenger*," she said defiantly. "A great writer."

"That's a Negro paper, isn't it?" asked Irene.

"The *Challenger* comes out three times a week," said Terrence, adding, even more awkwardly, "but we used to print six days a week before the War."

"Terrence gonna write a book one day that everyone will read," Coralee insisted. "One day. You watch." She pointed at me and Irene. "You all will be reading his book."

"Maybe my sister should sign him up as a client," said Irene with an icy look at me. "God knows her agency could use someone smarter than Charlie Frye."

Terrence turned to Ruby and Clarence, asking anxiously after the surgery, and amid even more uncomfortable talk of Clarence's bowels and viscera, everyone in the room, except for Serena, seemed to exude an unstable brew of shame and outrage. I excused myself and stepped into the hall, hoping like hell that Irene would not follow me and that Terrence would.

Eons seemed to pass before he came out, and we ducked into an empty hospital room next door. Terrence flung the door shut and took me in his arms, and we fell onto the scratchy gray blanket covering the hospital bed. He held me, pressed me to him as if he would etch my flesh on his palms forever, both of us breathing deep, seeking each other with our lips and tongues. His fingers fumbled with the buttons on my blouse and sought my smooth breast, my taut nipple.

"Oh, baby," I cried, holding his face in my hands, "I love you, baby, and I've missed you and you can't even—"

"I can. These last ten days, the feel of you, the touch, the smell . . ." His lips went up and down my neck. "I missed the way your eyes light up when you're happy, the way you crazy moan when I've got hold of you." He brought his mouth down to my lips, and his tongue sought mine.

I reached down and found where he was hardest, stroked him, and his breath came in sharp gusts. "Don't ever leave me again," I whispered against the curve of his neck, his small perfect ears. "I never want to spend another ten days apart. No matter what. Please come home, baby. I miss you. I don't want to live without you."

His hands splayed over my backside, clutched me, and his lips followed the rise of my breast. He murmured along my neck. "You make me crazy when I'm with you and crazy when I'm not with you." He kissed me again, a deep, searching kiss, until a loudspeaker in the hallway blared out and a hospital cart rattled near the door.

206 ☆ *Laura Kalpakian*

We got off the bed and stepped away from each other breath-lessly. I righted my bra, and buttoned my blouse, and smoothed my hair, while he tucked his shirt back in his pants and promised I'd see him tonight. I stepped closer to him, took his beloved face in my hands, and brushed his lips fleetingly one last time before I re-joined the disapproving others.

"I was just telling Clarence," said Irene, glaring at me as I en-tered the room, "that Summit Drive will probably fall apart in the next ten days while he's at home recovering. Roxanne, you've lost an earring."

"I'm sure it's in the car." I tasted Terrence on my lips, and my breath came involuntarily quicker.

Excruciating, inconsequential talk continued, more bowels, the old operation for cancer some years ago, Summit Drive, Ruby's Diner, what grade little Serena was in. Perhaps ten minutes later Terrence popped back in the room. His tie was still askew, and he had buttoned his sport coat.

"What's wrong with everyone?" asked Serena.

"We should let Clarence rest," said Irene, rising and picking up her handbag.

Everyone said awkward goodbyes with well wishes for Clarence's recovery. I offered Terrence my hand, which he held with exaggerated finesse. "Mr. Dexter. How nice to see you again," I said without looking at anyone else in the room.

"Miss Granville."

Irene did not speak to me all the way back to her car. She did not answer me when I spoke. I had to walk fast to keep up with her till at last we got to her enormous teal blue Cadillac. Once inside the car, she lambasted me.

"Have a thought back to Diana Jordan, you dumb cluck! It wasn't the arrest that finished her off, it was the Negro! She'll never work again! Not after the whole world knows she was sleeping with a Negro!"

"Terrence's brother."

Irene started to hyperventilate. "Did you actually meet this man the night of the raid?"

"Before that. He drove me to Pierino's one day last spring when my car was at Reg's. He has a Porsche."

"Oh, great god in the morning, Roxanne! You got in the car with a strange Negro because he had a Porsche? Have you lost your mind? Have you stuffed your brains up your twat?"

"I never knew what it was to be in love before this, Irene. I didn't know everything that can happen to you, body and soul—"

"I don't want to hear about body and soul! Stop! For god's sake, stop! Who else knows? I mean, other than all the servants at Summit Drive."

"Clarence would never tell anyone else. He's dead set against us. They all are. You saw their faces."

"And they should be! This is terrible. Scandalous. Who else knows? Jonathan, does he know?"

"Yes."

"One night Jonathan will drink too much and tell one of his Casa Fiesta sluts. 'Oh, guess what? Roxanne Granville is having an affair with a Negro!' You will be ruined in this town forever."

"Jonathan wouldn't—"

"Shut up. Who else knows? Who!"

"Thelma."

"Well, Thelma will keep her mouth shut, because she's a Red like the rest of them, and she has a lot to lose."

"She's not a Red. She never was."

"Shut up. Oh, Roxanne, you have gone too far! Don't do this. Don't. I beg of you. Have you thought what Leon would do if he knew? What Gordon would do? What it would mean to Empire? Oh, I understand it now, your whining when I called Clarence an old family retainer! You're turning into one of those radical women with your hair in a long braid and sensible shoes and signs calling for *Ban the Bomb* and racial equality." She caught her breath. "There never was any affair with Carleton Grimes, was there?"

"What else could I say, Irene?" I was blubbering now. "I couldn't tell you about Terrence. Could I say I'm in love with Terrence Dexter, and he has—"

"You'll be finished. Disgraced. We'll all be disgraced. Every client you have will leave you and you'll never work again. This is the worst kind of scandal you could possibly risk." She stopped the Cadillac at a red light and put her forehead against the steering wheel. I could hear her crying. I had never seen her cry, not even when Julia died. "You'll ruin all our lives."

"If I ruin it, it's my life," I said in a weak voice, undone by her tears.

"Have you thought what it could mean to Clarence when Leon finds out! How fast Leon will fire him? Thirty years at Summit Drive, and he will be gone!"

"He'd never fire Clarence."

"Really?" The light changed, and the car behind us honked. Irene wiped her eyes with her gloved hand, and moved forward. "Well, he certainly let Max and Simon and Nelson and Jerrold, and a lot of others, go without a second thought, didn't he? Fired them! Never mind their contracts. Oh, god, that's right! You're using that fool Charlie as a front for Max. Oh, sweet Jesus in the dandelions, Roxanne!"

"What?" I had never seen her so distraught.

"And I'll bet Charlie's not the only one, is he? All those successes you've been having! All that television, and the Maurice Allen script you just sold to MGM."

"Charlie's the only one. Honest."

"Just shut up. I don't want to know."

I babbled and burbled, and protested my innocence, and when that was obviously such a crashing lie, I fell apart entirely, the months of secrecy just peeled away from me, and I sobbed and gulped and wailed. How could I refuse Max when he had suffered so much? Between wet, wheezy gasps I told her how Kathleen Hilyard came all the way from Phoenix, and how Julia and I had cried our eyes out when we heard how Nelson died, and how Kathleen had lost everything, even Nelson's name, and all this got flummoxed up with what I felt for Terrence, and what he felt for me, and how we didn't mean to fall in love, but we did. I was mopping my face with my hands, mascara all over my cheeks, and still she did not say a word. Not a single damned word, just let me blubber and weep till at last she turned onto Clara Bow Drive and pulled in behind the oleanders.

She left the engine running. She was not crying now, though her perfect face was streaked with mascara. Ignoring everything I had just confessed, she said, "What if you get pregnant? Have you thought about that? A little chocolate drop of a baby?" Her voice was hard as little agates that she threw at me.

"I won't get pregnant." I wiped my eyes with the heel of my hand.

"We all say that."

"I'm not an unsophisticated fool. Julia took me to the doctor when I was in Paris. I have a diaphragm."

Irene laughed out loud. "And tell me, are you very careful and use it all the time?"

I hung my head. "Why can't people just love who they love? Why can't I be in love with Terrence?"

"Because there are things that are simply not done, no matter how much panache you have, or you think you have. I was so wrong about you. You are not a romantic. You are a goddamn fool, and you will come to sorrow, little sister."

"If I home-wrecked my way through a dozen married men, I wouldn't be any worse than Leon or Gordon. If I committed fraud or larceny or . . . or . . ."

"Those are acceptable human failings! Loving a Negro goes against the laws of nature."

"That's ridiculous. Gravity is a law of nature; love is not. He loves me," I insisted. "I love him."

"Are you really so stupid as to think that matters? You always say Hollywood is a house of straw, and you're right! One gust from the Big Bad Wolf, and you are gone. One little ember, and you are gone. One rainstorm, and you are gone. Don't you see? No one can save you. No one can save either one of you. You must end this affair."

"I won't."

She seemed to quiver with outrage. "All right, then I don't want to see you again, or talk to you, until you are finished with him. You choose."

Painfully I remembered giving Leon the ultimatum: *Denise or me. Choose.* I was firm with Irene, though not defiant. "I love him and I won't give him up."

"Fine. Then you've made your choice. Now get out of my car."

I was wearing only a black satin slip late that night when I heard the Porsche rumble up behind the house. I stood in the open door looking at the moon, a low-lying gold coin melting into the sea. Terrence leapt up the stairs and pulled me against his body, his hands sliding over the satin, my hands loosening his tie, undoing his belt while we kissed and wove our way inside, kicking the door shut. His pants hit the bedroom floor and we fell on the bed together. I wrapped my leg around his and got his shirt unbuttoned and put my lips to his chest, licking, breathing in the scent of everything I loved about him. His hand stroked my bare leg to the place where I was dampest and he whispered, "What's this, Little Liza?" And before I could answer he rolled underneath me, his hands guiding my thighs, and stroking my breasts, holding me firm till I cried out over and over again, and I flung my arms up high, my head back, like Galileo looking up at a whole new heaven.

CHAPTER TWENTY-ONE

Losing Irene felt like one of those Malibu mudslides where a whole chunk of my life had dropped off. *Splat.* For years we always had lunch together on Friday afternoons, and I always relied on her cool wit, her sophisticated insight. Besides, she was my sister. Jonathan, when I told him what had happened, took pity on me, insisting that he and I go for a drink at Ciro's on Friday afternoons to cheer me up. He liked to go to places where he might be recognized, and his eyes darted around the smoky bar while I bemoaned the loss of Irene.

"You know she's right about Terrence," he said without any special sympathy. He lit a cigarette and snapped the lighter shut. "You ought to break it off. He's no good for you. You're risking too much."

"We're in love."

"Oh, come on, how many men have you kept around till they quit being amusing? Oh wait, I forgot. Terrence is not amusing. Don't you ever get tired of his asking questions about what everything means?"

"I like that he's interested in what makes the world work."

"He doesn't care how it works! He wants to change it."

"What's wrong with that? I'd like to change it too."

"Look, Quacker," he said, keeping his voice low, "he's a

Negro; you're white. You can flout a lot of rules, but not that one. The point is, when you and Terrence get caught—and you will— you'll lose everything. Not to be ironic, but you'll be blacklisted. You simply cannot have a Negro boyfriend, Quacker. It isn't done. It's worse than anything you could possibly do."

"And love? What about being in love?"

"What about it? Look at Diana Jordan. She's been wiped off the face of the planet, hasn't she? Irv got his revenge. Someone might do the same to you. I'm sure you've made enemies."

Diana Jordan's fate was, to me, a living nightmare. Though Terrence and I seldom mentioned her or Booker, I know he felt the same. I lied outright. "I haven't paid attention."

"Oh, well then, I guess you haven't heard, have you? She finally got an appointment to see my father, and she went up to his office and flung herself at his feet, and said she was sorry about the black guy, she'd never go to another jazz club, and she would do whatever he wanted—whatever he wanted—to get another role in anything at all. Knowing my father, you can just imagine, can't you, what he—"

"I don't want to. Just go on."

"So the word is now that MGM is looking for some nice young actor of Diana's own age and race, someone they'll take off the star-farm, so it will be good for his career too. Soon you'll be reading all about it in *Secrets of the Stars*, how they fell in love and eloped! Surprise! And how they'll be living in domestic bliss in the Hollywood Hills. Isn't it romantic?" he added acidly.

"Don't you have any compassion? Diana will never be the same woman who took us to the Comet Club that night. How full of zest she was!"

"She was full of sex, Roxanne."

"Terrence and I are in love."

"No one cares. It's the sex people can't stand." Jonathan took a long, thoughtful drag on his cigarette. "Miscegenation and homosexuality are the unpardonable sins. No one gets forgiven for those sins."

With perfect timing (for me), Bob Mitchum walked into the bar. Conversations stopped, and as he passed by, people, even jaded Hollywood types, smiled and nodded. He recognized us, came over, gave me a quick, insincere kiss on the cheek, shook Jonathan's hand, and moved on. After that our waiter was more attentive.

"One day," said Jonathan, "when I walk into a room, people are going to halt and stare just like that. But in the meantime, I'm still waiting to get offered roles like they give to Marlon Brando or Monty Clift. Natalie got me into a special screening of *Rebel Without a Cause* last week, and I have to say, I could have done anything James Dean did."

We clinked glasses, sadly acknowledging Dean's death just the week before in a car crash. In a Porsche—a fact not lost on me. I moved the conversation back to Jonathan's favorite topic. "You're too sociable to be Marlon Brando, a brooding actor. All those Casa Fiesta parties? That's hardly the mark of Hamlet."

"I've quit the parties. Bongo's moved out."

"Really! Are you serious? When?"

"Oh, a couple of weeks ago. I'm sick of feeding the leeches. People have been using me my whole life. I'm going to see an analyst now twice a week."

These revelations struck me as a vast change in Jonathan's life, and I said so.

"The shrink has made me see myself in a whole new light. I'm an Oedipal mess, ignored by Daddy, abandoned by Mummy. Oh and remember my father's third wife? The one who seduced me."

"Please, don't remind me."

"The analyst said I should quit trying so hard to please others."

"But your charm is one of your great assets, you Duckling."

"Charm I wax on old ladies like Elsie," he scoffed. Then he brightened and did a scathing mimic of Elsie flirting with Phil Tobin at a recent Summit Drive dinner party. "Elsie's so hot to get laid, even Denise thinks it's hilarious. She makes fun of her all the time."

This was a sobering thought. "I thought she adored her mother. They were always a united front."

"I didn't say she made fun of her to her face. Behind her back, of course. Sometimes school has to let out, and Denise just needs to play a little."

"Who with?" I asked, alarmed.

"With me. We're good together, you know?" He blew a lazy smoke ring, ordered another drink, and steered the conversation decidedly elsewhere, leaving me with the creepy feeling, Peter Lorre creepy, that Jonathan and Denise were closer than they ought to have been. I had watched him go through so many affairs, I could have believed a fling. But if it were a fling, why wouldn't he just say he had bagged her? And Denise? Why would Mrs. Leon Greene bother with a measly actor, no matter how beautiful he was? I dismissed the whole thing as impossible.

I returned to Clara Bow Drive, late afternoon, surprised to see a strange car parked behind the oleanders, and to find Thelma drinking coffee and chatting with a sallow, well-dressed, dark-haired matron. Thelma cleared her throat meaningfully. "Of course you remember Simon Strassman's daughter, Susan."

I remembered her, but I certainly didn't recognize her. Simon's daughters were older than I, part of Irene's crowd. Susan Strassman hadn't so much aged as parched and puckered. She wore a dress cinched at the waist, the skirt and petticoats beneath so voluminous they brushed the doorway on either side as I escorted her into my office. Susan carried a sheaf of scripts that she set on my desk as she started off lavishing praise for my independence, a woman in a man's business, how brave I was, the long connections between our two families, how her father used to tell her family how cute I was, how smart, how talented, blah blah blah. I listened, saying little. I knew what was coming. I just waited for her to get there. Thelma had gone home for the day by the time she finally did.

"Please, please, Roxanne, find a front for my father. Marian told Mother you did it for Max. Oh, Roxanne, your heart would break to see Daddy. He's going crazy down there in Mexico with nothing to do but drink and quarrel. He's diabetic, and asthmatic, and he's killing himself, and driving my mother mad, and her health is buckling under the strain. He weighs three hundred and fifty pounds, and they had to move to a ground-floor apartment, and when he falls, my mother can't even get him back into bed. He's killing her, Roxanne. She won't leave him. If only he could be working again, think what it would do for him, for her." Susan collected herself, fumbling in her handbag for a handkerchief. "They're running out of money. I send them what I can, but I have a husband, you know? Kids. Please, Roxanne, Daddy always thought so much of you, but now I'm begging you to help him. To help us. If he can only work again, you'll save his life. I mean it!"

"Susan," I said at last, "I'll read these, but I won't promise you anything."

"I don't care how you sell them. Mother and Daddy don't care. He just needs to work again. To feel as though he has some hope."

"Sure, Susan. I understand. Leave me your phone number, and I'll call you. But don't come back here, all right?"

She wiped her nose. "The car is borrowed. Don't worry."

"So you do know what's at stake here."

"How could I not know what's at stake? My parents are living in Mexico and can never come home. I wouldn't ask if it weren't a matter of life and death. Really, Roxanne, my parents' life or death!"

The scripts were true Simon Strassman Westerns. Full of energetic derring-do, distressed damsels, laconic, straight-laced Good Guys whose underarms never darkened with sweat, lots of horses and dust and a gunfight at the end where the Good Guy wins, and the girl looks up at him full of chaste admiration. Still, it had not escaped my attention that though the Saturday serials in theaters had vanished, the form, now known as the "adult Western," was all over the television. These weekly serials were cheap and easy to make. Each episode could be shot in six days, max; unknown actors could be put under contract for two hundred fifty a week and made to work six days in a row while the network shot sometimes as many as thirty-nine episodes to fill up TV screens night after night. For the writers, the actors, and the crew, TV Westerns were the equivalent of chopping cotton, as Terrence said— downright servitude. But it was work, and people wanted to work no matter what. Warner Brothers Television was the main maw for TV Westerns, and I had a new contact there, none other than Ernest Todd, the guy I had met at the *Banner Headline* party whom Warner Brothers Television had seduced away from CBS. The next day I asked Thelma to type up two carbons of each. I called Jimmy Ashford.

"Hey, Roxanne! You've sold my script, haven't you?" In the background I could hear the tinny wail of an infant.

"No, Jimmy, but I have a proposition for you. Come by the office at your convenience."

Two hours later he walked through the door. I offered Jimmy the possibility that he might want to put Simon's Westerns under his name and I would sell them to television. I started to explain the risks, the Reds, and the need for secrecy.

"Fuck HUAC, and fuck the FBI! Of course I'll do it! We've had to move in with my folks at the walnut farm. I never want to see another walnut."

When he left I began to count all the people who had been sworn to absolute secrecy, including myself. Thelma and Terrence, Max, Marian, Simon, Leah, Kathleen, and Susan. These women obviously trusted one another, and talked or wrote often. But what about Susan's husband, or her sister, or the sister's husband? What about Kathleen's daughters, who were still just teenagers? What about all the ancillary people I didn't know? Jimmy's desperate wife maybe, telling a neighbor, or even his parents whispering how they happened to be suddenly solvent if these Westerns sold? All those people. Who might they talk to? How much, how far could they be trusted? How far could anyone be trusted? *Cue the thunder* rumbled through my heart and mind as I waded deeper and deeper into the rampant distrust, the prickly suspicion that had dirtied, corroded every imaginable relationship in Hollywood.

My sense of peril intensified when I drove up to Clara Bow Drive one afternoon and slowed to a crawl because some kids were playing kickball in the street. Across from our place, I passed a guy sitting in a gray sedan reading a newspaper. The car wasn't one I was used to seeing on the street, and why would a neighbor sit there reading? I turned to get a better look at him. He put the newspaper down and stared at me. He was a middle-aged white guy with a bad haircut and a squint.

"Did you see the gray sedan on the street?" Thelma asked when I came in. "He followed me from home this morning."

"Why?"

"He's FBI. I'm sure of it."

The blood drained from my head, and I slowly lowered myself into the chair across from her. "What does this mean?"

Thelma lit a cigarette. The match trembled in her hand. "I don't know for sure, but I'll bet the FBI knows Max is not in Mexico any longer. They could have observers in Mexico who noticed that Max wasn't hanging out at the same bars and cafés as the rest of them. They don't know where he is, or they'd be in Riverside."

"But we've been so careful!"

"We have to be even more careful. We have to be—" Thelma choked back tears. "Oh, god, I can't even think of the word."

"Vigilant."

"Vigilant." She took a deep, satisfying drag. "They know that I am a longtime friend of the family. They must think I will lead them to him. I work for you. You're an agent representing writers. And . . ."

"But could they have guessed about Charlie?" I lowered my voice to a whisper.

"If they haven't yet, they will. They may have bugged our phones. Be careful what you say on the phone. Listen for little clicks. They might have planted microphones here in the house." She lifted the desk lamp and looked under it.

A knock sounded at the door and I hesitated. "Answer it," said Thelma, going pale.

He wore a rumpled, cheap suit. With his squint he looked like Popeye, lacking only the pipe and the sailor hat. "Mrs. Smith?"

"You have the wrong house."

"No one here by that name?" His eyes lingered on Thelma, then darted over the living room that clearly served as an office. "I was told Mrs. Smith lived here. I'm looking for her."

"Look somewhere else."

We closed the door behind him. "We are screwed," said Thelma.

"We'll call him Popeye," I offered, my mouth dry with anxiety. "If we need a name for him, that's what we'll call him."

"You better tell Terrence. The *Challenger* is no stranger to the FBI."

I picked up the latest *Challenger*, which lay on her desk. All this fall, inflamed by the death of Emmett Till in August, the paper had blasted the travesty of the Mississippi trial that followed, the rhetoric escalating with every issue.

But when I went home and told Terrence about Popeye, he was less upset than I thought he'd be. "The NAACP is bugged for sure. The *Challenger* probably is too. J. Edgar Hoover has a burr up his butt about all of us. You get used to it."

"I don't want to get used to it."

"It doesn't matter what you want, Roxanne. You gotta be extra careful. Here." He took a matchbook off the table. "Let me show you an old trick Booker taught me." He tore the cover off a matchbook, rolled it up tight, and showed me how to stick it at the very base of the door when I left the house. "If anyone's been inside, you'll know it before you open the door."

"Popeye could come here?" My voice escalated to a near wail. "Find out about us?"

"They're the FBI, Roxanne." I knew when he called me Roxanne it was something important. "They can snoop all over your life, and they will. You and Thelma can't ever let down your guard."

"All right, but, baby, from now on you put the Porsche in the garage and close the door."

He chuckled. "Greater love hath no person but that they should give up their garage for another. Scripture, girl. Honest."

"Really? From the Church of Rick and Ilsa?"

"Chapter and verse."

Thelma certainly seemed to be the main target of Popeye's observations. He sometimes followed her home and parked outside her house in Tarzana. He followed me home only once—on a night, thank god, when Terrence was staying at Naomi Avenue to make a deadline. I gave Terrence Max's number and asked him to call from Naomi and alert him. Max was grateful, and he said he had a new script, nearly finished, but he would hang on to it. If anything happened to Thelma or me, he asked if Terrence would please let him know.

A few weeks passed and nothing happened to Thelma or me. But the kid who lived next door knocked on our door one afternoon to get his ball from our backyard, and he told us that Popeye had been asking up and down Clara Bow Drive for what people knew of us. Which was nothing except that Thelma drove a Nash, and I drove an MG. When Thelma took me out to Reg's to pick up the Silver Bullet after it was again repaired, Reg said that a man flashing an FBI badge had insisted on pawing through the MG, through the glove box, the trunk, under the seats.

"I had to let him look, Miss Granville," said Reg sorrowfully. "I got to keep my immigration papers clean, and I don't want no trouble."

"Sure, Reg. I understand," I said calmly, though I was seething. "Did he ask after Terrence Dexter at all? After Terrence's car?"

"No, miss. Only you."

I often wondered what the back seat of Popeye's Chevy must look like. Old newspapers? Apple cores? Bags of stale potato chips? Coke bottles? Did he read pulp magazines? Detective stories? Edgar Rice Burroughs while he sweltered in his sedan? We feared he might harass the mailman, so we got a post office box. True, he could harass the post office people, but he might need a warrant for that. I feared he might harass any clients who came to the office. I told Jimmy and Maurice to stay away. Charlie never showed up anyway. I met my clients at lunch dates, or for drinks at the most expensive places I could think of, places where a guy like Popeye would stand out just for looking like the dumpy little squirt that he was. But after that immediate, unnerving flurry of inquiries and poking about, Popeye became an intermittent rather than a continual presence. The fact that we never knew when he might turn up made him more scary, rather than less. He seemed a kind of ghost in our lives, and we feared him whether we could see him or not.

I was certainly unhappy to see his car on Clara Bow Drive one November afternoon when he followed me up to Laurel Canyon. I was going to Jonathan's to give him first glimpse at a script by Maurice Allen (one of Nelson's that Maurice had completed), a serious drama I thought would appeal to him. I pulled into the Casa Fiesta driveway beside Jonathan's car and turned off the motor. On the driver's side of my car was a big, old Packard. It had long scratches on the passenger's side. *That's the car I was driving when I rolled it down a ravine in high school.* I didn't know Leon still owned it, but then I hadn't been in the Summit Drive garages since the day I moved out three years ago. I looked up to the bedroom window and saw a curtain twitch, and a flash of bright blonde hair. I started my car and left immediately, watching Popeye in the rearview mirror all the way back to Clara Bow Drive. I watch the rearview mirror a lot more than I used to.

Jonathan telephoned me that night. His voice was theatrically upbeat as he cascaded reams of juicy gossip. Diana Jordan (who had indeed eloped) was about to work again. Bongo had been arrested for indecent exposure, and Jonathan had to call his own attorney, Adam Ornstein, to bail him out. People kept showing up at Casa Fiesta thinking the parties must still be going on . . . He nattered on and on. I made one-syllable replies. And then he said that Denise had dropped by that afternoon to rehearse. Though what they were rehearsing he did not say. "You understand, Quacker? You see what I am saying? Don't you?"

"Oh yes, I understand," I said before he hung up.

Terrence looked up from the bed, where he had the out-of-town papers spread out, comparing coverage. He took off his glasses. "What in hell was that all about? What's wrong with Jonathan? What does he want from you now?"

"Nothing," I said, unable to bring myself to put in actual words that I knew, deep down, that the longest friendship of my life had tattered into lies and distrust. On both sides. We each had a lot to lose.

CHAPTER TWENTY-TWO

Popeye wasn't there the afternoon that I drove to the Culver City post office to pick up a script that would change many lives. We had a key to this post office box, and Susan Strassman had a key, and that's how she gave us her father's scripts and how we paid her when we sold them. (And we did. My hunch about Warner Brothers Television and the adult Westerns was absolutely correct.) This envelope had in it just one script, and a note. *This one is different. Daddy has quit drinking and fighting and falling out of bed. Thank you so much, Roxanne. Love, Susan.*

Adios Diablo was indeed different—it was the story of an American railway inspector in 1915 who answers to corporate interests in the US. He goes to Mexico to make routine inspections, where he encounters the Mexican Revolution in all its chaos, turmoil, and drama. The story included a Mexican girl; not your usual lacy señorita, but a real *soldadera*, complete with a gun, a bandolier of ammo, and the kind of sexiness that Rita Hayworth does so well, brazen enough to make plain what she wanted from a man, but sufficiently simmering to sidestep the Hays Code. There was also a train wreck. And there was a Negro character: a middle-aged man who had fled Texas many years before and was vehemently on the side of the revolution. This man and the railroad inspector had to learn to trust each other, another strand of story that made it richer. Leaping up off the page, the film seemed to splash across my vision: the sound of the train wreck, the dust and smoke, the sacrifices of the men and women fighting the Mexican Revolution. And that, of course, was the whole trouble. The story wore Simon's old proletarian sympathies like a badge of honor. The hero was a man of conflicted integrity, the heroine was no shrinking virgin cowering in the corner, the struggle was that of people who had been oppressed for eons rising up against corporations who had grown fat and rich from their labor. All well and good, even heroic, but in Cold War America, any revolution looks like a call to Red arms.

I took it home, and Terrence read it, cheered to see that the black character was not a shoeshine boy, or an Uncle Tom, that no one did a jive dance or wore a turban. "This is exactly the kind of picture that will help America save itself."

"Agreed. But no one will make it today. *For Whom the Bell Tolls* could not get made now unless Robert Jordan was a sniper knocking off unwashed peons who want to deprive bankers of their nobly won gains."

"You should let Simon know so he doesn't get his hopes up."

"I want his hopes up. If he can write like this, he's come back to life."

The following morning I drove up through Zuma Canyon where, off a rutted road, Art Luke lived in a Quonset hut with a wife and a couple of kids. I remembered that he had grown up in a Mormon colony in Mexico and spoke fluent Spanish. He was just cantankerous enough that the story might appeal to him. When I got out of the MG, he was bringing his face up out of the engine of a pickup truck that was jacked up and had no tires. Joy lit his eyes. But, no, I hadn't sold another of his noir detective screenplays. We sat on camp stools around an outdoor firepit, and I told him the story of *Adios Diablo*, and who wrote it, and why that writer was living in Mexico.

"I remember Simon Strassman's Westerns. He's a hack. No

offense, Roxanne, but really, everything he wrote had a formula you could follow in your sleep. The Good Guy, the Bad Guy, the Sidekick, all that shit."

"You're right about most of his stuff. Jimmy's fronting for him for television."

Art's long jaw dropped. "Damn. So that's why Jimmy's buying a house. He said he'd got lucky, and that television was eating his stuff up."

"He did get lucky. Television is eating it up. I'm swearing you to secrecy. Routing out the Red vermin is still Hollywood's favorite sport. I'm offering you a similar proposition with *Adios Diablo*. Your name, Simon's work."

"I'm no Communist. I fought in the Pacific. Lie down with Reds and you wake up Pink. Guilt by association." He took the script from me and rifled through the pages. "You know I grew up in Mexico. My father met Pancho Villa. I still have family there. The Mexicans are still fighting the damn revolution forty years after they lost."

"Then you know why this is a great picture."

"What do you care about Mexico, Roxanne?" Art scoffed. "Why are you taking these risks?"

"I care about Simon. He's never written anything this good in all his life, and he deserves a chance to see it on the screen."

"*If* anyone will put it on the screen. Seems dubious to me."

I took *Adios Diablo* from his hands. "I have to get this copied, but if you're interested, come by my office this afternoon and read it. If not, I trust you'll keep everything I've said here confidential."

"I'd never rat out a friend. You can trust me."

"If I didn't believe that, Art, I wouldn't be here in the first place."

He showed up about four. He stretched his long, lanky frame out on the sofa and read. At six he knocked on my office door. "I wish to hell I had written this picture. I love the goddamned story.

I love the goddamned train wreck. I'd be proud to have my name on it."

"Good," I said, pleased that my intuition had been correct.

"Now, where in hell are you going to offer a script like this?"

I sent it to MGM, to Jonathan's odious father, where *The Devil and the Deep Blue Sea* was in preproduction, but MGM was not the least bit interested in *Adios Diablo*. Mr. Moore returned it to me within twenty-four hours with a terse note that read, *You must be out of your mind. Peons rising up against the railroad? Communist propaganda.*

One afternoon a few weeks later the phone rang, and instead of putting the call through, Thelma came to my door. Whoever it was would not give their name. She gave me a look of foreboding. I took the call in my office while she lounged in the doorway.

An ironic masculine voice said, "I understand you're having an affair."

Had Al Gilbert or some other slimeball sniffed out Terrence and me? "Is that so? Who with?"

"With me. I heard it from my wife. I am in deep shit, matrimonially speaking."

I laughed with relief and waved okay to Thelma. "Sorry, Carleton. Would it help if I denied it in *Variety*?"

He was calling about another script by one of my clients, a modest whodunit Paragon wanted to produce. Looking for paper to take notes, I picked up one of the many rejections for *Adios Diablo*. I described it to Carleton in glowing terms.

"No thanks, Roxanne. It's too Mexican, and anything with insurrection is like catnip to the American Legion and the Motion Picture Alliance. Believe me, I don't want John Wayne and Ward Bond sniffing around Paragon. Besides, you say it has a train wreck? Too expensive. Paragon is not MGM."

"MGM has turned it down."

He gave a rueful laugh. "And you want me to produce it?"

"Read it. Just read it. It's the most exciting script I've ever offered. Really. Stupendous. And we are lovers, don't forget."

"You are very persuasive. Send it over to Paragon this afternoon with your courier, and I'll read it."

Ha ha, I thought to myself, as I picked up my purse and keys, Carleton Grimes thinks I have a courier—or, more likely, he was trying to flatter me.

Ten days later Carleton Grimes called and asked me to meet him for lunch at Pierino's. Popeye was parked on Clara Bow Drive, so I left fifteen minutes early to give myself time to lose him in traffic. He drove a lumbering Chevy. I drove the Silver Bullet and drove it well, like Grace Kelly in *To Catch a Thief,* complete with broad-brimmed hat. I knew the shortcuts. I lost him, and I thought myself quite clever. Nonetheless, as I gave the keys to my car to the kid doing valet parking, I said, "If a frumpy guy in a gray sedan comes up and asks to see inside my car, and you let him, I will sue you from here to the rest of your life."

I sashayed in, and the waiter led me to Carleton's table, where the script of *Adios Diablo* sat on the table.

After the ordinary falsehoods of greeting, he said, "Tell me about Art Luke. Why have I never heard of him?"

"He's written a couple of detective pictures, and a monster flicker for Poverty Row, nothing especially memorable. But *Adios Diablo,* he's been working on this for years. He's passionate about it. He grew up in Mexico. His father met Pancho Villa."

"It's a fine story, Roxanne. Really. I have just the young director for it too, Sam Pepper. Heard of him?" I hadn't. "Mostly he's done TV Westerns, writing, directing, but the weekly episode— beginning, middle, end in thirty minutes—it's too narrow and finite for him. Sam needs a bigger palette. But this . . ." He thrummed his fingers on the script. "Train wrecks have been expensive since the days of Buster Keaton." Then he went off on a long aside about Buster Keaton and how much he admired him, and did I know him, and of course I did . . . As I kept up my end of this long, oblique conversation, I told myself, if the answer were simply no, I would not be here. Carleton was like a dragonfly, skirting over the reflective surface of the Hollywood pond, veering off into amusing anecdotes, returning to ask something more probing about Art, about *Adios Diablo*, talking about Paragon, still the Hollywood underdog, though not so underdog as to be down there with the Poverty Row boys. Why hadn't I taken *Adios Diablo* to Poverty Row? Well, because it wasn't B-movie material.

"I can see why you didn't take it to Empire," he said. "At least, I'm assuming you didn't take it there."

"Leon wouldn't touch this with rubber gloves and a surgical mask. The story is too bold. He's still operating under the 'Screen Guide for Americans' that Ayn Rand wrote in forty-seven."

Carleton looked thoughtful. "Hollywood has lost a lot of talent in the past few years, but Paramount, Warner, MGM, they can replace whoever they throw away. They can afford to groom younger writers and actors and directors. They can develop CinemaScope and Todd-AO, and VistaVision. They can part the Red Sea and rebuild the pyramids. Paragon doesn't have those resources. We have to choose everything carefully, make each picture count to remain competitive. But since Noah Glassman died last year, and I'm in charge now, I've got more leeway, but I also have more responsibility. Still, I'd like to do at least one big picture per year. Risky, yes?"

"Reckless," I replied, "but if it's a hit, one big picture can fund a dozen small ones."

"And make a new reputation. I want Paragon to be just that—a paragon."

I merely nodded. Carleton had his own rhythms.

"I so envy the people who were working in the silent era. They could make brilliant films with a couple of cameras, a few bathing beauties, and a pickup truck." He launched into yet another digression, and the lunch crowd at Pierino's had considerably thinned when he finally signaled for the check and said, "*Adios Diablo* is an extraordinary picture, full of color and character and great lines, and conflicted men and hard women. And an expensive train wreck. If we filmed in Mexico, Chihuahua or Sonora, we could do it."

So at last we get to it, I thought.

"I would want the writer on-set, on location for changes, rewrites. Art Luke would have to go to Mexico. That would have to be part of the deal. He'd have to stay there throughout the filming, or it's no go."

In Mexico, I thought to myself with a twinge of foreboding, there will be no agency services for the rewrites like we did with Charlie and Max. If Art got stuck, he'd be stuck. Except . . . Simon Strassman was in Mexico. Conceivably Simon might show up. That could go badly. Simon had an outsized ego to go with his outsized body, and he could wreak real havoc, even disaster. The disaster could wreck the picture. Could that wreck Paragon? It could certainly wreck Art Luke's career. Could wreck my career. "Sure," I said. "That sounds great."

"Let's talk particulars later in the week."

"Fine," I said as we both rose to leave, "but I'd like to add—I don't know who you're thinking about casting for the black guy."

"I'm always thinking about casting."

"There's a really great actor named Clayton Strong. You should look at him."

"What's he done?"

"Oh, the usual sword-and-sandal crap, but the question is: What can he do, given the opportunity?"

"That's the question we all ask of ourselves. If we're any good at all."

He picked up the check, glanced at it, and threw down a fifty-dollar bill with a show of panache, with what Julia would have recognized as a shimmering wake. Glamour.

CHAPTER TWENTY-THREE

I sat at my desk one overcast November afternoon, listening to Thelma's typewriter clack away, feeling glum and leafing through the newspaper. Unable to face the front page headlines screaming about Reds in government, Reds in the military, I turned to the society pages. There I found pictures of Leon, Denise, Jonathan, and Barbara Marsh all out together at the Cocoanut Grove, looking glittery and golden. *Fly Me to the Moon* wouldn't even premiere until February, or maybe even March, and already the publicity machine had started its inexorable grind. On the entertainment pages there were pictures of Jonathan and Denise at Griffith Observatory having a serious conversation with "real astronomers." They looked so intent they could have been Bogart and Bacall in *Key Largo*.

Thunder rumbled somewhere and rain pelted the windows. I dashed outside to the backyard and hurriedly took all the clothes off the line. Coming in through the back porch and the kitchen, I stopped and listened carefully. Someone was talking to Thelma. A voice I knew. I walked slowly into the living room and saw Irene wearing a chic red suit that warmed her pale complexion.

"I've missed you, little sister."

I dumped the laundry on the couch and ran to her, choked up

with tears. "Oh, Irene! I can't tell you how I've missed you!" I hugged her again and again while Thelma handed out Kleenex.

"I'll never approve of you and Terrence, and I still find it shocking, but as long as you don't ask me to embrace him as a brother—"

"I never did ask that, Irene," I said, wiping my eyes.

"Fine. I don't want to know anything more about him. Just like I don't want to know anything more about the writers you have fronting for your old Communist pals."

I quickly ushered her into my office, feeling the birthmark flush with guilt. I'd never told Thelma that Irene had guessed about Max. "You're wearing red," I observed.

"Yes. Gordon doesn't get to tell me what to do, who to see, or what to wear. He can't expect that from me anymore."

"I bet he loved hearing that."

"I'm the least of his problems, sad to say. I want to whisk you away."

"Where are we going?"

"Empire needs your help. Gordon wants to know what you think."

"He's never cared what I think."

"We're going to see a rough cut of *Fly Me to the Moon*. I told him if anyone might have some insight, it would be you."

"Ah," was all I could muster.

As we pulled away from Clara Bow Drive in Irene's Cadillac, I noticed Popeye across the street. I glanced over my shoulder, and yes, there he was, following us, a fact I did not bring to Irene's attention. Popeye now had her license plate number, and the make of her distinctive teal blue car, and there was nothing I could do about it. On the other hand, if I thought it out rationally, he'd certainly learn the car belonged to Irene Conrad, who was related to *the* Leon Greene, founding member and major nabob in the Motion Picture Alliance for the Preservation of American Ideals. She'd be safe. And then it occurred to me that I too was related to Leon

Greene, and perhaps the FBI wouldn't look too closely at the Granville Agency since my grandfather was pals with J. Edgar and Dick Nixon. That is, unless they believed Thelma Bigelow was a Communist spy trying to infiltrate the entertainment business, and spread Red propaganda using the Granville Agency as a cover. The burdens of secrecy, the murk and *merde*, the endless grate of fear of what I didn't know—and anxiety for what I did—made my innards knot.

"What's wrong with you?" Irene asked. "You look suddenly sick."

"I'm fine." But I rolled down the window a bit just the same, rain and all; I needed the fresh air.

Irene's Cadillac passed through Empire's elephant gates with a mere nod from the guard, and without waiting in line. (Popeye of course could not follow.) She parked in front of the ostentatious Executive Mansion and we ran through the falling rain (Californians never carry umbrellas). With only a breezy nod to the gorgon at the reception desk, we went to the screening room on the first floor. Gordon was making a few calls when we walked in, and he motioned to us to have a seat. I hadn't been in this room since I was in high school, what felt like a thousand years ago. As I sat down, the plush chair gave off a gentle whoosh of stale cigarettes and long-suppressed farts.

Gordon signed some documents, handed them to his secretary, and waved her away. He signaled the guy up in the projection booth. He said to me, "This isn't properly cut yet, and the gloss isn't on it, no music, except for that scene where we licensed the song, but I want to know what you think."

"Well, sure, Gordon, but why?"

"Aren't you the one who sat at the feet of the masters?" he snapped in his usual snotty fashion while Irene rolled her eyes.

Fly Me to the Moon and its witty premise relied on the audience finding Professor Bleeker endearing and exasperating, brilliant and myopic. Jonathan was perfect. The terrific delivery that I had witnessed on-set that day carried perfectly onto film. He might never play Hamlet, but he had a flair for this kind of comedic timing, like the younger Cary Grant. Maisie started out plain, but as the film continued she became beautiful by virtue of being smart, and being in love. But Denise was never plain, always a stunning beauty, and when Maisie spouted phrases like *oscilloscopic lenses* and *gamma refractions*, when complex equations configuring light years passed through her lush, pouting lips, Denise looked like an angel, but she sounded like a chimp. The comic effect was unintended. Would the audience believe that Maisie was smart enough to hoodwink her astrophysicist boss? Or that, given her extraordinary beauty, she would need to hoodwink him? The rest of the cast, including Barbara Marsh, was fine, but the story, as with any picture like this, fell squarely on the shoulders of the two leads, just like Clark Gable and Claudette Colbert in *It Happened One Night*. I winced to watch the scene where the shoeshine boy did his jive dance for Professor Bleeker.

During the picture Gordon smoked continually. Midway through, the director, Phil Tobin, came in and took a seat at the back, as did someone else I didn't recognize, the editor perhaps. When it was over and the lights came up, the editor (if that's who it was) left. Phil and Gordon and Irene looked at me expectantly.

"Jonathan was brilliant," I offered.

"Yeah, I was surprised," Phil conceded. "And he and Denise have good on-screen chemistry."

They have more than that, I thought to myself, though clearly I said nothing of the sort.

"The pacing is fine," I went on, "the sets are imaginative, and the dialogue is lively. Whatever else is wrong with the picture, it's not Charlie's script. Why am I here?" No one replied. "Leon's the boss. He's seen this footage ten thousand times. What does he think?"

Phil and Gordon exchanged uneasy glances. Gordon cleared his throat and called up to the booth. "You can go home now,

Steve. Thanks." The projectionist's light went out, and Gordon turned to me. "Leon says there are little weaknesses that only need to be adjusted. That's his word. 'Adjusted.' Leon says it is up to me and Phil and the editor to adjust. Leon says he did his part. Denise did her part. It's on us."

"The music might make a difference," I said.

"Who's our latest composer?" asked Phil.

"We don't have one. I liked Elmer Bernstein, but Leon nixed him as a Red. Personally, I don't give a good goddamn what people's politics are. Let the Reds sit in their little cells and plot world revolution or an Easter egg hunt for all I care, but for Leon, you're Red, you're dead." Gordon turned to me. "Give me some hope here, Roxanne. You're the one who learned at the feet of the masters."

This time he said it without irony or underlying sarcasm, and I was taken aback. "It's not a question of story. It's a question of image. If only Denise didn't look so vampy when she's supposed to be a scientific mind who devised this scientific plan to get her scientific man. How can you fix that?"

"If I could answer that question, I wouldn't be drinking heavily." He opened his bottle of Pepto-Bismol. "The premiere is already set—a gala premiere at the Griffith Observatory in February."

"How did you get the Observatory to agree to that?" I asked, impressed.

"The Leon and Denise Greene Endowment, a cool million dollars."

"A million dollars!" My jaw dropped to think of anyone just giving away that much money.

"Yeah, well, it wasn't my idea. I can tell you that. It's part of the publicity budget."

I let that sink in for a few minutes.

"Yes, ladies," he added, "the cool million came from the studio, not from Leon personally."

"Jean Arthur would have slain them in this role," I offered by way of nothing.

"You're living in the past. No one in Hollywood can afford to live in the past."

"Well, it's late, and I'm going home," said Phil. "I'll deal with this tomorrow."

"In *Banner Headline*," said Gordon, when he and I and Irene were left alone, "Denise's character was supposed to be a little harebrained—sweet, but not a great mind. This character . . . this film . . ." He coughed, a nasty, wracking cough, and stubbed out the cigarette.

"You shouldn't smoke, honey," said Irene. "It's bad for your ulcer."

"Denise Dell is killing me."

"Could you re-record her voice, maybe? Get someone else to speak her lines?" asked Irene.

"So we could call it *Singin' in the Lab* and have Gene Kelly dance?"

"The problem's not with the lines," I said, "it's with the mouth they come out of. Could you do some reshoots?"

"We can't reshoot, Denise is pregnant," said Irene as Gordon and I gasped in unison.

"Jesus Christ all Friday H!" he cried.

My heart knotted in my throat, and my mind whirled. The child of my grandfather . . . My aunt? My uncle? A squalling *infant* aunt or uncle? My grandfather fathered a baby? "I can't make myself believe this. Denise and Leon can't be having a baby!"

"You're not the only one with secrets," Irene added, though I couldn't tell if she meant that comment for me or Gordon. "Leon told me a week ago. Swore me to secrecy. Leon is delirious with joy. He's sure it'll be a boy, that he'll have the son he lost." She cast a tender, even a pitying look to her husband, knowing that Gordon would lose his treasured place as the son Leon lost. "Denise is in a rage. Leon is certain that once the morning sickness passes, she'll be happy, but he's delusional. Denise only ever wanted one baby, and his name is Oscar."

"When is it due?" I asked.

"June sometime."

"She probably thought at his age he was firing blanks," said Gordon. His brow creased uneasily. "Is it his? Maybe she . . ."

"You better keep thoughts like that to yourself," said Irene.

Was it Leon's? Or was it the child of a man much younger and more virile? A man like Jonathan Moore. At least since September, Jonathan and Denise . . . I looked from Irene to Gordon. Did they have the same suspicion? *Shut up,* I told myself, though I had uttered no word. *Shut up. Shut up. Shut up.*

"If Leon thought Denise walked on water before this, just imagine . . . just imagine." Gordon seemed to physically collapse inward; he reminded me of a cabbage I found last week at the back of the fridge. "She'll consolidate her power over him. She'll rule Empire Pictures. Really. She'll bring us down in ruins."

"The pregnancy won't be public till after the premiere," said Irene. "You can count on that. In fact . . ."

"What?" said Gordon, as he alternately flushed and paled. "What else do you know?"

"I'm sure Leon will tell you soon, but he wants the premiere moved up from February or March to January."

"January! I can't, we can't—"

"But you will, because Denise doesn't want to look pregnant when she steps in front of the press, the limelight."

Gordon rose, with difficulty it seemed to me. He gave a tight little sort of sphincter-smile, kissed Irene's cheek, thanked me for coming, for my time, and said he had to get back to work, and he'd be home late.

CHAPTER TWENTY-FOUR

parked the MG on PCH and went up the steps to my house mentally, physically, and emotionally bedraggled. Terrence looked up from the Royal, alarmed. "What's happened?"

I dropped my briefcase on the floor, kicked off my high heels, and went to his embrace. "I have some good news."

"You don't look like you have good news."

"I have some bad news too."

"Tell me the good."

"Irene made up with me. She came by the office, and we went to Empire."

"What's the bad news?"

"Denise is knocked up. Baby's due in June."

"Jesus! That'll be . . ." But words failed him. Words never failed Terrence. "Your aunt or uncle? Come on, sit down, Liza Jane. I'll pour you a drink."

He put a glass of Scotch in my hand, and I bolted it, letting the warmth suffuse inside of me. He wadded his discarded drafts for kindling, and soon a fire snapped and warmed the place. I put my feet in his lap and I told him that I feared Jonathan had fathered Denise's baby, that I was certain they'd been having an affair for months, though I had no proof except for the Packard in front of Casa Fiesta that day, and a glimpse of bright blonde hair in the window.

"Well, that sounds pretty damning."

"I think Irene and Gordon suspect too."

"Doesn't matter. You can't be sharing that outside these walls, Liza Jane. No good can come of it."

I sipped my drink. "I know. And there's other bad news. Irene took me to Empire to see a full cut of *Fly Me to the Moon* this afternoon. Jonathan is great. Denise is . . . well, she doesn't stink or anything. I hate to say it, but actually, she's a competent actress, but Maisie is supposed to be brainy, and Denise is too voluptuous. Audiences will look at her and think Professor Bleeker must be some kind of eunuch if he doesn't want to get her into bed. The casting is out of balance."

"Is that what Leon thinks?"

"Leon has tossed the whole thing back in the laps of Gordon and Phil and told them to fix it. Gordon knows he better by hell do just that, and it might be killing him." A knock sounded at the door. We both startled. "What if it's Popeye?" I whispered.

Terrence went to the door, and I stood behind him. As he opened it I felt like I was in a scene from *The Asphalt Jungle* or some other gritty noir film, because standing there in the rain was a tall, thin, hawk-faced man with long gray hair wearing a trench coat and a fedora. But behind his thick glasses, his eyes were a lively green.

"Jerrold!" I cried. "Jerrold Davies! What are you doing here! Come in!" I pulled him inside and quickly closed the door. He hugged me, and it was the old scent of Julia's Paris salons, of Gauloises, and clothes not washed often enough, and an unidentifiable whiff of something distinctly *artistique*, and full of bonhomie and élan.

"How good it is to see you, *chérie*! And now, you are so much more beautiful than you were at eighteen!"

"But . . . How can you be here? Are you in the clear?"

Jerrold put his finger to his lips in a conspiratorial fashion. He held out his hand to Terrence, and I introduced them. Then I went and stood beside Terrence, and he put his arm around my shoulders. Jerrold understood everything. *"Bon."*

We took his wet coat and hat and brought him to the fireplace and gave him a drink. "My mother was dying. Has died," he said. "My father died in fifty-two, and I had to stay in France. I did not say goodbye to my own father. This time? No."

Terrence and I both said how sorry we were about his mother's death. Terrence refreshed his glass. "But didn't the government revoke your passport?" I asked.

"I am someone else now. Someone French. Please do not ask who, or how I got this passport." He spoke with a slight lilt, not a French accent, but a way of ordering his words that was no longer wholly American. "I could not let my mother leave this world without saying goodbye. But have no fear; I was careful. I came in through Canada and took the train across to Vancouver. My brother drove up to get me. The border crossing in Washington is easy. We drove down to Portland, and I spent time with my mother. She was happy at the end. I did not go to the funeral, you can understand why, but I said my farewells. That's all that mattered to me. To her. Is that Nelson's old upright piano!"

"Yes," I said, not caring if it actually was or not.

"How happy he would be to know that you play it. Max writes to me often, how successful you are! Until he gave me this address, I thought you must be living in Beverly Hills."

"If she lived in Beverly Hills," said Terrence, "I'd have to drive a milk truck, wear a white uniform, and come to the back door."

Jerrold laughed. *"Oui,* that is certainly true. Your life here, I assume, is a secret you must keep from the world. You should come to Paris, both of you. There, it would not be so. The French are many things—arrogant, of course, utterly unsentimental, with long, unsparing memories—but they are always on the side of love. You would be happy there. I am happy there. I have an African wife, *chérie,* did you know that? My Annette."

"No. What happened to . . ." I struggled to remember his American wife's name.

"She left me, divorced me in New York. I don't blame her. It was terrible for a long time. I wasn't working. I was desolate, depressed, and angry and we were both homesick. Marriage is . . . well, in the best of times, marriage is taxing, and what we went through, that was the worst. I was so angry with Leon, so angry at being forced to leave my own country, torn from my career, my friends, my family, I thought I could never forgive him. But in truth, I'm grateful to him." Jerrold waved his cigarette. "Now I see it as fate. I will never return here to live, no matter what. Think how Americans would treat my African wife, how they would treat us both."

"No one knows that better than we do," said Terrence. "People look at us like we're Sodom and Gomorrah on the hoof."

"Do you still live in the same little Montparnasse flat?" I asked.

"*Oui.*" He laughed. "And I still use the Oscar for a hat rack. I am working, contented. My wife is teaching. She came to Paris years ago, as a student from Ivory Coast, and she stayed on to teach. We love Paris, but lots of my old Hollywood compatriots, they are not so fortunate. For some, to be driven from one's country is like a sickness, eating at the heart. Simon and Max were both dying down in Mexico. But now, thanks to you, Roxanne, they're working again. Everyone is so grateful to you."

"The money isn't even a fraction of what any of you used to make." I noticed the satchel he had put on the floor. I knew what was coming next. A script needing a front. Oh well—as they say, in for a penny, in for a pound.

"But working is what keeps a man alive. And that Leon would buy Max's picture! When Max wrote me that, I thought, Roxanne has pulled off an incredible coup!"

"Yes, well, I thought so too. I thought I was very clever and ironic, like Julia, poking a finger in Leon's eye when she financed your film, *Les Comrades.*"

"And now?" asked Jerrold.

"Now I think it was foolish of me. I'm sure Leon thinks I betrayed him. Maybe I did."

Jerrold's lined face relaxed into contemplation. "I have so many fond memories of Leon, of Empire, and all the good times at Summit Drive before he became so enthralled with Denise. His political judgment was bewitched as well, corroded with Communist suspicion. Julia would have never left him had she not been driven to the limit. She was devoted to him, and to you, *chérie*." He smiled tenderly. "I have brought you something that I found in your grandmother's apartment after she died. Something I could not let be offered for sale." From the satchel on the floor, he gave me an antique music box, burnished wood with an inlay of onyx and lapis in an intricate pattern.

"Oh!" I exclaimed, "I bought this for her at a watchmaker's shop on the rue Saint-Honoré for Christmas!" I opened it, and an elaborate, tinny version of "The Blue Danube" echoed out. Tears came to my eyes.

"Yes, it was the first Christmas I was in Paris, and I swear to you, without Julia—really, without the two of you, *chérie*—I might have shot myself, I was so devastated. But she created a genuine American Christmas, and you, you *gamine*, you did cartwheels down the parqueted hall. Do you remember?"

Of course I did. Jerrold and I spun our shared memories of Julia and Paris, and the soirées at the Parc Monceau apartment, the clever people who congregated there, Julia's genius at creating happiness and connection among so many disparate types. The time she had smuggled in a print of *Casablanca* from somewhere, how she hung a bedsheet in the drawing room, and showed it for three nights straight to a packed house, all of us crying our eyes out at the end, the airport scene, no matter how many times we'd watched it. As we talked, Jerrold broke out the two bottles of Sancerre that were also in the satchel and offered to make us some genuine

French omelettes to accompany it. I followed him into the kitchen, where, ever the director, he gave me instructions.

We three talked long and late into the night. Jerrold insisted that we must come to Paris. This was the best time to be an American in Paris. Ever since the Liberation in forty-four, the French, inasmuch as they loved anything, loved all things American, especially American jazz. "Sidney Bechet is a god in France! You remember when we went to see him, *chérie*?"

"I'll never forget it. I have his albums, and I love them, even if Terrence isn't that crazy about him."

"I like progressive jazz. My brother is a trumpet man."

"Your brother must come to France. They are mad for American jazz. France is good for American artists. Annette and I have been to dinner a number of times with Jimmy Baldwin. I see you have his book, *Notes of a Native Son*, on your shelves."

"Terrence is a writer too," I said.

"I'm a reporter for a hometown paper," he said. "Not a writer like James Baldwin."

"Few people are," said Jerrold. "Jimmy says he could never write in America, that being black stifled him there."

"But that's what he writes about," said Terrence, "being black in America."

"Yes, but he doesn't live in America. He lives in France." Jerrold sipped his wine. "Paris is the place to pursue your dreams. It's a place to be free as a man, as an artist. You and Roxanne could be openly in love there."

I reached over and put my hand over Terrence's. "I would go."

"And leave everything you've built up here?" asked Terrence.

"If you wanted to go, I would leave with you," I said.

Terrence shook his head. "Our lives are here. The battles I want to fight are here."

"Love should not be a battle," said Jerrold, "but all too often it is. I'm writing a film now, *The Oubliette*, about a French girl who falls in love with an African student, and both their hearts are broken. In the days before the French Revolution, the *oubliette* was a cage, a place where, if you were once cast there, you would be forever forgotten, but I am using the title more poetically. When their love affair breaks up, they both try to *oublient*, to forget; they each seek a place where they can forget the other. We start filming soon. You should come and help me. Paris is a wonderful place for artists and lovers."

I leaned against Terrence. "Maybe we should go. We should make the time. And thanks to Julia, I have the money."

"No, Liza Jane." He put an affectionate arm around my shoulders. "My mama didn't raise me to live off a woman, but I sure do enjoy the French lessons you teach." He winked.

The hour grew late, and Jerrold wanted to be out of Los Angeles before dawn. He was driving down to Riverside to see Max and Marian briefly, and then back to Portland. He gathered his hat and coat, and before he left he held me close. "You are like a daughter to me, Roxanne." He reached out and took Terrence's hand in his own. "Look after her."

"I do, though I can't always keep her out of trouble."

"Oh, most of that I make for myself," I said, tucking myself in the shelter of his arm.

"Trust each other," said Jerrold. "Don't let the world come between you. And when you come to Paris, you come to me first, you understand?" He gave me a last kiss on the forehead, pulled his hat down over his eyes, and walked out into rain that had diminished to a mere silvery drizzle.

Before I went to bed that night I put the music box on the desk beside the picture of Julia. I wound it up and listened again to thin notes of "The Blue Danube." I closed my eyes and just for a moment pretended I was back in that Paris apartment, a girl with so little care, such high spirits that she could bicycle through Paris on her way to finishing school and cartwheel down the parqueted floor. Where was that girl now?

CHAPTER TWENTY-FIVE

Humming "Silver Bells," I struggled up the stairs carrying my purse, briefcase, a bag of groceries, and a huge Christmas wreath looped over one arm. Terrence and I planned to go to Baja for Christmas (as we had for the Thanksgiving weekend), but I wanted the old, remembered scents. Julia always loved Christmas, and when I was a kid, the whole house at Summit Drive was festooned for the holiday, including a massive tree in the foyer and specially made wreaths on the doors. Julia shopped for months to get the perfect presents, not just for the family, but for the staff and friends, and there were parties galore. She created such a sense of festivity, especially in planning for the big Empire Christmas party held in the commissary on the winter solstice.

I hung the wreath on the mantelpiece, kicked off my shoes, changed clothes, put my hair in a ponytail, and set to work making dinner (thank you, Thelma and Fannie Farmer). I turned on the radio, KMPC 710, and hummed along with the infectious "Sixteen Tons" while I poked holes in the potatoes, and when the news came on, I listened halfheartedly to whatever the dreaded Soviets were up to. But I stopped chopping green onions and listened intently when the announcer spoke of a bus boycott in Alabama. All the Negroes in Montgomery, Alabama, were staying off the buses to protest an arrest the week before. I heard the Porsche rumble, rinsed my hands, and met Terrence at the door, alarmed to see he carried a battered suitcase as well as his briefcase. "What's wrong? Has someone died?"

He draped an arm over my shoulders and pulled me close. I could feel his warm breath on my neck. "Let's go inside."

He took his coat off, threw it over the desk chair, and retrieved some typed pages from his pocket. I turned off the radio, got us both a drink, and sat on the floor beside him, reading what he'd written. His column for the next day was about the woman in Alabama, a Mrs. Rosa Parks, who had been arrested the week before for refusing to give up her seat on the bus to a white man.

"Is that the actual law there?" I asked. "Legally she had to give up her seat?"

"It is. She's been arrested, fingerprinted, and released on bail. She's the secretary of the NAACP there, and between Thursday when she was arrested and the bail hearing on Monday, people in Montgomery organized themselves. Oh, you wouldn't believe what they did in such a short time! Mimeographed off thirty-two thousand flyers, strung them all over the city, and declared that on Monday, Negroes should refuse to ride the bus. That was days ago, Roxanne. They're still off the buses. They're gonna stay off the buses till they get some changes. It's mostly black folks who ride the buses, anyway, and the city of Montgomery is gonna feel the pinch, and soon."

"What does that have to do with the suitcase you brought home?"

"Mr. Branch's old college friend from the Alabama State College for Negroes telephoned him this afternoon. Mr. Branch called us all into his office to listen to Reverend Cooke on the speaker. He and some other leaders of the NAACP have set up the Montgomery Improvement Association, and they got a dynamic young preacher to lead it."

"But the suitcase?" I insisted.

"When we got off the phone, Mr. Branch just looked at me and said, 'You wanna go to Alabama, Terrence? We'll send you.'"

"But you wanted to go to Mississippi for the Emmett Till trial, and he wouldn't let you!"

"That was outrage. This is action. Black people just always expect the back of the bus. And that's where white folks expect to see them. But now, well, there's no one in the back of the bus, and there's not gonna *be* anyone in the back of the bus until those old habits, expectations, yes, even those laws!—till they get broken up and set to rights. This is gonna change what people think. What they expect to see. This is the first big step since Reconstruction."

"But what's the point of living in California if you're just going to go back to Alabama? We don't have laws like that here."

"Oh, come on, Roxanne! You and I can't even have a sandwich together without the locals looking for a rope. California ain't Mississippi, but it ain't heaven either, and it ain't like the old hymn where all God's children got wings." He finished his drink, stood up, and paced. "It's like there's a deep channel, a well of unrest and hate and ugliness that runs under this whole country. It's there. It's never gone away. Not just the violence visited on a boy like Emmett Till, but the daily violence, indignities that everyone expects, shit that no one can shake free of. Admit it, when you first met me, you thought I was Reg's help. You thought I should stand up and hotfoot it out there to tell Reg you arrived! People like me existed to park your car or pump your gas."

"I don't think that anymore, Terrence. Give me some credit for growing up."

"I do, baby! But it's like I've been saying to you all along! America has to grow up. We got one person, Mrs. Parks, saying, 'Enough!' Mrs. Parks knew exactly what she was doing. Exactly. She told Reverend Cooke she was thinking of Emmett Till when she refused to stand up so that white man could sit down. The Montgomery Improvement Association knows what they're doing.

And so does Mr. Branch. And so do I." He took a deep breath. "This is my moment, baby. I gotta grab it."

The stories rolled round in my head, awful stories of terrible things done to black men in places like Mississippi and Alabama. I'd seen it myself, here in California in the raid on the Comet Club, how much worse Negroes were treated. My heart constricted to think of the danger he would be in. There flashed in my mind a glimmer of why Coralee and Ruby and Clarence were so hostile to me. If I loved Terrence, and I did, if I was going to be with him, and I was, then I had to accept what being with him meant. "I hope you're not driving the Porsche."

"If those crackers see me in a Porsche, they're like to string me up before I hit the city limits. No, I'll ride the train."

"Where will you stay?"

"I got my trusty *Green Book* to tell me all the places that will feed and shelter Negroes in the Cradle of the Confederacy, Miss Scarlett."

"Please don't call me that. Not even as a joke."

"Sorry, baby." He reached out and ran his hands over my hair. "You'll be in danger."

"I'm in danger here. Right now. With you. What we're doing is dangerous."

"Not the same kind of danger."

"Oh yes, the same kind of danger. Why else would we have to keep ourselves a secret?"

"How long will you be gone?"

"Long as it takes."

"Long as what takes?"

"I don't even know the answer to that, Roxanne. I don't know what's going to happen. It won't be pretty, but it's necessary."

I will remember that night for as long as I live. Knowing he would leave in the morning impressed even the smallest detail on my heart and mind. We had dinner, and I gave him the Christmas present I'd been saving, a fountain pen with a solid gold nib. We made love, and when at last we released each other, sweaty, satiated, the sheets damp with exertion and scented with the tang of passion spent, I held him in my arms. I did not want to sleep. Neither did he. He lit up, and the cigarette glowed in the dark.

"This preacher who's leading the Montgomery Improvement Association, a Dr. King, he preaches out of the Dexter Avenue Baptist Church."

"You think that's named for your father's family?" I nudged him gently.

"You think any street in Montgomery, Alabama, gonna be named for a black family?" Terrence scoffed. He smoked in silence for a few moments. "The truth is, baby, I don't know the first thing about my father's family. Daddy never talked about Alabama, never told us any stories, except for a few war stories where he was a mechanic in France. None of his Alabama relatives ever visited Los Angeles. A letter might arrive now and then saying that someone had died or married. For a while there would be a fruitcake every Christmas, then that stopped."

"Didn't your family have to write to someone when he died?"

"He didn't die. I know I told you, that first day we met, that both my parents were dead, but it wasn't true. Really, he might just as well have died. One day he just didn't come home. His clothes were still in the closet, his shaving mug was in the bathroom—he left everything except the car and family savings. We never saw him again, and never heard a word from him either."

"Why didn't you tell me this before?"

"I've been saying he died for so many years, it just seemed like it was true. Anyway, what does it matter? He probably is dead by now, and I hardly remember him at all. Except for his hands."

"What about his hands?"

"He came home every night and his hands were seamed with grease, and Mama would say, go wash your hands and we'll eat, and he wouldn't do it. Like he was proud of them. He'd say you can't wash off black, and give Mama a look just daring her to make more of it. Some nights he'd go all around the table where the girls were doing their homework, and he'd leave grease smudges, dirt, oil from his hands all over their homework, all over the Baptist church bulletin Mama had in her typewriter. Sometimes she'd call him on it, and he'd take after Mama, and there would be a lot of noise and chairs falling over, that kind of thing, but he knew he never dared go too far, not with all her family nearby. You can imagine what they thought of him. Clarence especially. Clarence and the white gloves."

"Why didn't your mother divorce him?"

"Maybe *your* people divorce, Liza Jane, but not Addie Dexter. Out of the question. Truth to tell, we were all sort of relieved when he left. Life was easier. No more rages and cursing. The girls were older, but I was only six, and Booker was four. Mama already had a job cooking at Ruby's, so it wasn't like we were suddenly broke. The girls looked after us while Mama worked. We had to move to a duplex, but we stayed in the same neighborhood. Clarence stepped in to be a father to us. After a time, Booker and me just started saying our Daddy was dead. It was easier all round, at the school, you know? We said it so often, we came to believe it. The whole family. It quit feeling like a lie." He put out the cigarette, slid his arm underneath my shoulders, rolled me on my side and brought his lips to the back of my neck until I shuddered with delight. "Say me something in French, Liza Jane."

The next morning I managed to help him pack without crying, but when he snapped the Royal into its case, that's when I knew for sure he was leaving. I hid my tears, putting my head against his chest, and we held each other for a long time, while we murmured endearments and he hummed "Little Liza Jane." It was a bright December morning with clouds scudding high at the horizon, the sea gunmetal gray, and the uncaring waves pounding the beach. I carried the suitcase, and tucked my arm closer to his as we walked down the stairs, and bent my head against the wind as we rounded the corner. He lifted the garage door and put the Royal and the suitcase in the Porsche.

"I'm going to miss you, Liza Jane, miss this place, miss what we've got together."

"It will still be here when you come home. I will still be here. I will wait for you. Be safe. Come home to me. I'll never forgive you if you don't come home to me." I stood on tiptoe, flung my arms around his shoulders, and kissed him. "Here's looking at you, kid," I whispered before I let him go.

"I can't believe this!" I said to Thelma a few days later with the latest *Challenger* in hand. "Here's what the Montgomery Improvement Association is asking from the city. This is all they want, and they're being denied? Is it really too much to ask that the drivers should be courteous? Is that revolutionary? That they should hire black drivers for black neighborhoods and that the buses should stop at every block in the black neighborhoods like they do in the white neighborhoods? That seating on the bus should be first come, first served? Is that so outrageous?"

"Here's today's mail," she said, smiling. "Terrence's letter is on top."

Thursday

Little Liza Jane,

I have to rethink my every breath and step here. Which fountain to drink from, which window to go to for an ice cream, which door to enter. At least I don't have to remember to ride at the back of the bus. No one here is riding the bus. They walk. Miles and miles. As Dr. King says, the boycott is not just a right, a legal right, it is a duty. The Montgomery Improvement Association has set up places, lots owned by black businesses, and people come there, and drivers will take them to and from work. Any Negro with a set of wheels is driving. People can't pay the drivers, that would break the law, but they give money to the MIA, and they pay the drivers.

These drivers know they'll get arrested for going 29 in a 25 zone, for going 29 in a 30 zone. They'll arrest you for looking up or looking down. For speaking or humming or doing anything but shuffling along and whistling Dixie. I am in the land of cotton, all right. They arrested Mrs. Cooke for having a broken taillight that wasn't broken before the cop asked her to step outside the car to look at it. Then he broke it.

Write me at the address on this envelope, honey, Reverend Cooke's house. I'm moving out of the hotel after Christmas. His youngest son is at Howard University, and I can have his room. Reverend Cooke has been really good to me. Staying with him, I'll be closer to the MIA leaders, and he'll let me use his phone to call Ben Tupper with my stories. I can't use Western Union or I'm sure to be arrested as an outside agitator. My press card means shit here. White folks refuse to recognize me as a reporter. I can't even interview city officials. Newspapermen from all over the country, television cameras too, are crawling all over Montgomery, and they're labeled outside agitators, even the white guys.

Living with a preacher's family will keep me nice and proper. I'll have to watch myself for sure. When I see you next, baby, I'll probably call you ma'am, and I will surely rise when you walk in the room. (Any room except the bedroom.) Keep yourself sweet and safe, baby.

Love,
Terrence

PS: I have to tell you, Liza Jane, something strange. I keep thinking of my daddy, ever since I got here. He hardly ever crossed my mind at home in California, but here, I feel like I keep seeing him or his ghost or some such thing I have no word for. Not yet anyway. What would I say to him? What would he say to me?

His letters to me often held the germ of his published pieces in the *Challenger*, but they were far more passionate, unguarded. And if they were less polished, they were more vivid. We talked on the phone perhaps once a week, short, intense, expensive calls. Oddly, the phone calls were less satisfying to me than his letters. He always added some little intimate thought or endearment to his letters, but he could not always do that on the phone. He called from such public pay phones (undifferentiated voices and noise in the background, sometimes the stentorian roll of a church organ, sometimes honky-tonk guitars and the crack of billiard balls) that when I said I loved him, he could not really respond that he loved me too.

Living without him, I realized how much I had come to count on Terrence's sheer presence for the rhythms of everyday life. The sounds of the typewriter, his banging out old tunes on the piano, cooking together, washing the dishes, reading by the fireplace, going to bed together. I felt like a seed rattling around in the empty husk of my own life. I reminded myself of those lonely frontier women like Jean Arthur in *Shane*—look how strong they were. Surely I could do the same. I did the things that lonely women do, like defrost the fridge. I framed the two photographs Thelma had taken of us. I took one of them to bed with me and put the other on the desk. When I went out for a walk on the beach, Bruno always bounded over, looking all around for Terrence before settling for second best, me. One afternoon just before Christmas Mr. Wilbur brought out Bruno's leash and remarked that he was glad to see I had come to my senses.

"What do you mean?"

"Well, that colored man isn't around anymore."

"Terrence is not colored, Mr. Wilbur. If anything"—I touched my cheek—"I am colored. Red and white, you see?" I offered brightly, happy for the first time in my life to have a birthmark.

CHAPTER TWENTY-SIX

The family gathered on Christmas afternoon at Gordon and Irene's glass-and-steel Benedict Canyon home, for which I was grateful. I could not have endured lunch in the vast, antiqued dining room at Summit Drive with Denise Dell sitting where Julia once presided over Christmas.

Denise was in no mood to be gracious in any event. Cross and sulky, wearing a dress with a skirt so bouffant it ballooned across the couch like a peony, she glared at all of us, as if the whole Greene family were somehow to blame for her unwanted condition. (Which, Irene informed me sotto voce when I arrived, was absolutely not to be mentioned—a totally forbidden topic.) The person who might have been to blame for Denise's condition, Jonathan Moore, was attentive to her, and occasionally their eyes met, but there was no overt intimacy. Jonathan's lips might have lingered overlong on the cigarette he lit for her, and her fingertips might have lingered overlong when he passed it to her, but I was probably the only one who noticed. As we drank cocktails in the living room, Leon kept his arm around Denise, gazing upon her with the single-minded adoration usually reserved for Romans gazing at Caesar in the sword-and-sandal flicks.

Phil Tobin and his wife joined us. His wife, a bubbling font of energy, insisted on rounding up Irene's savage children to sing along while she played Christmas carols on the grand piano. I made myself a second martini before lunch and played with the slender gold bracelet I wore, my Christmas present from Terrence, sent from Alabama.

At lunch Gordon sat at the head of the table, Irene at the other end. Leon sat between Elsie and Denise. He patted her hand reflexively, encouraging her to eat, though she picked at her food, which had been expertly if soullessly catered. (I recognized as much now that I was cooking myself.) Jonathan and I sat across from them, and Phil and his wife beside us. The children were all at Irene's end of the table, at Leon's request. He doted on them, but they annoyed Denise. They would have annoyed a Botticelli angel. The youngest, Cindy, sat in a high chair banging on the tray. The twins were dueling with their forks. Gordon Junior picked broccoli off his plate and let it fall to the floor, where one of the white-gloved waiters picked it up and took it away. Then he dropped another piece. Irene told him if he did it again, she would have him spanked.

The waiters were all temporary help hired for the occasion. Negroes, I noticed. When the kitchen door swung open, I caught a glimpse of Eudonna standing there supervising the waiters and watching over the kitchen staff with a gimlet eye. Why wasn't Eudonna home with her own family? The question would never have occurred to me before Terrence came into my life. Then I thought of all those Christmas dinners at Summit Drive that Clarence had presided over. He had recovered from his operation in September and was back at work, but today, since Leon, Denise, and Elsie were here, surely he would have Christmas at home with Ruby and little Serena and their other grandchildren and their parents, with Terrence's sisters and their husbands and children. Maybe Booker was there with his trumpet, and maybe he was in a good mood, and maybe he brought his musician friends from the Comet Club, and maybe they were playing jazzy bebop arrangements of Christmas songs in the living room.

Why is it, I thought, that Clarence and Julia should so closely connect our families, and yet . . . I closed my eyes briefly and tried to imagine all of us at one long, noisy table, Clarence and Ruby and their children and grandchildren, Coralee and her husband and kids, Leon, Denise, Elsie, Irene, Gordon, their kids, Booker and the musicians, Terrence and the Cookes from Alabama, Mr. Branch, the Tobins, me and Jonathan, just celebrating Christmas together connected by the bonds of time, and affection, goodwill and respect. For a moment I could see it all before me, like some ghost of Christmas yet to come, and then Phil touched my elbow and asked me to pass the gravy. Twice.

PART IV

A HOUSE MADE OF STRAW

1956

CHAPTER TWENTY-SEVEN

In Southern California, once New Year's is over, it's spring. The narcissus pop up, the rains come, and the hills turn a tender, leathery green, and lupines and ice plants dot the headlands and canyons. That January, work settled into a certain amount of ho-hum with no major breakthroughs or excitement, except when Terrence's letters arrived, or, less pleasantly, the occasional appearance of Popeye. Thelma and I continued our routine precautions like the matchbook in the door, and we cut off all contact with Max and Marian. We all agreed that only in an emergency would we be in touch. How we would get in contact, we didn't say, and honestly, we didn't know.

Right after New Year's, Leon insisted on taking Denise to Tahoe. He offered to take Irene too, but she declined, even though she could have left her kids with the long-suffering Josefina. She stayed behind to be supportive of Gordon, on whose shoulders fell the unenviable weight of running the studio. She also had no wish to go to Tahoe, because Denise was still in such a rage that only Leon could stand to be around her. Even Elsie remained in Los Angeles to oversee the renovations at Summit Drive as builders and decorators swarmed in to create a second-floor suite for the soon-to-be infant.

Jonathan took a vacation to Key West and returned tanned and more handsome than ever. He and I were having breakfast in the dining room of the Culver Hotel, talking about plans for the up-coming premiere of *Fly Me to the Moon*. At Denise's insistence, it had been moved to late January. At Leon's insistence, Gordon was overseeing everything personally, right down to who would be arriving with whom.

"I'm paired up with Barbara Marsh. Part of the publicity love affair," said Jonathan, while we waited for our Bloody Marys (a hotel specialty). "I'm the star. I should be able to arrive on my own, but Gordon's such a skinflint, he won't spring for two limos."

"I sympathize. Gordon insisted I come with Charlie Frye. I fought him on it, but finally I said okay, as long as it's understood that I'm picked up first and dropped off last. I don't want Charlie coming to my house ever again."

Jonathan's eyebrow lifted expectantly. "Terrence is in Alabama fighting to keep people off the buses or something boring like that. You could . . ."

"No, Jonathan. That isn't going to happen. I've made my choices."

"You're going to be faithful to him? Really?"

"Really. I love him and he loves me, and he's doing important work there."

"Oh, Quacker, I liked you so much better when you were shallow and flip."

"You mean more like you."

"Exactly." He blew out a perfect smoke ring. "I'll be glad when the picture's finally launched and I can get rid of Barbara. She's a nice kid, but too inexperienced to be interesting. Soon as I can, I'm on to other lovers."

"Like Denise Dell."

For the first time since Jonathan was a fat, stuttering boy aban-doned by his mother, ignored by his father, and seduced by his stepmother, I saw something like actual pain cross his face. Not thwarted ambition or sulking petulance, but sadness. A look so swift

and fleeting that anyone other than I would have missed it altogether. However, he quickly gave an insincere laugh, raised his profile for an invisible camera, and spoke in a voice not at all discreet.
"I'd say that's a rather presumptuous question coming from a girl
who has made some very bad choices. Imagine what Leon Greene
would do if he knew you and the butler's nephew were living in sin,
if he knew that his granddaughter was no better than Diana Jordan."

I could feel my birthmark flushing. "It was just an observation."

"You should be less observant, Roxanne. I don't want to talk
about this again."

He had made his point, and I let it pass.

The night of the premiere, searchlights from the Griffith
Observatory raked across the sky, lighting it up probably all the
way to Catalina Island. As the line of limos inched up before that
stately institution, photographers and reporters flocked, and fans
pressed against the red velvet ropes that framed a broad red carpet
avenue. The publicity campaign for *Fly Me to the Moon* had been
unrelenting, and clearly, it was paying off. The million-dollar endowment to the Observatory itself, announced with great fanfare,
had garnered press from as far away as the *New York Times*, as well
as other major papers. Newsmen, photographers, and television
cameramen swarmed, eager to share with an adoring world this
incredible event: the best publicity money could buy. As our limo
pulled up, I thought, well, Gordon can congratulate himself on a
job well done, though I recognized (as did he) that this was an
applause-fest, and not a true test of the film's success. That would
be decided at the box office.

I've been attending premieres since I was allowed to stay up
past eight, so I wasn't especially excited, but beside me in the back
seat of the limo I sensed Charlie's almost quivering anxiety. I felt
for him a sort of solicitude that surprised me. I said brightly, "So
when you were warming the counter stool at Schwab's, did you
ever think you would see this night?"

"Of course I did. But I thought it would be for *Coast of Heaven*." He turned away from me.

"It still can be," I offered. "*Variety* said your writing was crisp and witty."

"Yes, well, they aren't my crisp and witty lines, are they? I'm nothing but a stooge for Max Leslie."

I glanced at the cap of the driver in the front seat and decided to say no more. When we arrived at the Observatory the driver jumped out and held the door for us. I stepped out into a gaggle of network and local television cameras, radio personalities with microphones, and press people. Hedda Hopper and Louella Parsons, shooting daggered looks at each other, took up their respective places of honor and smiled like the doyenne-dragons that they were. The renowned Dorothy Parker was on assignment for the *New Yorker*, and there were less stellar representatives from *Modern Screen*, *Photoplay*, and *Secrets of the Stars*. (Not Al Gilbert; he only did the slimy stuff.)

When Charlie stepped out beside me I could see on his face—no matter what had brought him here—that he was delighted to be part of this moment. I took his arm with some affection, and we turned, smiled, and waved to crowds lining either side of the broad red carpet while the flashbulbs sparkled, and people applauded our appearance: Charlie, handsome, beaming in his tuxedo, me in a ballerina-length, sea-green chiffon with a long chiffon scarf over one shoulder and the rope of Julia's pearls gleaming. I wore Terrence's gold bracelet over my elbow-length, three-button gloves.

According to Gordon's careful planning, Charlie and I were among the earlier arrivals—the newsreel, so to speak, before the main attraction. As we started up the red carpet, we turned and waved, absorbing a lot of anonymous attention, and I saw two older women deep in the crowd, two women who were not waving madly or jumping up and down with excitement. Smiling. Marian and Kathleen. They just stood there, like ghosts really, smiling ghosts, and honestly, when the next limo pulled up, they so swiftly melted into the crowd, I somehow doubted I had seen them at all.

Gordon rose from this limo and offered his hand to Irene, and then to Elsie as each stepped from the car. Gordon wore his worried-cobra expression, and Irene wore a white Balenciaga and sapphires, looking like the proverbial tip of the beautiful iceberg. Elsie still looked like a Victorian sofa. When, following them, Jonathan stepped out of his limo, he took his time absorbing the crowd's adulation all by himself before he offered his hand to Barbara Marsh, who sat in the back seat, waiting to emerge.

At last Leon and Denise arrived, bathed in applause. Denise shone in the spotlight, beautifully draped in a coat of white chinchilla; she did not show in the least. Leon in his tuxedo looked as debonair, bon vivant, and sophisticated as David Niven in *The Elusive Pimpernel*. As part of this glittering exercise, everyone smiled and preened along the red carpet and up the steps into the Observatory, where posters of *Fly Me to the Moon* adorned the walls.

When at last the curtain went up on the finished film, there were cute opening credits in keeping with the light comedic touch. It began with a panorama of the Griffith Observatory and a young guide showing a group of eager schoolchildren around. (An odd echo of the tense and intense *Rebel Without a Cause*.) *Fly Me to the Moon* was a comedy, and people laughed. The film was supported with a light, unmemorable score by Adolph Deutsch, an old friend of Leon's. Clever editing obscured some of the difficulties I had seen in the early version. Max's rewrites had considerably brightened the comedy, and I had to admit that Leon's addition of the ending scene with Maisie in an evening gown (and handsome Jonathan no longer looking frumpy) was a definite plus. Even Denise's inability to render scientific dialogue with conviction had about it a sort of charm, and she certainly knew how to flirt with the camera. This audience was ready to love her.

When the film was over, the applause was thunderous, and Leon stood up, turned around, and gestured with one hand to the lovely Denise Dell, still swathed in her white chinchilla, and with the other to the smoothly handsome Jonathan Moore. They both rose and took many bows to ongoing adulation.

We all moved into the main lobby, where a chamber orchestra played an up-tempo "Fly Me to the Moon" followed by a lot of other peppy standards. Champagne bubbled and caviar gleamed. Denise and Jonathan, side by side, collected praise, bestowed smiles, and held hands in victory while photographers snapped innumerable pictures. Leon and Elsie stood at their sides, looking, I must say, like the proud parents of high school graduates.

Irene, Gordon, and I moved to the edges of the crowd. I said, "I have to admit the movie was funny."

"Yes, but what were they laughing at?" Irene asked. "The wit, or Denise's delivery?"

"It's a comedy," said Gordon sourly.

"When do you think they'll publicly announce about the baby?" I said in a low voice.

"It'll be a while. Denise is still raging mad at being knocked up."

Gordon frowned. "Must you be so vulgar about it?"

Irene laughed her rippling laugh. "I have four kids. I have a right to be vulgar about it."

Sensing that they were hovering on the edge of a full-tilt quarrel, I stepped outside to get some air that wasn't swathed in cigarette smoke. I thought about Max writing away in that claustrophobic clapboard house that backed up to an alley in Riverside. I thought about Terrence down in Montgomery in his room at Reverend Cooke's, a gooseneck lamp on his desk, pounding out prose on the Royal. I thought about Simon in Mexico City, about Jerrold Davies now safely back in Paris, working in the apartment where a golden statuette served as a humble hat rack. I thought about Jimmy in his new tract house away from the walnut groves, about Art, who, with the money Paragon was prepared to pay him, was getting ready to move out of the Quonset hut. I thought about Maurice in the Hollywood Hills listening to his mother gripe about bagels. And of course, Charlie here, reveling in glamour and applause. Who would have ever believed that I, Roxanne Granville, would connect all these disparate lives? I stood at the top of the stairs and took a deep breath. The searchlights were all turned off, and the sky overhead was its own starry expanse, with no help from the phosphorescence of Hollywood or Empire Pictures.

(HAPTER TWENTY-EIGHT

The night of the premiere in Los Angeles, January 30, there was a bombing in Montgomery, Alabama. While the leader of the Montgomery Improvement Association, Martin Luther King, Jr., spoke at a big rally, someone threw a homemade bomb into his house, where his wife and baby daughter were. Terrence was at Dr. King's rally when he heard the news, and he ran to a nearby drugstore to call Ben Tupper, forgetting where he was and who he was, and three men yanked him out of the phone booth, which I guess was for whites only. They kicked him to the curb, and kicked him a few times after that as well. That too went into his story that ran in the *Challenger*.

To me he wrote more personally.

Liza Jane,

If I'm an outside agitator, well, time to agitate, damnit, and not just watch, witness, and write. I took the extra money the NAACP gave me and bought a prewar Ford. It's a bucket of bolts, but it runs. I bought it so I can drive to one of the lots owned by black businesses and pick up people and take them to their jobs. I drive. They talk. I listen. Their shoes are wearing out, but not their spirit.

But that car? That car! Roxanne, that is an experience that's seared into me for the rest of my life. I bought it off a white man, and god forgive me, I had to promise him, no sir, I wouldn't be driving no nigras to work. He called me boy. He was toying with me, all along, and finally said he wouldn't sell it to me because he didn't recognize me. I wasn't a local. I sure as hell wasn't about to show my California license. I had to get Rev Cooke to come down and buy it, and when he showed up, the cracker called Rev Cooke uncle. I wanted to punch his guts out. And I couldn't allow my face to show that I wanted to punch his guts out. I thought I'd have a hernia I was so goddamned mad. And he was still toying with us, cat and a pair of hapless black mice. After all that shit he put us through, he said that he would only sell the car to a white man. He wanted to be sure it wouldn't be used as a taxi for blacks who ought to be riding the bus. Rev Cooke telephoned a white pastor here in Montgomery, and he came and the cracker sold it to him.

Baby, just writing this I feel like I ought to take a shower and wash all that bullshit jive off of me, really, physically off of me. I miss you so much.

Love,
Terrence

PS: I think of my father living here, growing up here, and how going to war, how that must have shaken him to his core. He once said that before he was twenty he had never looked under the hood of a car, never seen anything but down the mouth or behind the butt of a mule. That's all I know of his Alabama life, but the more I see of the people of Montgomery, the more I want to know. Are these my people even if they're not my relatives? What brought him to California, and what took him away? It's late and I'm tired. I'll write more soon.

Once he got started driving every day, Terrence's *Challenger* stories were, each one of them, like the verse of an anthem. He wrote not just of the MIA and NAACP leaders, of council meetings and the like, but of maids and porters, pastors, mechanics, bartenders and barbers and waiters, of the Montgomery people he ferried in the Ford, people whose indomitable unity gave them courage that was strengthening rather than diminishing with each passing day.

THEIR SHOES ARE WEARING OUT
BUT NOT THEIR SPIRIT

That was the headline plastered across the *Challenger*'s front page announcing a Shoe Drive, to collect shoes for the people in Montgomery who were walking back and forth to work. Black churches picked it up, and radio stations too, though not the predominately white stations, nor the television networks. But in the pages of the *Challenger*, you heard the call, and all over Southern California people emptied out their closets to send shoes to Montgomery. Restaurants and shops and businesses set up pickup bins and started collection jars, *Send Montgomery Shoes*, to pay the postage.

I emptied out my closet. Thelma emptied out her closet. I called Susan Strassman, and asked her to call her sister. I did not dare contact Marian, but I wrote a note to Kathleen Bachman, assuming they had some kind of shoe drive in Arizona. I called Reg. I called Jonathan. Thelma cautioned me against asking any of the Clara Bow Drive neighbors, drawing attention to ourselves, but I did call Irene.

"I don't want to be involved," she replied, "but I saw that the *Times* did an article about your friend's reporting. 'Negro Reporter Brings Montgomery Bus Boycott Home to LA.' He's made quite a name for himself. You must be quite proud of him."

"I'm always proud of him. If he were white, he'd be nominated for the Pulitzer Prize."

"If he were white," she replied, "he wouldn't care who is or isn't riding the Alabama buses."

I personally delivered two big boxes full of shoes (as much as I could fit in the MG) to the *Challenger* offices. The receptionist thanked me and said that their circulation had doubled since their reporter, Mr. Dexter, went down to Montgomery. "Would you like a free copy of the paper, miss?" she asked.

"I subscribe. Thanks."

I went to Ruby's and sat at the counter. It was late afternoon, and on the jukebox, the Platters crooned their plaintive "The Great Pretender." The place was empty except for a group of high school students and two old men playing checkers. Coralee ambled out and asked what I wanted. "A root beer float," I replied. "I just delivered boxes of shoes to the *Challenger* for the shoe drive."

"Lah-di-dah. You want the Nobel Prize?" She made the root beer float and plunked it down in front of me. "What do you hear from Terrence?"

"He writes when he can. Calls now and then when he can find a pay phone."

"He calls you, and not me or Ruby or my sister?"

"We don't talk very long. It's expensive. Mostly he writes."

"He writes you letters and he sends us postcards? We, all of us, we say his name in church every Sunday. *'O Lord, bless and protect Terrence Dexter while he is braving hostile forces there in the Cradle of the Confederacy,'* and we ain't heard his voice? I call that shameful. Really. Shameful. He oughta know you're no good for him, Miss Granville."

"Please, Coralee, call me Roxanne."

"I only call my friends by their first names."

"I could be your friend. I want to be your friend. I want to be Ruby's friend."

"Listen to you! The great white hope come down here to bestow us with your friendship. Are we supposed to be grateful?"

"I don't want your gratitude. I don't want anything from you, except that you should believe me when I tell you I love him."

"Listen, missy, I never thought I'd be happy to see anyone I love go to Alabama, but if it means Terrence not around you, well then, fine with me. You put him in danger every time you go out with him." She lowered her voice to a hiss. "Every time you go to bed with him, you put him in danger. Every time you so much as look at him, you're saying to the world, come and take it out on this black man! Take out all your ugliness. All your fear. You wanna be my friend? You are crazy, girl. You are the living end. Remember Emmett Till." She ran her rag along the counter with frenzied effort.

"This is California."

"You think that really matters?"

"Yes. I do. It's not Alabama."

"It's not the pastures of heaven either, and all god's children don't got wings." She flung down the check on the counter, and as I reached for it, she suddenly gripped my wrist. "If you really loved him, you'd give him up. For his own good. For his own sake."

"I do really love him, and I can't give him up."

"Sooner or later, sooner or later, you and he, you're gonna be somewhere where some cracker just can't stand the thought, can't stand the sight, and they are going to kill him."

"Then let him leave me."

"He might just do that." She released my wrist.

I paid for the root beer float, and I put ten dollars in the jar by the cash register that said *Send Montgomery Shoes* before I walked out the door.

CHAPTER TWENTY-NINE

After the premiere of *Fly Me to the Moon*, Denise retreated to Summit Drive, where (Irene told me) she spent her days raging through all thirty-five rooms, rampaging at the servants, lashing out at Leon, and being cruel to Elsie. She put on some forty pounds in a matter of weeks, and when she wasn't making others miserable, she ate or cried or slept or read the reviews of *Fly Me to the Moon*. They were good, cheering. Critics praised the lively script, the wry performances. Denise, personally—astonishingly really—collected applause from none other than Bosley Crowther, the influential critic for the *New York Times*. Crowther was not usually kind to Empire Pictures, but here he said that Maisie's struggle with words like *oscilloscope* was part of her charm, indeed, part of her character. *Fly Me to the Moon* did well at the box office too. Max and Marian—I heard via Susan Strassman relaying messages with pseudonyms—were just as pleased as they could be. I heard nothing at all from Charlie, who, I assume, was in the Empire Pictures Writers' Building sulking. Had I guessed he was such a bundle of resentment and insecurity, I would have asked a chimpanzee to front for Max before I'd asked Charlie Frye.

And Jonathan? In the past four or five years, Jonathan had appeared in probably twenty films, and nobody had noticed him. With *Fly Me to the Moon*, effervescent fare that it was, critics and audiences suddenly woke up to his gifts; his comedic timing was impeccable. Superlatives rained down; the praise that washed over him was universal, and adoring. He wasn't Laurence Olivier (or Rowland Granville, for that matter) but he'd never have to wear another toga. He stood poised to be the next Cary Grant. To continue his winning streak, his agent insisted on another light comedic picture for his next venture, asking five times what he'd been paid by Empire. (Empire had not bothered to put him under contract for more than one picture.) With all these shimmering prospects, Jonathan terminated his Casa Fiesta lease in bohemian Laurel Canyon and rented a house in respectable Brentwood. I went to see it, not altogether surprised to find that it had been furnished by a designer, that it had a pool, a patio, a housekeeper, and glamorous neighbors. *Variety* gave him a big, fat headline when he signed for a film called *Aloha Express* with Paramount. They would start shooting in Hawaii in early summer, and ironically, Jonathan would have to learn to surf, at least enough to fake it before the stunt double took over.

He and I might once have been Ugly Ducklings together, but we no longer felt like Quackers. On those few occasions when we went out, he took me to high-profile restaurants and bars where the movie star Jonathan Moore was shown to the best table, and people nodded admiringly as he passed by. People came up to him just to shake his hand. We talked mostly of his successes, and the fact that Paramount had paid him four times his Empire salary. He never brought up Denise, and he never again evinced that moment when something like genuine regret, or caring, crossed his face as it had the time he had accused me of asking presumptuous questions.

I saw so little of him I was astonished one morning driving to the Culver City post office box to see a billboard advertising aftershave with Jonathan's handsome face and shirtless torso, staring into a mirror and beaming at the bottle of aftershave he held in his hand. I hadn't known that he was doing commercials. As I scooped the mail out of our post office box, I brightened to see Terrence's distinctive handwriting on the envelope, though when I read it, my heart broke and fear for him seemed to ice over my veins.

Tuesday

Liza Jane,

 Somewhere there's a blues song, or there ought to be, "Just got out of the Montgomery jail."

 Police crackdown on car pool drivers nabbed me for being black behind the wheel and having people in the car. When the cop saw my California driver's license, it was all over but the black eye and the bloody lip.

 In jail with me here was an old man named Moses Shaw whose father was born a slave. He and I had the same split lip and the same black eye from the same left-handed cop. Moses told me he had an old Model T out behind his barn that hadn't run since '28. He fixed it up and started driving it every day into town picking up people who needed a ride to work. This is his third arrest. He and I came up before the judge on the same day. The judge said he set Moses Shaw's bail low so Moses wouldn't be dying in the Montgomery jail and a lot of outside agitators and northern radicals (he looked right at me) bellyaching in the press how Alabama was unkind to their Negroes. He really said that. "Our Negroes," like we could still be deeded, stamped, delivered. Moses just said "Yes sir" to the judge, polite as pie, and when the judge asked him to sign, he made an X. He tipped his hat to me and Rev Cooke and said "See you round," and he left.

 I was told to leave Montgomery and that the judge and the law wouldn't answer for my safety if I stayed. My lawyer said if I knew what was good for me, I'd do just like Moses Shaw and say Yes sir to that white judge and get my black ass out of the court-room. If I was really smart, I'd leave Alabama altogether and go back to California. Another charge like this, and I could go to

*prison for sure. My bail was high, but Rev Cooke paid it. When
we went to get my Ford, all four tires were slashed, the battery was
gone, the ignition wires were cut, the front and back windows were
smashed into a million pieces, and there was no back seat, not even
springs. We just left it and walked away.*

> *Don't worry 'bout the black eye, Liza Jane. I've had worse,
and at least my nose wasn't broken, and I don't need stitches.*
> *Love,*
> *T*

Don't worry about the black eye? What about the Montgomery
judge who could send him to an Alabama prison? A judge who
would not look kindly on an outside agitator. I envied Coralee and
Ruby their faith in God, that they could ask God to protect someone they loved when they were powerless to protect him. What did
I have? *Here's looking at you, kid,* I murmured over and over whenever I thought of Terrence and feared for the danger he was in.

For the next two weeks, even if he couldn't drive, be part of
the action, he certainly knew how to witness and write. Terrence's
Challenger stories read like verses of "The Ballad of Moses Shaw,"
complete with photos. Terrence was on hand to record when
Moses Shaw got arrested again, but this time his Model T "got
lost." Next he hitched a pair of mules to a wagon and used that to
haul people. Arrested again, this time for driving an illegal vehicle
on the city streets, his wagon came back as kindling, and his mules
hadn't been fed in days. The sense of civic engagement, excitement, danger, and endurance in Montgomery bubbled off the
pages. Terrence published a stirring story describing when one
hundred fifteen people (fourteen ministers in addition to Reverend
Cooke) were indicted by a grand jury on an obscure 1921 law that
forbade boycotts. He recorded in colorful detail people, often in
big groups, going joyously to the courthouse to turn themselves in
for breaking that stupid law, a civic parade that became a celebration, a sight that uplifted and solidified the cause.

Terrence's letters were more personal. He described at length homes he had been invited into. Meals he had shared. Music he had heard. Church pews he had sat in. Cafés where he'd had sweet tea. Bars where he'd had cold beers. The people he had met and come to know.

> *Staying with the Cookes is like putting on a pair of glasses and all sorts of things come into focus that I didn't see before. When I tell people here that my father was from Alabama, they're so courteous, so warm that it feels like I've been adopted, even though I tell them I don't know nothing about him. People here have taken me to their hearts in a way I can't explain, except that*
>
> *Well, honey, I just came back to the page after dinner, and I'm just going to have to let it go at that. I can't explain.*
>
> *Love, T*

That night, I couldn't fall asleep, and when I finally did, in my dreams a shadowy figure appeared, old, stooped, his back to me, walking down a dusty road in a landscape I did not know. I called after him, but I didn't know his name, and he did not heed my voice or turn around.

CHAPTER THIRTY

From the beginning, Carleton Grimes made a big show of Paragon's commitment to *Adios Diablo*. He invited me to come to the massive publicity send-off from Union Station, a private train that would take everyone to El Paso, where they would be met by an armada of trucks and vans to cross into Mexico for what was supposed to be a thirty-six-day shoot. Hiring the private train, he told me, actually cost less than regular tickets and freight rates for all the cast and crew, which was over a hundred people, and the vehicles and sets and costumes. He had another consideration as well: With a private train, there would be no question of segregated cars once they crossed into Texas. I was impressed at his foresight; Leon would not have thought of that.

Two mariachi bands played lustily, wandering through the vast, vaulted station. Katy Jurado, Golden Globe winner for her role in *High Noon*, gave a speech in English and Spanish. *Adios Diablo* had no major stars (Paragon could not afford them), so Carleton asked for a favor from none other than Grace Kelly. Once word went out that the Oscar-winning actress would be there, the local television stations, radio, and fan magazine magpies flocked to the publicity event. Miss Kelly graciously allowed herself to be photographed with the cast, including Clayton Strong, who waved to me. (When he auditioned for the role, and got the part, Clayton sent a dozen roses to Clara Bow Drive with the message, *No more togas. Regards and thanks, Clayton Strong.*)

For Miss Hedda Hopper's note-taking benefit, Carleton Grimes introduced her to the new young director, Sam Pepper, and the writer, Art Luke. Sam Pepper flattered Miss Hopper. Art, a man not known for his charm, was short with her, and to make amends, Carleton described Art as the Gary Cooper of writers, a savvy choice that made Miss Hopper blush like a maiden beneath her flower-and-feather-laden hat. Carleton also had extraordinarily nice things to say about me, calling me the most interesting woman in Hollywood. Hedda insisted we have lunch sometime soon.

Was it possible to nibble a shrimp salad and be in mortal peril? Yes. Hedda Hopper was as effusive as she was dangerous, offering sotto voce confidences and all sorts of gossip, including who was sleeping with whom. God forbid she should allude to me and Terrence, or insinuate anything about Jonathan and Denise—not on behalf of Denise (or Jonathan for that matter), but for Leon's sake. My nerves made me break out in a rash along my back. As she held her little silver pen over a notebook, I remained perfectly *charmant*, but drank only Fernet-Branca. The bitter, medicinal tonic reminded me with every sip that my whole life, personal and professional, was based on duplicity of one sort or another, on lies, evasions, pretense, and subterfuge. I kept thinking that the very names she lauded (Hedda had done her homework)—Charlie with his coup at Empire, Maurice with his success at MGM, Art Luke's first major screenplay on its way to El Paso, Jimmy Ashford, who had just been made a lead writer on *Gunsmoke*—all four were equally pretending to be something they were not, fronting for men whose reputations Hedda had helped to torpedo. If she knew my role with these writers, she would tear me to shreds and put me on one of her hats. And if she knew I was shacked up with a reporter for the *Challenger* who was covering the bus boycott in Montgomery, what had happened to Diana Jordan would look like hopscotch compared to what Miss Hopper would do to me.

Popeye probably had an aneurysm a few days later when he was parked on Clara Bow Drive. A convoy of enormous tail-finned cars lined the curb and Hedda herself stepped out of a white Cadillac. She wore a peach-colored suit that dazzled the eye, long white gloves, and a hat with long peach-colored feathers that waved gaily when she walked.

"How quaint," she exclaimed, coming into the house, "to have your offices here on this lovely leafy street."

"We'd be pleased if you didn't mention that," said Thelma. "There are zoning regulations, you know, and we don't want trouble."

Thelma showed her into my office, where I greeted her. New desk, smart chairs, modern lighting, modern art, new curtains (closed) and no copy of the *Challenger* in sight. While the photographers were setting up (I only let myself be photographed from the left), Hedda and I chatted away, and when we parted, it was with effusive goodbyes and cheek-brushing kisses.

Her piece, when it appeared, was a confectionary gem. "Roxanne Granville, daughter of Sir Rowland Granville, the great British actor, granddaughter of Leon Greene of Empire Pictures, bravely struck out into a show business avenue of her own. The Granville Agency has championed the young and unknown, seeking out wonderfully talented, unsung writers who are rapidly rising in stature and numbers." In addition to some quotes from me and the flattering, even glamorous photograph, Hedda sought quotes from associates. Leon (or his office) complied with a sugared statement. Maurice Allen lauded my insight and excellent taste. Charlie said (probably ironically) that I knew how to recognize genius. Jimmy Ashford said the Western will live forever thanks to Roxanne Granville. Carleton Grimes said again, for print, that I was one of the most interesting women in Hollywood. Art Luke was in Mexico. Just as well.

"You know," said Thelma as we read the article, "I bet this is what it was like to run a speakeasy back in Prohibition. You know you're illegal, but you're offering up something everyone wants." The phone rang and she picked up. "Granville Agency." She turned to me, smiling, and put the phone in my hand.

"The trials are over," said Terrence, his voice laced with weariness, "and Dr. King's been found guilty of boycotting, and so have the others, including Reverend Cooke. Everyone's out on bail, and they're appealing, and it'll just go through the courts now, maybe all the way to the Supreme Court."

"That will take months," I said. "Maybe years."

"Yeah, so now it's just a question of endurance. And they will endure. Make no mistake of it. They will overcome too, but for now they will endure."

"Will you stay there and wait with them?" I asked, appalled to think how long he might be gone.

"I'm too restless to sit around while the courts churn through these motions. I'm coming home."

"Oh, Terrence! When?"

"I don't know. Soon."

"I'm here. I love you. I'll always love you."

The operator demanded more coins and cut us off before he could say he loved me.

CHAPTER THIRTY-ONE

We didn't see Popeye anymore after that blitz of praise from Hedda Hopper. I liked to think that J. Edgar himself called Popeye and said, "Popeye, there's no place on god's green earth a Red can hide from Hedda Hopper, and if she says these people at the Granville Agency are A–OK, well, that's good enough for me. Besides, this girl is related to my dear old pal, Leon Greene, so never mind staking out Clara Bow Drive, Popeye. Go torment someone else."

I gave this speech to Thelma, but she wasn't nearly as amused as I had hoped she would be. She didn't even laugh. She just said, "Ten days without seeing Popeye is just that. Ten days. Nothing more. We keep everything, all our precautions, just as they are." And with that she returned to her typing.

One early afternoon I came back to Clara Bow Drive from an appointment at Paramount and pulled up behind the oleander blockade. Humming "Little Liza Jane," my arms full of scripts, I opened the door, but everything fell to the floor when I saw Terrence sitting there, his elbows resting on his knees, a suitcase on one side, the Royal on the other, his gaze on the floor. He stood, with a kind of weariness that seemed to me etched into his face, into the marrow of his bones. He opened his arms to me, and I went to him, the joy of his homecoming flooding through me. I held him, my cheek against his chest, the sound of his breathing, the beat of his heart music to my ears, the pleasure of his name on my lips.

"I missed you something fierce, Little Liza. Something fierce. I took a cab from Union Station straight here."

"Go on, leave," said Thelma. "I'll cancel everything for tomorrow, Roxanne. Go take some time to be together." She put her arms around both of us. "Don't even pick up the scripts. Just go!"

As usual, we put the top up on the MG (otherwise, with a convertible, we were too conspicuous) and his suitcase and the Royal in the trunk. When I didn't have to shift gears we held hands, and when we reached PCH, I felt a glorious burst of happiness that translated into speed.

"You better slow down," said Terrence. "They'll arrest you."

I started to protest, but one look at his serious face, and I lightened up on the gas pedal. I kept (almost) to the speed limit as we drove north. The hillsides were awash in a dusty green and sprinkled with golden California poppies, wildflowers waning in the spring heat.

"I've forgotten all this," he remarked. "Forgot everything except you, Liza Jane." He put his strong hand on my knee, and my heart lit with happiness, and the conviction of being loved.

As we dashed up the stairs, Bruno saw us and started barking wildly, but he must have been chained up, because he didn't jump the fence. Terrence paused just briefly on the porch to look out over the beach, the sea, and the horizon, a view he had always loved. I opened the door (the matchbook still securely in place) and we dropped the suitcase and the typewriter on the floor and hungrily made our way to the bed, where the five months of our being parted had pent up in both of us. We made love swiftly, intensely, remembering each other's bodies with every possible sense: touch, taste, scent, words. We slept and woke, and had something to eat, and he talked in a roundabout, anecdotal way of his time in Alabama. I noticed right away that his speech had slowed in the months he'd been gone. Even the way he used language had slid into an easy vernacular, as if August Branch's insistence on correct usage had slipped his mind altogether. His talk was peppered with more biblical allusions than I remembered, and phrases I didn't recognize. What is a hissy fit? What is Hoppin' John?

We talked until other hungers came over us, and we made love again, slower, not so urgent, deeper and more tender, more gratifying. By the time I woke again, it was full dark, and I got out of bed, drank a glass of wine, read a little, and then came back and slid in beside him. I put my arms around him, whispered as he tossed and turned. "I'll always be here." He eased, and reached over and patted my behind before he slept again. I lay awake for a long time listening to the sound of his breathing, gratified that Terrence had come home to me unharmed, that he was home to stay.

But Terrence had brought a thousand strangers with him. These strangers filled up the house and spilled out onto the porch and down to the beach. Montgomery seemed to move into Malibu. Over a big breakfast he talked about the people he had ferried back and forth to work in his old Ford. Some were nameless but vivid. Some specific people I could see as clearly as if they stood in front of me, like a scrawny little firebrand named Miss Jessie, and people like Jo Ann Robinson, Ralph Abernathy, Martin Luther King, Mr. E. D. Nixon, the Reverend Elijah Cooke, Mrs. Cooke, the Cooke daughters, the Cooke grandchildren, Mrs. Cooke's great-aunt Patience and their neighbor Alice Washington.

Yes, Terrence was home for good, but he was significantly changed in ways great and small, not just his speech patterns. He sugared his coffee and used milk in it, when he used to take it black. He had put on weight. He said it was all those meals with the Cookes—Mrs. Cooke's cocoanut cake, Aunt Patience's snap beans, and Alice Washington's short ribs took him right back to childhood. He spoke of a Mrs. Gilmour's pork and greens and sweet potato pie. He spoke of music I had never heard of before, music he had never heard of before, for that matter, blues musicians who played in Montgomery bars and honky-tonks. He had brought back some records, Muddy Waters, Big Mama Thornton, Sister Rosetta Tharpe, music utterly unlike the sophisticated West Coast Cool of the Comet Club. On the old upright he thumped out some of their bluesy chords, repetitive progressions with a melancholy undertow and a rumbling bass line. He played for half an hour and then looked up and smiled. "Sorry," he said, "I just got lost."

"I missed you every minute you were gone," I said, going to him, putting my hands on his shoulder and my cheek against his hair. "I love you, and I will always love you. Do your worst. I will always love you best."

"My worst? What does that mean?"

"Just some lyrics rolling around in my head, I can't remember the song. Put a dime in the juke box, and see what you get," I said, as he turned to me, wrapped his arms around me, pressed against my breasts, ran his hands up under my shirt.

"You're not wearing a bra," he whispered, "not even a lacy one."

"I wanted to be ready for you."

His hand slid down between my thighs. "Are you ready for me?"

"Oh yes. I'm ready."

Later that afternoon Terrence took Charlie's surfboard out, but it was too cold to surf, and besides, Bruno jumped his enclosure and raced to the water's edge, mad with doggy delight to see Terrence home. Terrence splashed out of the water, lay the board on the beach, knelt, and greeted the dog. Shivering, his teeth chattering, he wrapped up in a towel and sat down beside me. I shared my body warmth with him, and Bruno plopped down on the other side. The brief saltwater swim seemed to have washed off the last of his weariness, and his old energy returned.

"You know, Liza Jane, I look out to that horizon and all I see is middle age staring at me. I'm twenty-seven, and I oughta do something now if I'm ever gonna do it."

"I thought you loved being a reporter."

"Alabama made me think. A reporter sticks to the facts of that one day, he sees things in dollops, this day, and that day, this fact and that. He writes it up in dollops. I keep thinking there's a book in this, in what I experienced down there. Because the facts themselves don't answer, don't tell the whole story. You gotta look beyond the facts. When you write a book, you gotta ask what things mean, make sense of the whole. What I experienced in Montgomery, it was biblical, Roxanne, biblical. I thought I was going down to Montgomery to report. I didn't know I was going to watch a whole city play Moses. In Montgomery they weren't just staying off the bus, they're leading ourselves out of bondage."

"Turn it into a novel."

"Oh no. In August Branch's world, you make stuff up, you going to hell."

"All right. Not a novel. Write about Moses Shaw. You made him into a powerful figure. Heroic."

"Well, he was heroic, baby, but that's just it. He went about being heroic just as if he was plowing a furrow. Up one side, down the other. He never protested his arrests, never fought back when they lit into him. He seemed unchanged. Like Job. How does a man live like that?"

"I don't know," I replied truthfully.

"He was old, with white nappy hair, broken teeth, sleepy eyes. He didn't talk much, and when they arrested him, he just said 'Yessir.' He couldn't read or write. He signed his papers with an X. But it was like he'd seen everything and this was his part and he was content with it. I admired him . . ." Terrence watched a gull circle overhead, and Bruno jumped up and chased it away, fearlessly returning to us like a champion. "I admired Moses Shaw, but I sure as hell don't want to be him, Roxanne. Every furrow he dug with that mule drove him deeper till he can't see out of it, can't see over it. Everything he did, every time he drove those mules into the city and picked people up, every time he was arrested, he did it without vision, or maybe even hope. His name didn't suit him. He wasn't a leader, a Moses looking for a sign from a burning bush. He just did this one heroic thing, not even thinking, not even knowing it was heroic, taking these people to work, just because it needed to be done, not that there was any reward or satisfaction in sight. But that kind of patience, it won't answer anymore. We'll never get what we want, what we deserve—what we need—and I don't just mean riding the bus and sitting where we damned well want to. I mean freedom for a man to be a man, and not a boy or a sexless uncle, or for a woman to be a woman, and not a victim, or a sexpot, or a fat old mammy. The absolute right to assume that our children deserve the same education as white children, that we deserve the same pay, and we'll never get that if we wait for it like Moses Shaw. Moses Shaw"—Terrence shook his head—"damned if he didn't just get to me, baby. More than anyone. More than Elijah Cooke, more than Martin Luther King. Moses Shaw taught me it's not enough to endure."

I ran my hand over Terrence's hair. "You need to write this book, baby. You do."

"He made me think of all those beaming colored folks who been standing at attention for two hundred years, smiling, Little Black Sambo, Uncle Ben, Aunt Jemima, Uncle Tom, like Clarence Goodall, just waiting to serve you fine white folks."

"That is a pretty cruel thing to say about a man who loved you like a father."

"Uncle Tom," he said again. "It's no worse than you've said about Leon rooting out the Red vermin. You can love someone without admiring everything they do. Clarence Goodall looked after the Greenes, your family, before he looked after his own. What else can you call a man who didn't have Christmas day with his own people for thirty years?" He stroked Bruno's shiny coat and stared out to the ocean. "I've been changed forever, Roxanne. Forever. I tell you when I tried to buy the Ford from that white man, and he put me through my groveling paces, all that jive shit, I wanted to kick that cracker's teeth in. But Elijah Cooke? I watched him—an educated, upright man, a wise man, a good man, a better man than that cracker could even dream of being!—and he *expected* to be treated like Uncle Elijah. He was ready. He knew what he had to do. And that cracker was ready. They were all ready to say what needed to be said. Just like everyone knew they would."

"Everyone but you."

"Everyone but me." Terrence shook his head slowly. "But you know what, Roxanne? When Elijah Cooke was done with his routine, with saying what that cracker wanted him to say, behaving like he was expected to behave, he looked at me, and with his eyes, he told me, you better do the same, Terrence. And by god, I did it. I hated myself, but I did it. I knew if I didn't, the suffering would spread far beyond me and this cracker. I did it. You see what I'm telling you?"

"I do. A year ago I would not have, but I do now." I leaned my head against his knees.

Terrence took a steep breath. He swallowed audibly. "I think my daddy grew up just like that. Up from slavery, but he couldn't wash it off. Maybe when he left us, he went back to Alabama where everyone expected his hands to be dirty." He paused and gulped with emotion. "Maybe that's why he left us."

I raised my head up and looked into his eyes. They were round with pain suppressed; his lips roiled briefly with words unspoken. He was shivering. "Let's go to bed, honey. Come on."

He threw the towel over his shoulders and picked up the board, and we started back toward the house. George Wilbur came out and called for his dog. Bruno, seeing we were going inside, ran to him. George put a leash on the dog and turned away without so much as a wave.

I went to the grocery store that evening and came back with champagne and steaks and all the newspapers—LA and out-of-town—I could find. (Terrence always liked to spread them out on the bed and see who was covering what.) I came up the steps and stopped for a moment, listening to him pounding on the Royal, the regular ping of the carriage, Muddy Waters low on the hi-fi, sounding from the inside, the slow insistent roll of the ocean on the outside. My heart soared with happiness: I opened the door, and he looked up from the Royal and smiled at me. *He feels it too,* I thought, *this happiness, this love, this strength we take and give to each other.* I went into the kitchen to pop the champagne and panfry the steaks. Even I could panfry a steak.

Later, finishing the last of the champagne by the fire, I said, "Does Mr. Branch know you're back?"

"No, but he knows I'm coming back."

"Let's go to Baja for a few days. We can just be ourselves there."

"Can't. I gotta lot of work in front of me."

"Can't it wait a day or so?"

"It's already waited a day or so. I'm here with you, aren't I?"

The phone rang and I reluctantly got up to answer, wishing immediately that I had just let it ring. Charlie Frye started lambasting me with every vile name he could think of, and then finally he blurted out in what sounded like a rush of tears, "Leon is going to fire me, Roxanne!"

"What? Who told you this?"

"It's gossip. All over the Writers' Building, all over the studio. People look at me like I'm a zombie, the walking dead."

"You have a contract." In the background I could hear a low buzz of voices and laughter. "Where are you?"

"Max Leslie had a contract, didn't he?"

"Please don't use his name."

"Your old pals Simon and Nelson had contracts! Leon hates me. He hated me from the time the picture started shooting. Leon knows I fronted for a Red."

"He doesn't know," I said with more conviction than I felt, since I was certain he had guessed. "Your name is on both scripts. You wrote them."

"Like hell. What about the rewrites? I couldn't do those until you started taking them out to Max's place."

"I never took them out there."

"Well, whatever the hell you did. Before that . . ." He fell into a weeping spasm.

"Where are you?" I asked again.

"I'm in a fucking phone booth in a bar, Roxanne. I'm drunk and I want my old surfboard back. I miss it. I want my old life back. I miss it. I wish I'd never met you. I wish I'd never heard of Max Leslie."

"Please don't use his name."

I heard the door of the phone booth squeal open, and he yelled out, "Max Leslie is not rotting down in Mexico! He's here in California turning out comedies for his old studio using a stooge for a front. A stooge who is about to be fired!" The door on the phone booth squealed shut, and Charlie started to hiccup.

I wanted to slap him for that, but I made my voice low and comforting. "*Fly Me to the Moon* is doing well, Charlie. It's a huge success. Why would they fire you?"

"I didn't have any real part in that picture. I was nothing but an errand boy for Max, and Leon knows it. I'm suing you and Leon and Empire."

"Rethink that. Remember Melvin Grant."

"Fuck him, fuck all of you! You talked me into fronting for a Red!"

"You said you were honored!"

"Well, I'm not honored anymore. I'm screwed! I'm sick of it. I'm sick of all the pretending, of the lying and sneaking around and the rewrites that had to come by way of Covina."

"Covina?"

"Yeah, you called me that night, remember?"

Only vaguely. And I surely did not remember telling him where I was calling from.

"I'm a damned good writer! You just never saw it. You never believed in me. *Coast of Heaven*—"

He rattled on about his masterpiece and how I had neglected it and him, and I wanted to say maybe they were firing him because he'd rather surf than work, but I could not be that cruel. I tried to soothe him, but finally he just blew himself out, like a storm, and I heard him sobbing against the phone, and with one last "Fuck you," he clicked off.

Terrence had sat silent through all this, his brow knitted. When I finally hung up, I felt weak, light-headed; he rose and came to me, put his arms around me. I sagged against him.

"Oh, Terrence, I'm scared . . . What have I done?"

"Come on, baby. It'll be all right. Charlie will sleep it off. Come to bed. It'll be a long day tomorrow."

We slept badly, both of us. We both woke before the alarm. I showered and made the coffee, and when Terrence came out to get a cup, he was dressed in the same rumpled, travel-worn clothes he'd brought home with him, and he carried the suitcase.

"You don't need to take all those clothes back to Naomi Avenue. I'll wash them at the office."

"No. I don't want you washing my shirts, doing my laundry. You're not a wife."

"I don't mind. I don't see it as some sort of comedown."

"No. I always take everything to the dry cleaner next door to the *Challenger*." He poured the coffee, laced it with milk and sugar. "Let's go. Are you still putting the matchbook in the door like I showed you?"

"Yes. Every time I leave the house."

"Good." He picked up the suitcase and went downstairs.

The MG, as if on its best behavior, started right up. "I'll take you to Naomi Avenue," I said, "so you can change before you go to work. I've never seen this famous place with its hot plate and garage."

"No. I'll go to Clara Bow Drive with you. I'll call a cab from there."

"I can take the time."

"No. I'll call a cab. It's better that way."

"What way?"

"Just let's go to the office."

"Why can't I drive you to Naomi? What's suddenly so wrong, Terrence?"

Terrence took a deep breath, like the kind you do when you're out there in the ocean, and you see a really big wave coming at you, and you know the only way to avoid its crashing down on you is to go under, deep down, to duck beneath the onslaught. "When there comes the day, Roxanne, that whatever's wrong or right with us is just you and me, well, fine, but it ain't that day now. Not in Montgomery, and not in Malibu, and it sure as hell ain't that way on Central Avenue."

"I don't understand." I took my eyes from the road and glanced over at him.

His gaze was straight ahead, his mouth firm, emotionless as a figure on a medallion.

"I been gone five months to Alabama, and when I come home, I cannot be driving up Central Avenue, or anywhere near it, with you in a fine little British sports car."

"Is it the car?"

Terrence gave a harsh, rueful laugh. "You are the living end, girl! Do you really think that?"

My birthmark flushed. "You don't want to be seen with me."

"It's not personal."

"You always say that." We rode in silence. The tension between us seemed to generate toxic fumes, or maybe that was just more trouble with the MG. "Are you ashamed of me? Of loving me?"

"I came to you first. I missed you something terrible. Isn't that enough for you?"

Terrence turned on the radio, and the Platters came on with "The Great Pretender." He turned his face away from me, and switched off the radio before it finished. He kept his gaze out the window.

"You are ashamed, aren't you? You are ashamed of me, of loving me!"

He didn't answer right away, and when he did, it was as if this were a question he had long pondered. "I suppose I am. I suppose I'm ashamed that I had to come to you before anyone else, before anything else. I should have gone to the paper. The *Challenger* needs me. I should not have come to my white girlfriend first."

"Aren't you going to tell me again that it's not personal?" I snapped. "It's pretty damn personal to me! Far be it for me to—"

"Don't do this, Roxanne. Don't make me choose."

"I'm not making you choose! But I want to know what's wrong with loving me!"

"Everything. Everything! Oh, Lord! Don't you get it? If I drive along Central Avenue with you, anyone who sees me, they're not gonna ask, 'Well, Terrence, tell us what was it like in Alabama during the bus boycott? How was the fight down there, Terrence? What did you think of all those folks walking back and forth to work, miles every day now for five months?' No, they're gonna say: 'Who was that white woman?' Can't you dig it, Roxanne? That's not what I want to talk about when I come back home!"

"Malibu isn't home to you?"

"No."

"Just where you get laid regularly, is that it?"

"Sure. That's it. Just drive, will you?"

We did not speak again until I turned on Clara Bow Drive. I pulled in behind the oleander barricade and got out of the car, and without another word to Terrence, I unlocked the door and went directly through to my office. I heard the dialing of the phone, Terrence calling for a cab. I wept quietly until the tears seeped between my fingers and mascara streaked my hands. I wanted him to come to me. To take me in his arms.

He knocked gently on the door. "I don't know when I'll be back. It depends on how much they need me at the paper." When I did not answer, he added, "I'll wait outside."

"Wait wherever you want."

"You can always tell the neighbors I'm the guy who mows your lawn if you need a reason for me to be in this neighborhood."

I heard him close the door, and ten minutes later I heard a cab pull up and drive away.

By the time Thelma arrived at the office, I was a sodden mess of tears, smeared makeup, red eyes, and mussed hair. Still blubbering, I told her about Charlie's phone call, and that he was being fired.

"All right," she said, "so Charlie's on the rampage. I'm not sorry to lose him for a client, are you?"

"No, but he might be dangerous now."

"He's always been dangerous, Roxanne. He's like Jonathan Moore. These are men who cannot see beyond their own shadows, who don't want to see beyond their shadows, who don't give a good goddamn for anyone but themselves, but Charlie Frye doesn't mean enough to you that you'd cry your eyes out over him. What's happened with Terrence?"

"Nothing."

"Horseshit. You were on cloud nine when he came home. Now look at you."

Wadding a Kleenex, I told her of our fight in the car this morning, and she shook her head.

"But can't you really see! Don't you understand what he's telling you? When he comes back—he's been writing about the Montgomery boycott for months, months of struggle, black people against white people, and when he gets back to the *Challenger*, he'll be the hero of the hour. You want him to drive up with a white girl?"

"But I'm not the enemy, Thelma! I love him!"

"Then have the wisdom to let him be! Jesus Jumping Christ, Roxanne! He'd look like a hypocrite. He owes it to the *Challenger*—and the people who read the *Challenger*—not to come driving back home with you." The phone rang. "If people knew how much love can hurt, they would take better care of their hearts," she said on her way to answer it.

I went to the bathroom to wash my face and restore my makeup, and when I came back out I heard Thelma desperately trying to placate whoever was on the line.

"Don't cry. Don't cry," Thelma pleaded. "Look, I don't know who. Jesus. Yes, you did the right thing. You both did. No, I'm not leaving you there alone. I'll be there in the next couple of hours." She offered more soothing words, then put the receiver down. "That was Marian." Her hands trembled as she held a match to her cigarette. "Max went out for a pack of cigarettes and a process server showed up at their door. Another subpoena from the Committee. If he ignores it, it's contempt of Congress. Marian packed up Max's passport, their checkbook, and a suitcase with his clothes, climbed out the back window, and waited at the end of the alley for him. She told him to leave right away."

"Where can he go? Mexico?"

"No, he'll never go back there. Probably England, if he can still use his passport. He'll leave the car at the San Francisco airport. She and I will drive up and get it sometime when . . . Oh, Roxanne! We were all so careful! How did they know where to find him?"

I sank down in the chair across from her, blistering my brain for possibilities. "Charlie?"

"Did he know about Riverside?"

"No, but he knew about Covina. I must have let it slip."

"Covina isn't Riverside. Maybe they traced Marian through her dead sister who lived in Riverside for years."

"Maybe they found out where Norman was."

Thelma's face went a ghastly gray, and she nodded. "They found out where Norman was, and they waited for Marian to show up, and they followed her home."

"That's why we haven't seen Popeye. They found out where Max was. That's what they wanted."

She reached in her desk drawer and took out her purse. "I'm going out to Riverside to get her, to take her to my place. You want to close up, and come with me?"

"No. I have to telephone Terrence and apologize for having a hissy fit."

Oh yes, I now knew what that was. Roiling with self-recrimination, kicking myself for how I had gotten everything wrong, I called the *Challenger* but I could not get through to Terrence. I called so often even the paper's operator lost patience with me, declaring that she had given him the message and would I please quit calling. The *Challenger* was beset with important calls. I wanted to say, hey, my call is important, but I didn't. I canceled my appointments for the rest of the day and waited for Terrence to phone.

When finally he did, late that afternoon, I could hear all the noise of the newsroom in the background and I knew he couldn't really talk. It was a short conversation. Even though I apologized at tearful length, I did not whine or ask when he was coming home. Terrence said I shouldn't worry about a little spat. He had to go.

"All right," I said, "I love you."

He said he loved me too, but his voice was neither rich with emotion, nor urgent with lust. Wistful, maybe.

CHAPTER THIRTY-TWO

Terrence Dexter was a returning hero. A photograph of Terrence and Mr. Branch ran two columns across the pages of the *Challenger*, along with a long, eloquent thought-piece about what the bus boycott had achieved, even though no immediate victory was in sight. The president of the LA chapter of the NAACP came to thank him personally; that photograph too was splashed across the front page, with an article about the boycott and its political and social significance written by none other than C. Vann Woodward, a famous historian. A two-column photo accompanied the *Challenger* piece about Jefferson High School students honoring him with a certificate of merit, and pastors of a dozen churches extolled him from their pulpits and in print. He recorded many radio interviews with those stations that played black music, talking about the appeals going through the courts, about the people still walking to work, the necessity of the Shoe Drive, the moral and civic strength of the Montgomery Improvement Association and their commitment to change. The major LA dailies, the *Times* and the *Herald-Examiner*, interviewed Terrence.

In all this time, I did not see him once. Talked on the phone, now and then, short conversations. I kept my promise to myself, no pleading for him to come home, none of that. I had other things to worry about as well. I had to cancel any appointments that took me out of the office because (given our situation) we could not hire a temp, so I had to answer the phones while Thelma was driving Marian all over the San Fernando Valley looking for a facility that would take Norman. Finally they found a sort of residential hospital, but before Marian could move him from Riverside, a lot of money needed to change hands. I told Marian I would personally pay whatever would be necessary to place him there. That she should not worry. When she said a thousand dollars, I blanched, but since we were on the phone, she couldn't tell.

I went to the bank late that afternoon and got out the thousand dollars, cash, from my savings account to give to Thelma the next day. By the time I finally got on PCH late in the afternoon it was one long, clogged artery. As I sped around big, lumbering cars, sometimes passing on the shoulder, drivers honked at me and waved their fists out the window. Sirens blared behind me as I quickly eased back into my lane, and cop cars sped by on the shoulder, lights flashing. I finally came upon an awful wreck; a produce truck had smashed head-on into an Oldsmobile, and cantaloupes and melons were splattered across the road, and ambulances were roaring away.

Traffic thinned out further north, but when my house came into view on the left, my heart stopped in my chest. I thought to myself: *Wake up, Roxanne, wake up, wake up . . .* Because surely, surely, surely this is some sort of awful nightmare. *Wake up.* A sheriff's car was parked behind my place, lights flashing. *Wake up.* It was blocking in the Porsche and Charlie's woody station wagon. *Wake up.* As I leapt out of the MG I heard Bruno yapping, squealing in canine pain.

At the foot of the stairs I found the cinched lip Wilburs. George held the struggling Bruno's collar. I raced up to find Terrence Dexter spread-eagle, facedown on the porch, handcuffed. Two cops standing over him, one with his foot on Terrence's neck. As long as I live, I will never forget that sight. As long as I live. And there was Charlie Frye, beat up, his knuckles bloodied, holding a handkerchief over his bleeding nose but satisfied. No mistaking that.

"Hey, Roxanne!" he cried. "I came to take back my board, and I looked in the window and saw this jungle bunny through the window and—"

"Let him up! This instant! For god's sake, take your goddamn foot off of him, and let him up!" I pushed the cop who had his foot on Terrence's neck, and he stepped back while the other one, the younger one, murmuring *Now, miss*, pulled me away. "I am Roxanne Granville. I live here! This is my place."

"Well, you was about to be robbed, miss, and—"

"—He broke in," said Charlie, waving a finger at Terrence. "I went in to stop him, and there was a fight and—"

"That's ridiculous! Terrence! Oh, Terrence, what's happened?" I knelt down on the porch. Blood from his nose dripped over the bright red slash on his lower lip. His eyes blazed with rage.

"You know this man?" asked the older cop, a laconic middle-aged white guy with crew-cut hair and heavy, dark jowls.

"Yes. He's Terrence Dexter!" I stood up. "Take those cuffs off him immediately."

The cop yanked Terrence to his feet. There were bloodstains on his shirt. My gaze was riveted to Terrence, whose face was a mask of cosmic pain. "We think this boy is a burglar. Your friend"—the first cop nodded toward Charlie—"tried to stop him, and your neighbors saw the fight and called us."

The Wilburs, still holding fast to the barking setter, came up the stairs. "We saw a fight. Heard it too," said Mrs. Wilbur.

"How could you! You know Terrence! You know—" But I did not go on, because of course they *did* know Terrence, and that was exactly why they'd called the cops. Bastards. I took a deep breath. I put my hand on Terrence's arm, and to the older cop, I said clearly, slowly, "This man has every right to be here. He lives here."

"He lives here?"

"Show him the key, Terrence. Terrence has a key. Undo his hands and he can show you his key!"

Terrence controlled his voice with difficulty. He spoke as though spitting pennies. "The key is on the desk. Or it was before the fight."

"I insist you take those cuffs off him."

"You show me the key, miss, and I'll think about it."

"Wait here," I commanded, pushing past them, pushing past Charlie, who blathered at me about being finished with me, and coming to get his surfboard back because . . . I ignored him, and stepped into the house. Carnage everywhere: Pictures on the walls were all askew and the andirons lay abandoned on the floor, except for the one that had smashed the coffee table in half. Cushions were strewn about, and the place smelled of Scotch from a broken bottle. Terrence's shirts lay splayed across the floor like lily pads on a sea of unrest. The desk chair was overturned, and the vase was broken, the flowers lying in a sodden clump on the floor beside the antique music box. No key in sight. Maybe he meant the kitchen table. I ran in there, eyes darting everywhere looking for that goddamned key. The chairs were upended and the radio had been pulled from the shelf, and the coffeepot had fallen off the stove and coffee was puddled on the floor. There was broken crockery and jagged bits of broken glass and the oven door gaping open, but where, where was the goddamned key? I went back out to the living room and thrashed through the mess where, beneath the framed snapshots on the floor, I saw a glint of brass.

I snatched that key up and ran back out to the porch. I put the key in the older cop's hand. "This is the key. This is his home. Take those cuffs off of him." Trembling, I turned to the Wilburs and screamed, "Get out of here! Get out and don't ever come back!"

"Now, miss," said the younger cop, a kid who still had acne scars. "No need to yell. Your neighbors was just thinking of you." He nodded to the Wilburs, who had not moved, and to Charlie, who had smeared the blood from his nose across his cheek.

"Everyone was thinking of you, miss, trying to keep your place safe. That's all." At a nod from the older cop, he unlocked the handcuffs on Terrence.

"Yes," Terrence growled through clenched teeth. "That's all."

"So . . ." the older cop said dubiously, "you two married?"

"No."

"He's your boy-friend?" He put unfortunate emphasis on *boy*.

Before I could answer, Terrence grabbed my shoulders, turned me around to face him, and brought his bloodied lips down to mine, kissing me, his tongue seeking mine, kissed me with the kind of passion that in other circumstances would have had my skirts up instantly, except this was not an expression of love or even lust. This kiss was a slap. An act of ownership, as though I were property to be disposed of however he liked. In front of these cops, and at the expense of my own pride, I let him do that to me.

"I'll be goddamned," said the older cop.

"Shit," said Charlie, going gray. "Jesus."

"No charges, right?" I said, rubbing Terrence's blood off my lips. "No burglary. No harm done."

The older cop considered this. Lit up a cigarette and considered it.

I turned to the Wilburs again. "Get your dirty butts off my porch and don't ever come back!"

By the time they had oozed down the stairs, taking Bruno with them, the cop had gathered himself, and he asked the younger one for a sheaf of papers. "Let's see now . . ." He ruffled through them. "We actually have made an arrest here already. We have the paperwork, see? We'll need your information, Miss . . . ?"

"Granville. Roxanne."

"ID?"

"Here, Roxanne," said Mrs. Wilbur, coming back up the stairs, her voice huffy with outrage, "you dropped your handbag. You should thank me," she added. Her husband called her down.

I rummaged about and found my driver's license and gave it to him, and he duly noted the information: age, address, phone number. He asked my occupation. "I'm an agent. Granville Agency. Charlie is my client."

"Your ex-client," Charlie snarled. "I'm done with you. I only came here because you kept my old surfboard all this time."

The older cop took his time while we three stood trembling with rage, anxiety, hatred, a bubbling gumbo of awful emotions I hope never to experience again.

"I dunno," he said as he gave me back my license. "It was a suspected burglary, and a definite fight. Property damage. I might still have to report this."

I swooped up my handbag, opened it, and found the envelope with the whole thousand dollars in it, which I counted out, one hundred dollars at a time into the cop's hand. His eyes widened as the bills piled up. The younger cop inhaled a great big breath. I was shaking, but I mastered my rage, controlled my voice, so much so that I might have been Edward G. Robinson himself. "I'm sure everything will be fine now, Officer. It was all a misunderstanding."

He shoved the money into his pocket, then regarded Terrence with a judicious frown. "Any harm done? What do you think? What about you?"

Please God. Please don't let him say, "What about you, boy?" I feared for the look on Terrence's face. I stood in front of him.

Terrence cleared his throat and spat the words out like phlegm. "No harm done."

"And the . . . ?" The cop motioned over his own face.

"Did you do that to him?" I burst out. "Did you beat him up?"

"No harm done," said Terrence, his voice guttural.

The older cop looked at the papers in his hand. "So, you're a reporter? Who do you report to?"

"The *Challenger*."

"Never heard of it."

"Oh shit," said Charlie. "Are you the guy who just came back from Alabama reporting on the buses down there for that colored paper?"

"Nah," said Terrence in a manufactured drawl. "Us all looks alike. Y'all thinking of someone else, boss."

I leaned against Terrence's bloodied shirt. He gave off an electric current that felt like it would fry me on the spot. He took a step to the side. He did not want my protection. To the older cop I said, "He has a key. He lives here. There was no burglary." I stapled a smile across my mug. "It's a simple mistake. Right? Charlie?"

"I guess I made a mistake." Charlie felt gingerly over his swelling eye. "How was I to know you and—"

"Shut up. It's a simple mistake."

"Well, maybe." The cop folded up the paperwork, and would have pocketed it.

I stopped him. I know how this works. I was not Leon Greene's granddaughter for nothing. I held out my hand. "No, I need you to tear that up and give it to me."

"But it's official."

"Not anymore, it's not. It just cost me one thousand dollars for it not to be official."

Reluctantly the older cop tore up his forms and put them in my hand. They gave Terrence back his wallet, but not before he opened it, took out the cash, and gave it to the kid with acne scars. He opened Charlie's wallet and took out the cash, and gave that to him too. They both went down the stairs, the older one whistling "Dixie."

Terrence walked to the rail that framed the porch. Stood there, clutching, roiling his fists around the banister.

Charlie's lip curled in disgust. "I don't care what you paid that bastard cop, Roxanne, the world's gonna find out you've been sleeping with a Negro, and you're gonna be murdered in the press, and I'm gonna laugh."

"Get the hell out of here," said Terrence over his shoulder. And at that Charlie and his surfboard went downstairs.

People who had been watching this fracas from the beach slowly broke up their little gawking groups, and went their own ways. The waves washed in and out. Otherwise everything was eerily quiet; a muffled sunset floated uneasily at the horizon. I moved to embrace Terrence, but he shook me off. He stood as though rooted, as though he were some ten-ton black marble idol. His face was devoid of emotion, but his eyes were alive with fire. I felt as though I were living in geologic time, waiting for the rough fissures of earth to creak and teeter and realign the universe. After an eon, Terrence finally turned to me. I wrapped my arms around him, held him, pressing my cheek against his chest. I could hear his heart thudding, and his breath rasping, as though choking down emotion he could hardly control. Then he let go of me and went inside. I heard the bathroom door slam shut.

I followed him in. As I picked up the photographs, broken glass cut my fingertip. Drops of blood fell to the floor as I went into the kitchen and put my hand under the faucet and stood there weeping till I turned the faucet off, and I found I could not breathe. I had to think about breathing. In and out. In and out like the waves.

Terrence came up behind me, put his hands on my shoulders, turned me in his arms, held me. "Look at the mess they've made of what we had, Liza Jane."

"They didn't! They can't!" I moved to kiss him, but he drew back. "Don't pull away from me, baby. Please. They don't matter. Let's go make love, honey. Make love like we mean it! Like we mean it forever and ever. Don't give them the power to hurt us."

"We've lived with that power every day. I'm surprised it took this long, really. We never had a chance."

"Yes we did! We do! We—"

"Don't you want to know why the key was on the desk?"

"What?" I ran my hands roughly over my face. "It wasn't on the desk. The key was on the floor."

"Don't you want to know why it was on the desk before the fight?" He spoke slowly. Carefully.

"I don't care why. I don't care, baby. I don't care about anything except you."

"I was returning it to you. I was about to write you a note when your boyfriend, Charlie—"

"He's nothing to me!"

"—saw me from the porch, and came bursting in to save the white girl's house from being robbed by a black criminal. That's his first thought. Any of them, that's the first thought. Criminals. It's still the same old story. No matter what. No matter where. What happened here tonight has happened before. And it will go on happening. It will never change. This was Charlie being white and me being black. This was the Wilburs being white and me being black. They been waiting for this day, ever since they first saw us together. They loved seeing that cop cuff me, rough me up."

"They are bastards and they can go to hell!"

Terrence shook his head wearily. "That's why I gave you back your key, baby, because even before Charlie burst in and attacked me for a thief, before that sonofabitch sheriff beat the shit out of me, I knew it'll never change."

"What? What are you talking about?"

"You really don't have any goddamned idea what I'm talking about?"

"I love you, Terrence. What else matters? You love me. We can—"

"No, we can't."

"We can!"

"Are you really going to tell me you have the strength to fight this shit on a daily basis?"

"Yes."

"Well, I don't. And I don't think you do either. I don't think you even know what's at stake. You don't know. How could you? Never in a million years. I came here to tell you goodbye, Roxanne. I came back here to leave off your key and write you a note telling you it's over before you got home."

I wanted to protest and fume and fight and swear, to pound his chest and fling myself across his body, but I stopped blubbering long enough to look deeply into his eyes; they could not have been more opaque if he'd had shutters pulled over them. "I don't understand."

"Exactly," he said quietly. He placed his hand on my birthmark. "You are always afraid that this is what people see of you, first and foremost, this color on your face, before you open your mouth, before they know anything else about you. That's how they remember you. The girl with the stained cheek. Being instantly judged for something you cannot change. Being black isn't a choice. I cannot change that. That bastard tonight with his foot on my neck, he was just loving the power he had over everyone like me, my daddy, my granddaddy, my brother. Moses Shaw."

"Oh, what has Moses Shaw got to do with me! With us! I don't care what all this means, I only want to hold you, to be with you forever!"

"It means I can't be who I am and come home to you. I can't do it. I've had enough."

"Look, I know I was wrong the other day. I understand why you didn't want to be seen with me, why you didn't want me to drive you back to Naomi Avenue." By now I was smearing snot and tears away from my face, wiping my hands on my skirt. "I'm sorry I didn't understand at first. I do now. Really. It's—"

"It's over. When I came back from Alabama, I wanted you, I needed you, I needed to hold you and love you and be with you."

"You love me! And I love you, and we—"

"I don't want to love you anymore." Terrence breathed a long, sad sigh, the longest, saddest sigh I knew I would ever hear if I lived to be a hundred. "The truth is, baby, I do love you. If I didn't, I wouldn't have brought the key back. I would have just dropped you like I've dropped a hundred other girls."

"So you're leaving me just because I'm white?"

He dropped his hands from my shoulders. "I don't have the

strength to explain everything to you, to fight every hour of my waking life just to be with you, just to take on the world that's going to kick the shit out of me because I'm with you. You are a battle I don't want to fight, Roxanne. I want to have my strength at hand." His dark eyes searched my face, and he held out his powerful right hand. "As a man, I can't do the things I need to do with you as my woman. You know I'm right."

"Didn't you ever hear of Romeo and Juliet!"

"If they'd lived, the world would have beaten them down, to pulp. To dust. They'd have lost each other anyway. That's the real tragedy, not that they died. And that's what the world would do to us. Maybe one day in the future it won't cost a black man and a white woman everything they have, every ounce of strength and sinew and courage just to love each other, but that day sure as hell ain't now."

"That's what you learned in Montgomery? You're leaving me because I'm white and you're colored," I lashed out, knowing how he hated that term, using it like the vicious little tool I knew it to be.

"I can't believe you said that, Roxanne. Are you willing yourself stupid?"

"A brave man would stand by a woman he loved!"

"Not if every time he looked at her he saw the very thing he needed to defeat. You compromise me. It's that simple."

I felt those words as though he had struck me. I could feel my birthmark throbbing with blood and anger. "It's not simple!"

"It's not, but I'm done talking about it. Some things you just need to know in your bones, and if you don't know it in your bones, you never will know it at all."

"People who love each other need to be strong together. We can be strong together."

"I can't, not anymore, not and do everything else I need to do. I don't have that kind of strength, and neither do you."

"I do!"

"I don't." He ran a hand over his face and stared at the dried blood on his palm. "I had to kiss you in front of them like I did to prove to those bastards that I had a right to be your man. They'll never grant me that right, and don't you mistake, Roxanne, it's theirs to grant. Not yours, and not mine. I'll never be humiliated like that again, as long as I live. I'll kill someone first."

"Oh, Terrence, please take your key back. Let's be strong together. Aren't you the one who's always saying if you stumble, if the person you love helps you, you're both stronger for it?"

"Yes, and if you're not, then it's time to just pull up your pants and go home. And that's what I'm doing." He swooped up his shirts that were strewn among the debris, and he left. The door closed behind him. I heard his footsteps down the stairs and the Porsche as he fired it up and drove away.

The taste of ash in my mouth felt gritty, and my skin seemed to be breaking up, and cracking open, exposing my heart, my liver, my guts to the pyre. Something inside me was burnt up, and gone forever, and I was living in the crucible of my own life. With shaking hands, I poured myself a stiff drink and swilled it, just like they do in the Westerns before they dig the bullet out. I stumbled into the bedroom and fell into bed, crying until finally an uneasy sleep put me out of my misery, though sleep was punctuated with bizarre dreams from which I would wake, remember, and ache. I hurt, physically hurt, like the night of the fight at the Comet Club. When I woke in darkness, and further sleep eluded me, I slid my feet into some sandals, wrapped myself up in a blanket, and waded through the carnage out to the porch, down to the dunes and the beach. I sat, my knees pulled up against my chest, my head resting there, so deep in anguish I thought I might dissolve altogether. The waves swept in and out in their careless fashion, and the moon finally paled against a brightening sky.

CHAPTER THIRTY-THREE

"**W**hat the hell happened here?"

My eyes blinked slowly open to see Thelma wavering above the bed, her face contorted.

"Roxanne, talk to me!"

Groggy with sorrow so thick it lay leaden on my tongue, I could hardly speak. I roused slowly and sat on the edge of the bed.

"Oh, god, Roxanne. Look at you. Tell me what happened. I called and called and got a busy signal. I knew something must be wrong. The phone was off the hook." Thelma went to the bathroom and dampened down a towel. She mopped my face while I sobbed out the story of yesterday. Was it only yesterday? I felt as though I had aged a decade. Thelma muttered over and over, *Oh god, oh god* . . . When I finished, she ordered me into the shower.

"I can't. I can't move. I'm dead inside."

"You can. You must." She went in the bathroom, started the shower, roused me from the bed, and walked me in there.

By the time I emerged, my hair dripping, clad in Terrence's robe, debris from the fight had been swept, much of it, into piles.

"Wear your sandals," she called out. "There still might be glass on the floor."

I lurched into the kitchen and fell into a chair. The Royal in its case sat on the table.

"I found it underneath the desk," said Thelma as she put a mug of hot tea laced with sugar and milk in front of me. "Drink. You need it." She sat down beside me, put her hand gently on my arm. I had never noticed she had such knobby knuckles, or that her veins stood up like thick blue skeins. "He'll come to his senses, Roxanne. Terrence will be back. He loves you."

I started to cry all over again, and confessed that I had given the bastard cop the whole thousand dollars I intended for Marian. "Can Marian wait a few days? I don't think I can go to the bank today. I don't think I can move at all."

"Of course. Drink the tea. I'll make you some breakfast."

"I can't eat."

"You can. You have to. You're going to need your strength, dear."

I ate, got dressed, moved like a zombie back out to the living room, picked up the framed snapshot of Terrence and me, clutched it to my heart, and cried. At lunchtime, Thelma put a sandwich in front of me, and she sat by my side till I ate it, still holding the snapshot she had taken of the two of us.

I dialed the number at Naomi Avenue. The phone rang and rang. I dialed the *Challenger* and asked for Terrence. The switchboard operator said he was no longer there. "What do you mean?" But she hung up. I dialed Ruby's and when she came to the phone, I said, "This is Roxanne, and I'm looking for Terrence."

"Oh I just bet you are!" She gave me a nonstop five-minute tongue-lashing, no chance to defend myself, and finished up with "Handcuffed like a common criminal! His neck under the boot of some peckerhead cop! This man is a hero, and because of you, he's beat up and disgraced? Disgraced! You been bad for him all along, and now this? You go to hell, missy, and don't you never come back. Don't you never come back here, that's for sure!" The phone clunked once as she banged it against the wall before she hung up.

I called again, and this time Coralee picked up, as if she had been standing at the ready, knowing I would call back. "You think a man like Terrence is gonna take that kind of shame, and just say, it's all right, just give me another fist to the face, white boy? Handcuff me, facedown with your stinking foot on my neck? Treat me like a criminal? You think a man with any kind of pride gonna take that shit?"

"He's been handcuffed before. He was arrested at the Comet Club! What about Alabama?"

"The Comet Club, he was swooped up with a lotta others just happened to be in the wrong place. In Alabama, he's arrested 'cause he's part of something big, something grand, something gonna make a difference in the way people get to live in this world! But your place? He was a black man in a white woman's house, a thief sniffing up a white girl, whupped by some peckerhead because he must be a burglar. His loving you done him in."

"So you do know he does love me."

"He was leaving you, missy. Oh yeah, you think I didn't know that? I knew. He was leaving you, no matter what. He was going there to do the right, the decent thing, and give you back your damned key, and write you some sort of damned note. That's what got him arrested. And now's he's gone, and he ain't coming back and it's your fault."

"What do you mean, gone? There's no answer at Naomi Avenue. The *Challenger* said he wasn't there. Where has he gone?"

"You think I'd tell you shit about my little brother? Hell no."

"What do you mean, he's gone?"

"He sold the Porsche, and he's took the money and he's gone far away from you, Miss Summit-Drive-Ain't-I-Special. He's gone far from you and all your people. He's gone"—sobs caught in Coralee's throat—"and he ain't coming back."

"Where? Where did he go? Oh, god, don't tell me he went back to Alabama. Did he?"

"I ain't telling you shit. No one in my family gonna tell you shit. I never seen my brother so broke up. His pride ain't never gonna be the same." She slammed the phone down.

An intense headache descended on me, as if billiard balls suddenly cracked inside my head, that sharp, unmistakable sound of the laws of physics smashing into one another, hurtling toward some unseen destination. I placed the phone on the hook and turned to Thelma. "He's sold the car and gone somewhere, someplace I can't reach him, where love can't reach and love won't matter. Maybe he went back to Alabama. To look for the father he hasn't missed for twenty years? Terrible things can happen in Alabama."

"Terrible things happen right here in Southern California."

"How will I live without him, Thelma? How?"

"I don't know," she said, "but you will. You will have to."

CHAPTER THIRTY-FOUR

⟫

I am a daughter of Empire, born on a movie set and raised by a studio mogul and his wife, so I knew from experience that despite the thousand-dollar payoff, that deputy would find a way and a place to sell his information. And he did. Within a few days the story splashed all over the gossip columns and movie rags. The prose was mostly tittering, *naughty-naughty* accompanied by a picture of me taken at some society event placed beside a recent picture of Terrence, the much-lauded reporter just back from Alabama. There we were, white and black, so that there shall be no mistaking just how *naughty-naughty* we had been. Additionally Al Gilbert for *Secrets of the Stars* dug up Terrence's mug shot from the Comet Club fracas, as well as the picture of me, Diana, and Jonathan from that same night, thus resuscitating that whole scandal with the salacious imputation that I had followed Diana's lead and her bad behavior. Hedda Hopper's column was particularly outraged as she described the "foiled burglary" at the Malibu home of agent Roxanne Granville. Charles Frye, screenwriter of the recent hit *Fly Me to the Moon*, had arrived at her house to find an intruder, one Terrence Dexter, "a reporter for the *Challenger* recently returned from helping to organize radical Negroes in Alabama." Hedda clearly took especial relish in finishing up with "Mr. Dexter had his own key to their love nest."

Irene called immediately. She ranted at me for tempting fate and how stupid I was, but when I started to cry, she stopped.

"He's gone," I wept, "and everything we had reduced to vulgar smut. A love nest? I want to throw up."

"Go throw up then, and get it over with, for god's sake. I'm sorry it happened like this, but I'm not sorry he's gone. You are better off."

"How can you say that? I love him, and I don't know how to live without him."

"The world is not well lost for love, little sister. Just ask Cyrano and the original Roxanne. Just like you, Cyrano brought about his own tragedy. This affair of yours was always bound for tragedy, and if you didn't know it from the beginning, well, grow up! That man was never any good for you. Give it a week and you'll be glad he's gone. For god's sake, use some of that panache you're always so proud of."

I hung up, went into the bedroom, took the bottle of Panache off the dresser, and wondered if it would kill me if I drank the whole thing.

Late that evening Jonathan telephoned from Hawaii, a crackling long-distance call. For ten minutes he rattled on about his own flourishing career, speaking in a voice so light it blew away like a soap bubble on a spring breeze.

"Quite the commotion you've raised," he said at last.

"You heard about it over there?"

"This is nineteen fifty-six, didn't you know? We're no longer relying on smoke signals. Well, don't worry, when I get back I'll help you find some nice white boy to marry, just like Diana Jordan."

"I hope you're not serious."

"Of course I am! How else is there to brazen it out? Has Leon torn into you yet?"

"Not yet."

Leon did indeed summon me. Even when I was most angry with him I never contested his right to power. No one did. That's why he continued to hold such power. I dressed carefully for the part. No black penitent for me. I was not sorry I had loved Terrence Dexter. I wore a coral-colored bouffant dress, just to prove I still had panache in addition to the cologne. I did my hair and makeup carefully, even though when I finished and looked in the mirror I knew it was only a performance, pretending to bravery I did not have, pretending not to collapse under the weight of Leon's disapproval. His rage would be easier to endure than his disrespect.

Clarence opened the door at Summit Drive, and coral-colored dress notwithstanding, I shriveled under his harsh gaze, his stoic bearing. Wordlessly he closed the door behind me, but he lost his senatorial self-possession, and his breath came in glacial gusts of anger. "I served this house, your family, for thirty-some years! I seen everything that goes on in this house! I kept its secrets, Mr. Greene's secrets and Mrs. Greene's secrets—oh yes, she had them! Who do you think introduced her to August Branch? She came to me, told me what she wanted to do, and I helped her do it. She put me in peril, my job in real peril. She knew it too. But I did it for her. I been everything the Greenes needed for thirty years, and I did it with my eyes open and my mouth shut."

I was jaw-drop stunned to hear that he had been the link between Julia, August Branch, and the NAACP, and I would have said so, but his escalating fury gave me no chance to speak.

"When I saw my nephew take up with you, I knew that everything I've done for this family, for the Greenes, that all my loyalty was going to be thrown right back in my face. I knew that you would break my family apart. 'Terrence,' I said, 'don't do this.' I told him more than once, we all did. We begged him to listen to us. Roxanne Granville is a Hollywood brat, nothing but trouble! She will ruin you, and you will pay a heavy price, heavier than you can ever know."

I wanted to lash out, and say, *Oh yeah, Uncle Tom? That's what Terrence thinks of you!* But I could not ruin a man's whole life acting out of anger. I wiped my eyes, careful not to smear my mascara. I

kept my voice steady as Bette Davis would have. "Why won't anyone tell me where he's gone?"

"After what you did to him! We're telling you nothing!
Everything I meant for Terrence and Booker to be, to become, to
launch them into the world like men, like men, I say! You undid
that."

"I didn't do anything! It wasn't my fault. I'm sorry."

"When are you and your people going to learn? We don't want
your sorry. We don't want your thanks."

"I'm sorry," I said again, tearing up.

"No one's ever gonna tell you where he's gone, Roxanne. No
one. No one wants you near him ever again. You were toying with
a real man for the first time in your sorry, spoiled life."

"We were in love, we are in love. It wasn't my fault," I insisted.

"Whose fault could it possibly be?"

I suppose there were three hundred years of answers to that
question, so when he turned away I simply followed him wordlessly up the stairs.

Denise stood poised on the staircase wearing a gingham mater-
nity dress. She was roly-poly, probably put on seventy pounds, and
was bloated from the ankles on up. The look on her face was a
mélange of menace and disgust. "A Nee-gro, Roxanne? Really.
Have you no shame?"

I started to walk past her with nothing more than Gallic dis-
dain, but all my ungovernable instincts kicked in. "At least I'm not
passing off one man's bastard brat as another man's child."

Clarence turned and walked away. He certainly did not want
to hear any more of that.

Denise paled to the same color as her blonde hair; her mouth
opened and she gawped before she managed, "How dare you talk
to me like that?"

"I know Jonathan Moore, and I know he bagged you. That's
his favorite word for the women he's had. You were bagged, pure
and simple."

"You shut up. It wasn't ever like that."

"You wanna bet?" I was pleased that I'd hurt her, cruel, small-minded as that makes me. I walked away, realizing I only had so much strength and I'd spent a wad of it with Clarence, and I wasn't going to squander the rest with that whore Denise Dell, not when I had to face Leon Greene.

He stood in front of the library's stained glass windows and held the newspaper in one hand, waving it at me like a matador. "Sleeping with a Negro! Unthinkable! You stupid, reckless girl! Look at what you've done!"

"What have I done? I fell in love."

"A Negro! A Negro agitator. And to think, this boy is Clarence's nephew!"

"Oh god, Leon! He's not a boy, and Clarence has nothing to do with it." The thought suddenly struck me. "You're not going to fire Clarence, are you? It was all my fault. Clarence didn't even know," I lied without blinking, and went on lying. "Clarence never guessed."

Leon paused and frowned. "That's what he said too."

"He's telling you the truth. It was all my fault."

"And aren't you ashamed?"

"No."

"You ought to be. You always act like the rules don't apply to you!"

"And who taught me that, Leon?"

His lip curled. "Don't blame me for your filthy actions! Your dirty sex secrets. My own granddaughter, sleeping with a radical Negro! Who writes for a radical paper, allied with the NAACP. The Reds are at the root of the NAACP, and—"

"You know nothing about the NAACP, and nothing about the *Challenger*, and absolutely nothing about Terrence Dexter, who is a good man, the best man I've ever known, the only man I've ever known who—"

"You have flouted the laws of nature and society—you have

tainted Empire Pictures with your disgusting sexual antics." Leon paced the library while I sat depleted and immobile listening to him rant for half an hour about the horrors of miscegenation, and how the NAACP roiled up race relations, aided by the Reds, about how I was no better than that slut Diana Jordan, never mind every advantage, every opportunity he had given me, including the house that I lived in and the office that I used. Oh, everything he had made possible rolled by like the opening credits with the theme of *The High and the Mighty* blaring over it. I sat through it all until he said that I had repaid him with malicious stupidity. That's when I stopped him.

"It wasn't malicious stupidity. I loved Terrence Dexter. I still love him, but he has left me, he's gone, and no one will tell me where or let me talk to him." I started to cry, and dug in my purse for a Kleenex. "There's nothing left to lose."

"On the contrary. There's a lot left to lose. Your scandal will smear all over Empire and hurt Denise."

"Hurt Denise?" I looked up from my Kleenex. "My heart is broken, my life is in ruins, the man I love has left me." My voice spiraled upward in disbelief. "And you're afraid I will hurt Denise?"

"I don't want her upset. This pregnancy has been hard on her. Any scandal of yours will hurt her too."

"Well, far be it for me to ripple the waters around little Dora O'Dell, the scheming bitch who wrecked your life and marriage—and not because she loved you, Leon! She's forty years younger than you!—she used you for her career."

"You will be respectful of my wife, the mother of my child."

Is it your child? The question trembled at my lips, but there are some betrayals you never recover from. I would not do that to him. I loved him too much. For all I knew he had guessed at her affair with Jonathan, and if he had, his pride would never let him admit it, not to anyone, perhaps not even to himself. Denise was having a baby, and Leon would love this child, be a good father. Hadn't he helped to raise me when my own mother couldn't stand the sight of me and my father had left the country? This child would be loved. What else mattered? As I slowly got to my feet, I considered telling him about Julia's note forgiving him, but decided against it. He did not deserve to know he'd been forgiven. After all, he had not called me here to offer forgiveness. And then, I had to admit to myself, that in truth, I had never really forgiven him for loving Denise. Why should he forgive me for loving Terrence? I just said, "Terrence Dexter is a good man who loved me. Why should the color of his skin make any difference?"

"You sound like an imbecile. You are a stupid, reckless girl, and you will pay for this indiscretion. No one will ever look at you in the same way again knowing you have been to bed with a Negro. It's disgusting. Your reputation will never recover." Leon went to the desk where once a French abbé had dispensed wisdom. He stood there, and the expression on his face had sent lesser mortals scurrying for nearly forty years. "I am finished with you, Roxanne."

"So at last I get tossed out with the other unfortunate, inconvenient people, like Julia, like Jerrold and Nelson and Simon and Max. Tell me, Leon, did you guess that Max wrote *Fly Me to the Moon*?" He did not reply, but his jaw went taut, and I ought to have been afraid, but I went on, taunting him. "Did you tell Denise, 'Look! I love you more than I love J. Edgar Hoover, Richard Nixon, and my pals John Wayne and Ward Bond! Pooks loves you more than he hates Communism! Think of it! For you, Denise, Leon Greene would produce a film he knew was written by a man he had destroyed.'"

He pressed his lips till they were white. "Max destroyed himself."

There was really nothing left to say unless I said, *I'm finished with you too, Leon*, and I could not bring myself to do that. I rose, collected my handbag, and sailed through the door, where I found Clarence right there, listening at the keyhole like a parlor maid in a melodrama.

CHAPTER THIRTY-FIVE

Charlie Frye's path to redemption (and revenge) after he was fired by Empire followed the same Shakespearean pattern that had played out in Congressional hearings beginning in 1947. However, Charlie was not called to testify and he took no oaths. No, the scandal of Roxanne Granville and her Negro lover had scarcely waned when Charlie carried the equivalent of a *Repent!* sign on Sunset Boulevard by abasing himself in print. In the pages of various mags and newspapers his story spooled out like this: Charles David Frye, an aspiring screenwriter and patriotic American, had been unwittingly recruited by his then-agent, Roxanne Granville, to put his name on a script written by Max Leslie—a low-down Red who had shown contempt for Congress and fled to Mexico. Charlie, insisting how truly, tremendously, and deeply he regretted his mistake, swore by the soul of Ayn Rand that there was (somewhere) Red taint, a Communist message hidden in *Fly Me to the Moon*, a film produced—and personally overseen—by Leon Greene, head of Empire Pictures, stalwart supporter of the Waldorf Agreement, and a founder of the Motion Picture Alliance for the Preservation of American Ideals. Asked if any other Granville Agency clients were fronting for blacklisted writers, Charlie Frye joined Vic Hale, and many other name-droppers more illustrious than he, and offered up his old comrades from the hungry days at

Schwab's, Jimmy Ashford, Maurice Allen, Art Luke, and "probably lots of others."

The scandal with Terrence had indeed hurt my agency, but this was the end. The Granville Agency, three years of my proverbial blood, sweat, and tears, was finished. The phone ceased to ring except for people calling to cancel meetings, cancel contracts, cancel long-standing negotiations, cancel anything in the present or looming in the future. That, or the press asking if I had any comment. I did not. My writers left in such numbers that I thought of lemmings jumping off a cliff. I wished I had taken my attorney's advice and insisted on signed contracts instead of agreements based on a handshake. But I hadn't.

MGM fired Maurice Allen, citing the Waldorf Agreement, though nothing connected Maurice to being a Communist other than Charlie's accusation. Maurice was philosophical about it. He called me and said he had known the risk when he took it. He had impressive credits now, and he was tired of writing; he wanted to produce. He was taking his mother and returning to New York. Daily, Thelma and I read every column inch of the trade papers like witches pawing through entrails, looking for word that Paragon Pictures had fired Art Luke, or that *Gunsmoke* had fired Jimmy.

"It might be different now," said Thelma philosophically after a few days had passed. "I'm cautiously optimistic. As long as the advertisers stay lined up for *Gunsmoke*, CBS might not care if Jimmy Ashford fronted for Lenin. Back in forty-seven when all this started, if you didn't work in the movies, you didn't work at all. But people aren't going to the movies like they did then. Audiences are more like pigeons roosting in front of their televisions. TV shows are just a middleman between the products and the pigeons. If Jimmy keeps his head down and his mouth shut and soldiers on, he might be all right. *Gunsmoke* is doing great. The networks need fodder for their shows, week after week after week."

"Look at this." I tossed *Variety* over to her. "Charlie's reward for doing his patriotic duty."

"So Irv Rakoff has taken Charlie on as a client. Fancy that."

"Yes, I wonder if Irv will snuggle up his dick to Charlie's tush."

We both laughed at that, though it was amazing to me that anything was funny, given our situation.

Interviewed separately by phone, Denise and Jonathan each were quoted in the press expressing outrage! Had they known *Fly Me to the Moon* had the least Red tinge, they would not have dreamed of being part of it! Had they known the writer was fronting for a Red, they never . . . and so on. They both blamed me. Denise added a few salty, indignant phrases decrying the betrayal inflicted by a thankless granddaughter on her entire family. Leon offered no public statement. However, Empire Pictures took out full-page ads in *Variety* and the *Hollywood Reporter* in what amounted to the Gettysburg Address of Denials. Empire maintained unequivocally they had no idea their ex-employee, Charles Frye, was anything but who he presented himself to be. In offering himself as a front for another writer, Charles Frye had lied, perpetrated fraud, and that was why they had terminated his services. They reiterated their long-held resolution that Empire would never knowingly have anything to do with anyone of a remotely Communist persuasion, and that *Fly Me to the Moon* was an outstanding example of good clean American values.

Not surprisingly, Gordon's ulcer flared or broke or burst or something awful, and an ambulance was called to Empire Pictures to take him to the hospital and emergency surgery.

When Irene called me from the hospital, she added, "I'm forbidden to see you, little sister, or telephone or even say your name, and given how sick Gordon is, I think I better go along with this."

"Sure," I said, resigned, and too battered to be more heartbroken. "I hope he gets well. He didn't deserve this."

Irene paused, clearly on the brink of a big fat *I told you so* . . . But she refrained and said goodbye.

Hedda Hopper (no doubt thrashing herself for having praised

the Granville Agency just a few months before) moved in for the
kill about a week after her initial article celebrating Charlie's patriotic exposé. She inserted a tiny note at the end of her column that
the Granville Agency operated illegally out of a house on Clara
Bow Drive, a neighborhood not zoned for business.

"I better call up my brother and see if I can deliver produce
again," Thelma said, tossing the page to me, Hedda's comments
circled.

"Ask him if he'll hire me too," I replied, looking up from the
latest issue of the *Challenger*, where, as usual, I searched for news of
Terrence. Jaylene Henderson was going to New York to record
with a new label. Booker's band was coming back after a West
Coast tour. The Comet Club had been raided again for drugs.
Ruby's Café advertised their lemon meringue pie. Jackie Robinson
got a lot of ink, as did Paul Robeson, as did the Shoe Drive and the
ongoing Montgomery bus boycott. Nothing by, from, of, or about
Terrence Dexter, whose name was gone from the masthead.

Tires screeched, and Thelma and I suddenly looked up,
alarmed to see an old Dodge pickup truck pull into the driveway,
blocking Thelma's Nash and the MG. Three or four men—maybe
fewer, maybe they just moved so fast they seemed like more—
jumped out of the pickup. They wore caps pulled down low over
their brows and old coats, though it was a warm day. We watched,
horrified, speechless, as swiftly and in unison they grabbed five-
gallon cans from the truck and quickly flipped the lids off and
splashed red paint over everything, covering the big window in
front of Thelma's desk so we could not see anything at all.

With a shriek I dashed to the front door and locked it, and
Thelma ran to the back door, locked it, and closed all the kitchen
windows. The two of us ran into the bathroom, the only room that
had a lock on the door. We crouched down, our weight against the
door, holding hands while we listened to the front window take a
blow from something heavy and shatter. Other windows shattered
too. The crashing seemed to go on forever. We heard male voices

call out threatening phrases filled with dirty names. "Dirty Reds! Go back to Russia!" Then the sound of tires peeling out. Then nothing at all.

We waited, crouched on the bathroom floor for fifteen minutes, fearing they might return. We got to our feet. We opened the bathroom door. The house was quiet. The neighborhood was quiet. We could hear birds. We came out of the bathroom and started slowly down the hall. The rooms that faced the backyard, the second bedroom, kitchen, and bathroom, they were untouched. The windows in my office that faced the front were broken and red paint had splashed inside, with broken glass and red paint gleaming across the desk and floor.

We timidly made our way to the living room, where shards of broken glass and puddles of red paint lay everywhere, across the floor, across Thelma's desk and her typewriter, splattered on the file cabinets and the furniture. The wet paint made awful little sucking sounds as it stuck to our shoes and we tracked it across the hardwood floors to the front door. I unlocked the door and opened it, and we gasped to find the long-decaying carcass of a dead dog lying there, and red paint all across the porch, the whole front of the house, glistening, still wet. Red paint spattered as well all over the MG, while lesser flecks dotted the Nash. The paint cans, still oozing, lay about. A big sledgehammer, itself covered in red paint, lay in front of the shattered front window. No point in calling the cops. We both knew that much.

I remembered Max Leslie sitting knee-deep in the vandalized swimming pool, red paint swirling in the depths. I could hardly catch my breath. "We have to get out of here. Fast."

"We can't leave without taking our files," said Thelma. "Our files are incriminating, and they could come back, whoever they are."

"We can't carry those cabinets."

"My nephews and my brother can. I'll call. They'll come right away." Thelma went back inside, crying.

I stepped over the dead dog. The flies stirred and buzzed. I walked over to the Silver Bullet as though I were afraid of waking it. No longer silver but streaked with red paint, inside and out. I gently traced my finger through the paint and remembered Max Leslie telling me I was too young to have a past I'd regret. Well, I was certainly old enough now.

PART V

THE OUBLIETTE

1956

CHAPTER THIRTY-SIX

Like the scarecrow in *The Wizard of Oz*, I had had the stuffing kicked out of me. I stuffed it back in, enough to get up and shamble haphazardly along, but without Terrence, without work, my life emptied of purpose. I bestirred myself enough to clean the seats and interior of the Silver Bullet by hand, and though they would never quite look the same, at least they weren't visibly stained with red. But for the exterior, I had to find a place that would repaint the entire car without asking too many questions. I finally found one and explained that it was a sorority hazing gone awry, which seemed to satisfy the guy. A week later I had the car back, no longer silver gray but a dark green.

Other than painting the car, the days, weeks of that early summer seemed to me blurred as though they got left out in the rain, mottled and muddied. Jobless, manless, unwashed hair, unshaved legs, and stinking of failure, I ate nothing but cornflakes and Hostess Sno Balls. I drank way more than was good for me. I slept way more than I should have, though I didn't wake rested. I read books without pleasure, or even much comprehension. I played the piano, plunking out some of Terrence's old tunes, vainly trying to ease the ache. The phone never rang except once a day when Thelma called to be sure I was still among the living. I moved the artwork that artists had lent me to the back bedroom. (Mercifully the red paint splashed across our furniture and desks had not reached the walls. Thelma's brother and nephews rescued the art-work as well when they moved our file cabinets to Malibu.) Methodically I went through the file cabinets, and in the big stone fireplace, I burned anything that might incriminate anyone who had dealt in my subterfuges. I'd regret it at tax time, of course, but it seemed necessary now. Other than that, I dealt with the death of the Granville Agency in a truly immature and unprofessional fash-ion by leaving everything in the hands of Adam Ornstein, my at-torney, who sent me stuff I had to sign. I signed it, sometimes without even reading it through. The past had been so hollowed out that I cared nothing for the future.

I kept Terrence's Royal typewriter on the table, beside the pic-tures of Julia and the music box. Sometimes I put my fingers over the keys, hoping to feel something of his presence; sometimes I put my arms around the typewriter, my head down, and breathed in the smell of ink and metal and ribbon. At night, I put the framed snapshots of the two of us under my pillow. I wore the gold brace-let day and night. I walked on the beach for miles, wearing dark glasses and a floppy hat. The Wilburs chained their dog up, and I could hear Bruno yelping. They kept him on a leash when they walked, and they always went south, away from me. I did not have to speak to them again. I missed their funny, eager dog.

I went to matinees, if not matins. At least in the movies I could step away from loss and failure. I sat through cartoons and news-reels, coming attractions with their blaring voices and gaudy music. I watched Poverty Row's offerings, including monster flicks by clients of mine and one of Art Luke's gangster films. But I also saw *The Searchers*, and even if I didn't like John Wayne, or John Ford, for that matter, I recognized an achievement when I saw it. I en-dured *The Man Who Knew Too Much*, and had "Que Sera Sera" etched on the brain. I saw *Rock Around the Clock*, and noted with some morsel of satisfaction that black and white musicians were actually playing together on the screen. That felt like a first.

I waded into the ocean every day, not swimming, not exerting my body against the sea, just letting the swells roll over and around me, fling me toward the beach, and cough me out on the sand. One afternoon I encountered a fierce riptide that carried me far to the north. I fought it, swimming vainly toward the shore that I could see but could not reach. I wondered if I was going to die out there, carried out to sea. Though my energy flagged, I struggled, and I was absolutely spent when I could finally stand up in the waves, only to be knocked down again and again as if the sea itself wasn't finished beating me up. Breathless and weakened, grateful to have escaped a watery death, I found myself on all fours, foam pooling around my hands and knees, remembering Terrence and the riptide, and how I had splashed into the waves, and we had rolled over and around each other, and how I had laughed to think of the rolling-on-the-beach scene in *From Here to Eternity*, and how at last I knew that experience. I wasn't laughing now, but blubbering with heartache and exhaustion.

I looked up, and in the distance I saw a figure on my porch, shimmering. I thought the rough ocean had shaken my brains loose, or that the afternoon light was playing tricks on my vision, but as I walked, staggered really, picking up my towel on the way, the figure on the porch did not evaporate. I cried out her name—*"Irene!"*—and flew up the stairs. I threw my arms around her.

She held me close, half laughing, half crying, and brushed the salty, sandy mess I'd made from her crisp summer dress. "I told Gordon it just wasn't fair to blame you for everything."

"I'm sure he disagreed."

"He did, but I don't care. He ignores me when I tell him that he should work less, that he should let up, so I get to ignore him."

"Is he well now?"

"He went back to the studio the day after he got out of the hospital. What does that tell you?"

"That he's not well and he doesn't care."

She looked around, frowned to see the snapshots of Terrence

and me on the desk, but she did not comment. "Why are all your file cabinets stacked up here?"

"What else was I going to do with them? I couldn't leave them at Clara Bow Drive, not after what happened."

"Oh, yes. I have this for you." She opened her purse. "It's an eviction notice for Clara Bow Drive, and a big fat bill for fixing the broken windows, and removing the red paint and the dead dog. Melvin Grant sent it to me because I signed the lease."

In his letter, Melvin Grant also wrote that he had personally talked the city out of suing me for zoning infractions, and the bill for those services would be sent separately. At least I wasn't evicted from this Malibu place. Ever since Leon had said he was through with me, I lived in fear of that.

"Melvin Grant will have to get in line to get paid," I said, flinging the letter to the desk. I went into the bedroom, peeled off my swimsuit, and put on some capris and a T-shirt. Sand still stuck to my skin.

"Denise had her baby yesterday," Irene called out. "A boy. Aaron Leon Greene."

"Leon must be ecstatic." I came out, toweling the salt water from my hair.

"Bursting with joy even though our uncle Aaron looks like a marshmallow with a face."

We both started laughing, and suddenly it seemed like old times as I got us two Cokes and we went outside. Sunshine and wind played over us, and we watched the distant surfers bobbing as Irene told me how she and Gordon had gone to the hospital with Leon and waited with him all night long while Denise went through labor.

"When they put that baby in Leon's arms, he started to cry, Roxanne. I have never seen him cry."

"Probably the last time he cried was in nineteen twenty-one when his first son died."

"He's absolutely besotted with this baby, like a man under an enchantment."

"That's what we used to say about him and Denise."

"Yes, well, Denise has no interest whatever in the kid. I mean, like none. She posed for pictures and that was it, handed him off to the nanny they've hired, and made a call to her hairdresser."

"Is the nanny one of Josefina's sisters?"

"Hell no. An Irish Catholic nanny. Mrs. Shea."

"Well, I'm glad Leon has the baby to take his mind off Empire's woes."

"Oh, those have all fallen on Gordon. Leon has other problems. The Motion Picture Alliance for the Preservation of American Ideals is debating a motion to evict him from the organization."

I felt my spirits collapse all over again, and I writhed inwardly. "I had not heard. Leon must be . . . I made a big mistake with Charlie. I should not have trusted him."

"You never should have done it at all. Any of it."

Perhaps this was true, but in these weeks I'd come to realize that taking on Max's work had proved to be the single most important decision of my adult life. Everything joyful, or shattering, the heights of happiness, the depths of despair, they were all allied to that one moment. Without *Fly Me to the Moon* I would not have had that lunch appointment at Pierino's when I took the MG to Reg's and Terrence drove me into town. I would not have gone to Casa Fiesta to insist that Jonathan audition for the role of Professor Bleeker, nor ended up at the Comet Club. I would never have seen Terrence again, felt his arms around me as we danced, or his embrace amid the brawl. Would not have fallen a little bit in love with him that very night. Certainly I would not have heard from Kathleen Hilyard, from Susan Strassman. And now? What had actually emerged from all those choices? What had happened to all those people I cared for? Thelma had told me Max was living in a squalid bedsit in England; Marian, homeless, was staying with Thelma indefinitely. The Granville Agency was utterly dead. My writers were disgraced, and worse, suspect, possible frauds fronting for Reds. Thelma was unemployed, probably unemployable. Like Basil Rathbone on the moors, creditors howled after me like the hound of the Baskervilles. My own grandfather had declared himself finished with me, and I had so totally lost the man I loved that I had no idea where he had gone.

As if reading my mind, Irene observed tartly, "Jonathan sure came out of this smelling like a goddamned rose, didn't he? The only one. How did that happen?"

"I don't know. Fortune favors the bold?"

"You don't hear from him at all?"

"I might never hear from him again. Jonathan's an opportunist, like Denise, and opportunity presented itself. He'll never look back."

"Oh, Denise might have met her opportunistic match in Jonathan, all right. And more than that." Irene made *tsk-tsk* sounds and rolled her eyes.

"Do you think . . ."

"I do," she said crisply. "So does Gordon. But there's certainly no proof, and absolutely no point in discussing it. Ever."

"I agree. Leon deserves his happiness with this new Aaron Greene."

She picked up her handbag. "I have to go. By the way, you look awful. I don't mean just like you washed out of the ocean like a piece of driftwood, which you did. What happened to all that L'Oiseau d'Or panache? Have you forgotten everything Julia taught you?"

"My L'Oiseau d'Or days are over. The Granville Agency is over. I'm a has-been at the ripe old age of twenty-five."

"Oh, don't be so dramatic. You'll think of something. You were never like the rest of us, just standing around waiting to get plucked and put on the marriage shelf. Oh no, Roxanne, you are complicated, but you are never dull. You are reckless and romantic, but you are always interesting."

"Not anymore."

"Well, you would be if you cleaned yourself up and did something with your hair. Get it cut."

"I don't go anywhere."

"Get it cut anyway."

I put my tanned hand on her pale arm. "Don't leave. Please. It's so good to see you again."

She glanced at her watch. "I have to. I have an appointment with the principal at Junior's school. They don't want him back next year, so I have my checkbook at the ready. I can't bear the thought of finding yet another school for him. Come to dinner on Friday."

"Gordon won't much like that."

"Don't worry. He may not even be home. Sometimes days go by and I only see him in the mornings, sometimes he's gone to the studio before I even get up. He's killing himself. If he is there on Friday, you'll be good for him, give him something else to get twisted about besides the studio. Besides, you'll be good for me. Come early and let's play tennis. You want to come to Tahoe next month with me and the children and Josefina?"

"No. But thanks."

"Oh, by the way, Carleton Grimes from Paragon Pictures called Gordon asking for your home number."

"What for?"

Irene shrugged. "Maybe he really does want to have an affair. You could use a good affair."

"I thought you didn't approve of adultery."

"You could use a good affair," she repeated.

"Not in the mood, sorry."

"Oh, you will be."

I walked Irene out to her car without contradicting her, but I knew, if she did not, that I was barely upright, that my heart was broken and my imagination might never be equal to another man, or another man equal to my imagination.

I came back inside and sat with my arms around the Royal for a while, till I heard a fluttering sound and looked up to see a moth bashing itself against the window. I moved swiftly to shoo it away and accidentally knocked the music box to the floor. I was sad to see that the bottom had popped off, and the workings lay scattered on the floor. Amid the tiny wheels there was a gold wedding band and a little envelope, the sort that might have been a baby announcement, with the words *Aaron Leon Greene, 1917–1921* in Julia's handwriting. Inside there was a lock of light brown curly hair tied with a thin, faded blue ribbon. The ring, I recognized, was the plain gold band Julia always wore, the one Leon had given her in 1911 before there ever was an Empire Pictures. I started to cry. For all her jewels, her antiques, the cars, the clothes, the furs, the Paris apartment, the Matisse on the wall, clearly these two things were her dearest possessions, and she kept them, secret, in the music box that had been a gift from me. I wept the harder, loving her, missing her, but as I dried my eyes, I could not help but wonder how she would have absorbed the news of another Aaron Leon Greene. Denise's son to have that name? Julia's heart would have split into tiny fragments. I put the ring, the lock of hair, and the scattered workings back in the music box that would never again play another tune.

A couple of days later, taking a break from pasting Green Stamps in the little book, I went out to the battered mailbox on PCH. Along with the usual bills and bad news, I found a typewritten French aerogramme with no return address. I tore it open, and my heart leapt with joy. Terrence hadn't gone back to Alabama! He was in Paris.

Dear Roxanne,

   Mr. Branch sent me newspaper clippings about Charlie and your troubles. He asked me to tell you that you did a brave thing finding fronts for friends who had suffered injustice. I'm writing to say how sorry I am about the agency. I know how hard you worked.

As you can see, I followed Jerrold Davies' advice and came here to write a book, to get distance between me and everything I've ever known. The French I learned from you isn't much use to me here in ordinary life, so every day is an adventure. At first I stayed in a crappy hotel on the rue Jacob, but then I met some bad cat musicians who had a summer gig in Nice, so I sublet the drummer's tiny Montparnasse apartment. It has a hot plate and a sink, and at least I don't have to share a bathroom. I wash clothes in the bidet. But in Paris no one cares where you live, and no one cares what you drive—no one has a car anyway. Everyone really lives in the cafés and bars. The Left Bank cafés are like theaters, and for the price of an aperitif you can watch for hours, and meet Americans you would never meet anywhere else. They're all writers, or they edit literary magazines or write for one, or they're stringers. I've sold some freelance pieces, but the book I'm writing takes most of my energy.

Everywhere here I see the African students and their girlfriends in their colorful clothes. Africans from Algeria and Senegal and Ivory Coast have their own cafés and restaurants, and white people eat there too. No one thinks anything of it. Here, when a bunch of us, white and black, are at a café, people just say les americains, not black or white. At the Ivory Coast café two weeks ago I saw Jerrold Davies and his wife, Annette. I had a long, lively evening with them. They thought for sure you were with me. I had some explaining to do. The truth was hard to tell.

I've found a little Left Bank theater that shows old movies with subtitles in French so I've finally been to your Church of Rick and Ilsa. I saw Casablanca with French subtitles. I saw it three times. At that same theater, I saw a lot of the films you've talked about. Jerrold and I and Annette went together to see The Ice Age that won him the 1940 Oscar. Watching these old movies is walking through your past, Roxanne, your imagination.

Jerrold lent me this typewriter, and he's given me part-time work helping out on the set of The Oubliette. *I'm grateful for the new experience, and the little bit of extra money means I can stay in Paris and finish my book. For the first time in my life what I write has to come to me, not me going to it.*

Terrence

What a wonderful reunion he must have had with Jerrold! *The truth was hard to tell* . . . Oh, Terrence, what truth did you tell them? That we loved each other, and that fate or circumstance or cruel people intervened? Or that we loved each other, and you were facedown on the porch, mistaken for a thief on the day you came to break up with me?

I read his letter so many times the ink smudged from my tears. I kept it under my pillow at night and in my pocket during the day. But within days my initial joy, relief shriveled when I realized there was no suggestion whatever that he would be coming back. He would not be coming back. Did he have someone else? Someone new? When I read that letter truthfully, I mean, telling myself the truth, I knew that Terrence, in moving to Paris, in writing the book he had wanted to write, had crawled out of the ruins of life in LA. He had found a new life. Clearly, he went out with new friends, black and white, and no doubt there were women. There was absolutely nothing in his note to suggest his heart was breaking over me. My heart was breaking over him. I needed my own *oubliette*.

One afternoon I took this tissuey aerogramme and put it in a big manila envelope, alongside Julia's plain wedding ring and the lock of hair from the first Aaron Greene. I took the cache of letters Terrence wrote me from Alabama, the two photographs of us, and the gold bracelet he had given me at Christmas, put all this in the envelope, and sealed it. I drove to the bank, where I placed it in the safe-deposit box that held Julia's diamond choker, the diamond ring, the ruby earrings, the rope of perfect pearls, and other relics from the past, from a life I needed to forget, a life no longer my own.

CHAPTER THIRTY-SEVEN

How could this meeting be anything but bad news? So bad Carleton Grimes felt it had to be delivered in person? I assumed he set this meeting for late, six o'clock at the Paragon commissary, because he didn't want to be seen publicly with me. I parked the MG and found the commissary; the place was closing, so I waited at an outside table where low, flowering hedges bristled with twittering sparrows. I felt like one of those dull birds, though I wore silk trousers, a silk blouse, and a much-needed spray of Panache. It was the first time in weeks that I'd left Malibu except to go to the movies, the grocery store, or Irene's house. Oddly, Gordon and I are actually getting along better than we ever did. Maybe misery loves company. Gordon is pretty miserable these days.

I saw Carleton from afar, and he waved. After the obligatory and totally insincere Hollywood hug, he said, "My wife wants to know if our affair ended badly."

"Everything that ends, ends badly. I speak from experience. Please tell your wife she's stuck with you, but I thought you were a terrific lay."

He chuckled. "Come, let's walk to my office." We strolled between the massive soundstages, mostly empty this late in the day. As I'd come to expect from him, Carleton chatted obliquely: He missed New York; California has climate but no weather (a distinction, I confess, lost on me). Then, somehow without my quite knowing how, the conversation moved to "You have quite the talent for trouble, Roxanne. I guessed as much when I saw you in that red dress, but I wouldn't have guessed you to be keeping a love nest with a Negro agitator."

"He was a reporter, not an agitator. And please, spare me the love nest. It sounds squalid. My affair with Terrence Dexter was not squalid."

"But it was scandalous."

"Only because people are narrow-minded."

"Yes, you offended the little corsets of conformity we all wear. Everyone gets along by sharing certain prejudices."

"Well, I don't share them."

He got out a cigarette. "I suppose Leon was horrified."

"Leon is not speaking to me."

"He should have been more forgiving of your love life. His was a scandal for a long time, though people will forgive adultery— maybe not the wife," he added, "but in this business, no one really cares if you're faithful or not. The Motion Picture Alliance is much less likely to forgive him for producing a film by a writer he had fired, a script"—he paused—"sold to him by his own granddaughter, who must have wanted him to look foolish or hypocritical."

I could feel the birthmark, my whole face, flushing with shame. And regret. I had nothing to say in my own defense.

"That disclaimer that Empire published in the trades, that was pretty disingenuous, don't you think?"

I shrugged, and put on my sunglasses.

"Leon's patriotism blinded him to a lot of things," Carleton went on. "Leon is something of a dinosaur. Meaning no disrespect."

"None taken." Where was Carleton going with this?

"This is a new era."

"Really? It feels like the same old lousy era to me."

"The picture business makes itself afresh every ten years or so. If it didn't, we'd still be back with silent films and Mabel Normand throwing pies in Fatty Arbuckle's face. Every new era means you have to ask new questions. Who's going to the movies, now, in nineteen fifty-six? Better yet, who is not going?"

I thought about this as we walked. "Well, the people who have to get up every morning and go to the factory, they stay home watching television. Like pigeons on a roost," I added with an internal nod to Thelma. I stopped and turned to him. "So who is in the theaters, Carleton?"

"The kids, teenagers, young people. They have money. They have cars. They have time. They want to get out of the house and go to the movies. These kids don't give a damn for Communism. They want sexy stuff. Look at *Blackboard Jungle*, *Rebel Without a Cause*, *Rock Around the Clock*, *To Catch a Thief*. We don't need Jesus Christ, pharaohs, and ten thousand extras for this audience. We need to make new kinds of pictures, like *Adios Diablo*."

"Really, Carleton? Teenagers coming to see a film about Mexico in nineteen fifteen? I mean, yes, it's a great picture, but you think kids are going to care about the Mexican Revolution? Meaning no disrespect."

"None taken. *Adios Diablo* is going to be a coup for us next year. Oscar fodder. Why do you look surprised, Roxanne? It happened for *High Noon*, didn't it? A little Western no one paid much attention to until suddenly, wow! Everyone sees it is a masterpiece!"

"It can happen again," I agreed, though I didn't actually believe that was true.

"Did I tell you I went down to Mexico myself? The shoot was way over budget and going on way too long. I wanted to have a personal look at the damage."

I was glad he was on my left so he could not see the birthmark flush with color while he talked at length. The set was chaotic. The delays had already doubled the cost of the picture. Some of these delays were the result of clashing egos and power struggles. Some had to do with acts of god, bad weather, and bad behavior, even rampant Montezuma's revenge among the cast and crew. While my own innards roiled, I commiserated without asking questions. Any minute now the accusation would unfold.

"You'll never guess who was on-set down there. Not on the payroll, mind you, but on-set. Simon Strassman, remember him?"

"Sure. I haven't seen him in years."

"Yes, that's what he said. He said you two were great pals when you were a kid. He has a very high opinion of you."

"How could he? I was just a kid." I stumbled in my high heels, and Carleton caught my arm. We had come to the Paragon executive offices, a stolid-looking brick building from the forties that now, only ten years later, looked totally passé and boring. It was late, nearly seven, and the place was deserted, the staff gone except for the security guard, who stood up when Carleton entered.

"My offices are on the second floor," he said as we started up a utilitarian staircase.

Just for a moment the thought crossed my mind—it was well after hours, and the building was deserted; was Carleton about to make an Irv Rakoff move on me? I didn't know him personally, and perhaps he had affairs, but surely Carleton would never sink to assault.

We walked through his secretary's office, and he opened the door to his own. I took off my dark glasses. I could not believe my eyes. There, sitting across from the desk, was Simon Strassman.

He resembled one of those old walruses with a drooping gray moustache, fat rolling off of every limb; even the pouches under his eyes were puffy and fat. I had not seen him since . . . I couldn't even remember. Though he was deeply tanned, he still looked pasty. His eyes were clouded, milky with cataracts. He rose to his feet with wheezy difficulty, but he opened his arms to me and called out my name. To be in his embrace was to be, fleetingly, a child again, with all those old certainties and comforts.

"But, Simon! What are you doing here? You shouldn't be here! If they know you're here, they'll—"

"Let them!" Simon made one of the big, expansive gestures I

so well remembered. "Let the flying monkeys come after me. I have grandchildren I've never met! I have grandchildren who won't remember me at all if I die in Mexico. No, really! Let them put me in prison. How bad can it be? I'm an old man. I don't care."

"But Leah?"

"Leah flew up. She's with Susan. Carleton was good enough to bring me back in his great big limo. We sailed through the border, and all the guard said was 'Yes, sir.' Not a single question." Simon gave an asthmatic chuckle. "Oh, Roxanne, I asked Carleton to set this meeting up. I just had to tell you how much it means to me, you can't even imagine, no really, you're too young to imagine! What it means to me to see the sets for *Adios Diablo*, to see the picture I saw in my head there in front of my eyes. *Adios Diablo* is the best picture I've ever written. Hell, it's like nothing I've ever written. That's what I got out of my five years in Mexico. A great picture and a liver that's failing me." He guffawed like this might actually be funny. "Sam Pepper, he's the new John Ford. You heard it from me! John Ford's at the end of his career, and Sam Pepper is on the way up! And Art Luke! Oh, Roxanne, you found the perfect guy to front for me. He's an irascible SOB. Just like me. We were the three musketeers!"

"They were," said Carleton, easing back in his chair. "In Mexico they all drank too much and talked too much, and each seemed to think he had personally settled the West. They wore out the typewriter ribbons making rewrites, putting in more sex, more violence, more . . . what's the word I want?"

"Dash," said Simon. "Art and I, we're going to write another great picture together. Even if I'm in prison."

Carleton walked to the glass cabinet, took out a bottle of Rémy Martin and three cognac glasses; he poured us each a splash. "To *Adios Diablo*!" We clinked glasses. "We're thinking about putting Simon's name on the credits, Roxanne. After Art's name, but right up there on the screen."

I lowered the glass from my lips. Surely I had misheard. "What?"

Carleton repeated himself, and across from me, Simon beamed like a big fat Buddha.

I said, "Are you out of your mind? Hedda Hopper will tear you to shreds. The American Legion will picket the theaters. The Motion Picture Alliance for the Preservation of American Ideals will see to it your actors never work again! I'm talking about the careers of everyone on the picture, the actors, the writer, the director. Even the script girl will never work again!"

"She'll be okay," said Carleton. "She's Mexican."

"And a little beauty," said Simon.

"I don't think you know what you're saying," I insisted. "They'll destroy you personally. They'll come to your home with red paint and the carcasses of dead dogs, believe me!"

"They might try to destroy me, us," said Carleton, "but I'm not such an easy target. For one thing I'm a lot younger than Leon, than Jack Warner and the rest of them, and my family are all WASPs from Connecticut. I wasn't here during the union turmoil in the thirties, the strikes, the informing, making propaganda films during the War. I'm a different generation of studio head. If the unions have to be dealt with, it's just part of the cost of doing business; it's not ideological for me. I didn't sign the Waldorf Agreement. Nine years is a long time to be settling old scores, selling out friends, painting one another Red, just to be able to work."

"Ask Dalton Trumbo," Simon muttered. "Ask Ring Lardner and Adrian Scott."

"But all the studio heads signed the Waldorf Agreement," I insisted. "Even Paragon."

"Noah Glassman died last year. I'm in charge now."

"Yes, but the rest of them haven't backed down."

"It was an agreement, or a declaration, or a statement—no one's quite sure what to call it. But it definitely is not a legally binding contract, especially not binding on me. The Waldorf Agreement never had the force of law, but as I said, everyone gets along by sharing certain prejudices. It was impossible to test in the courts, because, well, who had the endless legal resources to fight the studios?"

"And Dalton, Adrian, Ring, and the others, the Ten who took their First Amendment rights all through the courts," Simon said, "look where they ended up. Federal prison."

"It's time to test the Waldorf Agreement in the court of public opinion," Carleton went on. "For years now, you could get irrevocably smeared if just your name even appeared in *Red Channels*, or crossed someone's lips in a Congressional hearing. The only way you could defend yourself against libel was to testify in front of the Committee. The very people who held all the power. Damned if you do, and damned if you don't." Carleton put his feet up on the desk and looked thoughtful. "I'm going to take a different avenue. Think of me as Gary Cooper in *High Noon*. Will Kane, out there, one lone, handsome guy striding toward his destiny."

"Yes, Carleton," I reminded him, "and everyone deserted Will Kane. He was left all alone!"

"It's true, with Simon's name on the screen, there'll probably be threats, but at least if my experiment fails, I won't be going to federal prison."

"Simon will."

"So what? In Mexico I was committing slow suicide, and I didn't even know it. Leah was dying, and she didn't even know it. Now we're alive again, we've got our daughters, our grandchildren. If I'm arrested, the prison doctor will have to take care of my liver." This thought made him burst into laughter, and he and Carleton both lit cigarettes.

"There's another side to this too." Carleton brought his feet down. "With Simon's name on the credits, there will be lots of screaming in the press, lots of . . ." He brushed his Errol Flynn moustache and smiled.

"Publicity. You sly old fox."

Carleton chuckled. "I want you to be part of this, Roxanne. I want your input. It's only fair. There's a risk to you too. It's public acknowledgment that Art Luke was a front. The Granville Agency repped him."

"Well, I'm not an agent anymore. The Granville Agency doesn't exist. What does Art say?"

"Art fought in the Pacific. He's a brave man. He's agreed."

I finished off the brandy. "I've spent the last year having the FBI camped on my street and putting a matchbook in the door when I leave the house. I've been afraid that my phones are tapped. I've been afraid to be seen in public with a man I loved. I've been reviled by his family and shunned by my own. I've been called filthy names by strangers. I've cowered behind the bathroom door because vandals were attacking my house. I've lost everything, but at least now I don't have to be afraid anymore."

"What are you going to do next?" asked Carleton. "Someone as clever as you must have plans."

"I have no idea what I'll do next, but I have about six months to find out before I either go mad or go broke. Whichever comes first." I surprised myself with this admission. Candor doesn't come naturally to me.

Someone knocked timidly at the door, and when it opened, Leah Strassman poked her head in and smiled. Leah had always been stylish and petite, with strong features and jet-black hair. Now she was tiny and hawklike, her hair a dull salt-and-pepper, and her clothes fit her like a rumpled pillowcase. The years in Mexico had taken a terrible toll on both of them. We three had a great, tearful, heartfelt reunion while we lamented what had happened to Max, though at least I could tell them he'd found work in England, writing on *The Adventures of Robin Hood*. Leah offered the hope that maybe one day Max could come home again. I didn't contradict her, but I knew he hadn't any hope of that, not unless, like Simon, he resigned himself to the possibility of prison, and Max would never do that to his wife and son.

Susan Strassman came in to collect her parents. She put her arms around me and thanked me again and again. I started to tear up. Maybe I had done some good after all. Maybe I wasn't a total stinking failure.

When the Strassmans left, Carleton gave me a Kleenex. "Why?" I asked him.

"Because you've been crying and your nose is running."

"Not the Kleenex. Studio heads aren't philanthropic. They don't want to make old men happy. Money always figures in. Why did you decide to give Simon screen credit?"

"Spoken like Leon Greene's granddaughter. Come on, I'll walk you to your car. I admit," he said as we trotted down the staircase, "when I read the papers, all those confessions from your writer who fronted for Max Leslie, what was his name?"

"Charlie Frye," I said, hating the very sound of it.

"I assumed you had lied to me too. That you and Art had both lied to me. Hedda Hopper paid me a nasty personal visit, and I took a lot of shit from her because I'd said you were the most interesting woman in Hollywood. I was placed in the unhappy position of having to defend you. I had to assure Hedda that Art was true-blue, a veteran, the sole writer of *Adios Diablo*, or else let her believe that Miss Roxanne Granville had duped me too, just like she duped her own grandfather."

I could feel my birthmark flush with shame.

"People would think I had fallen for your pretty face, or that I'd lost my wits. A man in my position, I can't have that. After my talk with Hedda, I was so furious I almost recalled Art from Mexico, but if I did that, word would get out, and it would look like . . . No, I'd gone too far, and committed too much to the picture. I had to look as though I had faith in my own production. Which I did not. That's when I went down to Mexico to see for myself what the hell was happening, and there was Simon Strassman, large as life."

He fell quiet for a bit as though reliving that awful moment, and I wobbled alongside him.

"Simon wasn't shy about its being his picture. Everyone working down there knew who wrote the original script. Someone would blab, when everyone came back to Hollywood, someone, drunk—whether he was in Ciro's or some sleazy bar—someone would blab, and pretty soon the whole world would know that you and Simon and Art had all duped me. So, yes, I was plenty angry with the Granville Agency and with you. But"—he stopped to light a cigarette—"when I was down there, I also couldn't help but notice the great creative chemistry that Art and Simon and Sam Pepper have together."

We had come to my car, and I leaned against it for support. I wanted to get in and drive away, but I was too proud to squirm. After all, I had asked the question. I had to be able to hear the answer.

"That's when we got hit by one of those freak torrential rainstorms, and everyone just came together to save the picture, save the sets. The damage was awful, but the people were inspiring. When we were cleaning up the mess after the downpour, it was like the rain had washed away the past and I started to think about the future. Simon is one of those big, brash personalities. He could be good for publicity, especially if they come after him and arrest him—and I'm not being heartless, Roxanne. He agrees with me—it's a risk he's willing to take. Sam Pepper is no shrinking violet either. Art grew up in Mexico; he's a decorated veteran. It took all three of them to make this picture. I admire them, creatively speaking. Personally, they're each difficult, and they drink too much, but they're great together. And the studio has claimed the rainstorm as an act of god, and we will collect from the insurance company. So that eases the financial burden. So, yes, you're right. Studio heads always think of money."

"That still doesn't tell me why you'd risk Simon's name on the screen."

"I want *Adios Diablo* to be the most talked about picture of nineteen fifty-seven."

"Even if it's talked about because people hate it? Because it was written by a Commie? And a veteran of the Pacific helped cover it up?"

"We're in the middle of a sea change, something new and strange—not just the picture business. Everyone."

"I know a lot of people who read the *Challenger* who would agree with you."

"Ah yes, your friend wrote for the *Challenger*, didn't he? All those inspiring pieces about the bus boycott in Alabama."

"Yes."

"Ah. Well, even if the politics, the message of *Adios Diablo*, ties Hedda Hopper's knickers in knots and gives John Wayne constipation, it'll be the film no one will forget. It has the best goddamned train wreck since Buster Keaton made *The General*. Cost me a fortune."

I smiled. "I see you're not averse to risks."

"Neither are you. That's why I want to hire you."

"Me? I'm the biggest disgrace in this town."

"At the moment. That'll pass. You're a natural. The picture business is not for people with touchy pride or impeccable taste. It's not for weaklings, or people who want tidy lives. There's no eight-to-five, clock out, and go home. You have to live, breathe, eat, and sleep movies, so that even in your dreams you hear the wheels, the gears and sprockets of the cameras and editing machines and the whirr of projectors as the film threads through it. You're one of those people." He crushed the cigarette under his heel. "You were born to it. I want you on my side. On Paragon's side. Do you have other plans for the future?"

I gave an unconvincing laugh. "I don't have any plans at all. But what would I be doing? I don't have any talents."

"I doubt that's true. You recognized that *Adios Diablo* was a great picture. I'm sure I can find something to keep you occupied. Come see me next week."

"Do you mean it?

"I do. Just don't wear red."

CHAPTER THIRTY-EIGHT

~

I took Irene's advice and got my hair cut, and afterward, I went to a matinee of *High Society*. That very first scene, where Louis Armstrong and his musicians all sit at the back of the bus, that made me want to stand up and yell at the screen. And really, Bing Crosby as a cool jazz man? Don't make me laugh. Bing is a geezer, old enough to be Grace Kelly's father. If beautiful, fresh Grace Kelly was going to be stuck with an old man, she should have chosen Louis Armstrong—at least he had some grit and verve. I was still cranky when I got home from the theater, parked the MG in the garage, and opened the mailbox on PCH. No eviction notice— that was cheering. As for the rest of it, bad news and bills, I scooped those up to read later.

Along PCH I saw a Bentley coming north. It slowed and pulled off to the side, stopping right beside my mailbox, and the uniformed driver got out and opened the door to Leon Greene. I thought perhaps I was asleep, dreaming maybe. He was hatless, casually clad, still superbly tailored, though I could not read his expression. Even when he took off his dark glasses, I could not read his expression. Even when he opened his arms in a welcoming embrace. I was too stunned to speak, but I hugged him just the same.

When at last he released me, he said, "Roxanne, I have someone I want you to meet." He gestured inside the Bentley and a stern, white-clad woman got out, holding a tiny, blanket-wrapped bundle in her arms. Leon took the baby from her tenderly. "Meet my son, Roxanne. Aaron Leon Greene. Isn't he beautiful?"

What could I say? He was a baby. His little face above the blanket, and a baby cap protecting his head, he slept, utterly unaware of all the drama that had swirled around his coming into this world. I said all the things you're supposed to say to a new parent—beautiful, cute, adorable. When, to my chagrin, Leon put him into my arms, I held him in an unpracticed embrace as the white-uniformed nanny glared. She was middle-aged with severe features; a perpetual scowl had driven deep furrows between her brows, and the pinch to her lips was clearly of long standing.

"Mrs. Shea," said Leon, "we're going to take Aaron inside. Please wait here. I'll let you know when you're wanted."

"It's time for his nap," she replied.

"And he's sleeping, as you can see."

She glanced at her wristwatch. "And he's due for a bottle and a change soon."

"We won't be long."

Leon took the baby from me and hoisted him expertly to his shoulder. I led the way up the stairs to the porch and opened the door. I babbled nervously, asking him to ignore the untidiness while Leon wandered around, noting the movie posters, the file cabinets, some with dried red paint on them. He patted the baby's back rhythmically. He turned to the window and looked out to the ocean, where a late-afternoon banner of sunshine spread itself across the water. "I haven't been here in thirty years. The view is still the same."

"You know this place?" I asked, astonished.

"We used to film here—early pictures, silents. Making films in those days was like a party with your friends. You just put everyone in a couple of trucks with some cameras and costumes and went wherever you wanted. No one cared if you showed up in their orange groves, especially if you gave them ten bucks. The beach was free. I bought this place so we'd have somewhere to change costumes and drink. I paid cash."

"Which films did you shoot here?"

Leon shrugged. "Who can remember the titles? In those days we sometimes turned out twenty or thirty silent pictures a year. You could do a whole screenplay on the back of a paper bag. The talkies changed all that. You needed a script, actual words for the actors to say. But back then, since there was no sound, I could yell at the actors all I wanted while we were filming. Once, we had an orchestra, not a full orchestra, but a bunch of musicians right there on the beach, playing music to get the actors in the mood. It was a comedy, and the actors were building human pyramids on the sand while they played a lot of madcap music. Julia conducted, and the tide came up, and caught her unawares, splashed her, and all the musicians ran away to protect their instruments. The cameras turned on them to catch them all scrambling. I thought I'd die laughing. We all came back to this house to change clothes. We lit a fire and someone went out for sandwiches and beer. Such a fine time. Such good times those were."

I stood beside him, and looked outside as if actors still cavorted on the beach, Julia energetically conducting musicians, while Leon with a megaphone yelled at everyone and the waves frothed around their feet. "Why didn't you tell me this when I first moved here?"

"As you may recall, just then I did not want to discuss good times with Julia. I was furious with her. I mean, we had just returned from Wilkie's office, where I had to sit there and nod while she gave money away to the NAACP." He put his cheek alongside the baby's. "I'll dig up some of the old silent films. You can come to Summit Drive sometime and watch them."

"But you said—"

"I'm sorry I said I was finished with you, Roxanne. I said a lot of cruel things, things I didn't mean—or I did mean them at the time. I was enraged at the thought of you with a colored man."

All my ambivalent feelings for Leon warred and jostled like unsecured cargo on a storm-tossed ship. "Please, Leon, don't call him a colored man."

"Fine," he said sharply. "I didn't come here to talk about him."

I opened a window and welcomed the wind off the sea while Leon patted the baby's back and soothed his fussing with murmured endearments.

"I knew this baby would change my life, I just never guessed how much. Aaron has made me rethink everything I know, Roxanne, everything I believed in. Ever since I first held him in my arms, I've asked myself every day what's really important. The money? The reputation? The power of life and sometimes death? Love. Love is all that's really important. You're my granddaughter, and I've loved you all your life, and I will always love you. I want you to know you're welcome at Summit Drive anytime, and I hope you'll come. Often."

"What about Denise? She won't want to see me."

"She doesn't want to see anyone who can't help her lose weight and find the perfect script for her next film. She doesn't seem to care about the baby at all. She's eaten up with ambition." He added ruefully, "I recognize the symptoms. I wouldn't have before, but I do now. Denise is convinced that you set up the *Fly Me to the Moon* disaster from the beginning, that you planned it, that you wanted to bring us all down because you always hated her."

"I always did hate her, but I didn't set out to ruin her, or anyone else, and I'm sorry," I said truthfully, adding, "I don't regret helping Max, but I shouldn't have brought the scripts to Empire. I'm sorry, Leon."

"I'm sorry too, Honeybee. I'm sorry about Max too. Is he doing all right?"

Two months ago, two weeks ago I would have lashed out, *Fat lot you care!* But if Leon had changed and tempered, so had I. And too, living in England, Max had moved beyond the possibility of legal harm. His occasional dismal letters that Marian shared with me and Thelma also proved he had moved beyond the possibility of any hope that Marian might join him. He lived in one room, and he sent money to Marian, who was still living with Thelma in Tarzana. Norman had been placed in a facility nearby. "Adrian Scott got him a job in England with some of the other blacklisted writers, writing on *The Adventures of Robin Hood* for British television. It plays over here too, in the late afternoon, kiddie TV."

"Well, I'm glad to know Max is working anyway. Writers need to be writing."

"That's what Max said to me. That if he wasn't writing, he was dying."

"Composing or decomposing, one or the other, that's the writer's fate."

The baby yawned a great, wide-mouthed, satisfied yawn. He hoisted the baby to his other shoulder, where he left a pool of drool. Leon didn't seem to mind. The baby fussed, and with his little hands he tugged at the cap on his head, pulling it off and dropping it to the floor. I picked up the cap, and Leon put it in his pocket.

"See?" Leon said proudly. "Aaron already has a mind of his own. Mrs. Shea insists on the baby cap, but he hates it." He tickled the baby's chin. "Is that Nelson's old upright?"

"Yes. I think it is."

"I mourned Nelson, Roxanne, I did. And I know a lot of people were angry that I didn't go to the funeral, but I couldn't let people think that I was going soft on Communism, or that I supported his being a homo. I'd known Nelson for twenty years, but I cared more for my reputation than I did for my friends. It doesn't mean I love my country any less, and it doesn't mean I would ever embrace a Communist, but I wonder now . . . There are things I should have done differently. I should have called you right when I read those two scripts Elliott Dunne sent to Denise. I should have picked up the phone and asked what the hell you thought you were doing."

"So you did recognize Max's touch."

"Max wrote them, and you were fronting for him, and I thought you brought them to Empire to make me look stupid, or to give me a heart attack. Or both. I saw it as an act of betrayal."

In my own defense, I could only offer that I was angry.

"I was angry too. I should have sent the scripts back with a curt note. I never should have taken on the picture, but Denise thought Maisie was the perfect role, and she really wanted it. I wanted Denise to be happy."

"Do you still want her to be happy?"

"It's a marriage," he replied. "Marriage always requires compromises."

I didn't want to have to feel sorry for him, but I did. He had squandered love and time; he had broken up his marriage to Julia because he loved Denise, and now, it seemed, he had only dreary compromises to show for it. Well, they were not all he had. To watch him with this tiny baby was to see a man in love.

He walked around the room, patting the baby's back, and his gaze fell on the huge framed poster from the 1931 *Cyrano de Bergerac* starring Rowland Granville over the fireplace. He seemed to study it. "I used to think Rowland and Florence broke up just because they were young—she was only nineteen when they got married—or he didn't like living in California, or any other number of reasons. But now I think it was because Florence didn't know how to love Rowland, or how to love you, for that matter. She didn't know how to love anyone, because Julia and I forgot how to love her. I've been thinking about this for months now, even before this little boy was born." He kissed the baby's cheek and played with his nose. "It's a cycle that repeats itself, and what a terrible thing it was for Florence to grow up without a mother and father who loved her."

"It is a terrible thing."

"You speak from experience."

"I didn't have a mother and father, but I never felt unloved. I had you and Julia."

Leon smoothed the baby's wispy hair, and it seemed to me that he pondered before he spoke next. "What will happen to Aaron if his mother and father don't love him?"

"You love him."

"I won't live forever."

I peered at him more closely. While he still looked like Leon Greene, and carried himself like Leon Greene, he did not sound like the titan of Empire we all loved and feared. For the first time I saw that he was an old man.

The baby squirmed and started to squall. Leon put him on his shoulder, jiggled him, and made soothing noises. "Mrs. Shea will have a fit if she hears him. She's an absolute Nazi about his schedule. The whole house has to run on the baby's schedule. She was locked in a power struggle with Clarence right up until the day he left."

"Clarence left?" I couldn't have been more shocked if he had said the planets all fell from their orbits. "Did you fire him?"

"I didn't, but I would have fired him. I would have had to. He said unforgivable things to my wife."

"That doesn't sound like Clarence at all."

"Denise apparently made some sort of derogatory remark about his nephew, the one you . . . Why, how this came up, I do not know, I wasn't there, and Elsie isn't the most reliable witness, and no one will tell me exactly what Denise said, but Clarence blew up and cursed her. They got into a terrible fight, and then he just walked out. No notice, no nothing. Just dropped his keys on the floor and walked away after thirty years."

He went on about Clarence's disloyalty, about the domestic uproar following his desertion, but I scarcely listened. The news that Clarence had left Summit Drive struck me as inexpressibly sad, like the last sad domino falling from events I had set in motion. But

I also could not suppress a little joyful sensation that Clarence had proved himself no Uncle Tom, and that Terrence would have been proud of him. After living for thirty years in a houseful of people addicted to dramatic gestures, Clarence had indulged in one of his own.

The baby started wailing in earnest, and Leon said he had to go. "You'll come to Summit Drive, Roxanne, won't you? Come and visit Aaron?"

"Of course," I said, privately vowing that I would never go without Irene at my side.

"Do you need money? I know you haven't worked in months."

"I'm fine. I've got a job with Paragon. Carleton's offered me a job."

He looked slightly crestfallen. "You could always come to Empire, you know. You could have any job you like there."

"I know. But I would always be in your shadow there."

"I suppose I understand that. Suppose I have to." The baby squalled. "He's definitely hungry. I should go."

"I'm so glad you came, and I am happy to meet your baby." Together we walked outside and went down the stairs.

The driver turned on the motor as soon as we turned the corner, and Mrs. Shea stepped out of the car. "Mr. Greene," she cried. "I really must insist! His schedule! You're going to upset his bowels. Oh, his little cap! What have you done with his cap?" She took the blanket-wrapped bundle from his arms as Leon dangled the cap before her. She snatched it and got back in the car.

He turned for one last look at the sea, glancing at the garage. "I don't remember a garage."

"I had it built," I admitted. "You're going to tear the place down anyway."

"I'm not going to tear it down as long as you are happy here, Honeybee."

"Oh, I'm happy here, Leon! I love this place! I've been so worried you were so angry, you were going to evict me."

"I'd never do that. It's yours as long as you want to stay here. Can I ask one thing in return?"

"Of course."

He stepped away from the car so Mrs. Shea would not overhear. "Don't let my son grow up unloved. I need this from you, Roxanne. Promise me. When I die, please—"

"You're not going to die!"

He put an arm around my shoulders and pulled me so close I could smell the baby-smell still on his cheek. "I want you to be part of Aaron's life. Never let this little boy feel himself alone or uncared for. Love him, Roxanne, look after him. Irene doesn't much love her own children; how can I ask her to love mine? Please teach him how to love others, how to be strong and loyal. Teach him how important it is to love. Teach him how to be careful about whose heart he breaks, and who he lets go of."

The regret in his voice was heartbreaking, but his words rang for me with an echo reverberating from the past. *Life is short and love is long. Love is demanding and rewarding and aggravating, sometimes angering, but it is never finished or over, or done with, not even in death . . .* Julia's letter asking me to love Leon no matter what he had done.

"Wait here just a minute, will you? I'll be right back." I raced up the stairs to the living room, and in the desk drawer I found the letter, the request that three years before I had ignored. I ran back down to PCH and placed it in his hand. "It's a letter from Julia. She wrote it the month before she died. She sent it to me via Mr. Wilkie. She forgave you, Leon. She wanted you to know that. She wanted me to tell you she'd forgiven you, and I should have told you. I should have given you this letter years ago, but I couldn't. I was too angry with you. I could not . . ."

"Can we forgive each other, Honeybee?"

"Of course. Of course we can. She wanted us to look after each other."

"And Aaron. Will you look after him? You're the only one I trust. Will you do that?"

"Yes. I promise," I said, blubbering openly now. "Of course I will love him."

"Good." He kissed my forehead and looked at me with the old affection that so used to cheer my heart. "I trust you to do the right thing. To be brave. You've proved that."

Astonished, stunned really at the significance of his compliment, since my actions had exacted such a toll on him, I just stood there, speechless, as he got into the Bentley. The driver turned the car around and headed south, leaving me in the midst of emotions so tangled I wrestled with them for days as I thought about the past—not what had actually happened to me, but what could have happened to me if I had not had Leon and Julia to love me, if I had not had Max and Simon and Nelson and Jerrold to cheer me through childhood. My life might have been as blighted as my right cheek. And yet I escaped being unloved, and that escape seemed to me suddenly miraculous, and I saw my life strangely, as if I had somehow survived a shipwreck that had cast others into the loveless deep.

CHAPTER THIRTY-NINE

In that first month or so at Paragon, I made no new friends. Acquaintances, yes, but people were wary of me. As Terrence might have said, I didn't take it personally. After all, my scandals, plural, were well known, still fresh, and had been widely, publicly aired. Plus, I was closely associated with rival Empire. Still, everyone knew I was the person who had brought *Adios Diablo* to Paragon. That picture and its massive budget were the studio's great hope, and also, as everyone knew, its great gamble. But for the moment, only Carleton and I knew what he had planned for its 1957 release.

Carleton made up a title for me, head of the Story Department, and I spent my days reading, vetting, making suggestions for scripts, shaping material, suggesting casting and directors, rather like the work that Julia did for Leon for years. I was relieved there were no more producers with burn-pocked couches in my line of work, and I confess, I liked being part of studio life, the camaraderie of staff meetings with people who, whatever their differences, all loved making movies. From my old life on Clara Bow Drive, I brought only Thelma and two of the paintings I had borrowed years before. (I bought these from the artist and returned all the others.) I had a swamp cooler in one window, and the sluggish wheel turned and blew damp air around on these hot August days.

I had a big desk and a small conference area—couch, chairs, coffee table, and a bar, complete with ice trays in a little freezer and an electric percolator. And my own television set. Late afternoons Thelma and I often drank Campari and soda, or cold beers, and watched the half-hour series *The Adventures of Robin Hood* on the office television while we waited for the traffic to thin out. We couldn't tell what scripts Max had written, because of course, all the writers' names were fake, but we cheered the egalitarian principles each episode underscored. We sometimes left the building arm in arm singing the catchy theme song.

Outside of Paragon, life meandered on. The Wilburs moved away, and construction crews came in, razed their house, and started building something far more grand, from the look of it. My subscription to the *Challenger* lapsed. I did not renew. Even Irene gave up trying to set up blind dates. I turned them all down. I put my couture clothing in zipped plastic bags at the back of the closet. To be head of the Story Department at Paragon didn't require anywhere near as much socializing as being an agent—no obligatory galas, very few parties, so mostly I just went to work and went home. In place of our old Friday-afternoon custom, lunch at the Ambassador, Friday nights Irene and I had dinner at her house. Josefina had charge of the children, and Gordon was seldom home, though when I saw him I was continually appalled at how haggard he looked. There wasn't enough time in any one day to wield the kind of power Gordon Conrad now had, and there was never any time to shirk the ominous responsibilities that went with it.

One hot night in August Irene and I sat by their pool after dinner drinking iced champagne with our feet in the water. Gordon meandered out to the patio, just home from work at nearly ten. Irene rose and kissed him on the cheek. She went to the patio bar, got him a glass, opened a fresh bottle with a practiced pop, and refreshed all our glasses. "Eudonna's gone for the night, honey, but can I get you something to eat?"

"I had something at the studio." He took off his shoes and

socks, sat down, and wearily put his pale feet in the water. "I had to stay extra late tonight because Leon brought the baby to the Executive Mansion today to show him off. Work came to a halt, of course, so everyone could bow down to the little prince."

"Did Denise come too?"

"Hell no. That Irish nanny in her white uniform stood there like the commandant. But Denise came later in the afternoon." Gordon lit a cigarette. "She loves waltzing in, and having everything come to a halt so everyone can fawn over her. 'What can we get for you, Miss Dell?' 'Who do you want to see, Miss Dell?' Denise will get what she wants, no matter the cost in time or money to anyone else. She didn't even have an appointment with me, but she demanded that I drop everything—cancel a production meeting!—to sit there and listen to her berate me for an hour."

"What for?" asked Irene.

"Where was the Joan of Arc script I had promised her? I tried to tell her they're still—"

"Joan of Arc!" I choked on my champagne so it almost came out my nose.

"She's convinced she missed her calling with those Jean Arthur, Carole Lombard sorts of comedies and that really, she's a great dramatic actress."

"She couldn't say *oscilloscope*! How is she supposed to lead the French to victory?"

Gordon turned his gaze to me. His voice was even and acid. "I'd tell Denise Dell she was going to play the Virgin Mary and give birth to the light of the world. I'd tell her she was going to remake the rolling-on-the-beach scene in *From Here to Eternity*. I'd tell her she was going to play Ilsa in a new *Casablanca*. I'd swear to her that she would have lines like Bacall in *To Have and Have Not*, that we were rebuilding Rome on the back lot so she could play Cleopatra, that Mary Pickford will come out of retirement to kiss the hem of Denise Dell, America's new sweetheart."

"You're overworked, honey," said Irene.

"Goddamn right. There are days I wish I'd been a Red, and I'd be blacklisted and driven out of here forever. There are days I think I'll just go down in my own goddamned bomb shelter and never come out." His voice trembled with emotion. "Leon Greene was like a father to me, and like a good son, an obedient son, I stood by and watched him turn a great studio into an old man's plaything. I didn't question his judgment. I watched him demand loyalty oaths from everyone, but show no real loyalty himself. And now I'm the one who will bear the responsibility." He poured more champagne and drank it all down at once. He stood up, and his wet, bare feet padded toward the house. "Glory days, girls, as we rumble toward ruin."

To knock or not to knock, that is the question. Did we just walk in like we always had, or were we guests? Irene and I both felt apprehensive. I had not been to Summit Drive since that awful day in May when Leon had said he was finished with me. Irene was tense, because Gordon's health was cracking under the strain of his burdens at Empire, and Leon seemed not to notice, or if he noticed, he didn't care. There, in front of the front door that had once graced a French château, we stared at each other. Finally we just opened the door and walked in. A new maid who recognized Irene met us in the foyer. Summit Drive without Clarence was strange, but I was glad he wasn't there. I couldn't have faced him again. Not after the last time.

The maid led us to the French doors and pointed down to the tiered gardens, where Leon was pushing a baby carriage around the artificial lake. Mrs. Shea sat glowering under a nearby arbor. Irene and I waved and wandered downhill.

Leon was delighted to see us both, and we strolled with him while he chatted about the baby's many accomplishments. I hadn't walked these paths with Leon since I was a child, and I had the sense that time had somehow dislocated, gone off its accustomed tracks, the unsettling sense of playing at being a grown-up, as if I'd donned one of Julia's old hats and long silky shawls to put on a show for the swans.

"Leon!" cried an imperious voice. I was alarmed to look up to the house and see Denise framed in the French doors.

"I better go see what she wants," said Leon.

"We should leave," we said more or less in unison.

No sooner did Leon remove his hand from the baby carriage than Mrs. Shea instantly materialized. She consulted her watch. "The baby has another ten minutes for his walk. Then he will be fed." The baby seemed to hear this and resent it and started to fuss as she resolutely pushed him down the path.

The three of us walked back up the terraces to the house. We were about to say goodbye to Leon when Denise came down the stairs. She looked to have been poured into her dress, her bouffant skirt a lilac organza that lilted like a sail picking up a brisk wind.

"Leon," she said, flashing me a hateful look, "there was a phone call while you were out. Some relative of that Negro butler. She wanted to speak to you, but I told her we had no interest in anything she might have to say." With a final, frosty glare at me, she turned and started up the stairs.

"Why would Clarence's relative be calling me?" Leon said to us.

"Bad news or money," said Irene, "or both."

At the thought of bad news, my heart seemed to tighten in my chest. What if Terrence . . . "You'll call her back, won't you, Leon?"

"If it's important, she'll call back."

"Please, Leon. It was probably Clarence's wife, Ruby. She owns Ruby's Diner on Central Avenue. Please call and see what she wanted. For my sake. Please."

"All right, Roxanne. Let's go to the library, and I'll phone."

"I'll wait here," I said, feeling suddenly faint. I sat down in one of the Louis XVI chairs in the foyer.

"This is stupid," said Irene, after Leon had left us. "Why should we wait? Why do you care what Clarence's wife wants? I thought that was all over with what's-his-name."

"Terrence, Irene. His name is Terrence. It is over. He's left the country. But if . . . if there was something important, if something has happened to him, they don't have my number. They'd call here."

As we waited, Mrs. Shea wheeled the carriage in. The baby was squalling his little guts out by now. She lifted him out and carried him up the stairs as his wails amplified, echoing off the marble floors. They sounded eerie and lost.

Leon was gone quite a long time, and when he came down the stairs at last, he seemed to cling to the rail. He was pale and grim as he said, "Clarence's cancer returned. They operated, and just closed him back up. He's dying."

Both Irene and I took a few minutes to absorb this awful revelation, though my feelings were complicated with crashing relief that Terrence was not hurt or in trouble.

"Why would his wife call you?" asked Irene. "Clarence walked out on you."

"She didn't want to call. He did. I talked to him. He said he is a Christian and believes in forgiveness, and now that the end is near, he asked my forgiveness."

"And what did you say?"

"I said, of course, and thanked him for his years of service. He was a faithful servant. I said I'd never forget him. Besides"—he seemed to sigh—"Denise . . . might have started the fight with her unfortunate remark about his nephew."

"Terrence." I didn't want to shatter the peace I had achieved with my family, but I wasn't going to pretend he was just some nameless nephew. "Can't you, both of you, please just say his name?"

"Terrence," said Irene begrudgingly.

And in the same tone, Leon echoed, "Terrence."

I gave the keys to Irene. I was too upset to drive. I tried to fathom what this moment meant to Terrence's family. All those thirty Christmases that Clarence had stood at attention for the Greenes while his own family waited for him. How they must all begrudge us those Christmases, how Clarence himself must regret them as he now lay dying.

CHAPTER FORTY

The vast Baptist church was packed, everyone stifling in the September heat, sweating in their dark suits and dresses, their black gloves. I too wore black: a black sheath, Julia's pearls, and a broad-brimmed black hat that had been battered on the drive here with the top down. I arrived late due to traffic, and the choir was just finishing a hymn as I slid into the last pew at the back. Despite giving me some strange looks, people scooted together to make room for me in the pew. Far ahead, in the front, I could see the back of Leon's head, his wiry gray halo of hair, and beside him, Denise's bright blonde shingle. Irene and Gordon too sat there. They were not the only white people at the funeral, but they were the only ones up front with the family. Typical Leon.

The preacher gave long opening remarks, and Booker played several soul-stirring hymns, solos backed by his sax man and a pianist, hymns I recognized from hearing Terrence pound them out on the upright. The choir director signaled the organist; the choir and congregation stood, and everyone sang together. The lady next to me handed me a hymnal. She didn't need it, and I did. I wished I had one of those little fans all the ladies were using to cool themselves. The fans advertised the funeral home.

The sermon bidding farewell to Clarence Goodall was punctuated with a lot of lively input from the audience—I mean, the congregation—sobs, sniffles, laughter, shouts of *Amen!* The pastor was vivacious and mobile and spoke at length and lovingly of Clarence's devotion to duty, never mentioning that that duty was to a white family. He didn't mention the Greenes at all. He spoke of how Clarence had been a good father not only to his own children, but to his fatherless nieces and nephews as well, how his innate dignity touched and inspired everyone who knew him. I got misty listening to him tell Clarence's story as though it were a film unfolding, with certain peaks where he cued the musicians, and they played a few bars of something stirring, exactly like a movie soundtrack. Perhaps Terrence's church and mine weren't so very far apart after all.

"At the end of his life Clarence Goodall was an example of Christian fortitude amid the woes of the flesh," said the pastor, "which he met with unshaken faith and the hope of resurrection, and he surely has been admitted to a glorious heaven, where the righteous will be forgiven their sins, and rewarded for their strength of spirit, and shine forever in the light of Almighty God. Amen."

He nodded to a deacon and they closed the casket. I was so far at the back, I could see none of this, but I heard someone, a woman, break out in anguished sobs.

We stood for the closing hymn, "Amazing Grace," and six men stepped from the pews and moved to Clarence Goodall's coffin. They lifted it onto their shoulders and started up the aisle. One of these men at the front of the coffin was Booker. His face, when he saw me, turned to a granite mask of anger. And one of these men was Terrence. I had no idea he was back, and my heart raced, filled with *Hallelujah!* just to see him. As our eyes locked, Terrence's expression swiftly fluttered with a range of emotions I cannot describe. When he had passed by I found the verse in the hymnal, and I let my voice soar, though I knew I shouldn't be joyous at a funeral.

The congregation vacated the church in an orderly fashion, from the front to the back, so everyone had to walk past me in the last pew. I knew very few. Ruby, on the arm of her daughter, glanced at me with a look of chagrin. Coralee and her husband, frowning; Serena and her parents. Serena (who knew no better) smiled, waved. A woman who could only have been Terrence's other sister scowled at me. Mr. Branch, his wheelchair pushed by Ben Tupper, nodded to me sadly. I recognized Mr. Wilkie and his wife. Men and women, black and white, who had served at Summit Drive during Clarence's long tenure there murmured or nodded as they passed me. As for my own family, Gordon gave me a dyspeptic smile. Irene's eyes held something that looked like warning. Leon regarded me oddly, as if I were wearing a clown suit and a red rubber nose, utterly out of place here. As for Denise, she merely looked right through me, willing my atoms to disperse under her glare. Quite the best performance I'd ever seen her give.

From the church we all made our way to the parking lot out back, where the sun cooked down on the blacktop. Standing beside my car was Terrence Dexter. He looked thinner, or at least he'd lost the weight he'd gained in Alabama. He wore a smart, double-breasted dark suit, white shirt, and blue tie, with black polished shoes. His face remained serious, but his deep, dark eyes, I could tell, his eyes took me in.

"Is this your car? It looks like your car, but it's the wrong color."

"I had to have it painted," I said, feeling my way around each word as if it were a stone in my mouth. I could not bear to speak of the red paint, the dead dog. Not here. Not now.

"Can I ride with you to the cemetery?"

"Sure." I did not trust myself to say more. I could feel my birthmark flooding with color. I'm sure he could see it too as I got in behind the wheel and started the car.

The sprightly firefly MG T nosed into line with Leon's chauffeur-driven Bentley, behind all the other enormous cars with vast tail fins: Plymouths, Dodges, and Chevys. As a cortege, we followed the hearse to the cemetery.

"When did you get back?" I asked.

"I don't remember. A while. A month maybe. Six weeks?"

"Oh," I said, disappointed that it had been that long, and I never knew.

"Ruby wrote me how Clarence up and quit the Greenes, that he was dying. Soon as I got her letter, I knew I had to come back. I never thanked Clarence, never even recognized what he did for us after my daddy left, how he stepped in, as best he could. I wanted to thank him while there was time. I wanted to say goodbye."

"I'm sure he was happy to see you."

"Not at first. No, he was still real angry with me for taking up with you. Bone-marrow-deep angry. I had to ask his forgiveness."

"And did you?"

"I did. You don't split hairs or bluster, or make excuses for yourself, with a dying man."

"He loved you and Booker. I'm sure of that," I said, remembering Clarence's passion on behalf of his nephews in that last terrible exchange I had with him. I heard Terrence gulp, but only the engine murmured in the silence between us.

"I met Sidney Bechet while I was in Paris," he said at last. "I went with Jerrold and Annette a few times to hear him in one of those little *boîtes*. Seeing him play, being right there—how could I have thought he was anything but brilliant? I brought some records back with me, and I made Booker listen."

"And?"

"Booker's a West Coast Cool man. But I'm a Bechet convert. I guess I'm a convert to the Church of Rick and Ilsa too. I learned a lot from working with Jerrold on *The Oubliette*." He shook his head, and a tiny, audible scoff escaped his lips. "Pretty damned weird, my working on a film about an African man who falls in love with a white girl and tries to forget her."

"If you had put your address on the aerogramme, I would have written back to you."

"I didn't want you to write back. I didn't want to hear from you. I didn't want to think about you. I just wanted you to know I was sorry about your agency."

"I appreciated your note."

Like acquaintances, we offered pale inanities to each other, including the weather. Saying nothing of our shared past, Terrence and I seemed to be testing each other the way you would gingerly test a bruise. Does it hurt more? Does it hurt less? He was considerably less exuberant than he used to be; perhaps living in a foreign country had subdued him. But then, experience had subdued me too, and I hadn't been anywhere at all.

"How is Thelma?" he asked after we'd agreed the weather was unusually hot for September.

I rattled on a bit about our working life at Paragon, and he nodded. He asked after Max and I said he was in England, and at least he was working.

"And Jonathan. What's he doing?"

"I only know what I read about him in the papers. He's a big star now. He never calls or comes over. He stays away from scandal."

"Well, he isn't much of a loss to you. Just my opinion. You probably don't need him anyway, not to go out dancing, or play tennis. You probably have a new flame."

"I play tennis at Irene's. I don't go out much. I'm fine on my own. And you? Are you back with Jaylene?"

"Nah. She'll never be coming back from New York. Why should she? Her career's going great there. No, I'm on my own too."

As we followed the other cars and the MG's heat needle inched upward, we spoke of the Montgomery bus boycott, which was still going on while appeals to the convictions of Reverend Cooke, Dr. King, Jo Ann Robinson, E. D. Nixon, and the others dragged through the courts. Terrence had written articles about the political and historical significance of the boycott for the *Paris Tribune*. I mentioned my baby uncle, Aaron, but I didn't say that Leon and I had reconciled. I did not want to tread so close to the turbulent past. We were both carefully avoiding any suggestion of the intimate, saying nothing to indicate or acknowledge that our lives were complex, or that we had once loved each other, that we had laughed and quarreled, and raced naked to the water's edge by moonlight, that we had rested and roused in each other's arms, that we had played card games, and worked contentedly side by side, that we had been the warp and woof of each other's lives. None of that.

Finally I said, "I suppose you'll go back to Paris now."

He ruminated before replying. "It was a good place, a fine place, like Jerrold said. But I'm not Jerrold Davies, and I'm not Jimmy Baldwin. My life, the work I'm meant to do, I need to be here."

I was so happy to hear these words. I wanted to reach out and take his hand and bring it to my lips. I downshifted instead; the cortege had slowed.

"Got my old room on Naomi Avenue back, but not the garage. I don't need a garage for the DeSoto. I'm driving Ruby's old sedan. She has Clarence's car now."

"I can't imagine you in a DeSoto."

"Yeah, it's certainly not an eagle. Not even a firefly like this MG. More like an old sow bug just rolling along the street. But it gets me to work."

"At the *Challenger*?"

"I started there again last week."

"And your book?"

"I wrote it, Roxanne. I didn't finish it, and what I have is a mess, but I have enough to work with, to go on working."

"What's it about?"

He gave one of those rueful, almost unwilling laughs I so well remembered. "Truth is, I'm not real sure yet. Something to do with my daddy. I know that. My daddy and Moses Shaw."

"I saved all your letters from Alabama. You can have them

back if you want. For your book," I offered without looking at him.

"Thanks. I probably won't need them. I have all my own notes. I left them with Coralee when I went to Paris, and she saved them for me."

"I have your Royal," I said, hoping that I could hold the typewriter hostage.

"I have a new one. Keep it. Maybe you'll finally learn how to type."

The cemetery gates loomed as the cars in front of us entered, and the MG idled in line. We did not look at each other. I longed for the gifts of a real Cyrano de Bergerac, to be able to speak deathless dialogue, or the gifts of an Ira Gershwin, immortal lyrics that would tell Terrence how much I loved him, how my life had emptied of joy, of meaning when he left me. Now he was back and I felt like Joan Fontaine when she returns to Thornfield and sees Orson Welles sitting alone on the bench and Bernard Herrmann's music swells over them, but I had no music, no words, only the exhaust from other cars that soiled the air around us as the MG followed the cortege slowly winding along the road to Clarence's final resting place. The sun bore down, and the heat needle wobbled up toward the red zone.

"They'll bury Clarence not too far from my mother and my grandparents," Terrence mused, "and a lot of other family, Bowers and Prescotts, and Goodalls. I wonder if they'll bury me here too. If all our lives just end up in the same place, and in the same way, no matter what or how much we try to do."

I swallowed a great wad of unwilling emotion, not trusting myself to speak, wishing that a huge deer would leap out of the headstones, fly over us, antlers and all, and that we would clutch at each other reflexively and rekindle the flame we had so carefully guarded from everyone who would have blown it out. I parked behind the big cars and turned off the motor.

"Thanks. For the ride. Goodbye, Roxanne," he said as he got

out and folded the seat forward to protect the leather from the sun. He paused there, momentarily, before he turned and walked away. "Here's looking at you, kid."

Oh god, I thought, my heart crawling up into my throat: *This is it! Isn't it? This is the airport scene!* Can it be that the Church of Rick and Ilsa is a place without solace, with only the crumbs of strength you could sweep, hoard, muster, cling to so that you might endure the long, empty, loveless days and nights that would follow? *Goodbye. Our paths will not cross, and we will never see each other again!* Racketing through my whole body were emotions I had only ever seen onscreen, only ever felt secondhand, accompanied by popcorn. I used every ounce of strength I had to stifle anything remotely like a sob, or the temptation to call after him. Unsteadily I got out of the MG and walked toward the gravesite.

Terrence joined the other pallbearers gathered at the hearse. Together they shouldered Clarence's coffin, carried it to its final resting place, and lowered it to the ground in front of metal folding chairs lined up for the family. The chairs had gotten too hot to sit on, and men took off their suit jackets and placed them over the seats for buffers for the ladies.

At Julia's funeral, the few Negroes, badly outnumbered, had stood to one side. Here we few whites, badly outnumbered, stood apart, as though everyone had agreed to the custom that the races must be separate. Other than my own family, and the Wilkies, I didn't know any of the other white people. I stood between Irene and Gordon, with Leon and Denise to my left. A hot breeze moved the veils on women's hats and billowed out the preacher's robes. From some distance came the sounds of traffic as the world went on its heedless way.

Terrence stood behind his Aunt Ruby, looking across the grave to me. While the pastor spoke, Terrence's line of vision never faltered from my face, and mine never left his. Leon followed his gaze, and he turned to give me a hard look, which I ignored. I stared at Terrence Dexter, at his beloved face that I might never see again. I called on every L'Oiseau d'Or principle, on every bit of panache that Julia had taught me; I feared I might tremble or faint from the heat. I could not, I must not cry, because if I started crying, I knew I'd never stop. I reminded myself over and over, *I am Roxanne Granville, named for the heroine of a great play.*

When at long last this service ended, after the last "Amen," people broke into groups to talk, to greet and commiserate, to pay respects to Ruby and the family, and to slowly leave the cemetery in little family clusters. The crowd thinned, but I stayed put, unmoving, while Leon and Denise and the others began to walk away, Irene and Gordon too. Sunlight poured molten all around me. I could not move for watching Terrence, who also stood rooted, ramrod straight, and pensive for what seemed forever, as though eons lay between us. Ruby rose and took her daughter's arm. Terrence briefly kissed his aunt's cheek and gave a whispered word to Coralee, and then, circling the grave, he crossed the distance between us, which had seemed immense, crossed it as though he were diminishing not just space, but time, until he stood in front of me.

"The *oubliette* didn't work for me," he said in a voice that was clear and firm. "I went there to forget you, but I couldn't. I tried. I tried everything there was, and I could not forget you."

"I tried too. I could not forget you. I've missed you so."

"Do you still love me?"

"I never quit loving you."

"I never quit loving you, Roxanne, but we can't do it like we did before. We have to be braver than that."

"I know."

"We have to be stronger. We have to be willing to let the world say what it wants, and just insist on loving each other, on being together."

"I know."

"Are you ready to do this? Here? Now?"

"I am, Terrence. I'm ready."

"It won't be easy."

"I know that. I don't care. I don't want to live without you beside me. I don't care what it costs, or who hates us, or what the world tries to do to us."

"They'll try and destroy us. You know they will."

"They will try, but we won't let them. We are stronger and better together than we are apart. Oh, Terrence, Julia always said, 'The more strength you use, the more you will have.' I believe that's true."

"All right, then. We might as well take our stand here as anywhere."

"All right," I said. "I do."

"I do too."

Terrence offered me his hand, and I took it. I felt his warmth penetrate not simply the flesh of my hand, but the very fiber of my being. I looked up into his dark eyes. A smile tugged at his lips, and his gold tooth gleamed. We did not kiss. We were at a funeral, after all. Everywhere around us I heard a collective intake of breath, of shock. Everyone, black and white, stared at us as though they had been turned to stone. Someone, Booker, I think, shouted, *Don't! Don't do it! Don't do it!* I saw Leon go pale. I saw Denise's red mouth gape with outrage. I saw Irene roll her eyes, smile at me, and shake her head, knowing this was the most romantic act of my life, but it was not reckless. Far from it. Terrence and I walked on by together, crossing both space and time toward a future that would challenge and reward us for the rest of our days.

AUTHOR'S NOTE

In my family we take our movies seriously. Like Julia in *The Great Pretenders*, I took my eldest son to the movies when he did not weigh enough to hold down the seat. Bear sat through *Gandhi*—at age three. My youngest, Brendan, had seen *The Bridge on the River Kwai* three times before he was ten. They could sing all the songs from the Fred and Ginger movies, and they knew who wrote which tunes.

Every weekend we had marathon movie night because with the first royalties from my novel *These Latter Days*, I bought a VCR. I remember walking the aisles of the video store after we had plugged it in. I was overwhelmed. Hundreds—maybe a thousand movies! Blockbusters, obscure foreign films, classics, silents, comedy, noir, some I had seen recently, some I had seen as a kid, some I had never even heard of. All of them were suddenly mine to behold for $2.99. My sons, who were just little boys then, were a few aisles away, and I could hear them quarreling over which movies we would take home. I let each of them choose one. For myself, I was so paralyzed by the possibilities I could only walk out with *Gaslight* (1944) with Charles Boyer and Ingrid Bergman, a movie I had long heard about but had never seen.

But very soon our family trips to the video store required a bag to carry all the movies we rented. Our marathon movie nights were an education as well as entertainment, not just for myself but for my kids and their friends.

Despite a long-standing love of film and the darkened theater, I had never given much thought to the Hollywood blacklist era until the 1999 Oscars. The Academy gave a special award to Elia Kazan, the legendary director of *On the Waterfront* (1954), *A Streetcar Named Desire* (1951), and many other films, a man who, by any artistic standard, had contributed greatly to this art form. Outside of the event, cameras caught sight of protesters carrying signs decrying the award. Inside cameras circuited throughout, and you could see and sense the palpable tension as some of the celebrity-laden audience rose to their feet, applauding Mr. Kazan as he walked onstage while some remained seated, stoic, refusing to honor him. These conflicting reactions were based on Kazan's 1952 testimony before the House Committee on Un-American Activities (HUAC). Nearly fifty years later, so deep were the passions the blacklist aroused, many could still not forgive him. Kazan and many others "named names" of their former comrades in the Communist Party years before. Those named were themselves called before the Committee, and the people who refused to "cooperate" were universally blacklisted, ruining careers and wrecking lives.

The blacklist era (1947–1960) is a complex, difficult subject with tangled roots in the entertainment industry, in labor history and anti-Fascist movements during the thirties, as well as our alliance with Russia during the Second World War. Victor Navasky's *Naming Names* (1980) remains, in my opinion, the "bible" on the subject. This Columbia University professor painstakingly synthesized hundreds of interviews into a narrative that sought to explain not simply how an entire industry had so totally succumbed to fear, but why. A professor asks: *What happened and why?* A novelist asks: *What if?* A novelist has to condense and distill the historical past into currents that can lift and carry characters through the story.

I began to imagine a character caught in a web of old loyalties, and affections. Roxanne Granville had to be brash but conflicted. She had to be young enough to be reckless, convinced, as the young are, that bold gestures will be rewarded. She needed a past that would resonate, and so I gave her a unique childhood where she was informally tutored by a cadre of marvelous writers. I gave her a profession that would plunge her into the fear and suspicion that hung over Hollywood like red smog. For all her privilege and position, she also needed something that would give her a measure of insecurity. Without the stain upon her cheek, she would be a less interesting character.

Historical fiction always aspires to create vivid context around personal struggles. *The Great Pretenders* addresses social upheavals in what—on the face of it—appeared to be an era of happy conformity. I grew up during that fifties postwar boom in one of the new tract houses in the Southern California's San Fernando Valley, the streets all rigidly parallel, the neighborhoods uniformly white, televisions blinking blue in the living rooms. People took for granted that black and white families would not live in the same neighborhoods, or work for equal pay, or have equal opportunities. But by mid-decade, under all that bland assumption, new currents roiled. Radios blasted out the raucous, rebellious chords of rock and roll. The terrible death of fourteen-year-old Emmett Till outraged the nation. In Montgomery, Alabama, in an unprecedented collective action, citizens walked rather than ride at the back of the bus; they boycotted the buses for more than a year while their struggle went all the way to the Supreme Court. I wanted the reader to experience these contemporary upheavals as well as the political tremors besetting the picture business. I plunged Terrence Dexter, a reporter for a fictional LA paper, into the maelstrom of the bus boycott to experience it personally.

Ideally the human dilemmas that characters face should resonate beyond the pages of any novel. In this book those dilemmas are questions of aspiration and desperation, of betrayal, of loyalty, forbidden love, unregretted folly—in short, choices. Every life has choices. Truly, what are any of us but a handful of character traits tossed into a potful of historical circumstance? We are all obliged to respond, to fulfill or reject, to rise to occasions we could not have foreseen or imagined.

THE GREAT PRETENDERS

LAURA KALPAKIAN

DISCUSSION QUESTIONS

1. Uncontested assumptions about women's roles—sexism—constrict Roxanne's possibilities. So pervasive are these in the 1950s that she scarcely recognizes their effect. ("Isn't that what women have always been?" Jonathan quips. "Bartered, baffled, and dim but kissable?") After her encounter with Irv Rakoff, Roxanne begins to understand that these underlying notions are rooted in questions of power. How does she use that insight as she establishes herself as an independent agent? Does she fight sexism? Does she use it to her own advantage? How has the role of women in Hollywood changed? How has it stayed the same?

2. Born into Hollywood royalty, a milieu that values beauty in women above all, Roxanne Granville remains always at a disadvantage. How does the birthmark on her cheek affect her life?

3. These characters are constantly being challenged to make choices that can cast them into a net of lies, and potentially into ruin. They are asked to choose between families or lovers. Between personal loyalties or political principles. Between fronting for others, taking the credit, sharing the spoils, or maintaining one's own work. Who among them makes reckless choices? Who takes calculated risks? Do the individuals in the novel sometimes not know the difference?

4. "In Hollywood fame, money, reputation, friendship, even love and marriage are conditional, flimsy, and often for effect. No one is invincible." Is Roxanne's early observation borne out in the novel? What is the role of reputation in Roxanne Granville's Hollywood?

5. How important is the press in the book? Not just the *Challenger*, but the big daily newspapers, the scandal rags, the trade papers, gossip columns, the critics. Is Roxanne correct in describing the press and the picture business as "mutually voracious cannibals"?

6. Irene and Roxanne, though not actually related, are truly sisters, and yet their values remain very different. How do their values impact their bond? How and why are they reconciled? At the end of the book, do you think Irene will be supportive of Roxanne and her choices?

7. Many of these characters engage in socially unacceptable love affairs, not merely unwise unions, but outright forbidden. Are these people changed by the experience? Are there regrets or insights gleaned? What are the costs to the lovers themselves? To their families and friends? To their reputations? Are these the sorts of relationships that still, in our own day, extract a heavy price from anyone brave or foolhardy enough to engage in them?

8. Returning to LA after Julia's death, Roxanne's feelings for Leon remain ambivalent. She does not want to live in his shadow, and makes a great show of independence. Yet she makes many important decisions based on resentment, affection, respect, and other complex emotions she feels for her grandfather. Despite her bravado, why can she not quite free herself from Leon Greene?

9. Roxanne Granville assumes that black people exist to serve white people, herself in particular. The servants at Summit Drive, for instance, are mere backdrop for her. She never suspects that Julia contributes to civil rights causes. How and when does Roxanne start to question her assumptions? How does Terrence Dexter enrich her understanding of the way family and society work—and how they ought to work? Why are both Roxanne's and Terrence's extended families so vehemently against their affair? Does Roxanne's meditation on family Christmas day, 1955, seem utterly improbable for that era? And now? What do you think?

10. Terrence and Roxanne are each brought up with a serious set of doctrines, Terrence in the Baptist church and Roxanne in the Church of Rick and Ilsa. When they first meet they are utterly ignorant of the other's beliefs, even though they both quote "scripture." How essential are these beliefs to their relationship? Do they learn from each other? How?

11. The novel is bookended by two funerals. Roxanne comments on the theatrical aspects of each. Is she correct in thinking that they are similar?

12. Terrence Dexter, a seasoned reporter for the *Challenger*, goes to Montgomery, Alabama, to report on the bus boycott. What does it mean to him, personally and professionally, to be a participant in these events instead of just a witness? How does his time there affect his relationship with Roxanne? With his own family? How does it change him? Can you imagine the book he is writing? Would you want to read it?

13. Roxanne is fond of quoting Julia's maxim, "Glamour is nothing more than knowing how to talk fast, laugh fluidly,

gesture economically, and leave behind a shimmering wake." Do you think Roxanne ever quite figures out what her grandmother meant by this? Julia makes it sound easy; is it? Is this description of glamour allied to the notion of panache that figures so prominently in Roxanne's vision of herself?

14. Terrence says, "Leon Greene is absolutely right. Movies are powerful. They don't just reflect, they shape." Do you think this is true? Do you think that today's more diverse films still shape the way we live?

15. In 1958, *The Bridge on the River Kwai* won seven Oscars, including Best Picture and Best Adapted Screenplay, which was given to the author of the novel, Pierre Boulle. Monsieur Boulle did not even speak English. The actual screenplay was written by Carl Foreman and Michael Wilson, blacklisted writers who had fled the country, Foreman to England, Wilson to France. (Their credits were not restored until 1984.) Do you see parallels between *The Bridge on the River Kwai* and *Adios Diablo*? Why did Carleton Grimes not shut down production on *Adios Diablo* when he could, before the truth came out? Can you think of instances today where the tainted reputation of filmmakers or actors is enough to tank a multimillion-dollar movie?

16. "Max, Simon, Nelson, Jerrold, taught me, early on, that the dramatic core of any film is characters who are being tested. Whether high drama or slapstick, *High Noon* or *Duck Soup*, the characters don't have to be saints, they just have to be interesting, have interesting motives, and respond to unlooked-for challenges." Is this an accurate description of what makes a good film? Now that films are able to depict sex, does that alter the standard?

17. People in the novel are always talking about loyalty as a laudable value. Who are the loyal characters? What or whom are they loyal to? How are they tested?

18. Roxanne describes her job like being "the feeder in the zoo, the guy who walks around with the bucket full of meat and throws it at the lions, and the bucket of bananas for the monkeys and the bucket full of palm fronds for the giraffes. Occasionally I wear a pith helmet. It's a jungle out there." What sorts of havoc did television wreak upon the 1950s entertainment world? Why are Gordon and Carleton and Leon so afraid of it?

19. Who are the great pretenders of the title? Are pretenses, lies, and secrets all the same thing?

ACKNOWLEDGMENTS

First, a great round of gratitude and applause for Pamela Malpas, agent extraordinaire, insightful reader, and dear friend.

Many thanks to Danielle Perez, who inherited this project and brought to it her enviable editorial skills. She brought out the best in this novel.

Thanks too to supportive amigas and early readers Cami Ostman, Pam Helberg, Victoria Doerper, Tele Aadsen, and Connie Feutz. Grateful to Andrea Gabriel for website design.

A belated thanks for a long-ago delightful evening to Bob and Phyllis Joseph, who shared their Malibu memories.

Merci mille fois to my son Brendan for taking the time to drive me many places I needed to see, and to my son Bear for musical insight.

Lifelong gratitude to my mother, who shares the dedication of this book. She typed my novels—many drafts over many years. She has been my inspiration, and I like to think now that she is writing her memoirs, I have the opportunity to be her inspiration.

Laura Kalpakian has won a National Endowment for the Arts Fellowship, a Pushcart Prize, the Pacific Northwest Booksellers' Award, the Anahid Literary Award for an American writer of Armenian descent, the PEN West Award, and the *Stand* International Short Fiction Competition. She has had residencies at the Virginia Center for the Creative Arts, the Montalvo Center for the Arts, and Hawthornden Castle in Scotland. She is the author of multiple novels and over a hundred stories published in collections, anthologies, literary journals, and magazines in the US and the UK. A native of California, Laura lives in the Pacific Northwest.

CONNECT ONLINE

laurakalpakian.com
twitter.com/LauraKalpakian

Ready to find
your next great read?

Let us help.

Visit prh.com/nextread

Penguin
Random
House